'I've tried d  't work out.'

'And I've told you you're dating the wrong men.' Gabriel surveyed her. 'I bet you're going for nice, average men, with a nice, respectable job, and—'

'What's wrong with that?' Colour climbed Etta's cheekbones and she narrowed her eyes.

'Physical attraction is important too.'

'So what do you suggest?'

'That you date someone you feel attracted to in a *physical* way—where there's a spark.'

'I don't seem to meet guys like that. Maybe that gene is missing too.'

'I don't believe that.'

The last berry slipped on to the ring and he stood up and held the mistletoe circle, attached it to the waiting ring.

'Look up.'

A hesitation and then she did as he asked, her face tipped up towards him, her delicate angled features bathed in the flicker of light.

'Kiss me and I'll show you,' he said. 'The ball's in your court. Literally.'

His throat was constricted, his breath held in his lungs, and then slowly she rose to her feet and stepped forward until she was flush against him. Hesitantly her hands came up and looped around his neck; her fingers touched his nape and desire shuddered through his body. She stood on tiptoe and touched her lips against his in sweet sensation.

THE EARL'S SNOW-KISSED PROPOSAL

BY
NINA MILNE

First Published in Great Britain 2016
By Mills & Boon, an imprint of HarperCollins*Publishers*
1 London Bridge Street, London, SE1 9GF

© 2016 Nina Milne

ISBN: 978-0-263-92034-5

23-1116

Our policy is to use papers that are natural, renewable and recyclable products and made from wood grown in sustainable forests. The logging and manufacturing processes conform to the legal environmental regulations of the country of origin.

Printed and bound in Spain
by CPI, Barcelona

Nina Milne has always dreamed of writing for Mills & Boon Cherish—ever since as a child she played libraries with her mother's stacks of Mills & Boon romances. On her way to this dream Nina acquired an English degree, a hero of her own, three gorgeous children and—somehow!—an accountancy qualification. She lives in Brighton and has filled her house with stacks of books—her very own real library.

Family is a big part of this book so this is for my mum. Thank you for being a great mum, an amazing grandma, and for believing in me when I didn't believe in myself!

CHAPTER ONE

GABRIEL DERWENT STARED at his reflection in the opulently framed mirror of the lavish hotel room—just to make sure he hadn't inadvertently put his shirt on inside out or his boxers on his head.

But, no…his reflection gazed suavely back at him, its crisp white shirt correctly on beneath a midnight black tux, spiky blond hair free of encumbrance. No indication of the inner turmoil that had been tossing and turning inside him for the best part of a year. Not that he was complaining—the very last thing he needed was for the truth to be emblazoned on him for the world to see. For *anyone* to see.

Instead his fellow guests at the Cavershams' Advent Ball would see what they expected—the debonair, rugged, charming Gabriel Derwent, Earl of Wycliffe, heir to the Duke of Fairfax. No doubt there would be questions as to his prolonged absence from the social scene, but he'd deal with those as if he were without a care in the world. Ditto any queries about his split from Lady Isobel Petersen.

This was a fundraiser for a cause he believed in, but the whole idea of circulating, itty-bitty small talk and a face-off with the press made his jaw clench. Yet necessity dictated his actions… He needed the social backdrop to conceal the true reason for his presence—which was to start a quest, the idea of which banded his chest with bleakness.

Enough, Gabe. No way would he submit to despair. A childhood lesson well learnt.

The click of the hotel room door caused him to spin

round and he forced his lips to upturn. 'Hey, little sis.' Seeing her expression, he stepped forward. 'Is everything OK?'

Cora Martinez entered, her emerald-green dress shimmering as she moved. 'You tell me. I knocked twice and you didn't respond. I was worried. In fact I'm *still* worried.'

'No need to worry. You look stunning, by the way.'

A wave of her hand swept the compliment away. 'Don't distract me. I *am* worried. I've seen you once in nearly a year, I have no idea where you've been, and then you ring me up out of the blue to ask me to introduce you to the Cavershams. Next thing I know you get a last-minute invitation to this ball. I don't get it.'

'I know.'

Her turquoise eyes narrowed. 'That's *it*?'

Digging deep, Gabe pulled out his best smile. 'There is nothing you need to know except that I'm back.'

No way could he confide in Cora. What would he say? *Hey, little sis. Nine months ago I found out that I can't have children.* Life as he had known it had changed irrevocably—the future he'd had mapped out for years was toast. Thanks to the archaic legal complexities that surrounded the Dukedom of Fairfax, the title that had passed from father to son for centuries might now die out. Unless he could find a male heir who descended directly, father to son, back to an earlier Duke of Fairfax. Bleakness returned in a vengeful wave even as he forced his body to remain relaxed.

'Earth to Gabe…' Cora placed her hands on her hips, one bejewelled foot tapping the plush carpet. 'I'm *still* worried. I may be six years younger than you, and we might never have been close, but you're my brother.'

Never have been close.

The words were no more than the truth. They weren't close—Cora and her twin sister, Kaitlin, had been only two when he'd been sent to boarding school and after that he'd figured there was little point in forming close bonds with *anyone*, because closeness led to the agonising ache of missing people and home. Closeness made you weak and weakness rendered you powerless.

Her forehead crinkled. 'Is it something to do with Dad? Was his attack worse than I thought? Or are you upset about Isobel? Love can be really complicated, but…'

'Stop.'

Love was something he'd never aspired to—as far as he was concerned love was the definitive form of closeness and a fast track to complete loss of power. As for Lady Isobel… their relationship had been a pact. Gabe had always known his playboy lifestyle would have to end in the name of duty, and Lady Isobel would have been a dutiful wife. In return she would have had the desired title of Duchess and been the mother of the future Duke of Fairfax.

When he'd found out there was a possibility he couldn't fulfil his part in that, he had asked to postpone their engagement for a few months. True, he hadn't told her why, but she'd agreed…and then sold him down the river. She'd appeared on numerous talk shows on which she'd denounced him as a heartbreaker and a cad. But this was conversational territory he had no intent of entering.

'Isobel is history. As for Dad—I spoke with the doctors and his prognosis is good. The heart attack was serious, but the stent should prevent further attacks and Mum has taken him away to convalesce. I'll hold the fort in their absence.' Tipping his palms up in the air, he aimed for an expression of exasperated affection. 'So all is fine. There is no need to worry.'

Patent disbelief etched Cora's delicate features. Clearly his aim was off.

'Sure, Gabe. Whatever you say,' his little sister said as she turned for the door.

Five minutes, one grand oak staircase, several wooden panelled walls and more than a few intricately beautiful medieval tapestries later Gabe followed Cora into the impressive reception hall of the Cavershams' Castle Hotel.

Beautifully dressed people filled the cavernous room and the hum of conversation was interlaced with the discreet pop of champagne corks and the clink of glasses.

Next to him, Cora's face lit up with a smile that illuminated her entire being—a clear indicator that Rafael Martinez must be in the vicinity. Sure enough, within seconds her tall, dark-haired husband made his way through the throng to her side.

'Gabriel.' Rafael gave a curt nod.

'Rafael. Good to see you.'

His brother-in-law raised one dark eyebrow in patent disbelief and Gabe couldn't blame him. Although he had no problem with his sister's marriage, he hadn't exactly been around to offer his good wishes. On the other hand Rafael Martinez was undoubtedly more than capable of looking out for himself and his wife without assistance from anyone.

Gabe scanned the room, which glittered with festive cheer. Rich green holly wreaths adorned the stone walls and discreet choral music touched the air, heralding the first Sunday of Advent, the next day, and the arrival of Christmas in just a few weeks—the deadline he'd set himself to map out his options and discover if there was an heir to the dukedom besides him.

Not for the first time he cursed the legal convolutions that demanded his heir had to be derived from a direct male line only. If there was no descendant who matched the rules the title would die out; the idea coated his tongue with the bitter taste of the unpalatable.

Focus, Gabe.

Alongside the Christmas-tinged atmosphere he became aware of the attention and buzz directed at him, on his first public appearance for nearly a year. It came as almost a relief as his body and mind spun automatically into action. Time to walk the walk and talk the talk. It was crucial to ensure that the press didn't work out why he was really here this evening, and that meant he must speak to all and sundry so that no one would identify his real quarry.

A smile on his lips, he headed towards his host and hostess—they should be able to point him in the right direction.

Etta Mason stepped behind an enormous potted plant and hauled in breath so hard her lungs protested as she checked her mobile phone for the gazillionth time.

This had been a mistake of supersonic proportions. *Breathe, Etta.* It would be OK. Cathy was safe. Images of her beautiful, precious sixteen-year-old daughter streamed through her mind. From babyhood to teenagedom she'd loved and looked after Cathy—sure, it had been hard sometimes, but not once had she regretted the choice her sixteen-year-old self had made. Whatever it had cost her.

Safe. Cathy is safe.

She was at a sleepover with her best friend, and most crucially of all there was no way that Tommy could find her. Etta dug her nails into the palm of her hand. Cathy had managed without her father thus far and that was how it would stay.

Determination hardened inside her. She had the situation under control. So now she needed to get on with her job. This was an important event and she had promised Ruby Caversham that she would do a pre-dinner talk. Therefore skulking behind potted plants was really *not* on the agenda. Instead she would step out in her pink-and-white candy cane dress and… And walk crash-bang into a very broad chest.

'I am *so* sorry. Put it down to a combination of high heels and innate clumsiness… Thank goodness I didn't impale y—'

The words died on her lips as she took in the appearance of the man she had nearly spiked with her candyfloss-pink heels. Short dark blond hair, blue-grey eyes that caught the light from the wall-mounted candles and cast a strange spell

on her, a firm mouth that her gaze wanted to snag upon—
especially when a smile tipped it up at the corners…

Etta blinked. *Holy moly!* There could be no gainsaying
that this man had charisma. *Whoa…* Her brain cells finally
caught up and she stopped gawping as recognition sent out
a flare. The man in front of her was none other than Gabriel Derwent, Earl of Wycliffe, heir to the Duke of Fairfax.

Great! The first time she'd been poleaxed by a man
since…since *never*, and it turned out to be a man she despised. True, she didn't actually *know* him—but what kind
of historian wouldn't follow the exploits of a leading member of the aristocracy? A man whose ancestors had been
instrumental in the most gripping moments of English history.

In fairness, she had no issue with the playboy lifestyle
he'd enjoyed for years—it was his more recent actions that
had left her enraged. Nine months ago Gabriel Derwent
had renounced his playboy way of life, wooed Lady Isobel Petersen, wined her and dined her and taken her to
visit his parents—all of it recorded in celebrity magazines
worldwide. He had even been papped in a jewellery store,
scanning the engagement rings, and then…*kabam!* On the
verge of a proposal Gabriel Derwent had unceremoniously
dumped Lady Isobel and fled the country.

There had been a short but excited media outburst before the efficient Derwent publicity machine had rolled
in, and Etta had taken the plight of Lady Isobel to heart.
Etta *knew* how it felt to be deceived, to become enmeshed
in a situation only to have it exposed as an illusion, and
she could almost taste Lady Isobel's bitter hurt. A hurt inflicted by *this* man.

Her eyes narrowed as she returned his gaze.

His blue-grey eyes studied her face as he held out a
hand, and something sparked in their depths. 'I'm Gabriel
Derwent.'

For an instant her gaze snagged on his hand. Capable,

strong, thick-fingered…and suspended in mid-air. *Get with it, Etta*. The last thing she wanted was for Gabriel Derwent to believe her to be flustered by his presence.

Clasping his hand in a brief handshake, she mustered a cool smile. 'Etta Mason.' She ignored the surely imaginary lingering sensation from his touch.

'Etta Mason…eminent historian.'

The words were more statement than question, and for a daft second she wondered if he had been lurking by the potted plant waiting for her. How ridiculous was that?

'That's me.'

For a moment she recalled the sheer struggle it had been to obtain her qualifications: the constant exhaustion as she'd strived to combine being the best mum she could be with the hours needed for study and working part-time. So no way would she go for false modesty—she *was* one of the best in her field.

As his eyes swept over her appearance she clocked a hint of surprise and ire sparked. Presumably her outfit didn't match up with his idea of 'eminent historian'.

'You look surprised?'

There was a pause as he contemplated his answer, and then he lifted his hands in a gesture of surrender. 'Busted. I'll admit that my preconceived idea of a renowned historian didn't include a bright-pink-striped dress. But I apologise unreservedly. I shouldn't have made such a stereotypical assumption. So how about we start again? I'll forget you nearly impaled me with your shoes and you forget my stupidity? Deal?'

This was her cue to close this conversation down—make a light comment and then walk away. But the relaxed tilt of his lips vied with the determined glint in his eye. Gabriel Derwent was turning on the charm—and Etta wanted to know why. She certainly didn't qualify as his type. Gabriel Derwent had been linked with a fair few women—all beautiful, all famous and all shallow—and none of them serious until the Lady Isobel Petersen debacle. So why would he show an interest in *her*?

The idea was laughable—Gabriel Derwent and a historian. And not just any old historian but one who had been a single mother at seventeen. True, he didn't know that, but Etta knew the ballroom held plenty of women more suited to be the recipient of the dazzling Derwent smile. It could be that she was overanalysing, and that he charmed on automatic, but instinct told her otherwise and curiosity tickled her vocal cords.

'Deal.' There could be no harm in a conversation, right? 'So how do we do that?'

'How about you tell me a bit about yourself? A day in the life of a prominent historian?'

His interest seemed genuine, even if she didn't get it. 'Part of the reason I love what I do is that all my days are different. I recently helped an author research a historical novel. I investigate family trees…help organise historic events. I blog for a historic society, I've written articles, I've done guest lectures…'

'Ruby told me you were one of the most committed professionals she knew.'

'Well, I feel the same about Ruby. And Ethan. What they do for the kids their foundation helps is inspiring. I wish ─ ' Etta broke off. Her admiration for Ruby and Ethan Caversham and the ways in which they sought to help troubled teens—kids in care or on the street—stemmed from personal experience. How she wished she'd been able to turn to people like the Cavershams in her own time of need. But that was not a wish she had any inclination to share.

'What do you wish?'

Surprise touched her at the hint of perception in his voice—almost as if he too could empathise with the children out there who needed help—and for an instant an absurd flicker of warmth ignited her. *Ridiculous*. Gabriel

Derwent had come into the world housed and shod, with a whole drawer full of silver spoons to choose from.

'I wish I did as much good as they do,' she improvised. After all it might not have been what she'd meant to say but it was the truth.

'Ruby mentioned that you'd done some work for her?'

The words niggled Etta. Ruby always had a good word to say about others, but that almost sounded as if Gabriel Derwent had expressed a specific interest in Etta. *Could* he be interested in her?

To her irritation the idea set off a spark of appreciation, caused her gaze to snag on his firm mouth, sent a strange, long-forgotten tingle down to her toes. Jeez, she must be losing it big-time—the idea was nuts.

Focus on the conversation, Etta.

'I did. From time to time she deals with children who only have a name for their birth parent and want to know more about them.'

'So you're almost playing detective?'

'Yes—that's what's so fascinating.' Though that fascination held an element of the bittersweet—a reminder that all her research and effort hadn't unearthed a single clue as to the identity of her *own* birth parents.

A familiar ache kicked at her ribcage and she clenched her nails into her palms. *Enough. Accept it.* She would never know who they were or why they had abandoned her on a doorstep thirty-two years ago. *Move on.*

'What if you discover something people don't want to hear?' Now darkness edged his voice, and matched the shadow in his grey-blue eyes.

'I tell them anyway. It's better to know.' This she knew. After all, *her* adoptive parents had hidden the truth of her birth from her—hadn't even told her she *was* adopted. Instead they had woven a web of illusion around her life—a mirage that had been exposed when they'd had a child of their own and turned Etta out into the cold.

Enough. Accept it. Move on.

Aware that his grey-blue eyes were studying her expression with a penetration she wouldn't have believed a man of his reputation capable of, she summoned a smile. Hoped to combat the fervour her voice had held. Somehow their conversation had taken on way too much depth—and, worse, she had no idea how or why that had happened.

'After all, they say knowledge is power.'

'So they do.' Now his voice matched her lightness, and suddenly there was that smile again. Full of charm. And she wondered if she had imagined the whole other side to the conversation.

'And sometimes knowledge is just useful. I did one job for Ruby when a pregnant teenager in care wanted to find out her medical history.'

It had been a case Etta had related to all too well. How many times had she looked at Cathy and worried that genes she knew nothing about might have an adverse medical impact on her daughter?

'Although the other side to *that* coin is the fact that in the past no one understood genes and everyone got on with it. Sometimes I believe we have to make a leap of faith,' she said.

'And just believe in fate?'

So now they had plunged into philosophical waters. 'Sometimes. Don't you agree?'

A flare burned in the depths of his eyes. 'No, I don't. We choose our fate because we have the power of choice.'

The intensity of his voice prickled her skin.

Then his broad shoulders lifted in a shrug. 'Or at least that's what I choose to believe.'

Enough. The Earl of Wycliffe possessed more depth than she'd given him credit for, but that didn't alter anything. The man was at best a playboy and at worst a heartbreaking master of illusion. Etta still had no idea why he'd engaged her in conversation for so long but it didn't matter. So…

'It's nearly time for my talk and I really must mingle. Hopefully the more people I talk to the more people will enjoy my speech. I'll say goodbye.'

'I look forward to your talk and to chatting again afterwards.'

Really? This didn't make sense. Curiosity surfaced and she pushed it, her besetting sin, down ruthlessly. There were way bigger items on her plate right now.

Etta summoned up her coolest smile. 'I won't be staying long tonight, so in case we don't get a chance to speak again I'll say goodbye now.'

'And I'll say goodbye for now,' he murmured, so softly that she couldn't be sure she'd heard him correctly.

CHAPTER TWO

GABE WATCHED FROM a corner of the beautifully decorated ballroom as Etta Mason headed towards the podium with a sinuous grace. *Damn.* There it was again. The tap of attraction that had sparked when she'd first emerged from behind the potted plant earlier—a complication he hadn't anticipated.

In recent months his libido had been in hibernation mode. Plus the photo on her website hadn't prepared him for Etta Mason in the flesh, and the instant impact had caught him unawares. In real life her brown eyes were flecked with hints of amber and her generous mouth called for his attention. Glossy chestnut hair seemed to invite the touch of his fingers, and the slant of her cheekbones would cause envy in the heart of many a supermodel. But it wasn't only her beauty that had stopped him in his tracks—her expression had held a piquancy, a poise, that summoned notice.

Right now he needed to derail that train of thought and pull his libido under control. He required Etta Mason's *professional* expertise. Urgently. So this attraction needed to be sidelined.

Etta tapped the microphone and waited for silence, showing no sign of nerves as she waited for the hum of chatter to die down. She stood with poise and stillness, her sleeveless pink-and-white-striped dress emphasised the slenderness of her waist and the soft material of its skirt artfully swathed over the curve of her hips and fell to her ankles in sleek, diaphanous curves.

Her expression held calm, her tawny brown eyes looked directly out into the audience, and her lips curved upwards in a relaxed smile. The only small indication of tension was the way she tucked one short tendril of brown hair behind her ear.

'Ladies and gentlemen…I promise not to keep you for long. But before I begin I want you all to think about something that I feel is a staggering fact. Every single one of us here had an ancestor alive in medieval times, in Tudor times, in Victorian times.'

Gabe could almost hear the sizzle as the attention of the audience was caught.

'Some of us—' Did her gaze linger on him for a second? '—may have had ancestors who stood in this very room and feasted with kings. For others those ancestors might have been common soldiers or ale-keepers, stonemasons or cutpurses or highwaymen. We all have family trees, and all trees need roots. Tonight I want to think about what those roots mean to us. As you know this ball is a fundraiser for teenage kids who have had a pretty tough start in life for one reason or another. Many of those children say they feel rootless, or uprooted…'

As she spoke her voice vibrated with passion. She cared—*really* cared about her subject, and about these kids. It was something he recognised and respected in Etta Mason, in the Cavershams and in himself. An empathy that drove him to work with children who were victims of bullying and with the bullies themselves, to carry out charity work that he had not and *would* not make public.

It was not relevant to the here and now. And yet Etta's genuine concern was an additional point in her favour as her speech came across as heartfelt but delivered with a professional edge.

A sweep of her hand indicated her dress. 'I chose to wear this because it reminds me of Christmas and the traditional candy canes. Christmas is a time full of traditions—a time when families get together. As such, it is a difficult time of year for a lot of children in care and a lot of children who *should be* in care. The money raised today will help kids like those enjoy a better Christmas and help them towards a future in which they can hopefully put down some new roots of their own. So when it comes to the auction please dig deep, in the spirit of Christmas. Enjoy the rest of your evening, and thanks for listening.'

As applause broke out Gabe stepped forward. Decision made—he'd come here to assess whether Etta Mason could do what he needed and now he knew for sure. So he'd shut down the feeling of attraction and start on the mission he'd set himself.

A few purposeful strides and he'd cut through the people who clustered around her. As he reached her side, surprise sparked in the exotic brown of her eyes.

'Impressive speech.'

'Thank you.'

'I was wondering if I could have a word in private. We could stroll on the terrace before we eat.'

For a second he thought she'd refuse, in which case he'd fall back on his reserve plan, but after a fractional hesitation she nodded.

Five minutes later they stepped out into the clean, cold air and Etta gave a small gasp that undoubtedly denoted appreciation. 'It's beautiful!'

Potted greenery twinkled with fairy lights and lanterns hung over the tables dotted about the mosaic-paved terrace, casting a warm, magical glow whilst outdoor heaters combated the chill of the night air.

'The Cavershams know how to throw a party. There's outdoor dancing planned for later. It's a shame you have to leave early.'

A sudden image of Etta Mason in his arms as they glided round the moonlit mosaic tiles pierced his brain with a strength that sent a tingle through his body. Without thought his feet carried him a step closer to her, and a tantalising overtone of her vanilla scent teased his senses.

'Yes, it is.'

For a heartbeat he wondered if her mind had followed the same path as her brown gaze held his and flared with an intensity that caught his breath. Then the instant was over.

Her lips thinned and she muttered a *'tcha'* under her breath before moving away from him towards the wooden railings that surrounded the terrace. Once there, she turned to face him, arms folded. 'Why did you bring me out here?'

Her voice was tinged with suspicion—and who could blame her? Self-irritation coursed through his veins. He needed this woman in a professional capacity, and this conversation was way too important to risk it for the sake of a flare of thoroughly *unprofessional* attraction. Time to get back on track.

'I need a historian and you fit the bill.'

Surprise creased her brow as she assessed his words. 'Tell me more.'

Gabe kept his pose relaxed, indicating one of the wooden tables overhung with delicate white lit-up stars suspended from the glittering arbour. 'Shall we sit?'

'Sure.' Etta walked over and lowered herself into the chair with a wary grace.

Gabe followed suit, taking the opportunity to marshal his thoughts and line his words up like troops.

'I'd like you to put together a detailed family tree of the Derwent family, going back centuries. About eighteen months ago a much-publicised flood hit Derwent Manor and a lot of valuable items were destroyed—including a parchment that documented the basic Derwent family tree. A lot of the supporting documentation—ledgers that date back centuries—were also damaged and muddled up. Unfortunately I've now discovered that those records were never computerised. I'm sure some of the facts are a matter of public record but I wouldn't have the first clue how to access them let alone piece them all together.'

She leant forward, those amber-flecked eyes sparking with interest now, and for a perverse moment he felt chagrin that they hadn't been ignited by *him*.

'So you want me to put your family tree back together?'

'Yes. But in way more detail than the original.'

For centuries the dukedom had passed from father to son, and now that would come to an end. Which meant he needed to clamber up the family tree, delve down obscure branches and work out who might succeed to the dukedom after him, now that he knew he would never have a son of his own.

Frustration coated his insides. It was imperative that he understood his options—and fast. His father's recent heart attack meant the Duke and Duchess wanted him, the heir, to marry and produce a son at speed. That couldn't happen. But Gabe had no wish to trigger another heart attack in his father and the enormity of learning the truth might well do exactly that. So he had to come up with a strategy... a way to deal with it.

'There is another stipulation. I need it done by Christmas. I realise that this is a big job to accomplish in only a few weeks, but I'll do everything I can to help. As you may know my father recently suffered a heart attack. I'd like to present him with the family tree as a surprise gift.'

The animation left her face and she shook her head. 'I'm sorry. I have family commitments—I'm leaving the country in a couple of days on a five-week holiday.'

Disappointment weighed upon him. He'd done his research and Etta had seemed the perfect candidate. Now he'd met her, every instinct told him she would do the job right and fast. 'Any chance you'd postpone? I'd amply compensate you and you can name your fee.'

'It isn't about money. I'm taking my daughter on a cruise.'

Daughter. Somehow it hadn't crossed his mind that Etta might have a daughter—there had been no mention of a husband or children on her website—and for a second the idea of their existence twanged a chord of disappointment inside him. *No.* The whole attraction thing had been closed down. But on a professional level he wanted Etta Mason for the job. So…

'You're sure? Perhaps your husband could take your daughter and I'd pay for another family holiday.'

'There is no husband. Thank you for the opportunity, but I really can't accept the job.'

Now her words held regret, and a shadow that betokened disappointment clouded the amber of her eyes. Gabe frowned. Maybe he could change her mind—cruise or no cruise, he sensed she wanted the job. Time to utilise his reserve plan.

As if on cue the dinner gong pealed out and he rose to his feet. 'We'd better go in.'

Etta swallowed down a sigh. To trace the Derwent family tree ranked up there with her ideal job. Gabriel Derwent had offered her the opportunity to access papers and records of the past, to piece together a lineage that stretched back over centuries and complete a jigsaw puzzle of historical import, to lose herself in the life of people who had existed in times gone by.

On top of that a high-profile case like this would have boosted her reputation and it would have paid well. Nothing to sneeze at if ousting Tommy from her life ever involved a need for legal aid.

Tommy. Fear shivered through Etta—she would *not* let Tommy become part of their lives again. Nothing could compare with the importance of removing Cathy from Tommy's orbit. So this golden opportunity would have to be passed by. Yet disappointment twinged, compounded by an inexplicable feeling of chagrin that he looked so calm.

Which was further complicated by a memory of that moment on the terrace—that heartbeat of time when she had been aware of him with an intensity that had rocked her senses.

So all in all it was a relief to re-enter the warmth and grandeur of the hotel and join the throng of guests headed for the banqueting hall.

Once there, Etta stopped on the threshold. 'I'd better go and find my place.'

'I can help you there. You're at Table Five. Same as me.'

Etta frowned. 'No. I checked the seating plan earlier.'

'There's been a slight change to the plan.'

A flare of anger heated her veins at his sheer arrogance and she spun to face him—she would *not* be manipulated. 'Are you telling me *you* altered it? Ruby puts a huge amount of thought into these arrangements—you can't change them to suit yourself.'

'Relax, Etta. I asked Ruby if she would change it. You told me you had to leave early, and I wanted to make sure I got the chance to speak with you about the job.'

That made sense, and yet alarm bells began to clang in her head. She narrowed her eyes with suspicion. Gabriel Derwent was used to getting what he wanted, and right now he wanted her to take this job. Worse, he might have sensed how much she wished she could do just that. And even worse than that the idea of Gabriel as a dinner companion held a temptation she didn't want to analyse.

'Well, that's no longer necessary, so I think we should change the seating plan back.'

'Why complicate matters?' A nod of his blond head showed that most of the guests had found their places. 'Come on—it won't be that bad. I promise I won't mention the job again. We can chat about whatever you like.'

Clearly he'd found the charm button again. The persuasive lilt to his deep voice and the accompanying smile held definite appeal, enticing her own lips into an answering upturn.

Careful, Etta. Perhaps he believed he could charm her into the job. Perhaps she should prove him wrong. Etta Mason was impervious to beguilement—had long since accepted that romance was not in her nature, that relationships were not something she understood. So...

'Fine.'

Once at their table, she turned to greet the man on her other side, received his congratulations on her speech, and realised from the slight slurring of his words that he was on the road to inebriation. No matter—she'd manage. Because no way did she want to give Gabriel Derwent even a *hint* of encouragement.

Within minutes she'd set Toby Davenport off on a conversational trail upon which he told her all about his expensive lifestyle, his luxury holidays, and his yacht. Which left Etta free to add the occasional comment of encouragement whilst she savoured the rich flavours of the venison broth, appreciated the authentic tang of cloves and mace from the medieval recipe, and did her best to ignore her body's hum of awareness at the warmth and sheer presence of Gabriel on her other side.

Until his well-modulated tones broke into the Davenport drone. 'Sounds amazing, Toby. Etta, here, is about to go on holiday. Tell me, Etta—I'm intrigued. As a historian, do you choose your holiday destinations based on historical interest? You mentioned a cruise... Where are you going?'

Etta opened her mouth and realisation dawned—she had no idea of the answer. Her mind was a resounding example of the clichéd blank state. When she'd booked the cruise its destination had been the least of her criteria—availability had been her priority, because the idea of a ship surrounded by sea had felt safe. That was why it had been worth the remortgaging of her flat and the ransacking of her savings to pay for it. Cathy would be safe from her father.

Because visceral fear had flared inside her—a fear that had been dormant for sixteen years but that had been re-ignited the instant Tommy had swaggered back into her life days before.

Focus, Etta. Gabe had raised his eyebrows, and his eyes were shadowed with concern.

'Sorry,' she managed. 'Senior moment. I can't remember.'

'You're too young to qualify.'

'Clearly not. I'll let you know if it comes back to me.'

Come on, Etta. Change the conversation. Unfortunately her brain was still tuned in to Planet Blank.

Desperation loosened her vocal cords as she saw the challenge in his eyes. 'In the meantime, what about *you*? Have you got any holiday plans for Christmas?'

'No. I'll be based at Derwent Manor. My parents are away in France, so my father can convalesce, and I need to ensure that various traditions are upheld. Including the annual Christmas Fair at the manor. This year I've decided to introduce a Victorian theme—hopefully whoever I get to do the family tree can lend me some advice on that at the same time.'

Etta blinked. She *loved* to help with events such as this, and she'd bet Gabriel knew that. However innocent those blue-grey eyes looked as they calmly met her gaze.

'That sounds like a pretty full-on few weeks.' And a far cry from the playboy-style Christmas festivities she had imagined he would indulge in.

'It will be. In truth, running Derwent Manor is a full-time job in itself—my parents' whole life revolves around it.'

'And yours too?'

'Not my whole life, no.'

'But one day it will?'

'Yes.' The syllable was clipped, and she'd swear his

knuckles had whitened around the crystal water tumbler he lifted to his lips.

'That must be strange. To always have known what your job will be one day. For most children the perennial question is, What do you want to be when you grow up? For royalty or aristocracy that isn't a question—you've always *known* what you will be when you grow up.'

'Yes.'

It was impossible to read anything from the single word—yet she sensed a depth of emotion in the sheer rigidity of his jaw. Did Gabriel Derwent relish or resent his destiny? Speaking of which…

'You said earlier that you believed in the power of choice over the power of fate, but that's not true, is it? Fate has decreed that you will become Duke of Fairfax.'

'Yes.' As if this time he'd realised the curtness of his response he curved his lips into the famous Derwent smile. 'But I do have the choice to renounce the title.'

Etta placed her spoon down into the empty bowl. 'Fair enough.' Even if she didn't believe he'd do that in a million years. 'But not everyone has that sort of choice. Think of all the princesses in history who were forced to marry. *They* had no choice.'

'You don't know that. You could argue that they simply chose to do their duty. And some of them could have elected to give their life up to religion. Sometimes none of the choices we have are palatable, but they exist.'

Etta opened her mouth but he raised a hand to forestall her.

'I know that there are examples of people who have no choice. Innocent people caught up in a chain of events they can't control. But I'm not sure fate comes into it—perhaps they are casualties of sheer bad luck.'

'Fate versus chance?' Even as she said the words Etta wondered how they had ended up in this discussion. It was almost as if they were in their own bubble amidst the glitz and buzz of their glamorous surroundings, complete with fairy-tale elements.

The warning bells that had clamoured earlier renewed their alarm. But there was no need for worry. Two more courses and she'd be on her way. She'd never meet Gabriel again. This conversation was nothing more than a welcome distraction from her thoughts of Tommy. That was all. A distraction. If Toby Davenport hadn't been bent on a drunken flirtation with his other neighbour she would no doubt have been distracted just as effectively by *him*.

Liar, liar, candy cane dress on fire.

In truth Gabriel Derwent was casting a mesh of fascination over both her body and her mind, and panic trickled through all the other sensations. She couldn't remember the last time her body had responded like this and she didn't like it.

Before Etta could end the conversation she felt her minuscule evening bag vibrate under the strategically placed napkin on her lap. Foreboding shivered her skin even as she tried to tell herself it could be anyone. There was no reason to believe anything had happened to Cathy.

Pushing her chair back, she tried to force her lips into a semblance of smile. 'Excuse me. I'll be back in a minute.'

Don't run.

CHAPTER THREE

GABE GLANCED AT the empty space next to him and frowned. No bathroom break took *this* long. Euphemistically speaking, Etta Mason could have powdered a hundred noses by now. Plus her food would soon congeal. Could she be in trouble?

Not his business. And yet there had been an expression of near fear on her face when she'd left the table, and that had touched him on a primitive level. Fear had once been a part of *his* life, and the memories still lingered in the recesses of his soul. Plus, the more he could discover about Etta Mason the more likely it would be that he could work out a way to persuade her to do the job. All valid reasons to go and check up on her.

Rising, he smiled at his table companions. 'Be back in a second.'

He moved through the imposing doors and into the hall. A quick scan showed no sign of Etta. Could be she had headed somewhere more private to make a call. Could be he should just leave her to it. Yet his feet strode towards the lobby, which was a fusion of medieval detail and modern comfort.

He halted on the threshold, took in the scene with lightning assessment. Etta was backed up against a pillar and a dark-haired man stood over her, aggression in his stance. The man's expression held a malevolent smirk that Gabe recognised as that of a bully, of a man who knew he inspired fear in his victim. Tattoos snaked and writhed over the bulge of muscles that spoke of a lot of time spent pumping iron.

'Is everything all right, Etta?' Stupid question, because Etta Mason looked like a different woman from the professional, articulate, give-as-good-as-you-get woman he'd sat with at dinner. Her face was pale, her hands were clenched, and those tawny brown eyes held a mix of defiance and fear.

'Everything's fine,' the man said. 'So you can take a hike.'

'I didn't ask *you*.'

The man took a step away from Etta. 'And...?' The menace was palpable. 'I said take a hike.'

Etta moved towards the man, her whole being diminished as she approached him, fear in every awkward movement, and Gabe knew with ice-cold certainty that at some point this man had hurt her.

'Tommy, please.'

The man gave a short, harsh laugh that prickled Gabe's skin.

'That sounds just like the old days, Etta.'

'Enough.' Cold rage ran through Gabe's veins and he strode towards Tommy. 'The only person who needs to take a hike round here is *you*.'

'It's OK, Gabe. I've got this.' Etta hauled in an audible breath. 'Tommy, just go. Please. You've made your point.'

Tommy hesitated, his dark eyes mean, his fists still clenched, and Gabe took another step forward.

Then, 'Fine. This toff isn't worth messing up my parole for. But this isn't over. Cathy is *my* daughter and I *will* meet her. Whatever it takes.' Turning, Tommy walked towards the portcullis-style door and exited.

Gabe turned to Etta. 'Are you all right?'

'Yes. Thank you.'

She rubbed her hands up and down her forearms and

stared at the door as if to make sure Tommy had gone for good.

'Right.' Straightening, she tugged out her phone. 'I need to go.' A tap of her finger and then she lifted the phone to her ear. 'There's been a problem. Tommy turned up here. I'm on my way back now. I'll let you know what train I'm on.'

She glanced towards Gabe as if she was surprised he was still there and then she returned her attention to her phone.

'Taxi numbers…' she muttered under her breath.

'Where are you going?'

'London.'

Before he could even consider the import of his words his lips opened. 'I'll drive you there.'

Genuine shock made her jaw drop. 'Why would you do that?'

'Because I can get you to London way faster than the train, and I don't trust Tommy not to be waiting out there to follow you.'

The idea made her wince, and she rubbed her hands up and down her arms again, her brown eyes staring at a scenario that she clearly didn't like the look of. 'I'm not sure I should say yes, or why you even care, but I'd be a fool to refuse. Thank you.'

'Let's go. I'll find Ruby and explain you've had a family emergency.'

Ten minutes later Etta eyed Gabriel Derwent's deep red Ferrari and wondered anew if she shouldn't have caught a train, tried to hire a car—worked out some way to deal with this crisis herself. But the primitive need to be with Cathy overrode all else.

Logic told her that Cathy was safe with her friend Stephanie and her daughter Martha—according to Steph, Cathy and Martha were safely ensconced in Martha's bedroom, watching a rom-com. Common sense reinforced the idea—

there was no way that Tommy could track Cathy down there. And yet he'd found Etta.

Chill, Etta. That was hardly a huge feat of deduction. Her website had detailed her speech at the Cavershams' Advent Ball. As for her mobile number—anyone could get that from her work answer-machine. But she couldn't 'chill'—not when she remembered how she had cringed before Tommy and his delight in her reaction. Dammit, he'd *revelled* in her fear—a fear that filled her with self-loathing even as a tidal wave of memories threatened to break lockdown. *No.* The past was over. She had to focus on the present and her daughter.

So Etta wanted to be with Cathy as soon as possible and Gabriel's car offered the ideal solution. The problem was Gabriel himself came with the deal.

'All set?' The deep timbre of his voice held concern alongside a hint of amusement. 'You're looking at the car as if it's akin to a lion's den.'

Heat warmed her cheeks. 'I'm just wondering whether it's fair to put you to so much trouble.'

'I offered.'

This was daft—and a waste of valuable time. A nod and then she pulled the low-slung door open and slid into the luxurious leather seat. Fact: Cathy was more important than anything else right now.

Within minutes they were on the road. Etta looked into the shadowy darkness as the powerful car ate up the miles. Wind turbines loomed in the dark, turned by the Cornish winds, fields and farmhouses flashed past, and occasionally she glanced at Gabriel Derwent. His blond hair gleamed in the moonlight, and his focus was on the road, each movement easy and competent.

He glanced at her too, then returned his attention to the deserted road. 'I get the feeling you're not comfortable. Are you worried about your daughter?'

'Yes. But I know she's safe. You'll have to let me pay

you for this. I've dragged you away from an incredible dinner and moonlit dancing. I feel bad.'

'I told you. No need. Do you want to talk about it? The situation with Tommy and your daughter?'

Did she? For an odd moment a pull to do just that touched her. More madness—this man was a stranger, and not even her closest friends knew about that dark period of her life. 'There's nothing to say that you haven't deduced. You heard Tommy. He is Cathy's dad and he has decided he wants to see her. I don't want him anywhere near her.'

A small frown creased his forehead. Presumably he was wondering how she could ever have been such a fool as to have anything to do with a lowlife like Tommy.

'Has he ever been part of her life?'

'No.' Etta shook her head. 'I don't want to sound rude, but I don't want to talk about it.'

For years she had shut down the memories of Tommy and she had no wish to revisit them now—to expose her youthful stupidity, folly and weakness to this man. A man who clearly didn't know the definition of the word *weak*. Even now her insides felt coated with a fuzz of shame at her own behaviour, so best to keep the door firmly closed and padlocked with a host of security outside.

'This is my problem and I am dealing with it.'

'By running away on a cruise?'

Despite the softness of his deep voice, the words sent a flare of anger through her. 'I am *not* running away.' *Was she?*

'I'm sorry if that sounded harsh, and I know I don't know the details. I get you don't want to discuss them. But if there is one lesson I've learnt in life it's that running away is seldom the best option.'

No doubt it was easy not to run away when you were the Earl of Wycliffe. Etta bit the words back—the man was doing her a massive favour here. 'Thanks for the advice. As I said, it's my problem and I'm dealing with it.'

With that Etta leant back and turned her head to focus on the landscape. Conversation over. To her relief Gabriel Derwent let it rest. Even if she sensed that next to her he was still mulling over the situation.

But he remained silent until they approached the outskirts of London, where he simply asked for directions, and soon enough they pulled up outside Steph's house.

'Thank you again. I truly appreciate this and I owe you a big favour.' The idea was an irritant that she suspected would stay with her until she worked out how to repay the debt. 'In the meantime, I wish you a safe journey home and I apologise again for wrecking your night.'

'I'll see you to the door.'

'No! Really... Steph is waiting up and I'd rather go in quietly.' She pushed open the door hurriedly. 'Goodbye, Gabriel.'

Without looking back she scurried up the stairs and pulled out the spare key Steph had given her. Right now she just wanted to go and see Cathy and watch her daughter breathe peacefully. Yet at the door she turned for one last glimpse at Gabriel Derwent's shadowy profile.

'How did you sleep?'

Etta looked up from the pine kitchen table and smiled at her best friend. 'Fine.'

'Fibber,' Steph said. 'You must have been terrified when Tommy appeared.'

'It was scary, but...' *But from the second Gabriel Derwent had appeared she had felt safe.*

She had to get a grip—life had taught her that the only person to rely on was herself. She'd escaped Tommy once—she'd do it again.

'I'll be fine.' Etta gripped her mug of coffee and tried hard to believe her words even as she heard the hollowness of each syllable. 'How was Cathy last night?'

'Quiet. She didn't mention Tommy to me, though I'm

sure she has talked to Martha about it. She *did* say she doesn't want to go on the cruise.'

Etta sighed. Her usually cheerful, well-behaved daughter had changed since Tommy's arrival on the scene, and Etta couldn't blame her—she herself would do anything to meet her own birth dad. Or mum.

She hadn't even known of their existence until she'd reached fifteen and discovered the fact that she'd been adopted. Worked out that her whole life had been an illusion, a lie. That was why she had vowed never to lie to Cathy, believed that honesty was the best way forward. So as Cathy had grown up Etta had told her who her dad was in an age-appropriate way. She had never wanted Cathy to feel she'd been lied to—hadn't wanted her daughter to build up a fantasy picture of her father. Equally, when Tommy had turned up with his demand to see his daughter, Etta had told Cathy the truth—but she hadn't anticipated her daughter's reaction.

Cathy, caught in a web of confused emotions, wanted her father to be a wonderful man. Wanted to meet him, to bond with him, and the idea sent waves of terror through Etta's veins. No one knew better than she the spell Tommy could exert when he wanted to—she could imagine his spin, the story of his reformation, his interpretation of his past character as misunderstood rebel without a cause.

She gusted out a sigh as she looked at Steph. 'I know she doesn't want to go.' But the cruise had to happen, because Etta would not—could not—sit back and watch her daughter repeat her own mistakes. 'But we're going anyway.' She rose to her feet. 'Thanks a million for last night, hun. There's no need for you to stay. I know you need to get Martha to her singing lesson.'

'Stay here as long as you like.'

Twenty minutes later the click of the front door indicated their departure and Etta approached the bedroom where Cathy was staying.

Her daughter sat cross-legged on the bed, her long dark hair pulled back in a ponytail set high on her head. 'Mum—please, please, *please* don't make me go on this cruise. If Dad wants to see me badly enough to follow you to Cornwall then surely it's worth a try.'

Etta sensed her daughter's frustration and it tore her apart. 'Sweetheart, your father is not a safe person to be around.'

'Maybe he's changed.'

Before Etta could answer, the doorbell pealed and fear jumped up her throat. *Keep calm.* No way could it be Tommy.

Cathy leapt off the bed, clearly desperate for the very thing that held Etta petrified to the spot.

'Cathy—wait!'

Ungluing her feet from the carpet, Etta raced down the stairs after her daughter, reaching the bottom just as Cathy got to the door and peered through the spyhole.

'It's not Dad. It's some blond bloke.'

Disappointment drooped Cathy's shoulders and Etta moved forward and pulled her into a quick hug, her heart aching even as relief surged through her.

Cathy stepped back. 'We'd better open the door. Whoever it is he looks familiar. Good-looking for his age.'

Etta peeped through the spyhole and blinked. Blinked again in case of hallucination. But Gabriel Derwent remained in her line of vision. Casually dressed in jeans and a long-sleeved sweatshirt, he still exuded an energy that sent her pulse-rate up a notch. Be that as it may, she couldn't leave him standing on Steph's doorstep.

She pulled the door open and bit back a protest as he stepped forward and closed the door behind him.

'What...?'

'Apologies for the unannounced visit. There's been a development.'

'I don't understand,' Etta said, as foreboding prickled her skin. Surely things couldn't get any worse. *Could* they? 'What sort of a development?'

CHAPTER FOUR

GABRIEL HALTED, ALL thoughts of developments scrambled in his brain as he gazed at Etta. This was a completely different Etta from the previous night, and somehow even more full of allure in jeans and a short knitted cream jumper that emphasised the length of her legs. Shower-damp chestnut hair emitted a tantalising waft of strawberry, and fell in a glossy swathe around her unmade-up face. Her skin glowed and a smattering of freckles down the bridge of her nose was now revealed. For an absurd second his hands tingled with the urge to reach out and run his finger down the line. As for her lips—

Hurriedly he tore his gaze away and realised that they weren't alone.

A girl stepped closer to Etta and eyed him with a speculative gaze. There could be no doubt the two were related, despite the girl's long curtain of dark hair; her eyes were the same amber-flecked brown. Sisters? Or…

Etta stepped forward. 'Gabriel, this is my daughter, Cathy. Cathy, this is Gabriel—the man who kindly drove me home last night.'

Her chin tilted upwards as she met his gaze in an unspoken challenge, and he blinked away the surprise he knew had surfaced in his eyes. There was no point in pretence—he *was* surprised. In his mind Cathy had been considerably younger, and his brain whirred to adjust the parameters of the idea he intended to present to Etta.

'Good to meet you,' he said, and he held out a hand to Cathy, who surveyed him, her dark head tilted to one side.

'Are you…Gabriel Derwent?'

'The one and only.'

They were words he wished unsaid as he flinched inwardly at their bleak truth. One day he *could* be the one and only Duke of Fairfax—the last of the line. Yet he forced his lips to tilt upwards and could only hope the smile factor outweighed the grimace.

A small frown etched Etta's forehead. 'Cathy, could you go and get ready, please? Once Gabriel has left we need to get home and pick up our cases.'

Cathy heaved a sigh. 'I *told* you, Mum. It's not *necessary*. We don't need to *go*.' The muttered words held defiance underlain with resignation, but she headed for the staircase.

'Cathy. We'll discuss this later, but the bottom line is we *are* going.'

Once the teenager had trailed up the stairs Etta turned to Gabe. Her lips parted as if to speak but instead she just stared at him for a moment, her eyes wide.

Then she stepped back and gave her head a small shake. 'Look, I don't want to be rude, but I haven't got a lot of time. The cruise leaves tonight. What's happened?'

This would be a tricky conversation, and he'd be damned if he would conduct it in a hallway. 'I appreciate that you're busy, but we do need to talk. Properly. With you focused on what I have to say. I promise I will be succinct.'

A hesitation, and then she nodded. 'OK. Come through to the kitchen. I'll make coffee. It sounds like I'll need it.'

Gabe followed Etta into a spacious, airy kitchen with cheerful daffodil-yellow walls adorned with corkboards holding pinned artwork and photos. He seated himself at a big wooden table as she filled the old-fashioned kettle.

'OK. Hit me with it.'

Easy does it, Gabe. Instinct told him Etta wouldn't appreciate his next words, however he spun them.

'The press clocked our departure from the ball last night,

found out about our moonlit stroll on the terrace and discovered my ploy with the seating plan. They have decided you and I are an item. I thought I'd better give you the heads-up as there may be reporters outside your house.'

For a second she stood as if frozen, her lips formed in a circle of astonishment, her head tilted, waiting for the punchline. Then, when she realised none was forthcoming, she banged the kettle down onto the hob and sheer outrage etched her cheekbones with a flush of anger.

'*You* and *me*? The press thinks *we* are an item?'

Hmm... A hint of chagrin touched him at the sheer horror that laced her voice. 'I'm afraid so.'

Jeez, was it that bad?

'But that's ludicrous!'

'Why?' It wasn't what he had meant to say, but her expression of distaste had sparked a surge of irritation.

'Because...because it is such an impossible scenario.'

'Why?' Rising to his feet, he headed towards the kitchen counter, kept his gaze on hers.

And suddenly the atmosphere hitched up a notch. Or three. The look of aversion faded from her face and morphed into shock as desire ignited in her eyes. Gabe's mouth dried, and the tick-tock of a clock in the background pounded his eardrums as he moved closer—close enough that those damned freckles caught his attention again.

Her hands gripped the underside of the worktop so tightly her knuckles showed white against the marbled grey. As if the touch had pulled her back to reality she stepped back. 'It's impossible because it could never happen.' The quaver in her voice demonstrated the shakiness of her argument.

'Really?' He pulled his phone out and tapped the screen. 'Look.'

Etta stared at the images, and Gabe could almost see her eyeballs pop from their sockets on cartoon stalks as she swore under her breath.

'Yup. That's what *I* thought.' Gabe couldn't keep the smugness from his voice. Because some enterprising photographer had captured the moment he and Etta had met, as she'd emerged from behind the potted plant. There could be no denying the look of utter arrest on their faces.

'I'll track down whoever took that and disembowel him,' Etta muttered, before looking up with a tilt of her chin and challenge in her eyes. 'Because he is incompetent—clearly the light was odd, or the angle of the lens, or…or…'

'Or we saw each other and there was a mutual moment of appreciation.'

Her eyes rested on his image and for a heartbeat he would have sworn there was a glimpse of satisfaction on her face at seeing him equally smitten. Then it was gone and she straightened up.

'I'll stick to the mistake theory, thank you.'

Gabe raised his eyebrows. Maybe he should have let it go, but her sheer refusal to acknowledge the attraction prompted curiosity—along with his inner devil. 'Or you could admit the truth. You are attracted to me and vice versa. I don't have an issue acknowledging it.' He gestured to the screen. 'The evidence is right there.'

If the laws of physics had allowed, her laser glare would have shot his phone with its telltale images to smithereens. 'This may be hard for you to believe, but *I am not attracted to you.*'

Each word was exaggerated, and issued through clenched teeth, and yet Gabe knew she was lying.

'You don't *want* to be attracted to me.' And he wasn't sure why not. 'That's different.'

'Gabriel…'

'Please. Only my parents call me Gabriel. I prefer Gabe.'

'Gabe. You are not my type. I don't go for shallow playboys or men who lead women on and then break their hearts.'

Whoa. '"Shallow playboy" I'll own up to. But I don't lead women on.' *Ever.*

'What about Lady Isobel? You led that poor woman up the garden path, round the garden and a whole village full of houses. You made her think you'd marry her, then you bailed out in the public eye, broke her heart and humiliated her.'

Anger stirred inside him even as he accepted Etta's stance—Isobel had played her part to perfection, and most of the country believed in her false portrayal of Gabe Derwent as heartbreaker extraordinaire. In return she'd netted herself a packet and some great publicity. A month after that his sister Kaitlin had spotted her partying on the Riviera. It seemed as if Isobel had decided to break free—rebel against the role of duchess she'd been primed for and go for the money.

But forget Isobel. Right now Etta glared at him, one foot tapping the kitchen floor tiles. Gabriel met her gaze full on. 'I thought historians valued accuracy and confirmation and didn't rely on tabloid gossip?'

Heat touched her cheeks. 'A good historian looks at the available evidence and makes deductions. Are you denying that you led Lady Isobel to think you would marry her?'

'No. I'm not. But that is one fact. There are a whole host of other facts you are not privy to. Unlike Isobel, I intend to keep them private. However, I give you my word that it did not go down the way she claimed it did. I didn't break her heart.'

A pause, and then she lifted her shoulders in a small shrug. 'I accept that I may not know the full story. But I'm *still* not attracted to you. I appreciate you coming to warn me, and I'll explain to any reporters it's all a misunderstanding.'

'Actually, I have a different solution.'

Suspicion narrowed her eyes. 'We don't need a different

solution. We don't need any solution because this doesn't need to be a problem.'

'Fine. I have an *idea* I want to run by you. It benefits us both.'

The kettle whistled as she hesitated, and then she pulled a cafetière towards her and nodded. 'OK. Shoot. You've got a cup of coffee's worth of time.'

'Seems fair. I suggest we go along with the press. Run with the story.'

Her hand jolted on the plunger at his words and coffee spilt onto the counter. Etta ignored it. *'Go along with it? Run with the story?'* Her hands tipped in an exaggerated question. *'Why?* Why would we even do a two-minute walk with the story?'

'Because as my girlfriend you can bring Cathy and move in to Derwent Manor with me. You can put together the family tree. In return I will pay you a hefty fee and keep you safe from Tommy. Win-win.'

This way he would get his family tree done by the expert he wanted, she would get the chance to complete a project he knew she wanted, and she would be safe from Tommy. He figured it was pure genius. Etta looked at him as if she thought it was sheer garbage.

'That's nuts.'

'No, it isn't.'

'Yes, it is. For a start, how can you possibly guarantee our safety?'

'I have a number of qualifications in self-defence and a variety of martial arts.'

Once Gabe had worked out that no one was going to rescue him from the horrors of boarding school and the ritual humiliation the other students felt a prospective duke deserved, he'd figured he needed to rescue himself. The best way to do that had been to learn self-defence—and as it turned out he had an aptitude for it.

Etta shook her head, clearly unimpressed by the claim

as she mopped up the spilt coffee and poured the remains into two mugs. 'You don't get it. Tommy is a nutcase. He's a street fighter. He got put away for an assortment of crimes—drug-dealing, armed robbery, and a hit-and-run whilst fleeing the scene of a crime.'

'I'm not belittling any of that, and I'm not blowing hot air—I *can* protect you from Tommy. I didn't just do a few classes and get a few belts. I'm the real McCoy. There is no way I would offer protection if I wasn't one hundred per cent sure I could provide it.'

Her fingers drummed a tattoo on the counter, and her head tilted to one side as her brown eyes assessed him. 'It wouldn't work.'

'Why not?'

'You couldn't protect both Cathy *and* me because we won't be together all the time. Plus...' Her voice trailed off.

Gabe stared at her as his mind trawled the brief time he'd spent with Cathy. 'Plus Cathy doesn't want to go on the cruise because she wants to meet her Dad, and that would make her difficult to protect?' he surmised.

For a moment he thought she wouldn't answer, and then she exhaled on a sigh. 'Yes. Which is why the cruise is a good idea.'

'You can't keep Cathy on a ship in the middle of an ocean for ever.'

'I know that. But right now it works for me as a strategy.'

'I told you yesterday—running away is seldom a good strategy.' He had a memory of his eight-year-old self— the sheer exhilaration that had streamed through his body as he'd escaped boarding school. The terrified but deter-mined trek home to Derwent Manor, the blisters on his aching feet, the growl of hunger in his stomach. His igno-minious reception.

'Derwents do not run, Gabriel. You have let the Der-went name down.'

His explanation about the bullying had fallen on deaf ears.

'*Cowardice cannot be tolerated, Gabriel.*'

'This is a tactical retreat.'

'Don't kid yourself, Etta. A tactical retreat is a chance to move away so that you can regroup, because to stand your ground means certain defeat. You can't regroup on a cruise ship.'

Her mug made a decisive *thunk* on the counter. 'Enough. I've known you for less than twenty-four hours—I don't need your advice or analysis. This doesn't even make sense. There are other historians you could employ in a way that's much more straightforward and considerably less dangerous. *Why* offer to do this at all?'

It was a good question. From the second he'd seen her with Tommy a protective urge had kicked in. Nothing personal, but born from his own childhood experience of bullying, the taste of helplessness, the shameful desire to flee.

'My instinct tells me you are the right person for the job, and I don't like men like Tommy so it would be a great pleasure to kick him round the block. Several times.'

Her expression warmed even as she shook her head. 'That is a wonderful thought, but it won't work. I need Cathy off Tommy's radar.'

'Fair enough.' Turning, he paced the length of the counter. 'How about you stay here and Cathy goes on the cruise? With grandparents or another family member? I'll pay any difference.'

'There *are* no other family members.' Etta's voice was flat, clipped with sadness. 'Which is fine, because *I* will keep Cathy safe.'

'The best way to do that is to deal with Tommy.'

A small sigh escaped her lips and for a heartbeat vulnerability gleamed in the brown depths of her eyes, as if the idea of dealing with Tommy scared her.

'Whilst *I* keep you safe.'

Once again her fingers drummed on the countertop. 'I could ask Steph if she would take Cathy. And Martha, of course. The girls are at college together. I've explained the situation to the head and he is all right with me taking Cathy out as long as she takes some work with her. Martha could do the same. Steph is a self-employed illustrator, so she may be able to take work with her...' Etta shook her head. 'Sorry. I'm thinking out loud here.'

'That's fine with me.'

'I'll talk to Cathy first, and then Steph. *If* they agree I'll research your family tree and in return you will pay me and act as my bodyguard whilst I figure out how to deal with Tommy.'

'And we'll go along with the press angle of a romance between us.'

When he'd seen the article that morning his first thought had been that he'd better warn Etta. His next had been to consider whether this development might be utilised to his advantage. His *and* Etta's. After all, an alliance only worked if it benefited both parties.

'It works for us both.'

'How do you figure that?' Her voice held a certain fascinated curiosity.

'If the press believes we're dating it takes the spotlight away from you researching the new family tree. No one need even know that I am hiring you.' *Nor start to dig into my motivation for doing so.*

Besides, if his father got wind of his supposed 'surprise gift' he'd know something was off—neither the Duke nor Duchess had any interest in the family tree except in that it showed the unbroken direct line that he was about to snap with heart-rending finality.

'That hardly works for *me*. If I am working for you then I want recognition for that.'

'And you can have that recognition. In spades and shovels and pitchforks. After Christmas.'

'A fat lot of good it will do me then. By then my professional reputation will be in ruins. It will look as though you hired me because I was sleeping with you.'

A pause stretched into a silence and for a second Gabe knew with bone-deep certainty that their minds had tracked the same path to an image of silken sheets and bare skin, of touch and taste and…

'Supposedly,' Etta said, her voice a touch breathy. '*Supposedly* sleeping with you.'

'Not when they see your credentials and the results you provide. No one will blame you for mixing business and pleasure—you can spin the whole girlfriend deal into positive publicity. This is an opportunity.' One that any woman he had ever dated had *always* taken advantage of—a chance to glean celebrity coverage and rich pickings.

Her mouth opened in a circle of outrage. 'So you see this as a deal-sweetener?'

Gabe shrugged. 'Yes.'

'Not for me. I'd rather earn positive publicity through my *work*. So thanks, but no, thanks. I'll do your family tree. But I won't be your girlfriend. Fake or otherwise.' Her chin tilted in challenge. 'Take it or leave it.'

There was no quarter in her words and a hint of chagrin touched his nerves…along with a small burn of surprise. Not that it mattered. The most important objective had been achieved and he was a step closer to finding a future Derwent heir.

'I'll take it. We can tell the press I'm hiring you as a consultant for the Christmas Fair.' Yet her continued refusal to acknowledge their attraction prompted his vocal chords. 'But any time you change your mind and want to be my girlfriend—fake or otherwise—let me know. We can play this any way you want. It's up to you.'

CHAPTER FIVE

'ANY TIME YOU change your mind and want to be my girl-friend—fake or otherwise—let me know.'

The words, uttered in tones of molten chocolate, buzzed around Etta's brain and demolished each and every brain cell in their path.

Their whole conversation, with its undertone of aware-ness, had sent her body into overdrive. Her whole being tingled, sparkled, as sensations tap-danced on her skin.

Get a grip. Of some form of sanity.

Flirting with Gabriel Derwent was idiocy—the man had a master's degree in the art and she didn't hold so much as a pass. Yet her imagination danced with the possible scenario—what would he do if she took him up on the 'otherwise' option? Chose to join the ranks of his playboy play dates…? *Yuck*, said the tiny part of her brain that ad-vocated logic and common sense. *Yum*, shrieked her hor-mones, dizzy at the prospect.

The atmosphere in the room had accelerated to steamy and Gabe was so close. His eyes were dark with desire… dark as the blue of a storm-tossed sea. Breathing seemed problematic, time slowed in direct correlation to the leap in her pulse and her lips parted in anticipation.

Then guilt slammed in. *What am I doing?* Attraction led to loss of perspective, made you behave in ways so stupid and alien they changed your life, caused pain and loss. Al-ready for long moments she had taken her eye off the most important issue: Cathy.

Pressing her lips together, she moved away from him, all

too aware of the telltale jerkiness of her movements. *Focus, Etta.* No way would she give Gabriel Derwent any power over her—she would not relinquish even a jot of control. To any man. *Ever.* She'd experienced powerlessness first-hand already. Never again.

'I don't want to play at all. I want to keep my daughter safe. I'll let you know what is happening once I've spoken to Cathy and Steph. Provided all goes to plan, I'll travel down to Derwent Manor once Cathy is safely gone.' Holding out a hand she waited expectantly, but Gabriel didn't move to take it.

'I'm not going anywhere. Whatever happens, you need to go home to get your suitcases. There's a chance Tommy will be there, and it's a definite that the press will be. So I'll go with you. I'm your bodyguard, Etta, so you'd better get used to me.'

Just fabulous.

'And speaking of the press conference,' he continued smoothly. 'We'd better discuss a strategy. That photograph needs to be explained.'

There seemed little point in a reiteration of her the-photographer-got-it-wrong defence because it sucked. The previous night she'd thought she'd been poleaxed when she first saw him. Well, that was a freaking understatement—if she looked closely at that picture she'd probably spot the drool on her chin. Though at least Gabe looked similarly afflicted, and despite herself there was that funny little thrill. *Again.*

'I…' In truth she couldn't think of a single explanation, and he knew it. A smile quirked his lips and she was tempted to kick him in the shin. *Hard.* 'We need to stress that our association is strictly professional. That you are hiring me as a consultant for the Christmas Fair.'

'And hope they believe us and don't pick up on our body language?'

'There *is* no body language.'

'You're one hundred per cent sure of that?'

'One hundred and ten,' she stated. 'So there will be nothing for the press to pick up on.'

Even if she had to douse herself in an ice bath before meeting them.

'I'll go and talk to Cathy and then call Steph.'

Gabe watched Etta leave and felt intrigue mingle with surprise—most women would have taken him up on his offer. Especially given the flare of mutual attraction. For a second disappointment lingered at her refusal to acknowledge it, let alone act on it. But there would be other women—right now his focus was on business, not pleasure, so really he should feel relief at her decision to keep their relationship professional.

Glancing round Steph's kitchen, Gabe saw that Etta featured in the collage of photographs—an absurdly young-looking Etta with a woman he presumed to be Steph posing at a carousel. Etta held a dark-haired toddler, a miniature version of today's Cathy, and Steph held a blonde little girl of a similar age. There was another picture of the two women with their girls in school uniform, beaming with similar gap-toothed grins at the camera.

Gabe felt a two pronged searing of loss—for a past he couldn't change and a future he wouldn't have. The only photos he had of himself with his mother were publicity shots, and he would have no children to be pictured with. Fate had decreed that his body would let him down and the Derwent line would end. But perhaps there was still hope—perhaps there was another heir out there and Etta would find him. *That* was the goal.

As if on cue, the kitchen door opened to reveal Etta.

'Steph and Martha are thrilled, and Cathy is at least more enthusiastic than she was. Though she wants to speak to you alone. I don't know why. Maybe she wants to make sure you won't beat Tommy up too badly. Or—' she gave a sudden smile '—maybe she's checking you out as a suitable person for me to stay with.'

'I'll assure her that my intentions are strictly honourable.' *More's the pity*, whispered his libido.

Five minutes later Cathy entered the room and headed to the large wooden table in the window alcove. Gabe seated himself opposite her and waited as she surveyed him. Her assessment was direct, as if she were trying to decide how to play him. Fair play to her—it would be his own strategy in her place.

'So Mum will be staying with you?'

'Yes.'

'And you will protect her from my dad?'

'Yes.'

'It won't be necessary.' Cathy's chin tilted at an angle that mirrored Etta's line of stubbornness. 'Dad just wants to see *me*. I don't get what's so bad about that. He has changed over the past sixteen years. You'd think Mum would be glad.'

'I saw your dad last night, Cathy, and he struck me as potentially dangerous.'

For a nanosecond doubt entered her eyes, and then she shook her head. 'We're all *potentially* dangerous. Dad wouldn't hurt me. Or Mum.'

'Your mum is just looking out for you.'

'I get that. But I'm *sixteen*. Mum was pregnant with me when she was my age, and she had no one. She's always said she got where she is because people took a chance on her. So why won't she give Dad a chance?'

Gabe sensed deep waters closing in over his head. 'Cathy, this is something you should discuss with your mum, not me.'

'But I won't be *able* to discuss it with her because *I'll* be in the middle of the ocean. *You'll* be with Mum whilst *she* is dealing with Dad. You could help me, seeing as I've helped you.'

This was a girl after his own heart—a girl who saw the value of quid pro quo. 'How do you work that out?'

'You really want Mum for this job, and I could have got her to turn it down.'

'You could have,' he agreed. 'But it's not my place to influence your mum's decisions. I'm her employer. Plus, I'm sure your mum knows what she's doing with regard to your father.'

Cathy shook her head. 'Once Mum makes up her mind she digs her heels in. She'll never admit she's wrong about Dad. *Never*. Especially not if everyone keeps agreeing with her. *You* managed to persuade her to take your job instead of coming on this cruise. That's, like, *incredible*. You could try and persuade her to give Dad a chance.'

'I'm sorry, Cathy, but no can do. This is between your mum and you.'

A knock on the door interrupted them and Gabe turned his head to see Etta approaching the table. She looked professional from the tips of her smooth short chestnut hair that curved to touch the hollows of her shoulder blades to the tips of her black buttoned boots. The tailored two-toned blue tweed jacket worn over a matching dress gave a stylish twist to her authority. Seamed at the waist, the sophisticated shift with its V neckline emphasised both her slenderness and her curves and Gabe's breath caught in his throat.

'Sorry to interrupt, but Steph and Martha are back and we need to go and get our suitcases. And face the press.'

Cathy rose from her chair and threw one last glance of appeal at Gabe. 'At least promise you'll think about what I've said.'

'Think about what?' Etta asked, once her daughter had left the room, and then she shook her head. 'Forget I asked. That's not fair. Cathy wanted to speak with you privately. Just promise me she hasn't got any hare-brained schemes in her head.'

'If she has she didn't confide them to me. Plus, short of swimming the ocean, I can't see there is much she can do.'

'That's true.' Smoothing her skirt down, she hauled in a breath. 'So, shall we go?'

'Yes.' He rose to his feet and saw the pallor of her face. 'You don't need to be nervous.'

'Actually, I think I do. A certifiable nutter may well be lurking amongst that throng of press sniffing out a non-existent story.'

'The press will work in our favour. The last thing Tommy will want, if he is serious about seeing Cathy, is any confrontation recorded by the press. Plus, late last night he was in Cornwall—my guess is he won't have made it back here yet.'

'That's true.'

Etta looked marginally more cheerful, and a funny feeling of satisfaction that he'd erased at least one line from her furrowed brow touched his chest.

'Odds are he's sleeping off a session in the pub as well. He'd already been drinking when he found me.'

A small shudder shivered through her, as if the words had triggered a memory she'd rather forget. Gabe's guess was that Tommy was a mean drunk and his fists clenched—with any luck Tommy *would* turn up, and Gabe could make him wish he hadn't.

In the meantime… 'Don't mention Cathy to the press at all. The implication for Tommy will be that Cathy is with you at Derwent Manor—that way he won't try anything when she's en route to the cruise. And keep an eye out for April Fotherington—she's a good reporter but she'll be pushing the romance angle.'

'You can't push something that doesn't exist.'

Her tone brooked no argument.

One more sweep of her hand over her skirt and she nodded. 'Let's do this. Sooner we go, the sooner it's over, right?'

'Right. Let's get this show on the road.'

* * *

'And it *was* a pretty impressive show,' Etta admitted later to Steph, even as reluctance twisted her tongue.

The press had adored him, had seemingly accepted their professional status, and had taken Gabe's assurance that, with his father so unwell, romance was the last thing on his mind. That all he wanted was to ensure the Derwent Manor Christmas Fair was an unparalleled success, so that the Duke of Fairfax could be reassured that all was well. And so he had hired Etta Mason, renowned historian, to help ensure that his Victorian theme was historically accurate.

Only April Fotherington had been a little sceptical, but she had backed down when Gabe had offered her exclusive coverage of the fair.

'In fact he turned the whole thing into a massive publicity stunt for the Christmas Fair.'

'Definitely impressive,' Steph said, with an approving nod of her ash-blond head. 'And that's because he's a pretty impressive guy.'

Her friend grinned in a way that Etta could only categorise as sly.

'I still don't fully understand why you didn't take him up on the girlfriend idea.'

There were still some idiotic seconds when Etta wondered the same thing. 'Because it would be wrong. On so many levels.'

'And right on *so* many others. Honest, hun, I think you are *mad*! Imagine what fun you could have had. The pictures in the magazines, the fancy dinners, romantic champagne-filled weekends away...'

Steph wiggled her eyebrows and despite herself Etta grinned even as she shook her head.

'I don't *do* romance, Steph. You know that.' Maybe Tommy had beaten it out of her. Maybe it was a missing gene. Inherited from the birth parents she'd never known.

'Forget romance—you could have had some *fun* as his

fake girlfriend. You could have even more fun as his *real* girlfriend. I can tell you fancy him. Why not go for it?'

'I agree.'

Etta looked up as Cathy and Martha entered the room, laden with suitcases, and dropped them next to Steph and Martha's bright pink ones by the door.

'Steph's right,' Cathy continued. 'You *should* have some fun.' Cathy's pretty face grew serious as she came forward and perched on the arm of Etta's chair. 'Mum, I know how much you've done for me, and I know you missed out on loads of the fun that other teenagers and young women had because you were looking after me. Now's your chance to make up for it for a while. Have fun. Go to parties. Dress up. Dance the night away.'

'Cathy, sweetheart…' Her heart turned over with love for her daughter as she reached up to cup her face. 'I promise you that I have never once regretted all those nights of "fun" I supposedly missed out on. You are the very best thing that ever happened to me.'

That was the complete truth. Without Cathy, who knew whether she would have found the courage to leave Tommy, to run away in the depths of the night and find refuge on the streets. Without Cathy to care for would she have studied and worked and become the person she was? Probably not, was the answer.

'I don't need to dance the night away with anyone. Let alone Gabriel Derwent.'

As if on cue the doorbell rang, and Steph rose to answer it. Minutes later she ushered in Gabriel, followed by the tall, brown-haired Ethan Caversham.

Resolutely Etta kept her gaze on Ethan as she rose to her feet, yet despite herself she felt her skin shiver in response to Gabe's proximity, her whole body on super-alert.

'Ethan, this is so kind of you.' Gabe had asked Ethan to drive Steph, Martha and Cathy to the cruise ship as an added precaution against Tommy. 'I can't thank you enough.'

'It's no problem. Ruby sends her love and says you have to come round for lunch soon.' His face softened when he mentioned his wife in exactly the same way Ruby's did when she mentioned Ethan, and it filled Etta with a strange yearning—the equivalent of a child with her nose pressed against a sweet shop window, knowing she couldn't have a single sugar-coated mouthful.

'Sounds great.'

But now it was time to say goodbye, and Etta felt tears prickle at the backs of her eyes as she turned to her daughter. She thanked her lucky stars that whatever genes she was missing she had never once had any inclination to abandon *this* precious part of her life.

'Cathy, sweetheart. Have fun, and take care, and listen to Steph, and do all your college work, and…'

Cathy hurtled into her arms and wrapped her arms around her waist. 'Mum, I'll be fine. *You* take care—and *you* look after her,' she added, turning to glare at Gabe.

'I will,' Gabe said, his voice serious, and Cathy gave a small satisfied nod.

Then, minutes later, they were gone.

Pull it together, Etta. This was the right thing to do. Her daughter would be safe. That was all that mattered.

'It's OK to be upset.'

Gabriel's voice held a sympathy that surprised and distracted her from thoughts of Cathy as she turned to face him.

'I know. And I know Cathy is sixteen—she's definitely old enough to do this. It's just that we've never been apart this long before. A weekend here and there, but otherwise it's been her and me all the way.'

His face held an unreadable expression, and a hint of sadness whispered through his eyes. 'Then she is very lucky.'

'I don't know… I've always felt bad that she doesn't have a family.' Familiar sorrow touched her that she'd been unable to provide Cathy with grandparents. Only birth parents who had abandoned Etta at a day old and adoptive parents who had turned her away when she'd refused to give up Cathy.

Your choice, Etta. We'll take you back, but surely you can't want to keep a child who carries that man's genes? Her adoptive mother's words had slammed her with clarity—the reason her parents hadn't been able to love her was because for all those years they'd raised her they had believed her to be tainted by the genes of her unknown birth parents.

Etta pushed the memories down fiercely—what was done was done. Over the years she had come to realise that her parents hadn't *chosen* not to love her. They had entered into adoption with every intention of loving her—had truly believed they could take in a child who didn't share their blood or genes. And maybe they *could* have loved a different child. Just not Etta.

Enough.

Such thoughts were unproductive at best, depressing at worst. Now she had Cathy, and that was all the family she needed. She had Steph, other friends, a career—a life that she had built brick by painstaking brick.

Etta lifted her shoulders. 'But it is as it is, and I know I'm lucky to have her. Cathy is a fabulous girl—really together, caring, bright—' She broke off. 'Sorry, I sound like one of those dreadful mothers who goes on and on about their precious little darlings.'

'No, you sound like someone who gets on well with her child, and that's something to be proud of.'

'Thank you. Cathy and I *do* get on well. That's why I'll miss her. Especially now, with the run-up to Christmas. We go a little Christmas mad—we decorate the flat to within an inch of its life and I get the biggest tree we can cram in. Oh, and last year we had an inflatable Rudolph on the patio. Hard to imagine, but there it is!'

Embarrassment struck. This man was an aristocrat. His Christmases were undoubtedly posh, expensive affairs, and here she was rabbiting on about plastic tat.

'Anyway, I'm sure your Christmas is far more sophisticated.'

A shrug greeted the comment. 'I'm not much of a Christmas person.'

Etta blinked. 'How can you *not* love Christmas?'

'It's not my thing.' His expression was closed, as if he regretted his admission. 'It's not a big deal.'

But it *was* a big deal. Christmas was about love and family and peace and goodwill. 'So how are you going to plan a Christmas fair if you're full of *Bah humbug* rather than Christmas cheer.'

'That's different. This fair has been an annual tradition at Derwent for the past one hundred and fifty years—since Victorian times. Which is why I am introducing a Victorian theme this year. It's never been themed before, but I think it will attract bigger crowds, which will mean more money coming in. There will be re-enactors, Victorian games for the children...'

His deep voice vibrated with enthusiasm, but more than that it resonated with determination that the fair would be a success—an extravaganza. Almost as if he wanted, *needed* to make a statement, to impose his own brand on the fair. Purpose showed on every hard plane of his face, and his attitude a far cry from that of an idle aristocrat. His sheer aura sent a frisson of an elusive something through her body.

'It sounds incredible, and I'll help in any way I can— especially as we've told the press that you're hiring me as a consultant. Plus, I'll need to get my Christmas fix from somewhere.'

'But your priority is the family tree.'

'Of course. The sooner I get started the happier I'll be.'

In fact Etta realised she hadn't given any thought to what happened next, because somehow since Gabe's arrival into her life everything had moved so fast. Under *his* orders. 'So the sooner we set off to Derwent Manor the better.'

'We'll go tomorrow. It's better to stay in London tonight, until Ethan lets us know they are safely aboard. Just in case something unforeseen happens.'

Panic clutched her, tightened round her chest. 'You don't think Tommy could…?'

'Could have found out about the cruise? I don't see how, but it's best to be prepared for any contingency. If he *is* around, Ethan will deal with him.'

Curiosity flickered. 'So you and Ethan must be good friends?'

Was it her imagination or did he hesitate ever so imperceptibly before he answered.

'I only met him a couple of weeks ago. Cora knows the Cavershams well, so I asked her for an introduction in the hope of persuading them to give me an invitation to their Advent Ball. It snowballed from there.'

Curiosity bubbled. 'And on the back of that you asked him to drive Steph, Cathy and Martha to the cruise ship?'

'Yes.'

Etta waited, but clearly that was it.

Instead of elaborating Gabe glanced at his watch. 'If you're ready we should leave now. The hotel is booked.'

'I'll pay for it. We're only staying in London because of Cathy.'

'It's all part of the job package. The deal we have is all-expenses-paid, and we'll be discussing the parameters of the job over dinner.'

'But that doesn't seem fair—really, I'd rather pay…'

His eyebrows rose in a look of surprise that was almost comical—presumably he wasn't used to women offering to pay their own way. Yet if she didn't she would feel like one of *those* women, and the idea swirled in a conflict of sensation inside her tummy. His words still echoed her brain—*'Any time you change your mind and want to be my girlfriend—fake or otherwise—let me know.'*

Not happening.

'Really. Really. *Really.*'

Now amusement touched his face, and she knew he had read her mind. 'And *I'd* really, really, *really* prefer to pay myself. Don't worry—there is no hidden meaning to this. If it makes you feel better it's tax-deductible.'

Etta hesitated, then nodded. Perhaps she could have a word with Reception and work out a way to settle the bill once they got there.

As Gabe pulled into a space in a public car park in central Mayfair he glanced across at Etta. 'It's a minute's walk from here.'

'Where are we staying?

Snapping his seatbelt undone, Gabe named one of London's most prestigious hotels.

'We can't stay *there*.'

'Why not?' No woman he knew would pass up the opportunity.

'Because it will cost a fortune.'

'That is not your concern.' Though the mutinous line of her lips indicated otherwise. 'There's little point in refusing—it's booked and paid-for already.'

Her eyes narrowed, but she unclicked her seatbelt and minutes later they emerged into the crisp, cold dusk. The streets were adorned by spectacular Christmas lights that arched over them in a glittering extravagant swirl of stars and planets.

Etta exhaled on a gasp of wonder. 'It's incredible. Every year I forget how fantastic it is.'

Every tree was festooned with brightly lit baubles. The smell of roast chestnuts mingled with the aroma of mince pies, and a group of teenage carol singers tinged the air with festive songs.

As they joined the bustling throng of Christmas shoppers Etta paused outside each shop window. Every single one was filled with a different festive theme. One designer shop was festooned with greenery and foliage, and enormous red bows, and another was more minimalist, with hundreds of square white presents dangled in an eye-catching concentric design. Another boasted a tableau of angels and cherubs…another depicted an incredible 'partridge in a pear tree' ensemble, made up of different fabrics and beads. But Gabe derived more pleasure from the intent look on Etta's face, as if she were taking mental photographs of each window.

They approached the hotel, where eight abundantly lit gold Christmas trees filled the balustrade above the entrance. The windows blazed and sparkled with strings of dazzling lights, and liveried hotel staff waited to usher them through the ornate revolving doors and into the foyer.

Etta stood stock-still as she gazed at the Christmas tree inside, and Gabe didn't blame her. The enormous realistic-looking spruce was placed in the middle of a carousel straight from Victorian times. Each brightly painted horse seemed to have a character of its own, and each one somehow gave an illusion of movement. The tree itself towered over the signature sweep of the hotel's grand staircase. Hundreds of blown glass ornaments rested amid the branches, and as he stepped closer Gabe could see that each one depicted an aspect of a funfair: a stick of candy floss, a windmill, a toffee apple, a hoopla ring…

Next to him, Etta stirred herself out of her trance. 'Awesome. I could stand and stare at it for hours.'

'And you can. But let's check in first.'

They walked across the marbled floor to the impressive long reception desk.

'Hi. I have a booking under the name of Derwent for a suite with two interconnecting rooms.'

'Yes, I have that right here.'

A bellboy hovered, took their bags and led them to the state-of-the-art lifts. He escorted them up to the eighth floor and opened the door of the suite.

'I've got it from here,' Gabe said, and waited until the youngster had gone before he took Etta through.

Etta stepped into the enormous, beautifully furnished room and stopped. 'This is amazing, but it isn't necessary. You didn't need to book a suite.'

'It's safer. My guess is that Tommy will head down to the Manor, but if he has tracked you to here I'll feel better able to control the situation in a suite.'

'But… I…' Genuine worry creased her features into a frown.

'I really don't understand the problem. I can afford this.' Impatience warred with the novelty of an implied accusation from a woman that he was spending too much on her.

'I understand that, and I don't want to seem ungrateful, but this morning at the press conference you waxed lyrical about Derwent Manor and your family, and your commitment to raising money for its maintenance. That's what the Christmas Fair is about. Yet here you are, squandering Derwent money on this hotel when we could easily have stayed somewhere else at a fraction of the price. I understand that you work for the estate, but I don't see how you can justify your lifestyle with your commitment to maintaining the manor.'

'I'm not "squandering Derwent money".' Gabe exhaled a sigh, irritated to find that the judgement in Etta's tawny eyes had touched a nerve. 'I don't draw my money from the Derwent Estate. I have my own investment business.' He'd decided long ago that he needed independence from his parents, and it turned out he had a real financial flair. 'The money I earn from that funds my lifestyle.'

'Oh.'

There was no mistaking her surprise—in fact her jaw had headed floorward and he gave a rueful twisted smile.

Her tawny brown eyes, soft with contrition, held his as she stepped towards him. 'I'm sorry. I made a judgement based on insufficient evidence. I had you down as nothing but a shallow playboy, living off Daddy's money. Turns out that wasn't the full picture.'

Now she was closer, and one small hand reached up and rested on his forearm. The touch fizzed against the cotton of his shirt. The moment stretched, the scent of strawberry shampoo assailed his nostrils, and as she looked up at him, then closed the gap between them, the urge to kiss those full lush lips nearly overwhelmed him. The approval in her eyes warmed his skin and a warning flare was set off in his brain.

He did not need Etta Mason's *approval*. Annoyance banded his chest. There had been no need to tell her about his company, to volunteer information. As for the urge to kiss her—he'd be damned if he did. Etta had made it clear their mutual attraction was not welcome and he would respect that—wouldn't risk spooking her. Not when the new family tree was on the line. The ball was in her court—it was her choice what to do with it.

Stepping back, he kept his voice light. 'Well, now you know. I'm a shallow playboy living off my own money.' Another step back and he glanced at his watch. 'Our table is booked in an hour, so I'll meet you back here then.'

For a second she stood as if frozen, then one slim hand rose and touched her lips. 'Sounds like a plan.'

Etta practically leapt across the room and dived into her bedroom. The click of the lock turning was more than expressive of her feelings.

CHAPTER SIX

ETTA STARED AT her flushed face in the enormous chrome-framed mirror that reflected a positively palatial art deco bathroom—white sinks embedded in beds of marble, snow-white towels hanging from gleaming heated rails… Somehow she had to get a grip. It was as if the surroundings had somehow turned her light-headed. The surroundings or the man who had provided them.

Enough. She loathed these sensations he induced. Back in that empress-worthy lounge, with its sleek modern furnishings and sumptuous cushioned sofas, she had wanted him to kiss her. *Again.*

Time to take control. No way—*no way*—would she lose her hard-won self-respect and throw herself at Gabriel Derwent. She would *not* give him any vestige of power over her—would not let these giddy feelings sway her, make her take her eye off what was important. She was a professional, a career woman, a renowned historian—not a foolish teenager as she had been with Tommy. When she had allowed feelings and sensations to override all sense and decency.

Never again.

That moment earlier had been an aberration—nothing more. Brought on by the emotional intensity of the past days and by yet another of her misconceptions about Gabriel Derwent being tumbled down. From now on in it would be professional all the way.

One blissful shower later and she gazed at her wardrobe choice, then pulled out a midnight blue fifties-inspired evening dress. Perfect. Long-sleeved, with a straight demure neckline, and a fun flared skirt, cinched at the waist with a vintage belt.

As she buckled her high-heeled Mary Janes her mobile rang.

'Steph. Is everything OK?'

'Everything is fine,' her best friend said cheerfully. 'Ethan got us here safely. No sign of Tommy and the cruise ship is awesome. The girls are in seventh heaven and I'm about to embark on a cocktail. So don't worry about anything.'

Ten minutes later Etta dropped her phone into her vintage evening bag and headed for the lounge. Bracing herself for the inevitable impact, she opened the door and instructed her lungs to breathe.

Gabe stood by an enormous arched window against the magically lit backdrop of Mayfair. His blond hair glistened with the remnants of a shower, and she stood mesmerised as he shrugged a dark grey jacket over a pristine white shirt. The expensive material seemed to mould to the breadth of his shoulders and she gulped. Without her brain's permission her gaze dropped to the triangle of skin at the apex of his chest and a small shiver ran through her.

For a crazy moment she didn't care about self-respect or professionalism. She wanted to walk across the room and press her finger over that patch of bare skin.

Well, tough. That wasn't happening.

As he turned she forced her features into neutral and fixed a cool smile to her lips. There was a silence, and then, his jaw clenched, he stepped forward. 'Let's go,' he said.

'Right behind you.'

And what a view that is, whispered a small, defiant unprofessional part of her as they descended the grand staircase.

The hotel glowed with a mingling of wealth and Christmas cheer, and the sheer decadence of the art deco foyer

was completed with a chandelier that threw out beams
of diamond-white light that played and sparkled over the
wreath-laden walls.

Lights and baubles arched over the entrances, fluted pillars trailed tiny iridescent lights, and floral displays spread
their magnificence over glass-topped tables and filled the
air with heavenly scents. Just for a moment Etta relaxed,
almost wishing this were a real date. *Almost.* After all, her
track record with dates was hardly stellar.

They walked towards the entrance to the restaurant—a
curtained doorway that rippled with a dark green tasselled
fabric. Etta stepped through and gasped...

The vast vaulted ceiling gave the room an organic simple
feel, and the predominant colours of green and brown gave
the area an enchanted sylvan warmth. Walnut tables with
slate placemats dotted the floor around the centrepiece—
a bare-branched tree with stars hanging from every polished wooden limb.

'This is fabulous,' she said as a waiter led them to their
table.

As they walked she became aware of the looks directed
at them—or rather at Gabe—and her step faltered slightly,
though he seemed oblivious.

'Is it difficult?' she asked, once they were seated on
green leather chairs.

'What?'

'Being recognised all the time?'

'You get used to it. My parents always taught Kaitlin
and me to use the attention if we could, but also always
to be aware of how our behaviour could impact upon the
family image.'

'What about Cora?'

'Cora pretty much avoided *any* publicity—even as a
child. My parents had to focus on Kaitlin and me as Derwent ambassadors.'

'I'm with Cora on that one.' Etta glanced swiftly around

and resisted the urge to wriggle in her seat. 'What about *my* behaviour? If I eat with the wrong knife will that impact on you?'

'You're looking at it the wrong way. You should be thinking how to use the situation to your advantage. Most women do.'

'Isn't that a bit cynical?'

Etta studied the menu. Her tastebuds cartwheeled, already jumping about in anticipation as she read the selection. Each item was a seasonal delicacy that offered local fresh produce with a twist.

'No. It's the truth. But I don't mind if my date can score a bit of beneficial publicity—good for her. As long as she doesn't lie or smear me in any way, I don't begrudge her.'

No wonder he'd assumed she would jump at the chance to pose as his girlfriend. 'Well, I don't want to exploit your name or your title. In any way. In fact I hope that the press were thoroughly diverted from the scent this morning. If April Fotherington saw us here she would *definitely* get the wrong end of the stick.' The reporter was renowned for her ability to track down celebrities and unearth the juiciest of stories. 'She has pulled off some pretty big celebrity scoops.'

Amusement gleamed in his eyes. 'So you're a celebrity gossip magazine reader?'

'I'm not. Well, I am—but only because of Steph. She reads them avidly and I end up browsing through them too.'

'You two are really close?'

'Yup. Steph is like family.' Her mind flashed to the birth parents she'd never known, to the adoptive parents who were now lost to her, and to the younger sister she'd barely got a chance to know. *Close it down.* 'Like an older sister, really.'

'How did you meet?'

'At a mother and baby music class when Cathy and Martha were small. The rest of the group didn't exactly approve of me—I was a seventeen-year-old with a toddler. But Steph looked out for me. Actually bothered to talk to me. If it hadn't been for her I'd have cut and run. Anyway, Steph was a single mum too—she'd adopted Martha after her marriage broke down.'

That was another reason why they had connected. Steph had shown Etta that adoption could be a *good* thing—her relationship with Martha was honest, open, and full of love.

'She's ten years older than me but we clicked, and Martha and Cathy bonded instantly, so our friendship took off from there.'

'You're lucky to have each other.'

'I know. We are totally different, but it doesn't seem to matter. Steph would love all this.' Etta glanced round the room. 'She'd agree with you that I should take complete advantage of you.'

Oh, hell. Had she said that? The words took on a double meaning that she hadn't planned, and now the words kept tumbling out.

'I mean…I mean she thought I should take you up on the girlfriend idea and enjoy the publicity and the dinners and a romantic getaway. A *fake* romantic getaway obviously.'

Stop the talk. Now.

'I've told you it's not too late to change your mind.'

Lazy amusement touched his voice and she narrowed her eyes. No way would she let him think she regretted her decision.

'The ball's in your court,' he continued.

'That's where it's staying.' Yet her tummy did a loop-the-loop at the depth of his voice, the way his dark eyes rested on her lips. 'I was talking about *Steph*, and as I said she and I are chalk and cheese.'

'So Steph would go for the shallow playboy type?'

'Yes.'

'But you won't because…? Remind me again.'

'Because there is more to attraction than the physical side of things.'

Really? asked her sceptical hormones—after all, in the last few years there had been no 'physical side' at all. With anyone. Just a sad series of failed fizz-free dates that had culminated in nothing. And before that there had been a couple of tepid relationships that were best consigned to the 'bedroom disaster' category of her memory banks.

'So you admit there *is* a physical attraction?'

'I…' Darn the man! 'That is irrelevant.'

'It seems pretty relevant to me.'

'I said there has to be *more* than physical appeal.'

'Sure—I agree. Conversation is useful too. You and I don't seem to have any problem there.'

'That is still not enough.'

'It works for me. What's wrong with a few days of fun, no strings attached?'

'It's just *wrong.*'

The idea of letting go, revelling in sensation, was impossible to imagine.

An echo of her mum came: *'Never cross the line, Etta.'* Any line. Even the smallest of childhood fibs had been a heinous crime. Her first Valentine, when she'd been aged ten—an innocent offering—had drawn forth horror. Her parents had made her tear it up into little pieces and told her she must have behaved with 'promiscuity' to attract it. She'd had to look the word up in a dictionary, and even now the remembered burn of shame seared her soul. Even though she'd come to understand her parents' actions—they had been on a constant lookout for her unknown genes to show themselves.

'So you disapprove from a *moral* viewpoint? You shouldn't.' The amusement had vanished now and his voice was edged with cold. 'I am still in touch with nearly all the women I've dated. They aren't mindless bimbos. They are all passionate and fun-loving and we had good times—in bed and out. They did nothing *wrong* and neither did I.'

'I understand that, and I *don't* disapprove. It just doesn't make sense to me. What's the point of entering into a short-term relationship with no future?'

'That's like saying, "What's the point of going to a party?" just because you know it will end.'

'You can't equate a party to a relationship.'

'Why not?' His mouth quirked up, and the teasing glint was back in his blue-grey eyes.

'Because a party is a social gathering and a relationship is a…a connection between two people.'

'Exactly—and those two people can define that connection in whatever way they want. They can make an agreement, an alliance, a pact to last a few days or a lifetime. You scratch my back, or whatever bit you choose, and I'll scratch yours.'

Her back positively tingled in response, and her tummy turned to hot, gooey mush at the thought. His smile expanded and a wave of relief washed over her at the arrival of the waiter with their entrées.

As she thanked him, and inhaled the exquisite aromas that arose from her plate, she gathered her thoughts. She would not back down on this. Would not let the ledge of certainty she'd always camped out on crumble.

'Nope. You've got it wrong. Relationships *can't* be a pact because relationships involve emotions and you can't control those or agree on them. Emotions don't remain static. You may enter into the pact with the best intentions, but feelings could develop. How do you know you won't fall in love with one of these short-term women or vice versa?'

Ha. Etta forked up a mouthful of her starter and exhaled a small huff of pleasure. The seared venison had a smoky juniper taste, and the tang of elderberries and the crunch of walnuts in the salad made her savour each bite.

Gabe took a sip of wine. 'So you wouldn't have a fling

with me because you're worried you'd fall in love with me or I'd fall in love with you?'

'*No!* Because neither of those things would happen.'

'Exactly. So what's the problem?'

Etta narrowed her eyes. 'We are talking in general. *I* wouldn't have a fling with you because you are not my type.'

'Oh, yes. I'd forgotten.'

The drawl was underlain with a molten heat that warmed her skin.

But she would not succumb to attraction or distraction. 'You haven't answered the question. How do you know one or the other of you won't fall in love?'

'The time frame, for one. I keep my flings short. And I'm very clear upfront about the terms of agreement. The only thing on offer is short-term fun—love is not on the table and neither is my title.'

'So you aren't planning on marriage?'

That didn't make sense. Surely the future Duke of Fairfax had to get married in order to ensure the continuity of the line.

'Not with someone who isn't within my social circle.'

Outrage rendered her near speechless and she could only gawp at him as the waiter cleared their plates and served them their main course. '*Excuse me?* So you believe all these wonderful, liberated women of yours…are *beneath* you? That they aren't worthy to be the Duchess of Fairfax?'

An answering streak of anger flashed lightning-like in his stormcloud-grey eyes and Etta was aware of a strange exhilaration.

'That is not what I said. You're a historian. Haven't farmers and shepherds always wanted to marry farmers' daughters? Women who understand the truth of farming—the back-breaking labour, the weather, the hours, and the work. Or do they want to marry someone who thinks farming is all about sweet little lambs?'

'So you're saying us common people think being a duchess is all about wearing a tiara and going to balls, and a true aristocrat knows it's more than that?'

'Something like that. Marriage is an alliance, and I need to ally myself with a woman who will understand what Derwent Manor means to me—who won't see the house as a money-eating pile better given over to a heritage trust. A woman who will enter into a life dedicated to fundraising and ensuring Derwent Manor remains in the family.'

His large hand reached for his wine glass and for a second his eyes dropped to the amber liquid. His lips set in a grim line, as if the idea filled him with bleak rather than happy thoughts.

'And you think a "commoner" won't be up to the job.'

'Don't twist my words. I just think it would be *easier* for someone used to it. And it will make everyone's life easier if I marry someone who will get on with my parents. Someone who fits.'

'So you're marrying to please your parents?' That seemed impossible to believe of a man of his strength.

'No. But I can't see the harm in marrying someone they approve of.'

A funny little pang assaulted Etta—that ruled her *right* out, then.

'It will lessen the chances of adverse publicity and make working together easier. I'm all for an easy life.'

'What about love?'

Gabe shook his head. 'Love isn't in the equation. It's not a factor. It's not on the table because I neither require love nor offer it. I believe my alliance is more likely to endure without it. Bottom line, love is not relevant.'

She couldn't help but wonder why he believed that. Of course he needed to marry—she understood that—but it all sounded so clinical. Presumably the Duke and Duchess had made an 'alliance', and expected their son and heir to do the same. Yet Gabriel wouldn't bow to their wishes if he didn't want to—ergo, he was more than happy to comply. And yet…

'Is this what you *want*, though? A cold-blooded alliance? It seems a far cry from "having fun, enjoying yourself, no strings attached". What about liking and physical attraction and warm, passionate women?'

'Of course liking is important, and so is physical attraction. But long-term I need someone who shares my goals and understands that there is more to life than my "shallow playboy" existence. So I'll be offering something different to my wife and expecting something different from what I get from my flings.'

'But…' It still seemed wrong.

Leaning over, he topped up their wine glasses. 'Enough of my attitude to love and marriage,' he said. 'What about yours?'

Etta took a sip of the golden liquid with its overtones of elderflower and narrowed her eyes. *Botheration!* The last thing she wanted was to discuss her inadequacy, her missing gene, her inability to connect romantically. Yet she'd sat here and interrogated Gabe on *his* attitude to love without compunction. Fair was fair.

CHAPTER SEVEN

GABE CRADLED HIS wine glass, watched the swirl of emotions crossing Etta's face—the crease of her brow, the angle of her cheekbone, the quick gesture to tuck a tendril of chestnut hair behind her ear—and wondered how a business dinner had morphed into this. Perhaps he should shut this down now, but he didn't want to—he welcomed the distraction from his own thoughts and the prospect of his marriage.

It was a merger that would now have a key component missing. Children. His hopes and expectations had dissipated to dust, but marriage was still a necessity. The manor would need a duchess and if—no, *when*—he found another heir, that man's wife would need a role model. Because Gabe had every intent of persuading this heir to take his duties and responsibilities seriously; he owed it to his name, to the estate, to find a way forward. But tonight he wanted to forget that.

'When you're ready.'

Her shoulders lifted. 'My attitude to love and marriage is easy enough to encapsulate. They aren't for me.'

'Why not?' Surprise made him raise his eyebrows—somehow he'd expected someone as vital as Etta Mason to embrace love. Assumed her antipathy to a short-term fling sprang from a desire for a waltz over the happy-ever-after horizon.

'I'm not made that way. I'm truly happier on my own. I'm in charge—I don't have to ask anyone's permission or compromise in any way at all. If I want to get home and change into my PJs, curl up on the sofa and watch a history film and eat cereal I can.'

'So you're choosing sugar-coated flakes over sex, love, and companionship?'

'No! I'm choosing independence and being happy on my own over the pointless pursuit of romance.'

'How can you know it's pointless?'

'Because I've tried. For a while I felt that I needed to find a man and marry him for Cathy's sake, so she could have a dad. But then I realised that wouldn't be fair to anyone. Most of all me. I prefer to be on my own. I've done just fine without a man in my life.'

As if realising she might be protesting too much, she sat back and then picked up her knife and fork to pierce her last piece of fish.

'Maybe you haven't met the right man yet. Every man isn't a Tommy.'

'I *know* that. This is nothing to do with Tommy. I know most men are decent individuals. I *liked* a lot of my dates— I'm still friends with a couple of them and I happily danced at their weddings. But romance isn't my thing and I'm OK with that. I like my independence.'

'I get that, but…' But he couldn't help but wonder if, for Etta, independence equalled safety, and whether her willingness to give up on all aspects of a relationship was due to the damage Tommy had inflicted.

'But what?'

There was pride in her voice, as if she dared him to pity her.

'I think it's a waste. I think you're missing out. You've decided against long *and* short-term relationships.'

'I haven't decided anything. It's just how the custard cream has crumbled.'

'Maybe because you're dating the wrong type of guy?'

'So let me guess… You think I should be dating a guy like *you*?'

Gabe shrugged. 'Why not? If romance isn't for you maybe you should consider what someone *like me* can offer. Instead of dating the type of guys you think you *should* be with.'

The words rang across the table and she flinched. 'I do not want what you can offer. Anyway, what's wrong with dating suitable guys? This coming from a man on the look-out for a "suitable" wife.'

'That's different. You've stopped looking—you've given up. I don't want love, but I'm still up for sex and companionship.'

'Well, I don't need those either. From anyone.' Reaching for her glass, she lifted it and took a gulp of wine, placed the crystal flute down and exhaled on a sigh. 'This isn't a topic I want to discuss.' Her words dripped ice. 'Perhaps we could make this business dinner a tad more businesslike.'

Good job, Gabe. Slow hand-clap, please.

Etta's love life was *zip* to do with him—so why was he rocking the boat when he needed her on board. He cut a piece of tender fillet steak, alongside some of the buttery, floury potato terrine and balanced the forkful on the edge of his plate.

'So let's talk business.'

Business. Business, business, *business*. The byword, the watchword—the *only* word.

It was a mantra Etta repeated to herself every waking second the following day, until they drew up outside the imposing exterior of Derwent Manor. Relief washed over her—now she could get to work, down to *business*, and forget the stupid conversation of the previous night.

Mortification mixed with sheer horror—she'd pretty much admitted to a physical attraction, had laid out the sorry state of her love-life and witnessed his reaction: shock mixed with compassion. With a dose of psychoanalysis. *If romance isn't for you maybe you should consider what someone* like me *can offer. Instead of dating the type of guys you think you* should *be with.*

The words had stung then and the memory of them stung now. The smarting was worsened by a trickle of temptation to cross that line and succumb to their attraction. Become one of those liberated, passionate, and warm women he'd waxed so lyrical about.

Enough. *Business.* No more personal conversations or even thoughts. To be on the safe side she'd requested breakfast in her room and had feigned sleep for the entire journey to Derwent Manor.

Now, as she faked a yawn, she gazed at the manor and nearly choked—of course she'd seen pictures, but nothing could have prepared her for the sheer grandeur of the Elizabethan-style building. The turreted, many-windowed stone building was immense, on a way more opulent scale than the word *manor* suggested.

'It's so big!'

'There was a manor on this site as far back as the thirteenth century, but the building was pretty much scrapped and rebuilt in 1590. It took eight years and who knows how much money. Then in Victorian times it had another makeover—thanks to the Duke at the time cashing in on various industrial schemes. Nowadays we live in some of it, display other rooms to the public and desperately try to pay the maintenance. Kaitlin, Cora, and I used to picture the house actually *eating* money.'

Etta tried to imagine the heating bills, the maintenance costs, and quite simply couldn't. No wonder the Derwents had to dedicate their lives to raising money.

'What do you want to do first?' Gabe asked. 'I could give you a tour, or...'

Etta opened the car door. 'Actually, I'd like to get started. So if you can show me to the records room that would be fantastic.'

Ten minutes later Etta surveyed a room piled with dusty

tomes. Shelves adorned the walls and humidifiers stood in two of the corners. An enormous ornate desk was tucked into another corner, stacked with piles of papers and old photo albums.

'I think this is what is known as one damp mess,' Gabe said.

'To me it's like a treasure trove, waiting to be opened. So if it's OK with you I'll get stuck in.'

'Not until we discuss some security measures. By now Tommy will know you're here. Press coverage wasn't huge, but there was an online article saying that I'd hired you and a bit about the fair—he may well have read it.'

Her anticipation at the prospect of losing herself in the fascination of the past came up against the reality of the present, and fear shivered through her. Tommy was going to be livid when he realised Cathy wasn't with her, and the thought of his anger unearthed a swathe of memories. The thud of her heart, the futile entreaties, the pathetic ways she had tried to appease him.

Gabe muttered an explitive under his breath, stepped forward, and encased her hands in his.

Etta allowed herself one brief instant of reassurance and then pulled away as the feeling of reassurance turned to something else—a heat, an awareness of the feel of his skin against hers...

Business. 'I'm sorry. I'm fine.'

'This room is safe, and it doesn't lead directly onto the grounds. Here.'

Automatically Etta stretched out a hand and he placed a white box in her palm.

'It's a panic pendant. You press the button and an alarm runs to my phone.'

'Thank you.'

Yet even as she looped the pendant over her head Etta knew she must not become dependent on Gabriel—must work out a strategy to be rid of Tommy herself. Because once the job was done Gabe's bodyguard duties would cease.

But right now she was safe, and there was a project to embark on. 'Right. I'm going to get started.'

The hours passed by in a welcome blur. A part of her was aware of Gabe's presence, but he didn't interfere as she inspected and stacked and sorted and dusted and felt the comfort of centuries of history envelop her. As she sifted through the records she could almost *feel* the people in them starting to come alive in her mind.

Until… 'Etta. I think you need to stop before you collapse.'

She rose to her feet from where she'd been inspecting a tottering pile of ancient-looking papers and wiped a hand across her forehead. 'What time is it?'

'Dinner time.' Gabe pointed at a plate of now rather limp-looking sandwiches. 'Especially as you haven't touched lunch.'

'I did mean to eat them. I'm sorry. I got completely absorbed.'

'So I can see. But I'm making an executive decision. You need to stop. I haven't even shown you where you're going to sleep. So, come on, I'll show you your room, then you can freshen up and give me a progress report over dinner.'

'OK.' Etta looked down at herself and grimaced. *Filthy* didn't quite cover it.

As she followed Gabe out of the records room and down a long corridor she took in the faint air of dinginess in the peeling wallpaper and the slight smell of must and damp. Then Gabe pushed a door open and Etta blinked.

'This part of the house is open to the public,' he said.

The contrast was marked: a gleaming oak staircase curved upwards with imposing elegance, polished furniture from times gone by sat on shiny wooden flooring, and gilt-edged portraits adorned the walls.

Etta trailed her hand along the carved oak as she

mounted the richly carpeted stairs, and peeped into rooms resplendent with tapestries and velvet and history.

'Here we are.' Gabe unlocked a door marked Private and they stepped through into a shabby hallway. 'All our money is poured into the upkeep of the estate and the public areas of the house. So I'm afraid you won't be staying in historic splendour yourself.'

'These rooms are still part of history. I'm guessing they were the servants' quarters… Perhaps one of my ancestors worked as a scullery maid here.'

Gabriel pushed a door open. 'Hopefully you'll be fairly comfortable in here.'

'Of course I will.'

The room was simply furnished, but it was clean, and although the walls could have done with a coat of paint there were fresh flowers on the dresser and the eaves and cornices were a reminder of ages past.

'I'll knock for you in half an hour. The bathroom is across the hall.'

Half an hour later Gabe watched Etta seat herself at the large wooden table in the airy well-equipped kitchen. She was dressed in jeans and an oversized jumper, her chestnut hair hung in damp tendrils round her make-up-free face, and she looked absurdly young.

She inhaled appreciatively as Gabriel ladled beef casserole onto a pile of wild rice and handed her the plate. 'This smells divine. Did you make it?'

'Not me. I can cook, but not to this standard. Our housekeeper made it. Sarah has been here for years, and she is always thrilled when one of us comes back to stay.'

In truth, Sarah had been one of the people he'd missed most when he'd been at boarding school. She was one of the few people who had ever hugged the Derwent children.

'So you don't live here?'

'No. I've got my own place in London.' One day, when

he married, he planned to renovate one of the old empty houses on the estate. No way would he expect his wife to live with his parents in the manor, however suitable she might be. No way could *he* live with his parents—the idea was impossible to picture.

'It must have been amazing to grow up here. I felt thrilled for Cathy when I got us a place with a tiny patch of lawn and her own bedroom. So all this space and the gardens… It must have been magical.'

'I didn't really spend that much time here.' He kept his voice deliberately even.

Etta's forehead creased. 'Where were you? I thought the Derwents lived here pretty much all year round?'

'I went to boarding school at eight and I spent a lot of the holidays at various camps.'

Camps to toughen him up. His parents had been appalled when their son and heir had run away from boarding school. His gut still twisted when he remembered the first step in their 'toughen up Gabe' regime—they had sacked his nanny, who had also looked after Kaitlin and Cora.

In truth Megan Anstey had been more of a mother to him than the Duchess had ever been, and he could still taste the grief, feel the tears pounding the back of his eyelids. Tears he'd held in because he'd known if he'd cried his parents would blame Megan, would hold back her references. So he'd uttered a polite, formal goodbye, and later that afternoon he'd been driven back to boarding school.

The entire journey was etched on his memory. Suppressed tears, the tang of grief at the loss of Megan, and the pang of guilt at the consequences to Megan of *his* actions. The realisation had come that if he hadn't let Megan close then he wouldn't be feeling this pain and neither would she.

Then, as the car had sped over the country roads, he had felt the clench of fear in his gut at the knowledge of what awaited him: the glee-edged cruelty and ritual persecution from the bullies. He'd loathed himself for the sheer helplessness he'd felt. Had made a decision that his parents were right—his only option was to toughen up. One day he would make up for his error to Megan Anstey, but he wouldn't let her or anyone else close again. And one day he would take on the bullies and he would win.

Both those days had been a long time coming, but one of his first acts when he'd had money of his own had been to track Megan down and give her a substantial cheque. As for the bullies—eventually he'd got tough enough to fight.

'Oh.' Etta's delicate features were scrunched into an expression of perplexity. 'I can't imagine how that must have felt. I don't think I could have sent Cathy away, missed so much of her childhood.'

'*All* the male Derwents go to boarding school.' Though he had vowed with intensity that he would never send a child of *his* away. Though now that wouldn't be an issue. In any sense of the word. The now familiar ache tightened his chest.

'That must have been tough on your mother.'

He doubted that—his parents had been remote figures all his life. Oh, he knew they were proud of him—proud of his looks and charisma, proud to have produced a healthy male heir. But they had barely registered his absence as a person.

'Did you want to go?' Etta asked, her eyes wide with a mix of curiosity and sympathy.

It was impossible to lie—not when he remembered the bleak horror of those first years. Until he'd learnt to fight back, form alliances, and never show weakness.

'I accepted it,' he stated flatly.

'That doesn't answer—' She broke off as the doorbell rang: a hard, insistent peal. One slender hand rose and rubbed her chest, as if fear had clasped her heart. 'Tommy...' she whispered.

CHAPTER EIGHT

GABE ROSE TO his feet. 'Wait here.'

The temptation to do just that showed on her face, but then she shook her head and pushed back her chair. 'If it's Tommy it's my problem. You're here to guard me. I'm supposed to deal with him.'

Admiration surged inside him—Etta was whiter than milk, and he could see the fear in her eyes, but her back was ramrod-straight as she moved from behind the table.

'All right. But remember if it *is* Tommy I will not let him hurt you. OK?'

A slight hint of colour returned to her cheeks. 'OK,' she repeated as the doorbell rang out again in staccato buzzes. 'But be careful.'

'I will be.' Gabe smiled as an adrenaline buzz kicked into his veins.

They walked through the kitchen and down the corridor to the front door. Gabe tugged it open, unsurprised to see Tommy slouched against the jamb, dressed in jeans and a leather jacket. The dark-haired man smiled—a slow sneer—and Gabe tensed, ready to push Etta behind him.

'Where's my daughter?'

'Not here.' Etta's voice was breathy but clear.

'Then where *is* she? We need to discuss this, Etta. Cathy is my daughter too.'

'There is nothing to discuss.'

'But there is, darlin', there *is*. I've talked to a lawyer and now I want to talk to you. You know it's better to give me what I want.'

Etta flinched, then nodded. 'Ten minutes. We're in the middle of dinner.'

Gabe led the way into a small anteroom.

'Dinner?' Tommy said. 'Very cosy.' His dark blue eyes darted between Etta and Gabe. 'Guess she hasn't got you between the sheets yet, then?'

'Enough.' Gabe moved forward and in one seamless move slammed Tommy against the wall. He saw the surprise in the other man's eyes and revelled in it. 'Let's keep this clean, shall we? Say what you need to say and get out.'

He released his grasp and for a second he thought the other man would go for him—he saw the malevolent gleam in his eye. *Bring it on.*

But then Tommy shrugged, walked over to a chair, and sprawled in it. 'I want to speak to you alone, Etta.'

'No.' Etta folded her arms across her chest. 'Whatever you need to say you can say it in front of Gabe.'

'Whatever?' The word dripped with malice. 'Perhaps we can take a trip down memory lane? I can tell the toff *exactly* what you like and the best way to make you listen.'

Against all probability Etta's complexion took on an even deeper pallor.

'If that's how you want to spend your ten minutes, feel free. But the clock's ticking, Tommy,' Gabe told him.

'Say what you need to say.' Etta's voice was low, but steady, and Gabe hoped the reminder of his presence had helped. 'I've consulted a lawyer too. You're not on the birth certificate. You have no parental responsibility.'

'But I can apply for a court order. Or… Cathy is sixteen-if she wanted she could even move in with me.'

'She'd need my consent until she was eighteen.'

'That's a technicality and you know it. I think in real life there won't be anything you can do about it.' Tommy smiled and settled back in the chair. 'You know I always hated the idea of a family, but now I'm thinking maybe I was wrong. I *like* the idea of having a daughter—someone who carries my blood, my genes—and I believe I have the right to be part of her life. Teach her my ways and my beliefs. You took that opportunity from me, Etta—you ran away and you took away my chance to be a dad.'

'You didn't *want* to be a father.' Etta's voice was tight, and her hands rubbed up and down her arms. 'You punched me in the stomach to try and get rid of the baby.'

Gabe's blood chilled and he stepped forward even as Tommy shook his head. 'That was *your* fault, Etta. You defied me and you know I don't like that. That's something Cathy will need to learn too. It's something I had to learn from *my* father, and it's a tough lesson but an important one.' He rose to his feet. 'Of course I would never hurt Cathy—I'm a reformed man. You see how I didn't lay a finger on your toff, here. I came because I want to give you a heads-up. Let you know I'm coming after my daughter. You took her from me once—now it's my turn. You and me…we've unfinished business. I owe you, and another thing my old man taught me is to always pay my debts.'

Etta stood as if rooted to the spot, her tawny eyes shocked, and anger made Gabe's fists clench. 'You've said your piece. I'll see you out.'

As he walked Tommy to the door Gabe held tight to his anger—yes, his foot itched to boot the man as far as he could kick him, but that wouldn't help the situation.

'Don't come back.'

Gabe shut and locked the door and made his way back to the kitchen. Etta was standing exactly where he'd left her, his arms wrapped around her body, shivering, her lip caught between her teeth.

'He's gone.' Gabe moved towards her. 'Come into the lounge. I'll light a fire and get us a drink.'

Ten minutes later he rose from the fireplace as the logs caught and the flames crackled into a blaze. The scent of pine invaded the air and Etta released a small sigh, as if the warmth gave her comfort. Gabe strode to the lacquered drinks cabinet, selected a bottle of cognac and poured a generous measure into two balloon glasses.

'Here.'

Etta reached up from the depths of the armchair she had curled into. 'Thank you.'

'You're still shivering.' Gabe pulled his thick knitted jumper over his head and handed it to her. 'Put this on until the fire kicks in.'

A hesitation, and then she accepted it. 'Sorry. Tommy really spooked me this time.'

'No need to apologise. The man is clearly, as you said, a first-class nutter and downright scary. I'm sorry you ever hooked up with him—it must have been hell.' The memory of her words, the revelation of how he had hurt her, still iced his veins, made him want to force Tommy to his knees to grovel before her.

'It was.' The words were simple. 'But I'm glad he came here today.' She straightened up and tugged at the sleeves of his jumper so she could pick up her glass. 'Because it's made my decision. I know how I'll deal with Tommy.'

'How?'

'Exactly how I did sixteen years ago. I'm going to run—take Cathy and disappear.'

'Or you could stand your ground.'

'I can't fight him. You saw it for yourself—he's a nutter. No amount of restraining orders will stop him—even if I could get one. I won't risk Cathy, and it won't be for ever. Tommy is a criminal, through and through. All I have to do is run until he gets himself put behind bars again. Cathy and I can take off—go backpacking somewhere or relocate for a while.'

'And then what? What happens when he gets out of prison the next time?'

'I'll deal with that when it happens.'

'No.'

Gabe realised he'd said the word with way more force

than he'd intended. But he knew that this was not the way to deal with a man like Tommy—with any bully. He had first-hand experience, and as an adult he'd done enough work with children—both bullies *and* the bullied—to know that running away, showing fear, kept the cycle going.

'It won't work. I get that you're scared, but running will make Tommy worse. He relishes your fear. He didn't need to come here today, or stalk you to Cornwall. If this was only about Cathy he'd contact her. This is about making you suffer.'

'Well, he's good at that.' The bitter undertone spoke volumes about her bleak memories. 'But I don't care about me. It's Cathy I'm scared for. And that's why I'll run. To keep her safe.'

'You don't have to do that. Not when you've worked so hard to get where you are. Don't throw it all away.'

'I won't. I'll just be putting it aside for a while. You don't get it, Gabe. None of it matters more than Cathy.'

'There *is* an alternative.'

'What? I kill him? Tempting, but unfortunately not feasible.'

'Call his bluff. I don't think he has any interest in Cathy—he just wants to punish *you*. Let Tommy see Cathy.'

'Excuse me?' Etta thunked her glass down on the side table, the expression in her tawny eyes morphing from incredulity to anger.

'I don't mean hand her over. I mean set up a supervised meeting. From what I saw of her, it seems to me that Cathy is a strong, intelligent girl. And that you and she have a strong bond.'

For a moment envy touched him as he tried to imagine his own parents forging any bond with their children except one of duty. He remembered the photos on Steph's walls, depicting the years of Cathy and Martha's childhood.

'Am I right?'

'Yes.' Etta's expression softened. 'Cathy has some teenage moments, but she has got a great outlook on life. She worked hard, got excellent GCSEs, and she has a plan for her future, great friends. That's the point. I won't let Tommy ruin that.'

'Then maybe you should trust her. And yourself. You've brought up a very together, bright young woman. Trust her to see Tommy for what he is. Then he loses his power over you.'

For a scant second she considered his words as she swirled the cognac round the glass and watched the dark golden ripples. Then she shook her head. 'You don't understand. You *can't* understand. You are Gabriel Derwent, Earl of Wycliffe, one day the Duke of Fairfax. You have a long line of ancestors at your back, two parents, two siblings—a whole family tree. Cathy has *me*. I'm her entire family tree. So of course she wants a dad.'

'It doesn't always work like that.' Gabe figured that one mum like Etta completely topped two parents like the Duke and Duchess in the parenting stakes. 'Cathy won't want a dad like Tommy.'

'Tommy knows how to turn on the charm. I know that all too well. And it's not only that. I'm not excusing any of his behaviour, but he did have a rough time himself—everyone knew that his dad was an evil man who beat up his wife *and* his kids. Tommy got the worst of it—it was like his dad hated him. Cathy will feel instant sympathy for him. I can picture it all now. Tommy will present himself as the reformed convict or the wronged rebel. He'll admit his sins, tell Cathy he wants to make it up to her, and Cathy is susceptible.'

'Maybe so. But Cathy loves you—her bond is with *you*. You won't lose her to Tommy.'

Etta shook her head and the sadness on her face twisted his chest.

'Bonds break, Gabe.'

Her voice vibrated with emotion and Gabe wondered exactly what bonds she meant.

'Especially around me,' she added, so softly he wasn't sure he'd heard the words. 'But you're right. I won't lose Cathy—if I have to run to the ends of the earth, I will.' She lifted her glass to her lips and drained it. Then she rose in one lithe movement. 'Thank you for having my back with Tommy, and thank you for the drink. Now it's business as usual. I'm heading to my room and I'll be back to work first thing.'

Relief that she was backing away from further confidences mingled with his frustration that she would give up her hard-won life. But he had to back off—Etta was not someone who had come to him for advice, not one of the kids he tried to help. She was an adult, and so far she had done fine without him. Yet it took enormous effort to hold himself back from holding forth.

'OK. I'll be next door. Any problems, bang on the wall.'

Two weeks later Etta glared at the wall—exactly as she did every night. Right now she was suffering a veritable *multitude* of problems.

Not so much in the daytime, because then she could throw herself into work. The Derwent family tree fascinated her during waking minutes; the only niggle to her absorption was a nagging feeling that somehow Gabriel was orchestrating her work. There was nothing she could pinpoint as such, and it might well be that her thoughts were skewed by her constant awareness of him. An awareness she loathed for that very reason—it made her lose perspective.

As did her inability to sleep. Every night—every time she closed her eyes—Tommy loomed behind her lids. With every creak she imagined him sneaking through the darkness of the house. Worse, though, were the images of him finding Cathy. In the depth of night the scenario spun out… Tommy getting ever closer to the cruise ship, boarding…

And as each nightmare wove its dark spell the urge to bang on the wall grew ever larger. Stupid, stupid, *stupid*. Every instinct warned Etta that Gabe represented danger— and yet he made her feel safe, and she wanted him to chase away the shadows and the spectres of her imagination.

Not happening.

Instead she would do the mature thing—get up, get dressed, make a soothing cup of herbal tea and get an early start. Especially as she had unearthed some very interesting facts in the past few days.

Five minutes later she tiptoed to the door, holding her breath as she pulled it open.

One step onto the scruffy carpet of the hall and she stopped short as Gabe's door opened and he stepped out. Etta nearly swallowed her tongue. Dark blond hair sleep-tousled, blue-grey eyes fully alert, he pulled a dark grey T-shirt over his head, allowing her a glimpse of the glorious expanse of his chest.

There it was again—that stupid spark that she couldn't seem to douse. Wrenching her eyes from the golden skin, Etta turned away.

'Are you OK?'

Questionable. 'I'm fine. I couldn't sleep, so I thought I'd make myself a cup of herbal tea and start early.'

'OK. Give me a second and I'll come with you. You can give me your daily update early.'

'Sure.'

Etta glanced at him, further convinced that there was something odd about all these updates; they seemed out of character. She'd watched Gabe over the past weeks and the man worked like a demon. But what she had also noted was his ability to *delegate*, not to micromanage but to trust his staff to carry out the tasks necessary to convert the manor into a Victorian Christmas masterpiece. Yet with the family tree he seemed interested in every minute detail.

Tea in hand, they entered the records room and Gabe pulled a chair up to the desk. Etta braced herself, inhaled the now so familiar tang of citrus soap and pure Gabe—almost as necessary as her first coffee of the morning.

Focus, Etta.

'I've discovered something really interesting. I haven't mentioned it before because I wanted to be sure, and now I am. I've found a whole new branch of the family. It's one I originally thought had died out, but in actual fact this man here—' she pointed at a name '—married again and had a son. Very soon after that he died and his wife remarried. I think everyone must have thought this son was actually from her second marriage, but he wasn't.'

'Are you absolutely sure?'

'Yes. I've done extensive research, and I've got copies of various records. Although he took his stepfather's name, and inherited his property, I'm sure that he actually belongs on the *Derwent* family tree.'

Gabe scanned the enormous rough diagram Etta had put together. 'Looks good.'

'It's better than good.' She tugged a piece of paper towards her and skimmed her finger down the line of names. 'His line goes all the way to the present. I mean it's pretty convoluted—he's your cousin practically a million times removed, and I doubt he even knows he is even distantly related to you, but he is. Linked directly back to the 5th Duke.'

His body stilled and for a heartbeat a blaze of heat streaked across his eyes, gone so fast she wondered if it had been a mere trick of the light.

'Fascinating,' he stated. 'I've never so much as heard of this branch of the family tree. You're doing a fantastic job. Next I'd like you to follow the branch we discussed yesterday. I want to find out more about my Great-Great-Great-Aunt Josephine—she sounds like a real character.'

'Sure. Anyone who singlehandedly fought off a band of desperate ruffians with a borrowed sword is worth a mention.'

Etta frowned... Had there been a hint of strain in his voice? Plus, surely her discovery warranted a bit more discussion and considerably more interest. By her reckoning, given the intricacies of peerage inheritance laws, this distant cousin could well be next in line to the Dukedom after Gabe. 'Will you do anything about the distant cousin?'

'As you said, it's unlikely he has any idea who the Derwents are.' Gabe's voice was dismissive. He rose from his chair. 'I wonder if you'd like a break from the family tree today? In your other role as fair consultant I need your help with the Christmas decorations, and you have been holed up in here for days.'

Etta hesitated, sensing his reserve, wondering if she'd hit some sort of nerve. But if she had it clearly wasn't a nerve he wished to discuss. Perhaps her reference to this new branch of his family tree had reminded him of his need to settle down, to abandon his playboy lifestyle and find his suitable wife. Maybe he regretted turning away Lady Isobel...

And maybe this was Gabe's personal business and as such none of hers. 'I'd love to.'

Relief tinged his smile. 'Good. Come with me. I need you to cast an eye over the tree, and also I'm setting up some stalls so people can make their own Victorian wreaths and ornaments...'

It was impossible not to admire the dedication he'd given to tackling the Victorian theme, and admiration filled her at how much he'd achieved in so short a space of time.

As she followed him into the Great Hall she slammed to a stop as she gazed at the Christmas tree and her jaw dropped. She gawped. It was the most enormous spruce she'd ever seen, but what held her speechless were the ornaments that hung from it.

'They aren't actually antique Victorian—they're vintage Victorian-*style*.' Gabe's voice held satisfaction and appreciation. 'But they're beautiful, aren't they?'

Etta stepped forward and gently touched a stunning angel decoration. 'This is incredible…'

The balloon-shaped ornament contained a Victorian-style chromolithographic angel holding a candle. Its lavish trimmings included vintage tinsel ribbon as well as narrow chenille, antique beaded ribbon and more beautiful spun glass. Further up the tree a vintage-style Santa Claus with a frosty glittery beard hung, framed inside a gold paper medallion.

'Forget incredible. Each one is *exquisite*.' She glanced round the room. 'You've outdone yourself.'

He really had. In true Victorian-style greenery abounded—spruce, cedar, ivy and holly was draped and hung and garlanded over the furniture…the walls…the banisters and chandeliers in a beautiful sweeping display. The scent of cedar infused the air and made her tingle with the spirit of Christmas. Garlands of cranberries and popcorn, tinsel and paper chains streamed over the ceilings and coloured glass lamps shone in the darkness of the early December morning.

'The Victorians really did know how to push a whole flotilla of boats out. But I couldn't have done all this without my staff and all the helpers.'

'Too right, Gabe,' came the cheerful tones of a young man who had entered, laden with a basket of logs.

'Sam. How did the match go?'

'We won. It was a hard game, and I got me leg bashed in when a dirty b—' He glanced at Etta and blushed. 'When one of the opponents took me down. But he was too late. I managed to pass the ball, just like you said, and we got the try.'

He deposited the logs by the fireplace and he and Gabe did some sort of complicated high five.

'Oh, and Dad sends his regards and says to tell you that he'll be here early for the fair. He'll set up the lights and then he'll be on standby, and Mum's cooking up a storm.'

'Sounds fabulous. I'll drop in to see them later.'

'Cheers, Gabe. Catch you later.'

It was incredible, really. There was no side at all to Gabe's interaction with his employees—no feeling of a social or class divide other than a difference in accent and no feudal spirit, as such. And yet she sensed that his employees felt a fierce loyalty to the man who would one day be the Duke of Fairfax.

Everyone was working all-out on the fair—none more so than Gabe—and they worked with an easy camaraderie that indicated a long-term two-way friendship and respect. The kind instigated by a man with integrity and a genuine loyalty to his land—not a shallow playboy.

Gabe headed over to a corner piled with boxes. 'I'm going to set up some tables for people to make their own wreaths and decorations. Could you help me put together some samples?'

'Of course.'

He lifted a cardboard flap in one deft movement and looked at the contents. 'I thought these were wreaths.'

'What are they?'

'Mistletoe balls.'

Etta couldn't help herself. Despite the knowledge that it was puerile she chuckled, and in response his expression morphed and his lips quirked up into a smile.

'Oh, Lord. I *am* sorry,' Etta said. 'I'm behaving like a schoolgirl. Please show me your mistletoe balls.'

With that his lips parted and he started to laugh, and Etta joined in. A full-blown, belly-deep laugh that only eventually subsided.

'OK. Let's try again,' he said as he took various items out of the box, along with a set of instructions.

'I've done this before.' Etta pulled out a strand of wire and some string and handed it to him. 'You need to bend the wire into a circle and then twist the string round and round in loops until it's all covered. Then do the same again and join the two of them together to make a round shape. Twist the mistletoe around it, thread the berries and roses on and voila!'

'You make it sound easy.'

'It's a little fiddly, but it's a great idea for the fair. Kids *and* adults will enjoy it.'

As she twisted the wire she cast one more look around the room. 'For a man who doesn't like Christmas you've really surpassed yourself.'

'This is nothing to do with my feelings about Christmas. This is about making the event a success.' His tone of voice was firm as he bent his golden head to the task. 'This is a work project, aimed at maximising publicity and making money for the manor.'

'But it's not only about money—it's about the celebration of Christmas. I don't see how you can produce this and *not* have a tiny tendril of Christmas spirit buried somewhere.'

'Nope.' The sigh he puffed out was filled with exasperation. 'Why does it matter to you?'

It was a good question. 'Because I don't understand it. You have parents, siblings... Derwent Manor is an idyllic place to celebrate Christmas—you have everything I was desperate to give Cathy—and yet you say Christmas means nothing to you.'

Every Christmas she'd felt that surge of guilt, wished that Cathy had kind, loving grandparents, thought about the adoptive sister she'd barcly known. Rosa... Small blonde Rosa—Etta's sister, Cathy's aunt.

'It doesn't feel fair.'

There was a silence, and then he picked up a piece of mistletoe, his movements deliberate. 'Things aren't always how they seem.'

Before he could elaborate his mobile phone shrilled out and he picked it up.

'Kaitlin.'

CHAPTER NINE

PHEW. RELIEF HIT him at the sound of his sister's voice. The last thing he wanted to do was swap Christmas memories with Etta. The obvious choice was to lie and back up the misleading articles the Derwent publicity machine rolled out every so often. Extol the supposed virtues of an aristocratic Christmas complete with family traditions and a sumptuous tree.

But he didn't want to fib to Etta—not when she clearly had a few Christmas demons of her own lurking…a fact betokened by the wistfulness, sadness and guilt that had skimmed over her expression. Yet the idea of sharing the details of Derwent Christmases didn't sit well with him— the awkwardness, the stilted conversations, the knowledge that his parents had little to say to their children other than homilies, the lack of joy or fun…

'Gabe?'

His sister's voice pulled him back to the present.

'You OK, Kaitlin?' It occurred to him how rare it was for him to receive a call from his sister, especially in the past year.

'I'm fine.' Her voice was flat. 'I wondered if I could come back while the fair's on. Maybe help out?'

'That would be great. The only reason I didn't ask you is that Mum and Dad said you wouldn't be around because you had commitments with Frederick.'

Kaitlin's romance with Prince Frederick of Lycander was well-documented, and the tabloids were poised, waiting for an engagement announcement.

'Are you both coming?'

'Nope. Just me, if that's OK?'

Gabe frowned. There was an almost desperate undertone to Kaitlin's voice—a far cry from her usual serenity.

'Of course it is. This is your home and you can come here whenever you like. You don't need my permission or anyone else's.'

Though maybe that wasn't strictly true—he had little doubt that his parents were as avid as any reporter for news of an engagement, and would barricade Kaitlin from the manor until it came, if necessary. An alliance with royalty would have whetted the Derwents' ambition.

'Thanks, Gabe. I'll let you know my ETA.'

'OK. But I should warn you: April Fotherington will be here covering the fair.'

A sigh of resignation travelled over the miles. 'Please don't tell her in advance that I'll be there. I'll talk to her, but I'd rather do it off the cuff. I don't suppose you could announce *your* engagement, or create some sort of diversion? Something to take the heat off me?'

His frown deepened as worry kicked in—his sister usually revelled in the heat of the public's glare, shone in the spotlight with an even ' .ighter glow than he did.

'Hold on, Kait. Is there something I should know?'

'Everything's fine.'

'You don't have to say that.'

'Yes, I do. I don't think *you're* fine—I don't even know where you've been the past nine months—but you won't tell me what's wrong, will you?'

'No.'

The laugh she gave was brittle. 'There you are, then. I'm fine. But you *can* give me some advice.'

'Shoot.'

'Do you think I should marry Prince Frederick?'

Talk about a loaded question… But Gabe sensed that if he didn't answer now Kaitlin would never ask again. 'He has a lot to offer. He's a prince, and he seems like a nice guy. You would have a more than comfortable life, and you were brought up to be a princess. You'd do an amazing job. Your children would be well off and privileged. You'd have fame and fortune and the opportunity to do some good.'

'In other words you think it would be a good alliance?'

'Yes.'

'Thank you, Gabe. I needed to hear that.'

Her voice had regained a level of serenity, yet he felt a qualm twinge.

'I'll see you soon.'

Gabe dropped his phone into his pocket and dismissed the doubt. His reasoning was spot-on—an alliance with Prince Frederick of Lycander would ensure Kaitlin's happiness.

A glance at Etta showed her with her head discreetly bent over the mistletoe decoration as she deftly threaded red beads into place. Brain whirring, he walked across the room, re-seated himself and picked up his own creation.

'Kaitlin is coming to the fair,' he said. 'I'd appreciate it if you don't mention your role in researching the new family tree to her.'

His sister knew as well as he did that his parents had no interest in their ancestors, and he didn't want Etta's suspicions to be aroused. Especially now she had served her purpose.

Emotions seethed in his gut—emotions he had in lockdown even though the name of the man who might found a new Fairfax dynasty reverberated in his brain. Matteas John Coleridge.

Enough.

A small frown creased her brow and he could sense her curiosity.

'OK. I won't say a word.'

'Appreciated.'

'No problem.' Another bead was threaded, and with the

air of breaching a conversational chasm Etta said, 'So, you never got round to telling me why you are so *Bah humbug* about Christmas.'

Reprieve over.

'I'm not *Bah humbug*. I'm just indifferent. Christmas hasn't ever been a big deal in our family. When I was a child I thought the best bit was the Church service in the morning—I loved the ritual of it…the words…the tradition. But after that it was always business as usual. The staff all used to have the day off, but Sarah always left us something to heat up.'

The awkwardness of those childhood Christmas lunches would live with him for ever.

'You must have enjoyed the presents? All children love to open their stockings.'

'My parents didn't do stockings. Their view was that presents should be functional, and we all understood that it was more important to put money back into the estate rather than accumulate useless clutter. They forbade us from giving them presents or giving each other gifts as well—they always said the best present we could give them was the forfeiture of our pocket money.'

Etta looked as though she were picking her words carefully. 'I get that the estate is important, but presents don't have to be expensive…'

'Inexpensive gifts came under the "useless clutter" umbrella, I guess.'

In all honesty the lack of presents hadn't been an issue. What he'd hated was the lack of any enjoyment. There had been no sitting down to watch a film or play board games, no laughter, nor much conversation, even. Though he knew he had little to complain about—he'd been fed, clothed, warm and safe.

'It's no big deal. There were times when we entertained over Christmas—that was much more festive.'

Although soon enough Gabe had understood that each

occasion served a purpose, or forged an alliance, all with the idea of furthering the House of Derwent. So he and Kaitlin had learnt how to perform, how to charm and behave as befitted a Derwent, and that way he'd finally won his parents' approval—the holy grail that all three children had always craved.

'Tell me about *your* childhood Christmases.'

'There's not much to say. I was an only child for years, and Christmas was always quiet. I vowed that one day I'd have loads of kids—that I'd marry someone with an enormous family and Christmas would be packed with frivolity and fun and festivities.'

The look on her face was wistful, as if she could see that dream Christmas before her.

'That didn't pan out, but Cathy and I always have a fab day. We get up at dawn and open our stockings—lots of fun gifts, like mugs, chocolates, jewellery... Then we have a pancake breakfast and a long walk before we cook Christmas dinner with Christmas music turned up high. We eat, open more presents, watch films, play games, eat chocolate... It's a great day. I do my best to make up for the lack of family.'

He threaded another bead onto the wire ring and eyed her. Curiosity percolated through him as to why she'd given up on her dream. 'It's not too late for you to marry and have more kids. Not because you want a suitable dad for Cathy, but because it's what *you* want.'

'I told you—marriage is not for me. As for more kids... I have considered adoption, but I know what a big step that is to take.'

It was a step he would never take; because it wouldn't be fair. The law stated that an adopted child could not inherit his title. So no way could he adopt a son and bring him up on an estate he could never inherit. And somehow to adopt a girl just because her gender meant she couldn't inherit seemed wrong.

For a second, desolation touched him, but he pushed it away, focused instead on Etta. There was no reason why she couldn't have the future she'd once envisaged. 'Perhaps it's the right step for you? But what about the other part of that dream? The husband and the in-laws and the whole big family Christmas?'

'It's not going to happen. I think I'm missing the necessary gene.'

Her voice was light but it masked sadness, and now the air felt awhirl with dreams that had bitten the dust. Both his and hers. Dreams of families seated around dining tables, children opening presents under the Christmas tree… His dreams couldn't be resurrected, but maybe hers could.

'Rubbish.'

'No, it's not! I told you. I've tried dating and it…it doesn't work out.'

'And I told *you* you're dating the wrong men.' He surveyed her. 'I bet you're going for nice, average men with nice, respectable jobs and—'

'What's wrong with that?' Colour climbed her cheekbones and she narrowed her eyes.

'Physical attraction is important too.'

'I don't see why that can't grow with time.'

Gabe raised his eyebrows. 'For *real*? Has that worked for you so far? *Sheesh!* You told me you've ended up dancing at your dates' weddings to other women. Not the best track record.'

'So what do you suggest?'

'That you date someone you feel attracted to in a physical way—where there's a spark.'

'Maybe that gene is missing too.'

'I don't believe that.'

The last berry slipped onto the ring and he stood and held up the mistletoe circle, attached it to the waiting ring.

'Look up.'

A hesitation and then she did as he asked, her face tipped

up towards him, her delicate angled features bathed in the flicker of light.

'Kiss me and I'll show you,' he said. 'The ball's in your court. Literally.'

His throat constricted, his breath massed in his lungs, and then slowly Etta rose to her feet and stepped forward until she was flush against him. Hesitantly her hands came up and looped around his neck. Her fingers touched his nape and desire shuddered through his body. And then she stood on tiptoe and touched her lips against his in sweet hesitation.

Her lips parted in a sigh of pleasure and he deepened the kiss. For a heartbeat she hesitated, and then her body relaxed, melted against his, and he pulled her closer, inhaled her vanilla scent, tasted a tang of peppermint. Then sweetness morphed into more—into a fierce intensity of sheer sensation as need grew.

Until she pulled away and stood with eyes wide as their ragged breaths mingled.

'I...'

Panic filled the tawny brown eyes and her lips twisted into a line that spelled mortification.

Gabe tried to pull his frazzled brain cells together—knew he had to stop her before she ran.

'It's OK, Etta.'

'No. It isn't. That was unprofessional and wrong...'

'It wasn't. It was a kiss. Between two consenting adults who are attracted to each other. It wasn't wrong. It was a kiss to show you that you aren't missing a gene.'

Etta shook her head, swiped her hand across her mouth. 'I want to forget this ever happened.'

The day of the fair dawned cold and crisp. Etta woke up and assessed the weather with relief. The sky was clear—a bright blue studded with the cotton wisp of a few clouds.

It would be cold, but there would be no need to move everything inside.

Swinging her legs out of bed, she let her brain list her extensive to-do list.

On the list was meeting Kaitlin Derwent. Gabe's sister would fly in early the next day. Curiosity resurfaced as to why Gabe wanted to keep the new family tree secret from his sister. Surely that took the idea of a surprise present a step too far? Not that Etta would ask him—she had gone out of her way to avoid any non-work-related conversation with him since The Kiss.

Mortification still roiled through her tummy at the memory—how *could* she have kissed him like that? A sheer cascade of desire had overwhelmed every iota of sense and she had given in, lost perspective and thrown self-respect aside. *Stupid.* And worse was the fact that for Gabe it had been nothing more than an object lesson, to show her that she could feel passion. Well, Etta didn't *want* to feel passion—or at least not on that scale. It was too much, too dizzying, too everything.

Thank goodness that in two days she'd be out of here—away from Gabe and his ability to unsettle her. Instead she'd be on board a cruise ship, reunited with Cathy.

Excitement fizzed inside her, but like it or not it was underlain with a soupçon of sadness. A sadness she *always* felt at the end of a project. The second she saw her daughter again all thoughts of Derwent Manor, family trees and *especially* Gabe Derwent would flee her brain. She knew it. It had to be like that. She couldn't let passion overcome family bonds ever again. Especially now. Because once the euphoria of seeing Cathy faded she needed to explain the relocation plan to her daughter.

Fifteen minutes later there was the familiar knock on the door that heralded Gabe.

'Morning. You all set for the day?'

As ever, no sign of tension was on display, and not for

the first time she envied his ability to surf over all circumstances with unshakable confidence. The same confidence
that meant he appeared to have had no problem whitewash-
ing The Kiss from his memory banks. Not that it had been
a capital letter event in his opinion—and that thought in-
tensified her humiliation a hundred fold.

'Ready and looking forward to it.'

A few hours later and the fair was in full swing; Etta gazed
round at the incredible display on offer. It was easy to believe that she'd stepped back in time.

Inside the manor, the staff were kitted out as Victorian
servants. Parlour maids in simple black dresses, chamber-
maids in print dresses, both complete with frilled apron and
cap, bustled about, engaged in their household tasks, and
they were all able to discuss the duties expected of servants
in the Victorian era.

Sarah reigned supreme in the hustle and bustle of the
kitchen, in the throes of the preparation of a lavish Christmas
dinner. The scents were evocative of Christmas—cranberries
bubbling over the fire, the aroma of chestnut, sugar and can-
died fruit mingling with the savoury scent of roast turkey and
freshwater smelt. Families watched and asked eager questions.

Etta glanced round and saw the lengthening queue for
Christmas punch. It looked as if they needed some help.

As she approached the table Eileen, a teenage girl from
the village school who'd volunteered her services, smiled
in relief. 'It's manic! I'm not allowed to handle the rum,
and my mum came over all faint, and…and…'

'You're doing a grand job. Hand over a spare pinny and
a hat and I'll get mixing.'

Soon enough the good-natured jostle of the queue became manageable, with everyone happy to hand over the
cost for a plastic cup of Roman Punch—a judicious mix of
rum and lemon and near frozen dissolved sugar.

'I'd better move on,' Etta said as she saw Gabe gesturing to her to follow him.

'Thank you for that,' he said as they exited the kitchen.

He smiled down at her and the world seemed to shrink. The sounds of the fair faded and his smile warmed her, curled her toes, and that wretched kiss sprang to the forefront of her mind. His eyes darkened, the same way they had when they'd locked lips, and a stupid feeling of gratification streamed through her veins at the knowledge that just maybe he *did* remember those magical moments.

Hold it together. Even if Gabe had been affected it would *not* be a smart move to grab the man and have a replay.

'No problem. It's the least I can do.'

As they stepped outside into the crisp air she gestured around.

'You must be thrilled—the place is packed and people are having an amazing time.'

The outside area buzzed with noise and laughter overlaid with the exquisite sound of the local choir, whose pure voices filled the air with Christmas carols. Children raced around a designated part of the lawn with hoops and sticks, and in another part a boisterous game of quoits was underway. The smell of roasting chestnuts tantalised her tastebuds, and everywhere Victorian re-enactors roamed chatting to the visitors.

'It's a true extravaganza! A day everyone will remember.'

There was that smile again, and she would swear her hair had frizzed. Time for a breather.

'I'll go check out the stalls. I want to find extra gifts for Cathy and Martha and Steph.'

He frowned.

'I'll be fine, Gabe. In two days' time I'll have to fend for myself.'

The words were a timely reminder as she headed off.

Authentic-looking Victorian toys glinted in the light of

the December sun, and delight filled her as she browsed the beautifully crafted spinning tops and Victorian dolls. Her gaze landed on a stunning jewellery box that Steph would adore. As she ran her finger over the glossy wood, with its inlay of mother-of-pearl and gold leaf, she could picture her friend's appreciation of the two-tier box.

But before she could ask the price her neck prickled and she spun round.

'Hello, Etta.'

Tommy stood there, dark hair slicked back, a leather jacket over a white T-shirt, a swagger in his stance.

'Fancy seeing you here. I knew I'd get you alone if I was patient. I've been watching you.'

His voice was low—friendly, even—but Etta recognised the underlying menace. Tommy was at his cruellest when he sounded his most pleasant, and a cold drop of fear ran down her spine.

'Hardly alone,' she reminded him, her hand darting to the panic button round her neck. *No.* She would not cause a scene—would not cast a shadow over the success of the fair.

'But minus Sir Toff. I wanted another chat.'

'I have nothing to say to you.'

'But I want to talk to you. In person. I *like* the personal touch, Etta. You know that. You remember my personal touch, don't you?'

Now fear burned cold and she stepped back, unable to help the instinctive movement. 'This is getting old, Tommy. Please leave.' Brave words, given that her insides were roiling.

'But this is a new message—a Christmas greeting. I've decided that this Christmas should be a nice family affair— you and me and our daughter, sitting down to a nice roast dinner, cooked the way I like it.'

'You've lost the plot, because that is *not* happening. You're not family.'

'I think Cathy might disagree. That's why you've hidden

her away isn't it? But I know you'll be spending Christmas with her.' Then his expression altered. 'Ah, here comes Mr Toff now.'

Relief doused her in a wave as Gabe arrived, the warmth of his muscular body next to her shielding her. 'Get off my land. Now.'

'It's a public event, Toff. My money is as good as anyone's. And I'm sure you don't want to cause a scene.'

'I have no problem with a scene. You're leaving now. Either of your own volition or with my assistance…'

Malevolence lit Tommy's eyes and Etta tensed, braced herself in that old familiar response.

His dark eyes rested on her for a second and then he stepped back, his hands in the air. 'Nice try. But I don't brawl any more. I'm a nice, peaceable man who has seen the error of my ways. All I want is the chance to be a father.'

He winked at Etta and bile rose in her throat.

'I'll be on my way…but I'll be seeing you. Happy Christmas!'

With that he vanished into the crowd.

The whole confrontation had taken no more than a few moments, but those minutes had left her encased in a mesh of terror.

Gabe was on his phone, giving a description of Tommy and asking for confirmation that he'd left the grounds.

He dropped his phone into his pocket. 'You OK?'

'I'm fine.' Aware that a few spectators were nudging each other, Etta forced a smile to her face. 'Absolutely fine. Isn't it time to judge the Victorian Christmas reindeer?'

Gabe hesitated.

'It's OK, Gabe. This is my problem now. Our deal is nearly done.'

CHAPTER TEN

GABE EXHALED HEAVILY. His muscles ached, but the clear-down was finally finished, with everything set in place for a rerun the following day.

'Thank you, everyone. The day was an outstanding success. You have my heartfelt thanks and I've put my wallet behind the bar in the pub. Drinks on me tonight. Go and enjoy.'

There was a cheer and the staff filed out, leaving just Etta and himself in the enormous marquee that held the restaurant. Exhaustion smudged her features and dust smeared the jeans she had changed into for the clear-down. She'd worked like the proverbial trooper—she'd served food, played games, and done more than her share of lugging crates and boxes. But he was pretty sure her pallor had *zip* to do with work and everything to do with Tommy.

'Come on. We definitely deserve a drink.'

Now her lips turned up in a smile and his breath caught at her sheer prettiness; there was an ageless quality to her beauty—the kind that came from character and poise.

His palms itched with a desire to swirl her into his arms and kiss her, take her mind off Tommy. *Bad idea, Gabe. Been there, done that.* And whilst their kiss had blown his mind, it had spooked Etta—she'd been clear that she wanted to forget it. He didn't get why, but instinct told him the reasons were complicated. If Etta wanted to act on their mutual attraction it had to be her decision, not his.

'A drink sounds good—and I have just the thing,' she said.

He followed her to the kitchen, where she headed to the fridge.

'I know it's probably not as high-quality as you're used to, but I picked us up a bottle of bubbles. To toast the success of the fair.'

The unexpectedness of the gesture halted him in his tracks.

'Don't look so surprised.'

'I *am* surprised. The Derwents don't go in for celebratory gestures because success is a given. Thank you.'

'You're very welcome. That must be hard,' she added. 'To always expect to succeed.'

'I've never really thought about it.'

'Hmm. Well, I don't always succeed, and I'm not sure how successful our dinner is going to be either. I told Sarah she didn't need to cook for us today—she needs to go home and put her feet up, ready for tomorrow. So I made something yesterday! Don't get your hopes up—it's not exactly haute cuisine. Just macaroni cheese and salad, but...'

'Etta, stop apologising. This is a lovely gesture.'

And in truth he didn't know how to handle it.

She pulled the macaroni cheese out of the fridge and put it into the oven, while he opened the sparkling wine, the pop of the cork reverberating round the room. He poured the frothing golden liquid into two crystal flutes and handed one over.

'Cheers.'

'Cheers. To a successful alliance. Your new family tree is done, the fair is on its way to success, and after tomorrow I'll be out of your hair.'

There was a hint of strain to her smile, and he put his glass down on the counter.

'You must be looking forward to seeing Cathy again. I'll drop you at the airport as planned.'

Etta was flying out to New York to meet up with the cruise ship.

'Actually, there's no need.'

He raised his eyebrows. 'It's no bother—it's all part of the contract, and I want to make sure you get on board safe. Especially now Tommy has turned up. Again.'

'No. I mean there's no need because I'm not going. I've decided to stay home. Tommy made it clear that he intends to gatecrash Christmas, and I can't risk leading him to Cathy.'

'You can't let Tommy dictate your actions. Even if he did make it to the cruise ship, Security would deal with him. Hell. I'll speak to the captain.'

Etta shook her head, her chin tilted outward. 'Thank you, Gabe, but I'm still staying put.'

'Then Tommy wins.'

'No, *I* win. Because I know Cathy is safe.'

'So what happens after Christmas? Are you *never* going to see Cathy again?' He knew he shouldn't sound so angry but frustration clenched his jaw, caused him to pace the tiled kitchen floor.

'Of course not. I'll work out a way for us to meet up and then we'll take off for a while.'

'What about her education?'

'It will be like an early gap year. She will be experiencing life.'

'What about money?'

'I've still got some savings left, and I'll let my London flat out… I'll waitress. I'll manage. It won't be for long— I *know* Tommy will end up behind bars again.'

'You cannot let Tommy screw your life up. At least give Cathy a shot at meeting him and recognising him for the creep he is.'

Her face flushed and her hands clenched into fists. 'You don't understand, Gabe. You can't.'

'Try me.'

'I will *not* let Cathy's life be tainted or flawed by that man. He's evil. He…' Her voice caught, and her brown eyes were dark with a maelstrom of memories. 'He is capable of charm—he weaves a spell that sucks you in. He will pull Cathy in.'

'You don't *know* that.' Why was she so stubborn about this?

'No, I don't. But no way will I risk it.' The laugh she gave was mirthless. 'Think about it like an investment strategy. This is a commodity I will keep safe at any cost. I know Tommy. He entices you in but once he's enmeshed you it all changes. He hurt me, Gabe, and worse than that he made me believe I deserved it. That I was nothing.'

The anger that swept over him shocked him with its extremity. If Tommy were here right now he would crush him. Yet he sensed there was something more at stake here than Etta's fear that Cathy would be sucked in.

'I understood why you ran from him when you were a teenager. I don't understand why you would run now. Not without giving Cathy a shot at seeing what a loser Tommy is.'

'I can't. I won't take the risk.'

Her voice was flat. Gabe studied her closed expression and realisation struck. Etta was terrified that she would lose Cathy—believed that Cathy would forsake her at the drop of a hat.

'I've made my mind up, Gabe, and I won't discuss it further. Please—can we drink fizz, eat macaroni cheese, and think about the fair tomorrow?'

The tiredness in her voice swayed him into acquiescence— that, alongside the knowledge that it was her decision to make. Their deal was nearly over and he had other fish to fry. A twist of his gut was a reminder of his own Christmas plans and what he needed to be focused on—the future of the Dukedom of Fairfax was at stake.

'Fizz and macaroni cheese it is.'

Distraction therapy at its best.

The second day of the fair dawned even brighter, and Etta was determined to enjoy the day and keep all thoughts of her lonely Christmas to come at bay.

As she entered the kitchen she paused in the doorway at the sight of Kaitlin Derwent, seated at the table.

Every bit as stunning in the flesh as her photographs indicated, Kaitlin was dressed in a gorgeous hand-embroidered dress that brought out the Titian shade of her hair and showed off a figure that combined svelteness with curves. But before Etta could even register envy Kaitlin rose and smiled a poster-girl smile that she couldn't help but return.

'You must be Etta. Gabe told me how much help you've been with the fair.'

Etta glanced across at Gabe, who was standing at the counter pouring cereal into a bowl, and her heart gave its familiar annoying hop, skip, and jump. This would be the last time she witnessed the Earl of Wycliffe at breakfast, and she allowed herself a sneaky glance at the breadth of his torso, the strength of his features, the spike of his blond hair. A glimmer of regret struck her—the first man in years her body was interested in and she'd passed up the opportunity to follow it up.

Ridiculous. No regret necessary. She'd made a mature decision not to succumb to an over-the-top attraction.

The Kiss flashed into her mind. *See—an exact case in point.* The Kiss had been a humdinger and very much over the top.

Turning resolutely back to Kaitlin, she smiled. 'I've had a great time.'

'I need to freshen up and then I'll be ready for duty.'

'We'll catch up properly later,' Gabe said with a small crease on his brow as he watched his sister leave the room. He turned to Etta. 'I need you to stick with Kaitlin today.'

'She may not want me to do that.'

'Tough. I want to keep an eye on both of you, and that will be easier if you're together.'

'Fine.'

She could only hope Kaitlin wouldn't mind. After all,

Lady Kaitlin Derwent was used to a social circle way more sophisticated than Etta's.

As it turned out, Kaitlin seemed more than happy to hang out with her, and Etta could only stand back in admiration as the red-haired woman walked around the fair, exuding charm.

'Come on,' Kaitlin said eventually. 'I'll buy you a drink.'

Minutes later they were seated at the back of the marquee.

'So, how have you got along with Gabe?' Kaitlin asked.

'Fine.'

The redhead hesitated. 'Are the two of you an item?'

'No. Absolutely not. No. *Ick.*'

Ick? Where had *that* come from? Etta took a gulp of punch, welcoming the hit of rum as Kaitlin's perfectly arched eyebrows rose.

'Hey, Gabe's not that bad. Most women would bite your arm off for the opportunity to spend time with him.'

'I'm not "most women".'

'Well, he's not most men. I know Lady Isobel didn't do him any favours, but Gabe is a good man. Bet he hasn't told you about his charity work.'

'What charity work?'

But before Kaitlin could answer she looked across the tent and muttered a most unladylike curse. 'What's wrong?' Etta asked.

'April Fotherington is headed this way.' Kaitlin stood up. 'I'd rather face her outside.'

Once they were on the lawn Etta saw the dark-haired reporter sashaying towards them with a predatory gleam in her eye.

If Kaitlin was nervous it was impossible to see; her lips were upturned in a smile of welcome with a hint of coolness. 'April. Lovely to see you.'

'And such a surprise. My sources had you at a function

in Lycander, with Prince Frederick and the rest of the Lycander Royals.'

'It was a last-minute decision.'

'Hmm… I hope all is well with you and the Prince? I did hear a little rumour that the Lycanders had been hoping for a match with a Princess.'

'I'd like to think that the Prince will make up his own mind about his marriage.'

Kaitlin's voice was even, but Etta could sense the tension that vibrated from her body.

Before April could answer Gabe arrived, his body seemingly relaxed as he stood next to his sister in definitive alliance.

'So no rift?' April persevered.

'None.'

Kaitlin's composure was enviable—due, no doubt, to a lifetime in the public eye.

'Hmm…' The reporter's tone hinted at scepticism. 'I'm glad to hear it. So, what about your Christmas plans? Will you be jetting back to Lycander for the Christmas Eve celebrations? They are spectacular. I was there last year, covering a story on the Prince and Sunita Greenberg—the model he was supposedly serious about. Before *you* came on the scene, of course.'

'Of course.'

Again her voice was level, but now a slightly strained quality had entered Kaitlin's smile and Etta could sense the effort it took for her to hold her body poised.

Gabe stepped forward. 'Easy does it, April. You're here to cover the fair—not grill my sister on her personal life.' There was a steely undertone to his voice.

'Good point.' April turned her green gaze, alight with calculation, to Etta.

Great. Unfortunately she *didn't* have a lifetime of experience in the public eye, and a feeling of foreboding prickled her skin.

'I *do* have a question about the fair. Etta, you have done a fabulous job—the Victorian theme is spot-on...accurate to the last detail...'

The 'but' loomed, travelling at warp speed, and Etta braced herself.

'But I am a little confused. You've been here for over three weeks. It seems a little over the top for a consultant role. Makes me wonder if there's something else going on here... Any other aspect to your role...'

Keep calm. This was a fishing expedition—April couldn't know about her work on the new family tree and was way more likely to be angling for a romance story.

Etta opened her mouth, summoned the evasion. 'Well... fairs like this need a lot of planning.'

'I understand that. But your role wasn't to plan the whole event, but simply to consult over historical accuracy. I'm not sure I understand why that necessitated such a long stay here. I was wondering if maybe you were hired for something else. Maybe you're writing a book, Gabe? Or maybe...'

Etta's mind raced. Any minute now April would mention the possibility of her researching a new family tree and she knew her face would give away the truth.

Then Gabe stepped forward and took her hand in his, gave it a squeeze that conveyed warning. 'OK, April. We're busted.'

Say what? They were?

Apprehension sliced at her tummy even as she did her best to keep her expression neutral. No need to panic. Clearly Gabe was in possession of a plan.

'I did hire Etta to help with the fair, but once she'd been here a few days...well, we got to know each other better and what we saw we liked so...'

'So the two of you are an item?' April's gaze skittered from Gabe to Etta and back again, suspicion mingling with the hope of a nice juicy story.

Etta remained stock still, her head awhirl with disbelief. Gabe wasn't in possession of a plan—the man was clearly possessed.

Suspicion won out and April shook her head. 'And you've just stayed buried in the countryside for weeks? I haven't heard even a whisper of gossip. No fancy dinners? No parties?'

'The fair took precedence. But I'm going to make it up to Etta. We're off on a Christmas break to Vienna. Surprise, sweetheart!'

Ah! Surprise was an emotion she could do! Right now she could be more surprised than anyone. 'Vienna...?' she whispered.

Sweetheart?

'Yup. What do you think?'

She thought she wanted to clock him on the head, pull on her trainers and leg it over the horizon. An alternative would be to identify this fabrication as being exactly that... But Gabe wouldn't do this without good reason. Right?

'Um...I sure am surprised,' she managed.

April's gaze was focused on her. 'You obviously weren't expecting this? You must be thrilled to be Lady Isobel's successor.'

Fantastic. This gets better and better.

Good reason or not, she would not go along with this.

But before she could open her mouth Gabe kept right on.

'Lady Isobel is the past—it's the present I'm most interested in, and I'm looking forward to Christmas with Etta. But right now we need to get on with our fair duties.' He turned away and then back. 'Oh, incidentally, I believe that this also explains Kaitlin's sudden arrival on the scene. Am I right, sis?'

Kaitlin didn't so much as blink a perfectly made-up eyelid. 'Busted too!'

An expressive lift of her elegant shoulders and a full-wattage authentic Kaitlin Derwent smile accompanied the words. AKA the barefaced lie.

'I spoke to Gabe and curiosity got to me. I wanted to meet Etta in person.'

Etta gave up, pasted a smile on her face and watched the Derwents in action. Waited until the reporter finally left to cover the fair and then spun round to face Gabe. 'What the—?'

'Not now. People are watching, and April isn't a fool. I'll explain later.'

Etta was pretty damn sure that steam must be rising from her in visible waves. 'No, you won't. You will explain right now,' she hissed. 'We can go into the private bit of the house. I'm sure everyone will understand that we need some privacy, given our "relationship".'

Kaitlin glanced from one to another. 'I think Etta has a point. I can hold the fort at the fair. You clearly need some quality time alone together.'

CHAPTER ELEVEN

GABE WOULDN'T EXACTLY call this 'quality time'. He watched as Etta strode up and down the already threadbare carpet, practically sparking with anger.

'What the *hell* did you think you were doing? Because there is no way in this universe or any other, parallel or perpendicular, that we are going to Vienna.'

No preamble, then.

'I was salvaging the situation. A minute later and April would have rumbled the family tree surprise for my father.'

'So? Who cares? I get it you want it to be a surprise, but this is a bit extreme, don't you think?'

'Look, I understand you're angry.'

'Angry? I'm *livid*. I'm a *thesaurus* of angry.'

Each furious pace showed that.

'But it's done. At the time it seemed like the best solution. It helped Kaitlin out and...'

And it meant he could keep his role of bodyguard, make sure Etta remained safe from Tommy whilst she perfected her relocation plan.

'Now the whole world thinks we're an item. Exactly what I *didn't* want.'

'I know, and I apologise for that, but I had hoped Christmas in Vienna would make up for it.'

Etta screeched to a halt. 'Why would you think that?'

'Because it will beat spending Christmas by yourself, missing Cathy and hiding from Tommy.'

Etta narrowed her eyes. 'I didn't even know you were going to Vienna.'

Neither had he until a few days ago, when he'd discovered that Matteas Coleridge lived in Vienna and played the cello in a renowned Viennese orchestra. The knowledge had triggered a visceral need to see the man who might one day step into his shoes. Just see him—Gabe had no intent of making contact. Not yet. But he wanted to see him in his own environment.

'It seemed like a good idea. Rather than rattling around here on my own.'

'Why take *me*? What's in it for you? I can understand why you'd take a real girlfriend, but why me?'

Because taking a girlfriend would effectively take the spotlight well and truly away from his real motivation. He had a lot of respect for April's tenacity and instinct for a story. If she got wind of the new family tree there was a chance she'd pull the real story together.

There was also a chance Etta would do the same—hence his first choice of girlfriend *wouldn't* have been Etta. But he'd had to move fast and he had decided to take the risk. Yes, she knew Matteas Coleridge's name, but there must be lots of Matt Coleridges in the world, and with any luck she wouldn't even realise that it was the name of a member of a twenty-piece orchestra. If she did, he'd deal with it.

'I have my reasons.'

'Now is *not* the time to be a man of mystery. I'm sure you do have your reasons—I want to know what they are.'

'No.'

Hands slammed onto her hips. 'No?'

'No. This is the deal on offer. You let April run with this romance story until after the New Year. You come to Vienna with me. In return I extend your contract and pay you an additional fee. I'll throw in the bodyguard service as well. An added bonus is that you'll lead Tommy far away from Cathy. That's the deal. If you don't like it, don't accept it. Feel free to call April. Tell her it's off, that you've changed your mind. Tell her the truth—tell her I made it up.'

'If I do that what would you do?'

'Find another girlfriend and take her to Vienna.'

Even if the idea didn't sit well with him, given his reason for going to Vienna it would be simpler to have a fake girlfriend rather than a real one.

'So the ball's back in your court.'

The following day Etta gazed around at the interior of the private jet. En route to Vienna. Disbelief sat alongside her consideration as to whether or not she had lost her mind.

How had Gabe manoeuvred her into a position where she had actually *agreed* to this hare-brained scheme? Well, firstly there had been the sheer impossibility of any explanation to April. How to clarify why she'd gone along with it all, posed for photos, agreed to everything? Plus the idea had filled her with discomfort—it reeked of snitching, and it would drop both Gabe and Kaitlin in it. Mind you, she had little doubt that Gabe would pull himself out, no problem, but still…

Then there had been the internal debate: Christmas in Vienna, versus Christmas holed up in her flat or at an anonymous motel? True, Vienna came with the price tag of Gabe, but if she didn't go he'd take someone else. And she loathed the concept—her fingers had curled into fists at the thought. Not from jealousy. But from anticipated mortification. Everyone would think she'd been passed over for a newer model.

In addition, the element of curiosity had popped right up—every historian's instinct inside her told her there was something off about all this. *Why* did Gabe want to go to Vienna? *Why* didn't he want anyone to know about the new family tree?

And lastly her treacherous body had seen some definite potential benefits. Benefits endorsed by her conversation with Steph.

Her best friend had been thrilled for her. 'Go for it,' she'd instructed. 'For once in your life, Etta, let your hair down, put on your dancing shoes, and do the Viennese waltz. Quit worrying and go with the flow.'

Cathy had advised much the same. 'Mum, I am *so* happy for you. Now we can all enjoy Christmas because we know you won't be alone. Enjoy yourself—and don't worry.'

Easier said than done. Worry was paramount as she gazed round the luxurious interior—somehow the idea of a spacious airborne room, complete with sumptuous leather sofa, a boardroom table, reclining seats and a screen that might grace any home cinema, represented the utterly over-the-top level of her own emotions.

No, not her emotions. This was all about her physical reactions—the rapid rate of her heart and the acceleration of her pulse as she gazed at him now, completely at his ease, his blue-grey eyes on her as she curled her legs beneath her in a false posture of relaxation.

His mobile rang and he glanced at the screen. 'Sorry, I need to take it.' Phone to his ear, he said, 'Cora, thanks for the callback. You need to call Kaitlin. I reckon she could do with some twin input—she actually asked for *my* advice.'

A pause.

'Yes, that's exactly what I told her. To consider it an alliance, a merger.'

A longer pause, and Etta couldn't help but hear the agitated squawk that emerged from Cora's end.

Then Gabe shrugged. 'I told it how I saw it. Kaitlin is cut out to be a princess. But I figure I'm not the authority on marriage—you're the one who has walked that walk to the altar.'

More talk and then he raised a hand in a gesture of affectionate exasperation.

'Spare me the lecture on love. Talk to Kaitlin.'

He disconnected with a shake of his head and Etta couldn't help but grin.

'You're close to your sisters.'

The observation sent a thread of sadness through her veins as a sudden image of Rosa strobed through her brain. The adoptive sister she hadn't seen for seventeen years.

Gabe shook his head. 'Not really. They were only two when I went to boarding school, so we never got close. And now we're adults we have pretty much gone our separate ways.'

'Why don't you do something about that? You're lucky to have siblings. Plus it's clear they care about you.'

His blue eyes held hers with an arrested look that bordered on startled. 'It is…?'

'Yes—it *is*. I don't mean to pry, but it sounds like Kaitlin isn't OK and that she came home to see you and ask your advice. And you *do* care about her—one of the reasons you stepped in with April was to help Kaitlin.'

'*One* of the reasons.' Gabe's voice was hard. 'Don't read something that isn't there. I stepped in with April to protect my own interests. Helping Kaitlin was a bonus.'

Why was he so resistant to the idea that he was close to his sisters? 'So you wouldn't have helped her if it hadn't benefited you too?'

'I didn't say that. I'm just telling it as it is. We aren't a close, touchy-feely family.'

'You say that like it would be a bad thing if you were. I don't get that at all.'

Because *she* would love to somehow turn the clock back and be part of Rosa's life, and it made her mad that Gabe was bypassing something so important. The man was lucky enough to have family on tap and he didn't seem to care.

'It works for me.' Gabe looked at her, his eyes still angry. 'You said you were an only child "for years". So presumably you now have a sibling?'

For a moment she was tempted to deny it. *Not accept-*

able. Bad enough that she wasn't part of her sister's life—to deny her existence would be wrong. Even if her parents *didn't* count her as being Rosa's sister. After all she didn't share the same bloodline—hadn't been in Rosa's life since Rosa was three.

'Yes. A sister. We've lost touch.'

'Then why not get *back* in touch?'

'It's complicated.'

And now she was regretting the whole conversation—Gabe's relationship with his sisters was none of her business. But now she'd made it her business and she'd opened up a conversational bear pit.

'Complicated how?'

'It doesn't matter.'

'Yes, it does. You've given *me* a hard time about my lack of brotherly support and now it turns out you've lost touch with your sister.'

Hmm... It seemed she'd touched a nerve, but Gabe had a point. What to do now?

Etta squared her shoulders—she would give him the facts. Or at least some of them.

'My parents gave me an ultimatum when I was pregnant. Them or the baby. I couldn't give my baby up and I haven't seen them since. Rosa was three at the time.'

The scene was still etched on her memory banks, however many times she'd tried to erase it.

Rosa in her mother's arms, the three-year-old's chubby legs wrapped round her mum's waist. The daughter her parents had always craved—blood of their blood. Her dad standing behind them. A tableau of the perfect family; no need nor space for Etta.

Her adoptive mother's voice. 'You can come back, Etta, and we'll do our duty by you. But not the baby. Give it up for adoption.'

'I can't do that.' The taste of tears as they rolled down her cheeks, her hands outstretched in plea. 'I know I've

done wrong, messed up big-time with Tommy, but I can't do that.'

There had been no relenting on her parents' faces.

'You have to. That baby has Tommy's genes—how can you want to keep it?'

Black knowledge had dawned—a dark understanding of why her parents had been unable to love her—they had always seen her as tainted by her unknown genes.

'I want to keep this baby because I already love him or her, and I don't care whose genes she has. Please try to understand. This is your grandchild. A part of me.'

She'd waited, but her parents had just stood there, lips pressed together. Rosa had looked on, knowing something was wrong, her lower lip wobbling. So Etta had taken a deep breath, stepped forward and dropped a kiss on Rosa's head, felt the little girl's blond curls tickling her nose.

'Goodbye, sweetheart.'

With that she'd left, one hand protectively cradling her tummy even as panic washed over her. All the time hoping, praying that they would call her back. But they hadn't.

Etta blinked, emerged from the vivid clarity of the past and saw that Gabe was hunkered down in front of her chair. She realised a tear had escaped her eye and trickled a salty trail down her cheek.

He reached out and caught it on the tip of his thumb. 'I'm sorry, Etta. I can't imagine how that must have felt but I'm pretty sure it sucked.'

The temptation to throw herself on the breadth of his chest, inhale his scent, take reassurance and safety and comfort nigh on overwhelmed her.

Pull yourself together. She'd come to terms with her past long ago.

'No need for you to be sorry. It is what it is and I've come to terms with it. I'll never regret the choice I made.'

The idea of giving Cathy up had been an impossibility— her own birth parents had abandoned her, and maybe they'd had reason to, but she would not—could not—do that to her child.

'But I do regret that Cathy has no grandparents. And I regret Rosa not being part of her life. That's why I get mad when I see sibling relationships going to waste.'

He remained in front of her. His hand covered hers and awareness sparked.

'So Rosa must be nineteen...twenty now?'

'Yes. I send my parents a Christmas card every year. In case they ever want to meet their granddaughter.'

'Maybe you need to try and get in touch with Rosa directly. Could be your parents haven't told her about you *or* the Christmas cards.'

'That wouldn't be fair to anyone. Gabe, you don't need to come up with a strategy. My parents and I—we made our choices and we need to live with them.'

'Rosa didn't make a choice. I'm not advocating a reunion with your parents—I think what they did was wrong—but Rosa is different. She should be given a choice.'

'I won't be responsible for causing complications in Rosa's life. Or my parents'. That's my choice. Just like it's yours whether or not you build a closer relationship with Kaitlin and Cora. My point is that I envy you the opportunity to do so. I think you should build on what you have with Kaitlin and Cora.'

'Cora doesn't need me—she is incredibly happy.'

'Closeness isn't just about being there when someone needs you. You don't always have to be Mr Fix It.' Though now she came to think of it, that was what Gabe was—always looking for a solution, the optimum strategy.

'Right now there's nothing to fix. Cora's marriage seems to be working out.'

'Even though she has made a technically unsuitable alliance? With someone out of your social circle?'

'Actually, no. She has married someone with immense wealth—that's an asset. And it turns out Rafael also has connections with the elite of Spanish aristocracy, though the jury is out on whether *that* is a useful commodity or not.'

'But that isn't why Cora married him. She married him because she loves him. You can see how much they love each other.' She'd seen it at the Cavershams' Advent Ball—it was the same connection Ruby and Ethan had.

Gabe shrugged. 'His money will endure and grow. Rafael Martinez is a billionaire, with an incredibly astute grasp of business opportunities. His connections are handy. I assume Cora thinks love is a bonus.'

'No! You're missing the point. Cora probably thinks the *money and connections* are a bonus. She loves him regardless of those and she would have married him if he were penniless.'

'He wouldn't be Rafael Martinez if he were penniless.' He shrugged. 'I see what you're saying, Etta, but I think they'd have been wiser to leave love out of the equation.'

'So you believe they're kidding themselves? That in reality they have married each other for money and titles and connection but they won't admit it?'

Why was he so anti-love? So sure every relationship was based on barter or an exchange of assets?

'Yes. And I think one or both of them will be hurt when the bubble bursts.'

'And you think it will be Cora?'

'Yes.'

'So what are you going to do about it?'

'Ram Rafael Martinez's teeth down his throat if he messes with my sister. Is that supportive enough for you?'

'Actually, I was thinking you should spend some time with them, and then you'd see that they actually love each other.'

The pilot's voice came over the intercom, smooth and clear. 'About to start the descent into Vienna.'

Relief touched Gabe's face—clearly this conversation

wasn't something he felt comfortable with. Etta knew she should leave it—knew it was none of her business—but as she looked across at him she felt an urge to know why he was so resistant to closeness, what made him tick.

Stop, Etta. The old adage that curiosity killed the cat had some truth in it. Best she leave well alone and focus on Vienna and more immediate concerns. Such as how to face four days as Gabriel Derwent's Christmas girlfriend.

Yup, she must have been insane to agree to this—and yet as she gazed out the window of the jet anticipation swirled within the tumult of panic.

CHAPTER TWELVE

HOLY MOLY, MACARONI! Etta gazed round the suite, sure that her eyes must have bugged out. 'This is…' Words failed her.

The suite was even more impressive than the hotel's lobby—a vast, glittering golden parquet enclosure with stucco ceilings, enormous chandeliers and mirrored surfaces that refracted and shone.

But this… 'You could fit my entire apartment in here three times over.'

'Courtesy of April,' Gabe said. 'She pulled some strings and managed to get us this.'

'Why?'

'I don't know, but I have my suspicions. No doubt she'll have a source here keeping an eye on us.'

'Oh.'

Etta looked around the sumptuous room, decked out with renaissance lavishness. Gold curtains and tassels and brocade all combined to display elegance and luxury, and more chandeliers abounded. The panelled domed ceiling and intricate plaster cherubs spoke of the hotel's origin as a Viennese palace, but the main feature of the suite, seen through two enormous mirrored sliding doors, was the bed. Ornate and splendid, its carved headboard was a work of art in itself, and thick, sumptuous bejewelled curtains were draped around the super-king-sized bed.

Bed. In the singular. Yes, it was big enough to house a family, but it was still *one* bed.

As if he read her thoughts Gabe's lips upturned in a mixture of amusement and rue. 'We'll need to share it. If

April has a source the last thing we want is a story questioning why one of us is sleeping on the sofa.'

He had a point, so she needed to focus on the size of the bed... No, she needed to forget about the bed. Because all of a sudden the memory of The Kiss fermented in her brain, her pulse racked up a notch, and her skin heated.

Wrenching her gaze from the four-poster, she headed towards the window and gave a cry of delight. 'Look, Gabe! It's snowing.'

The white flakes swirled down lazily and landed among the shimmer of Christmas lights and crowds of Christmas shoppers.

'It's beautiful,' she whispered, and turned to find him right behind her.

Her breath caught at his proximity and an insane yearning hit her for this to be real. For them truly to be here on a romantic getaway. For a moment the possibility hovered in her brain. Hadn't he said all those weeks ago that the ball was in her court?

No. Too dangerous, too risky, too much.

'So, what's the plan?' she asked.

'You tell me.'

'This is what Cathy and I usually do—we take it in turns to choose something. Write it down on pieces of paper, put them all in a hat and then take turns picking them out.'

Gabe blinked, and instantly Etta felt foolish. 'But obviously *we* don't have to do that. It's a tradition with me and Cathy, and this is my first holiday without her in sixteen years, so... Old habits die hard.'

'It's fine. Let's write some things down. The only thing I have already done is book tickets for a Christmas Eve concert at the Schönbrunn Palace.'

'That sounds magical. Which orchestra?'

His jaw tensed, but his voice was light as he named the ensemble.

'Oh, I'll research that...'

'It's two days away. How about we get on with this papers-in-a-hat thing? Have you even *got* a hat?'

'Of course I have a hat. It's December. I have a bobble hat! With a reindeer motif.'

Ten minutes later Etta pulled out a piece of paper with Gabe's scrawl on it.

'Shopping,' she read out. 'You want to go *shopping*?'

'I was being nice.'

'You mean you thought *I'd* want to go shopping? For what? I mean, I want to go to a Christmas market or two, but that's not what you meant, is it?'

'I assumed you'd want to hit the shops. My treat.'

'*Your* treat? Why?' Hurt strummed inside her. 'You've known me for weeks—you know that's not what I would do even if this were a real fling. Which obviously it's not going to be.'

Gabe ran a hand down his face. 'I guess I feel I owe you. I tricked you into a situation you didn't want to be in. I figure you may as well have some of the benefits. Seeing as you've chosen to pass on others.'

For a fraction of a second Gabe's gaze skittered towards the bed and Etta felt heat touch her cheeks. Without permission her imagination ran riot—if this were a real fling she was pretty sure they'd be spending most of their time in that very bed. As for shopping... She'd bet good money that lingerie was usually on his list.

The idea sent liquid heat to her tummy and she forced herself to hold her ground and his gaze. Prayed he couldn't read her thoughts. 'OK. Thank you. But how about you agree to being dragged around lots of museums instead? Although first you get to choose something you really want to do.'

'Anything?'

His gaze raked over her and Etta knew he'd made a pretty accurate perusal of her brain. Words failed her. Her mouth opened but no response would come out.

Eventually he took pity on her. 'Ice-skating sounds like a plan. Outdoors, cold, energetic… Sounds like what I need right now.'

Him and her both, but… 'I've never ice-skated before.' And the idea of making a fool of herself in front of Gabe didn't appeal.

'I'll teach you. It'll be fun.' His smile widened. 'Unless you're chicken, of course?'

'I'm not chicken. I'm *cautious*. My parents weren't very keen on risk, and since having Cathy neither am I. I've always been worried that if anything happened to me there would be no one to look after her.'

The words made her pause. They had been true enough when Cathy was small, but now… Now she felt a surge of irritation with herself. Was she really such a worrier that she wouldn't go ice-skating for fear of…*what*, exactly? How had that happened?

'Let's go.'

'Good girl. What's the worst that can happen?'

'I fall over and someone skates over my finger and—'

'I won't let that happen. Come on.'

They walked through the grandeur of the lobby and through the small revolving doors onto an illuminated street. The cold flakes of snow sizzled on Gabe's upturned face and next to him Etta gasped.

Above them hung shimmering sheets of sparkling lights that twinkled and twisted and glittered in a cascade of light. The shops were lit up too, literally wrapped in Christmas lights in the shape of a bow, and bedecked with silk ribbons and pine branches. The smell of roast chestnuts mingled with the aroma of traditional *glühwein*—a heady mix of wine, cinnamon and cloves.

'Incredible…' she breathed as they mingled with the shoppers.

'So, Christmas market first, then ice-skating—or the other way round?' He looked down at the map.

'Market first,' she decided. 'Just in case I end up in hospital.'

'Ye of little faith. I told you I'll keep you safe.'

'Martial arts expertise is *not* going to stop me falling on my backside.'

'Ah, but my expert intuition will. OK, we'll do the market first. We can easily walk to the one outside the Hofburg Palace and then walk to the rink.'

'Lead the way and I can look at all the lights. Look! Each street is different. There must be literally millions of LED lights throughout this city.'

Etta was right—the brilliantly lit streets boasted stars and garlands in a display that caught his breath. But in truth it was Etta who affected his lung capacity. Dressed in black jeans and a dark green jumper with a snowflake motif, under a brilliant red coat that emphasised her slender waist before swirling out to knee level, she looked beautiful. Back in the hotel Gabe had wanted to pick her up and kiss her senseless and he still wanted to do exactly that. But he wouldn't because it needed to be Etta's decision.

A ten-minute walk brought them to the immensity of the Hofburg Palace, its sandstone walls and green domed roof a mix of architectural styles—Gothic alongside Renaissance, with Baroque and Rococo thrown into the mix.

'It's a place full of history.' Etta's face lit up with enthusiasm. 'Though it's hard to believe that a family, even a ruling one like the Habsburgs, actually *lived* in something so enormous. It occupies fifty-nine acres and it's got 2600 rooms. Sorry. I am *so* boring to go on holiday with. I read up on everything and spout facts and…'

'It's fine. I'm interested.' His words were true, but more than that he was enjoying the way she waved her hands around to make a point, the enthusiasm on her face, her appreciation of the sights.

'Lucky for you. Because it's one of my hat choices. And I really want to visit the Sisi Museum—it's all about the Empress Elizabeth... Her life was fascinating and tragic.'

'It makes Derwent Manor look minuscule.'

Etta tipped her head to one side in consideration. 'I know it's very different, but have you ever considered the idea of handing the manor over to a heritage trust? You could still live in it, but the enormous upkeep costs wouldn't be borne by your family.'

'No!' The idea filled his Derwent soul with repugnance. 'Derwent Manor belongs to the Derwents. To hand it over to an institution would feel wrong—the land is our land, the rooms are ours, the history is ours.'

And yet thanks to him perhaps once he was gone the manor *would* be handed over, because the new Duke might not want to live in it. This Matteas Coleridge might not feel any loyalty to the property at all—why would he? *No.* Somehow, by hook or by crook, he'd imbue Coleridge with pride in his lineage. Bring him up to scratch.

'Derwent Manor will remain privately held.'

Etta's eyes scanned his face. 'OK. I just wondered if there isn't a part of you that resents the fact that you will have to live your life a certain way in the name of duty.'

'Nope. Not a particle.' It was hard to explain the deep tie he felt to his ancestral home, his abiding need to preserve it at any cost. And yet he'd let it down...

But right now he didn't want to think about his inability, his failure to his land and home. Didn't want to think about Matteas Coleridge—the man he was here to see. There was little he could do right now, and he wasn't even sure what he would achieve by an observation of the man who might one day wear the Fairfax coronet. Better to focus on Etta and her glowing features as she turned towards the market.

'I don't even know where to begin—and apparently this is one of the smaller markets. It's all so magically Christ-massy.' Etta pulled her phone out of her coat pocket. 'I have to send some pictures to Cathy. Look at those Christmas decorations! They are exquisite.'

The hand-painted baubles hung in colourful array, glinting in the December sunshine. Next door to them was another pristine white stall where beautifully crafted reindeer jostled with snowflakes and the walls displayed intricately embroidered Christmas stockings. Brightly coloured shelves were decked with snowman figurines and snow globes.

'And the candles! They smell heavenly.' Etta darted from stall to stall, her enthusiasm evident in the way she gently touched the wares, considered her purchases. 'I know I won't see Cathy for Christmas, but I've promised her we'll have our own Christmas once...once we're settled.'

Her gaze challenged him but Gabe said nothing. Clearly Etta hadn't abandoned her run-from-Tommy idea, but Gabe let it go. Her explanation of her adoptive parents' behaviour, the information she'd shared about Tommy, had given him an understanding of her decision even if he didn't agree with it. Etta had had to face such a lot on her own.

His chest tightened at the thought of the sixteen-year-old Etta, terrified and alone. But from somewhere she had found the strength to escape Tommy once, with no help from the parents who should have supported her. Gabe knew his own parents would have been the same—their way or the highway. Well, Etta had chosen the highway and travelled that road to success—he couldn't blame her for running now.

'What do you think of this?'

She held up a chunk of soap for him to smell and her proximity sparked desire as he bent his head to inhale the sandalwood aroma.

'I like it,' he murmured, but as he straightened up his gaze rested on her face. 'Subtle, but tantalising. Spicy with a hint of sweetness.'

Her face flushed as awareness shimmered in the air—

the same awareness that had glimmered into being the very first time they'd set eyes on each other. Only now it hummed with a deeper note, its pull stronger.

Etta blinked once, and then again, and shook her head slightly. 'Speaking of sweet…' She gestured to a bakery stall. 'Those smell divine. I need to try something but I can't decide what. There's gingerbread, and apparently that is a must, but I want something savoury too. Maybe a pretzel or…' She glanced at yet another stall and inhaled with appreciation as she read from the blackboard. '*Kartoffelpuffer.* They smell amazing. Shallow fried potato pancakes. Mmm… What do you think?'

'I think we should have both—savoury *and* sweet. We're on holiday, after all.'

'Sounds good to me. Let's eat.'

They walked through the rest of the market, both quiet now. The silence was comfortable, and yet Gabe noticed that Etta took care to keep her distance—presumably as aware as he that the slightest touch could cause them to combust. In truth he would welcome it—he wanted Etta, but only if she was fully comfortable with the idea.

'Ready to skate?'

Fifteen minutes later they had approached the outdoor rink.

Etta peered through the panelling. 'Look…' she breathed. Skaters of all ages, all shapes and sizes twirled and pirouetted in a display of expertise, to the strains of classical music that lilted from the outdoor speakers.

Ten minutes later Gabe and Etta approached the ice.

'So tell me—exactly *how* good are you at this and how much are you going to show me up?' she asked.

'I'm not an expert, but I can hold my own. I've played ice hockey before, so I'm more of an ice athlete than a dancer.'

'Hmm… OK. Let's give this if not a whirl then at least a wobble.'

Etta stepped onto the ice, pushed off with far more bravado than sense, and gave a yelp as she pitched forward. Without hesitation Gabe glided over and grabbed her round the waist, pulled her up, and held her steady.

The people around them receded and all there was was *this*. The feel of Etta in his arms...the warmth of her body against his...the smell of strawberry...the scratch of her bobble hat against his chin. She tried to move backwards, nearly lost her balance again, and clutched his arms.

A small gurgle of laughter escaped her lips. 'This is awkward.'

But it didn't feel awkward to him. 'It doesn't have to be. All you have to do is hold on to me and you won't fall.'

Her eyes widened and for a long moment their gazes locked. He saw the uncertainty in her eyes, along with a flare of heat that flecked the tawny gold with amber.

'I... You... What is happening to me?' Her voice was low and vibrant with a hint of anguish.

'The same thing that is happening to me, and it's OK to feel it, Etta. There is nothing wrong with attraction.'

'I know that in theory—but I haven't felt like this in a long time, Gabe, and I'm not sure I like it.'

'I'm not Tommy. I would never hurt you.'

'I know that. I promise I do. But...'

'It's OK, Etta. I don't want you to feel pressured in any way at all. Whatever you decide to do with this attraction I'm good with it.' He smiled down at her.

Her laugh was shaky. 'That darned ball is still in my court?'

'Yes, it is.'

'Then let's skate.'

The snow had stopped and glints of late sunshine dappled the cold whiteness of the ice. Gabe's arm around her waist felt warm and right and it played havoc with her senses. The exhilaration of gliding on the smooth ice, the laughter in his voice as he instructed her, the passion in his eyes as they rested on her caught her breath in her throat, filled her with female joy.

Gabe wanted her and he was honest enough to admit it. Suddenly Etta was tired of the pretence. The attraction existed and it was impossible right now to regret it. It enveloped them in a mesh of anticipation, and each movement, each word was filled with innuendo and sensual overtones. Each touch sent her pulse a notch higher, brought another hint of desire into play.

Time seemed to float by as he instructed her, clasped her hands in his and skated backwards, towing her along. He encouraged her, teased her, praised her, and all the while his eyes conveyed a message of need and desire until her whole body was heightened to fever pitch, every sensation on alert.

A warning alarm tried to clang in her mind, telling her that this was too much, but as the crisp air nipped her cheeks, as the swirling snow fell in magical flakes around her and the Christmas music added cheer to the air, it was impossible to think that this could be wrong.

All her life she'd believed in what her parents had imbued her with—she was inherently flawed, programmed to do wrong, her natural instincts would lead her astray and into wrongdoing.

Tommy had proved them right—she'd entered into that relationship like a fool. But Gabe wasn't Tommy and she wasn't that teenage girl any more.

'I think you're ready to let go now,' Gabe said. 'Skate by yourself.'

Etta braced herself and pushed off and gave a small squeak of delight. 'I can do it!'

Exhilaration surged through her as she glided forward in a smooth movement, the classical music adding rhythm to her advance. Next to her Gabe grinned, and desire spiked inside her.

NINA MILNE   139

'This deserves a glass of Viennese punch. I'll meet you in the middle of the rink.'

As they made their way across the ice Etta knew what she wanted and exactly what to do about it.

If she had the guts.

Minutes later she held a steaming mug and sipped the sweet, hot brew—a mix of tea, sugar, rum and brandy.

The scent of cloves wafted upwards as Gabe lifted his mug. 'To new experiences.'

Etta nodded, and her stomach looped-the-loop as her nerves jostled and twanged. *Now or never.*

Balancing carefully, she placed her own mug down on the stand, took Gabe's from his grasp, and placed it next to hers. 'I can think of another new experience I'd like to try.'

With that she glided forward, reached up, and pressed her lips against his.

Sensations zapped her body in a warm molten stream as synapses pinged and went into overload. For the first time Etta knew what a timeless moment was. Her body moulded to his as his lips played feather-light havoc with her senses. Touched her own lips with a sweetness that morphed into an intense vortex as she parted her lips and he deepened the kiss. Her hands looped round his neck and his large hands spanned her waist and pulled her even closer to him.

When finally he ended the kiss he rocked back, though his hands still anchored her to his body. 'Any more new experiences you want to try?'

His deep tones danced over her skin and she released a sigh of sheer anticipation as she batted her eyelashes at him in exaggerated flirt mode. 'Hmm… Perhaps you could help me out?'

'Let's go.'

Her whole being was now consumed by a need he seemed to empathise with fully as they tugged their skates off, fingers made clumsy by haste. But eventually they entered the dusk of the Vienna evening. Snow whirled down once more, and Etta marvelled that it didn't sizzle as it landed on her heated face, on lips that tingled from sensory overload. The lights looked even more magical now, and she slowed her quick march for a few minutes to listen to the jaunty medieval carol being strummed by a busker with a harp outside the festively lit shops.

Back at the hotel, they crossed the lobby, went down the corridor and into the suite. The door closed behind them and she stepped forward, straight into his arms, lifting her face for his kiss.

But although he wrapped his arms around her waist, his eyes were serious as he looked into her face. 'Etta, are you sure about this?'

'Yes. I haven't felt like this in years, and I want this.'

Caution etched his forehead with a frown and she knew why.

'You once told me I was a fool to give up on sex, love, and companionship. Love and companionship aren't for me, but you've convinced me sex is worth a shot. I want to join the ranks of your liberated passionate women who can do a fling.' She wanted to know she wasn't still living her life as if her parents watched and waited for her to screw up. 'So...' She smiled up at him. 'What are you waiting for? The ball is in *your* court, Gabe Derwent.'

'Now, *that* isn't a problem at all.'

The smile that accompanied the honeyed words was downright sinful, and her skin shivered in response.

'Let's start like this...'

His hands dropped to the belt of her coat and he unbuckled it in one deft movement and shucked the woollen garment down over her shoulders.

'I think we can get rid of this too...'

Seconds later her jumper joined her coat in a colourful pool.

'Your turn.'

Without hesitation, her fingers trembling with unabashed greed, she slid her hands under the pure cotton of his top, heard his intake of breath as she touched his skin, ran her hands over his glorious chest.

'Come on.' In one clean movement he scooped her into his arms. 'It would be a shame to waste that bed. Let's move this over there.'

A few strides later and he'd laid her on the decadent bed and was looking down at her, his eyes dark with raw desire.

She reached up and pulled him down next to her.

CHAPTER THIRTEEN

ETTA OPENED HER eyes and blinked as she absorbed the vast stuccoed ceiling, the deep gold of the folds of curtain that hung from the bedposts. Then the ornate splendour was obliterated by memories of the previous night and warmth swathed her body with a flush of remembered pleasure, joy and wonder tinged with a hint of anxiety.

What should she do now? What would one of Gabe's liberated women do?

Turning her head, she looked at Gabe—took in the strength of his bare chest, the sprawl of his long limbs tangled in the sinful silk of the sheet—and something tugged at her chest.

Whoa, Etta. Don't mix up the physical and the emotional. That way lay stupidity of Mount Everest proportions. What Gabe had given her last night was the realisation that she was capable of passion, of the giving and taking of pleasure, and for that she owed him a debt that she wouldn't fuzz with any other feelings.

He opened his eyes, went from drowsy to instant alert, and his lips curved up in a sinfully decadent smile. 'Morning, gorgeous.'

'Good morning.'

As if he sensed her hesitation he reached out. 'It is—and I know how to make it even better.'

His deep chocolate drawl with its wicked note of laughter dissolved the remnants of her reservations. 'Hmm…that sounds like a proposition I'm happy to explore.'

'Exploration was exactly what I had in mind.'

And then Etta got lost in the magic and the sizzle and the sheer exhilaration of the moment, until the dawn light had given way to bright Viennese winter sunshine that streamed through the gap in the brocade curtains.

Eventually… 'What shall we do today?' Gabe asked. 'I think we may need to add more options into the hat. But, whilst spending the whole day in bed has its plus points, I don't want you to miss out on Vienna. So over to you.'

The temptation to remain in bed was nigh on irresistible— but way too dangerous. She was Etta Mason, eminent historian, and she would not let herself forget that. Outside the hotel was a city that she had always wanted to visit, and she wouldn't be distracted from that.

Yet somehow her mood didn't lend itself to visiting a museum, or even the historic splendour of a palace. 'I'd like to go on the giant Ferris wheel. Apparently it's an experience not to be missed.'

'Leave it to me.'

By the time Etta emerged from the luxurious magnificence of a marble bathroom that was big enough to do the Viennese waltz in, complete with domed ceiling and chandelier, Gabe was standing at the window of the lounge, dressed in jeans and a thick knitted dark blue jumper.

'All sorted,' he said. 'Let's go.'

The sky was clear and their breath mingled white in the cold air as they stepped onto the busy Viennese streets, walked side by side, and Etta marvelled at the difference twenty-four hours could make. Now her awareness of Gabe had heightened into a knowledge of exactly what would happen if she succumbed to temptation, and the added frisson sent a small shiver through her.

As if still attuned to her body, he turned to look down at her—and there was that smile again…enough to bring heat to her face and a vague echo of her mother's disapproval. *No.* There was nothing wrong in what had happened last night and *zip* to be ashamed of.

They approached the amusement park and Etta tipped her face up to view the imposing, truly giant Ferris wheel silhouetted against the Viennese landscape. She absorbed the hustle and bustle of the fairground, the excited shrieks of kids and adults as they braved the roller coaster, the scents of pastries, schnitzel and hot dogs mingled into an evocative mixture.

'I've hired a private gondola,' Gabe said, '1897-style. Plus a champagne breakfast.'

'What a lovely idea. Thank you.'

Looking up, she smiled at him just as the click of a camera made her whirl round.

The man gave her a thumbs-up. 'Looking good, Gabe.'

A fleeting frown touched his face before the Derwent smile took its place. 'Now you've got your picture we'd appreciate some privacy.'

'No problem. As long as I get the heads-up on your dinner plans.'

'No deal—because we haven't decided as yet.'

The photographer discreetly moved away, presumably content with his picture, and Etta composed her features. 'So we have photographers following us around?'

'I figured it was better to arrange a photo opportunity—with any luck, that will be it for the day.'

'You told the photographer we'd be here?' It was an effort to keep her voice light, to remind herself that the reason she was here was to play the part of Gabe's temporary girlfriend. It made sense that he had given the photographer the information.

'Yes. I always figure it's better to have a good relationship with the press—usually if I tip them off they take a photo and then leave me alone. I should have mentioned it.' He shrugged. 'I guess I'm so used to the publicity I don't think about it. Sorry, Etta.'

'It's not a problem.'

She was tempted to ask if he'd booked the Ferris wheel

ride for the benefit of the press coverage, as proof of their relationship, but she pressed her lips together and held the words at bay. It didn't matter, because Gabe always saw the bigger picture and always liked to be the one who painted it.

'It is if you're upset.'

'An angle you didn't consider?' She'd meant to utter the words lightly, but she recognised the note of hurt. 'Sorry, Gabe, that came out wrong. I'm not really a public person unless it's to do with my job, but for the next few days this *is* my job.' It was a reminder to herself as much as to him. She grinned up at him suddenly. 'And I intend to enjoy it.'

'Good, because so do I.'

Etta followed Gabe to the front of the queue and soon they boarded a red gondola. The simple interior had wooden slatted walls, and light streamed in through the six windows to illuminate an elegant round table set for two. Champagne flutes glinted in the winter sunlight and silver cutlery gleamed next to pristine white napkins. The aroma of coffee tantalised, and an array of breakfast items topped the damask tablecloth—*semmeln*, pats of creamy butter, glass jars of apricot jam, ham and boiled eggs.

'This looks amazing. But I'm not sure we'll be able to eat it all on one rotation of the wheel.'

Gabe shook his head. 'Each rotation is about thirteen minutes. We get to stay on for six rotations, so we have plenty of time to eat and enjoy the view.'

His eyes rested on her as he said the last words and her tummy turned to mush.

'Shame there are so many windows so all I can do is look.'

Her legs threatened to turn jelly-like and she sat down as the wheel began to move slowly. Gabe seated himself opposite and poured her a glass of bubbly, followed by a glass of orange juice. 'Cheers.'

Etta clinked her glass against his and then sipped the

golden liquid. 'This is madly decadent. Steph and Cathy would definitely approve.'

'How are they?' he asked.

'Loving the cruise. The Caribbean was an enormous hit, and Cathy says she wants to live in New York one day.'

'You must miss her.'

'Yes. But…'

But not as much as I'd expected. There came that familiar nudge of guilt-laced panic. Because, like it or not, she suspected the reason for that was sitting opposite her. *No need to panic.* Given the choice she'd be with Cathy for Christmas, and soon enough she *would* be with her daughter and they would embark on a new phase of their lives. Gabe would be a treasured but distant memory.

'But what?'

'But I need to get used to it.' Etta improvised with a different truth. 'Cathy is growing up, and it could be that she *does* decide to live abroad for a while, and that's how it should be. I don't ever want her not to do something because she's worried about me.'

'You're a great mum. You know that, right?'

Warmth touched her at the sincerity in his voice. 'I've done my best.'

'It can't always have been easy. Seventeen and on your own with a baby.'

'It *wasn't* easy.' There had been times when fear and panic and sheer exhaustion had threatened to overcome her. But through it all she had known she could never give up Cathy. She had wanted to give her baby everything her own parents—birth and adoptive—had failed to give Etta. 'But I wanted to give Cathy the best I could—both in terms of love *and* lifestyle.'

'You could be a role model for young single mothers. Or for teenagers who are having a rough time. You pulled yourself from a dark place. I know how much you could help some of the kids I work with—' A shade of annoyance crossed his face as he broke off.

'The kids you work with?' Kaitlin's words came back to her. *Has he told you about his charity work?*

Gabe hesitated, reached for a roll and buttered it, as if debating whether to close the conversation down.

Then he gave a lift of his broad shoulders. 'It's no big deal but it's not something I publicise. I work with a charity and I offer self-defence classes for kids who've been bullied or have suffered physical abuse. Sometimes the bullies come in as well. Often the reason they're bullying others is because they've been bullied or abused themselves—it's a vicious cycle that needs to be stopped. A lot of them come from difficult backgrounds and are in care, or they're on their own and isolated.'

'So how long have you done this charity work and how come you haven't publicised it? Surely that would be advantageous?'

'It's a personal thing.'

'Personal?' Etta surveyed him across the table as her mind pieced together various comments he'd made. She made a leap in the dark. 'Were you bullied at school?'

His body stilled and she was pretty sure it wasn't in reaction to the gentle lurch of the gondola as the wheel it made its way round.

'Yes. Again this isn't public knowledge, and I don't want it to become so. But I'd rather you knew the truth than speculated.'

Etta shook her head. 'I won't tell or speculate. But…that must have been hell. I…I guess I didn't think someone in your position would ever be bullied.'

'My boarding school was rife with bullying, and in fact I made the perfect target. The older boys decided I was stuck-up and needed to be taken down a peg or two.'

His voice was matter-of-fact, but Etta's heart twisted

at the image of an eight-year-old Gabe, his blue-grey eyes filled with fear, being hurt.

'It was a long time ago, Etta.'

Maybe, but she was pretty damn sure he still carried the scars. 'How long did it go on for?'

'Until I got old enough and skilled enough to stand up to them.'

'But that must have been *years*. Why didn't you tell anyone? Your parents? A teacher?'

'Telling a teacher would have made it worse—the teachers wouldn't have been able to protect me twenty-four-seven. Plus, that would have been snitching.'

'What about your parents?'

No answer. And as Etta studied his expression she suddenly knew with utter certainty that he had told his parents and they had done nothing.

'As I said, it was a long time ago. I dealt with it, I learnt from it, and now I'd rather not talk about it.' He made a gesture to the window. 'We're nearly at the top.'

Conversation closed.

Reaching across the table, she covered his hand, hoping her touch conveyed sympathy and admiration as she gazed out at the panoramic view of Vienna. Her breath caught in her lungs, but Etta was unsure whether it was due to the incredible landscape from two hundred feet up or the feeling of warmth that Gabe had confided as much as he had—trusted her with such personal information.

'It's amazing.'

Equally as amazing were the next two days that soared by.

Minutes spun into hours, time cascaded in a fairy-tale warp and Etta lost herself in an exquisite maelstrom of sensation with every sense heightened.

The sights of Vienna were bright and vivid, with the boldness of modern art displayed in opulent baroque backgrounds. The smells and tastes of schnitzel, *glühwein* and *apfel strudel* and the dark richness of coffee lingered on her tastebuds.

And throughout it all there was Gabe. His lightest touch caused her entire body to hum with desire and the nights were filled with the touch of silken sheets, his warmth and strength, his gentleness and laughter and the intensity of shared passion.

Until somehow Christmas Eve arrived, and from the moment they woke Etta sensed Gabe's withdrawal.

There was no laughter or teasing, no fleeting touches that spoke of intimacy. It was nothing she could encapsulate in words, but it was in the tension of his shoulders, the clenching of his jaw, the distance he kept between them as they walked to the Schönbrunn Palace for the concert.

'So we tour the palace and then go to the Orangery for the concert?' Etta knew the answer, but for the first time in days the silence between them was laced with awkwardness.

'Yes.' Gabe had his hands deep in the pockets of a grey overcoat that topped a charcoal suit. As if aware of the brevity of his reply, he added, 'The tour is guided and people are split into groups of ten.'

'It should be great. The Orangery is meant to be magnificent. It was built in 1754 by Franz I and it's very baroque. Joseph II used to have banquets there, with illuminations in the citrus trees, and Mozart conducted his singspiel *The Impresario* there in 1786—'

Etta broke off. Why on earth was she trying to fill the silence by spouting like a tour guide? Perhaps to counter the clench of misery in her tummy. It was an irrational sadness. Was this the etiquette of a fling? To start to pull back as the end approached? Maybe it was a strategy she should emulate—after all, once Christmas was over it would be time to get on with her real life. This was an interlude, with no more bearing on reality than the fairytale it was. Only this fairy tale didn't end in happy-ever-after. It ended with no strings attached, never to see each other ever again.

But no matter. Right now there was Christmas Eve to be enjoyed, in this incredible setting that would stun any fairy-tale princess, and she would make the most of it.

The palace was lit up, shining in all its splendour, and the Christmas market outside was a hive of bustle and cheer. The enormous Christmas tree was simply decorated with white lights and overlooked a life-size hand-carved nativity scene that imbued Etta with a sense of awe.

But as their tour of the palace commenced for once Etta couldn't find it in her to marvel at the Imperial splendour. Even as she gazed on the most magnificent of ceiling frescoes, the grandeur of the white-and-gold rococo decorations, and the incredible crystal mirrors that created a near magical illusion of blurred other dimensions, her entire awareness was focused on Gabe.

Her antennae registered his tension, growing like a fast unfurling plant, until finally she said, 'Gabe, is something wrong?'

CHAPTER FOURTEEN

GABE FORCED HIS body into a more relaxed stance—not an easy task when every muscle seemed filled with tension, every sinew torqued with strain.

Pull it together and answer the question.

He smiled down at Etta's concerned expression. 'No. Nothing is wrong.'

Except for the fact that in mere minutes he would see the man who might one day bear the title that Gabe had believed would pass to his own child. It wasn't a big deal— dammit, he was *glad* Matteas Coleridge existed, relieved that there was a possible alternative heir so the title would not die out. Yet right now anger and bleakness pulsed inside him because fate had decreed that he couldn't have children.

Enough. Whingeing at the unfairness of life was pointless and ineffective.

'I'm fine.'

'Are you sure? You seem different, somehow.'

'Not me.' Gabe dug deep and discovered the famous Derwent charm, the smile, the expression. But Etta's frown only deepened. 'You're imagining it.'

Turning from the searching look in her tawny eyes, he studied the blue and white porcelain on display and tried to quell his sense of impending doom.

Tour over, they completed the two-minute walk to the Orangery. Once inside, he waited until Etta had settled herself onto a comfortable seat below the glittering extravaganza of the chandelier and seated himself beside her. The orchestra, dressed in eighteenth-century costume, were already assembled, and Gabe's heart pounded his ribcage as his eyes scoured each member.

There he was. Gabe rested his gaze on a stocky, brown-haired man, cello in hand, his eyes closed as if in inner preparation for performance. Visceral pain sucker-punched Gabe so hard he expelled a breath, and Etta turned to look at him.

With immense effort Gabe leant back in the chair and forced his voice into action. 'It should start any minute.'

To his relief, before Etta could respond the conductor rose to his feet and started to speak. Minutes later music swelled around them. The classical pieces fluted and strummed through the air, mingled with motes of history, and it was almost possible to imagine that Mozart himself stood on the stage.

But somehow for Gabe each and every glorious note evoked images of the children he'd once thought to have, and grief and loss for a now impossible future swirled in his gut.

On some level Gabe registered the next couple of hours. The choice of pieces was a perfect mixture of the haunting and the lively, and the conductor was both knowledgeable and witty. When a pair of ballerinas came onto the stage they were greeted with a universal murmur of appreciation, and after their performance applause rang out. Next up was an opera singer, whose voice soared and dipped with notes so pure and melodic that Etta gasped next to him.

Yet throughout, his whole being was attuned to Matteas Coleridge, his body feeling cold and hot in turn, taut with the fight-or-flight instinct.

At one point he became aware of Etta's glance and then her hand reached out and covered his. *Damn.* No doubt she'd sensed his discomfort, and for a moment he wanted to accept the unspoken comfort she offered. *No.* That way lay weakness; he would not allow any closeness with Etta other than their physical connection.

He had to pull himself together and man up, and so gently he pulled his hand away. Forced his emotions into shutdown, made himself focus on Matteas Coleridge with calm. Then he turned to Etta with a smile, refusing to acknowledge the hurt in her brown eyes.

'The finale should be magnificent,' he murmured. Almost as if he were speaking to a chance acquaintance.

In truth the finale was more than magnificent—the Viennese orchestra played in complete harmony, with an intensity that left their audience spellbound and captivated, and when the last strains of the music graced the high-vaulted room there was a moment of silence before a standing ovation.

But even the beauty of the music couldn't permeate the ice he'd generated around his emotions, and Gabe was glad of it.

'Back to the hotel for a late supper?' he suggested.

'Sure.' Etta looked up at him, her eyes narrowed slightly. 'I just want to pick up a programme on the way out. It'll make a great souvenir.'

Gabe considered a protest, then decided against it. Etta might well simply buy the programme and not study it in detail. So he merely nodded, waited whilst she purchased the glossy bound booklet, and then they set off through the Viennese streets back to the hotel.

Gabe knew he should try and manufacture some sort of conversation but somehow it seemed beyond him—perhaps once they were back at the hotel, surrounded by the chatter and bonhomie of their fellow guests, it would become easier. But he did derive some strange solace from Etta's presence as she walked beside him, their steps in time as they passed the still brightly lit shopfronts, and after ten minutes they reached the now familiar environs of the hotel.

'Can we pop upstairs quickly before we eat?' Etta asked.

'Sure.'

Once in their suite Etta vanished into the bedroom, slid-ing the door shut behind her. Gabe walked to the window and looked out into the Viennese night. Matteas Coleridge existed; he'd seen him in the flesh and his mission to Vi-enna had been accomplished. No, not fully. It was Christ-mas tomorrow, and he wanted the day to be special for Etta—however unfestive he felt himself. Then, after Christ-mas, he would go home and face the music.

Gabe frowned, wondering what Etta was doing. It was unlike her to change for a meal—especially as she had looked pretty smokin' in the green dress she'd worn to the concert.

As if on cue the door slid open and Etta stepped forward, halted on the threshold of the palatial lounge area. Forebod-ing issued him with a qualm. She hadn't changed—stood tall in the simple green dress, which was given a twist by the fall of its asymmetric hem which emphasised the length of her legs. She had the concert programme folded open in one hand, and as he met her tawny gaze he flinched in-wardly at the hurt that lurked behind anger.

Gabe steeled himself—he'd known this was a possibil-ity and he had a strategy in place.

'Why didn't you tell me?'

'Tell you what?'

'That "Matt Coleridge", a cello player in that Viennese orchestra, is Matteas Coleridge, your newly discovered distant cousin.'

'I didn't think it was important.'

Disdain narrowed her eyes. 'That doesn't fly, Gabe. You must have known I'd be interested. Is that why we're in Vienna?'

'In part. I was curious. And when I found out he was in that Viennese orchestra I figured, why not? I wanted to get away for Christmas so why not Vienna?'

Nice and casual. No big deal.

But Etta wasn't buying it—that much was clear from the frown on her face and the twist of her lips.

'But you didn't want anyone else to know? Not your sister, not April, not anyone?'

'No. Poor bloke—I wouldn't want to unleash April onto him just because I wanted to satisfy a curious impulse. As for Kaitlin… She has enough on her plate.'

'You don't get curious impulses.' Etta's voice was tight. 'If you don't want to tell me what's going on, fine, but don't insult my intelligence. You didn't want anyone to even *know* you'd commissioned the new family tree. Why not?'

'That's my business. I hired you to do a job—you did it and you've been paid. Subject closed.' A small voice told him that this was the wrong approach. A louder voice informed him that he was being a complete arse.

'No.' Etta strode forward, her pleated skirt swirling in the angry movement. 'The subject is *not* closed. I don't understand what's going on, but I know I've been manipulated. You hired me as your cover—your fake girlfriend. What happened?' Her voice broke and she gave an angry shake of her head in denial. 'Is that what all this has been about? You and me? An additional cover to make it real for April's spy, so no one suspects why you're really here?'

The revulsion in her tone was directed in equal measure against him *and* herself.

'That is not true.' He didn't want her to believe that—not when he knew what a leap of faith it had been for her to trust her feelings, trust her physical instinct. 'I wouldn't use you.'

Disbelief gazed back at him from her eyes. 'But that is *exactly* what you've done. You used my professional expertise and then you used me. This whole fling has been an illusion, created to throw dust in everyone's eyes for reasons of your own—a master strategy.'

Damn it. He couldn't let her believe that, but the alternative…the alternative was to trust her. She had already worked out some of the facts...could already do damage.

As if she could read his thoughts she gave a small scornful laugh, devoid of all mirth. 'Don't worry, Gabe. I won't go blabbing your secret to April or to anyone else. We had a deal and I'll keep my part—I'll even keep up the fake girlfriend charade for the next couple of days.'

She rubbed her hands up and down her arms, and for a second she looked lost.

'But I don't care who April's spy is—we aren't sharing that bed. And I will be out of here on the first available flight on Boxing Day.'

Let it be.

That always worked. Only it didn't. He couldn't let Etta believe he'd used her, that the past days had been fake, an illusion.

'I can't have children.'

The words reverberated, caromed off the patterned wallpaper and lingered in the air, each syllable a portent of fate. The act of saying the words out loud banded his chest with harsh reality, and his lips twisted in a grimace as he took in her expression.

Etta's mouth opened and closed, and shock etched each delicate feature even as her tawny eyes filled with compassion and near-empathy. His gaze twisted from hers. He didn't want her pity—couldn't bear to see her commiseration.

'Gabe...'

The programme fell from her grasp, swished to the floor, and as if the soft thud had galvanised her she closed the gap between them. She reached up and cupped his jaw in her palms, angled his head so their gazes locked.

'Look at me. I'm *sorry*. More sorry than words can express.'

The sincerity of her voice and the feather-lightness of

her touch mingled and grief threatened to surface. Gabe shoved it down—no way would he give in to misery.

'It's OK. You don't need to say anything.' Gently he lifted his hands and removed hers, squeezed gently and then let go and stepped back. 'I've had a while to come to terms with it.'

'How long have you known?'

'Nine months. Since then I've seen three separate experts—top men and women in their field. I've looked into treatment options, but I am one of those rare cases for which they don't believe treatment will result in success.'

The bitter tang of disbelief was still there—he'd been so sure he could fix the problem.

'So the unbroken father-to-son Fairfax line will be broken. But what worried me most was the idea that the title might die out altogether. Thanks to the convolutions of the law and the way the Fairfax peerage was originally set up the title can't be passed on via a female. So any children Kaitlin and Cora have can't succeed.'

'So that's why you hired me?'

'Yes. I needed you to find out if there was anyone out there to succeed me. You found him—Matteas Coleridge. The possible one day Duke of Fairfax.' Try as he might, he couldn't keep the acid note from his tone. *Stupid.* He had *wanted* another heir to be found, for Pete's sake. This way there was a chance for the future. 'Potential founder of a new dynasty.'

The words made her flinch. 'Gabe. This sucks. You must be devastated. Why didn't you tell me?'

'Because no one knows. I wasn't sure how the news would affect my father's health. I was worried it would tip him into another attack.'

'So is that why you split with Lady Isobel?'

'Yes. Isobel and I have always known our parents wanted us to marry—we talked about it when we were young and we agreed it suited us both. She wasn't interested in love any more than I am—she wanted a title, the position of duchess, to be the mother of a future duke. She was very clear that she wants children, so I figured it was probably worth making sure I could back up what I had on the table. When I found out the truth I knew we couldn't go ahead and get engaged as planned. But I still thought there must be a fix—a treatment of some sort. So I told Isobel I needed to postpone the engagement and I took off for America, because I figured it would be easier to avoid publicity there whilst I got the problem sorted.'

'But Isobel must have been curious?'

'Isobel didn't seem to mind—after all, what difference would a month make?'

'So what happened?'

Gabe shrugged. 'You've got me there. I have no idea. Next thing I knew she gave that press conference without any warning at all—the one that denounced me as a heartbreaker. I called her and she said she was sorry but she didn't want to get married any more, and she'd figured the best way to get herself out of it was to stage that interview.'

Etta looked at him with narrowed eyes. 'Why didn't you expose her?'

'Because there was no point. I hadn't been totally upfront with her, she would no longer want to be my a wife, so why stand in her way? There was nothing in it for me. And it meant I didn't have to tell her the truth.'

'So what will you do now?'

'Explain the situation to my parents. Following Dad's heart attack my parents are understandably keen for me to marry and produce the next Derwent heir. They need to know that although I can't do that there is another possibility—that way the family can take Matteas in, groom him... Could be my parents will ask me to abdicate my position so they can take him in hand.'

The whole thought made the blood turn to ice in his veins but it was an option that had to be considered. Now that he had seen Matteas in the flesh he knew it to be a feasible reality.

'No. They wouldn't—they couldn't do that.'

'If he's the right type of guy they could do *exactly* that. If they think it is better for Derwent Manor, for the future of the title of Duke of Fairfax, of course they will.'

'And will you agree?'

'Possibly.' Though every emotion revolted, he knew that in reality he would have no choice. 'If I agree that it's best for Derwent.'

'But what about what is the best option for *you*?' Etta's voice was gentle. 'What about you, full-stop? All you seem to care about is the effect on Derwent. You must be devastated on a personal level about not having children. Have you taken the chance to grieve for yourself?'

'Grief won't provide a solution. One way or another Matteas Coleridge might.'

It almost helped to speak the words out loud as he paced the carpeted floor.

'Option one: I remain in line for the title, marry a suitable duchess, look after the estate and imbue Matteas and his family with centuries of heritage. Or I stand aside now and he takes my place when my father dies. It depends on Matteas.'

'No, it doesn't. It depends on *you*. In any case, your parents will *want* you to succeed them. You are their *son*. They *love* you.'

Gabe shook his head, touched by her misplaced certainty. 'The Derwents don't work like that. Love isn't in the Derwent vocabulary. My parents will transfer their loyalty to Matteas if they believe he is a worthy heir.'

'That *has* to bother you.'

'They believe the future of Derwent is more important than all the emotions and dramas of today.'

'But it still must hurt to believe your parents could transfer their feelings so easily. I *know* it does, so don't try and con me into believing you aren't feeling *something*.'

'There is no point in giving in to feelings.'

'Maybe. But those feelings exist, however much you suppress them. If you don't want to talk about it I truly get it.' Etta hauled in a breath, met his gaze square-on. 'I was fourteen when my mum fell pregnant with Rosa. When she was born I worked out that something wasn't right... There were questions Mum couldn't answer, or the answers she gave didn't ring true. Also they were different with Rosa than they were with me—tactile, demonstrative, loving, *happy*. They adored her—truly adored her—and it was as if I didn't exist any more. They wouldn't even let me help look after her.'

Gabe could see the remembered hurt and bewilderment on her face and he stepped towards her. This time it was her turn to step back, with a small shake of her head.

'The point is I eventually worked it out—I'm adopted, but they hadn't ever told me. I asked them and they admitted it. Like it wasn't a big deal. But it was—one minute I had an identity, and the next, *kaboom*, the whole facade tumbled down, leaving *me* as the debris.'

Gabe knew how that hurt—the collapse of a lifetime's belief—and the pain on her face caused his chest to tighten as he imagined a teenage Etta, caught in a maelstrom of pain and confusion, hurt and anger. So much made sense now—her fear of losing Cathy's love, her belief that Cathy would transfer her love to Tommy.

'Etta, I'm sorry.'

'That's not why I told you. I told you because you're treating something devastating as something logical, and it isn't. You thought you had a future and now that future has been snatched away from you. Well, I thought I had a past and that was ripped away from *me*. And it sucks. This I know.'

Warmth touched him that she had shared something so

personal, so distressing, in order to help him, and for an instant he almost felt an urge to allow the emotions he'd leashed so tight for months to run loose. But that would mean letting Etta closer, and he'd let her close enough. Anything further would smack of weakness—but he was in control and he would find a strategy to move forward.

'Come here. I appreciate what you have told me, and I promise you that it outweighs anything I'm going through. I will deal with my parents—however it pans out, and whatever goes down. But right now there is one thing I need you to know.'

He stepped forward, cupped her jaw in his hands, and tilted her face towards his.

'I *didn't* use you in the past few days. I *didn't* sleep with you to pull the wool over April's eyes. I slept with you because I wanted to.' He smiled, wanting—*needing*—to change the mood. 'I still do. And it's important to me that you believe that.'

She surveyed him, her brown eyes soft with emotion. 'I do. I do believe that—and thank you for telling me the truth. I promise you can trust me, and if you want to talk— not about strategies and logic but about how you *feel*— I'm here.'

'Thank you.'

That would happen when hell froze over—he wouldn't know where to begin, even if he had any desire to invite Etta to a pity party.

'In the meantime, let's skip supper and go to bed.'

CHAPTER FIFTEEN

GABE ENTERED THE bedroom where Etta still slept, curled on her side. One hand pillowed her cheek and she looked so beautiful his heartstrings tugged.

She opened her eyes and surveyed him drowsily before she rolled onto her back and then pushed herself up against the ornate splendour of the headboard.

'Merry Christmas,' he said, surprised to feel anticipation unfurling in his gut as she grinned at him.

'Merry Christmas!' A stretch and she inhaled appreciatively. 'What *is* that heavenly smell?'

'Rise and shine.' He tugged at the duvet and she snatched at it. 'I ordered Room Service. Pancakes, Viennese-style. I know it's not the same as having Cathy here, but I thought it might help to have your traditional breakfast.'

Her smile illuminated the whole room and made him feel about eight feet tall.

'Thank you, Gabe. I'll be out in two minutes.'

'Take your time—and wish Cathy a merry Christmas from me.'

True to her word, minutes later she sat opposite Gabe and looked at her heaped plate. 'Wow!' The thick golden pancakes had been torn into bite-sized pieces, sugar-dusted and piled into an artistic tower. Berries bedecked the concoction and gave the dish a festive edge.

He wiggled his eyebrows. 'I thought you might be hungry after last night.'

'You thought right.'

She dug into the pancakes and nearly moaned at the

light texture, at the taste of custard and sugar melting on her tongue.

'These are *amazing*. But now it's your turn for a present.'

Sudden discomfort made him shift on the brocade chair. 'You didn't need to…'

'I wanted to. It's Christmas.'

One more spoonful and then she rose and went over to the cabinet, returning with a beautifully quilted deep red stocking, embroidered with an image of Father Christmas—presumably purchased from one of Vienna's numerous Christmas markets.

'Here you are. Happy Christmas. I'm sorry if it's a bit over the top. I thought that because you said your parents didn't do stockings…'

'Thank you.' There was a small awkward moment. 'Really. I'm not sure what to say. The Derwents aren't very experienced in receiving presents. But I really mean the thank you.'

'The best way forward is to open them.'

Her small chuckle, the eager expression on her face, suddenly made it easy to smile and Gabe grinned at her.

'Here goes!'

He delved a hand in and tugged out his gifts. First a bottle of Viennese wine, then sandalwood soap, a snow globe, and chocolates.

'Etta, thank you. I'll always remember my very first stocking.'

For a millisecond a cloud hovered: the realisation that it would in all likelihood be his last, that he wouldn't ever hang up a stocking for his own children.

As if she'd read his thoughts she reached out and quickly touched his arm, before reseating herself opposite him. 'I know you will have thought about this, but not being able to have birth children doesn't mean you have to give up on having a family. You can adopt.'

'No, I can't. Adopted children are prohibited from inheriting a title or the land. I won't bring up a son on Derwent

Manor and then tell him he can't inherit because he's adopted. It wouldn't be fair. As for adopting a daughter... It wouldn't feel right to deliberately adopt a girl just because she couldn't inherit anyway.'

'I truly believe if you tell the truth from the start it wouldn't be a problem. If my parents had done that I think it would have made a monumental difference to our relationship. For them *and* me.'

'I won't take that risk. I know what it feels like to face the prospect of watching another man take over the land I have learnt to love.' It was exactly the scenario Gabe now faced. 'The Derwents have to have children to further the Derwent line.'

'I don't believe that. Surely you want children for yourself? Because you want to be a dad?' Etta frowned. 'Is it that you don't want to adopt because you don't want any children who don't carry your blood?'

'No. It is truly the children I am thinking about.' His lips straightened into a grim line. 'If I inherit the title I can't adopt. If I stand aside I won't marry at all. My "shallow playboy life" can continue apace. But let's not talk about this—it's Christmas, after all.'

For a moment he thought she'd pursue the topic, but then she nodded. 'OK.'

'Good. I've got a gift for you as well.'

Etta's face creased into puzzled lines as she accepted the small wrapped piece of card and opened it. '"Max Woodstock, Martial Arts Master",' she read out.

'I want you and Cathy to go and get some lessons. I want to know you can defend yourself. Max is the best. I've spoken to him and he'll teach you himself. Lifetime of free lessons.'

'Thank you.'

Etta rose and came round the table, wrapped her arms round him. The unfamiliarity of being hugged caused him to tense for a moment, and then he followed suit, inhaled her vanilla scent as her hair tickled his nose.

'That's incredibly thoughtful.'

'Knowing martial arts makes you walk taller, with more confidence, and you'd be surprised how far that alone goes in getting people to back off.' People such as Tommy. 'Now, let's go and enjoy a Viennese Christmas.'

'Maybe we could go to the service at the cathedral?' Etta suggested. 'I know it's not the same as a country church, but it would at least be one of your traditions.'

So they strolled the illuminated Viennese streets, called out greetings to strangers, all smiling and full of festive cheer. Horse-drawn carriages clip-clopped down the road, the horses' breath showing in clouds in the crisp December air. They stopped to join a cheery crowd that surrounded an outdoor piano-player whose fingers flew over the keys with breathtaking skill.

Then there was the cathedral, dominating the skyline with its four towers and famed roof tiles in a colourful zig-zag pattern that depicted the coat of arms of the Austrian Empire. Gargoyles spouted water in figurative defence of demons, and the Gothic portals displayed a wealth of detail that had absorbed Etta's attention for nigh on an hour on their previous visit as she'd examined the biblical scenes, beautifully portrayed with glorious symbolism, alongside the more macabre winged sirens, entwined dragons and two dogs with a single shared head.

In truth, Gabe had been more captivated by her absorption than by the undoubted craftsmanship. He'd studied the focus in her brown eyes, the curl of her chestnut hair against the delicate nape of her neck, her grace as she'd hunkered down to examine a detail more closely.

The interior of the cathedral was filled with people, a mixture of those there for the Christmas service, and tourists enthralled by the statues, frescoes, and paintings. The ambience was weighted with history, and above them the immensity of the arched ceiling inspired awe.

It was an awe that resounded throughout the beauty of the service—in the language that rolled out from the ornamental pulpit and the sound of the choir soaring and swooping in choral harmony, touching the air with a feeling of universal peace and goodwill.

Once it was over they mingled with the crowds and headed to the entrance, though Etta lingered to study the thoughtful figure of St Augustine with a book, mitre and an inkwell, leant down to peek at the self-portrait of an unknown sculptor under the steps.

'I want a last look. That's the trouble—there is so much in the world to see, but I fall for places and I want to come back.'

'Like the café?'

The one Etta had fallen for on day one and insisted on returning to.

'Exactly like the café. I'm a creature of habit.' Her smile was rueful. 'So can we go back there today? I checked and it's open on Christmas Day.'

They entered the café, a historic haven, chock-a-block with tradition and frequented by philosophers and royalty over the years. High vaulted ceilings, painted archways and splendidly covered seats sprinkled with damask cushions gave the coffee house a regal glory. Notes tinkled from the piano as jacketed waiters glided over the floors with silver trays held aloft with stately expertise.

'I can't believe I can be hungry after that breakfast, but I am. I'll have the Viennese potato soup with mushrooms followed by a piece of *sachertorte*.'

This brought a smile to his face—Etta had also completely fallen for the torte that Vienna was famed for—especially the café's speciality: a dense chocolate cake with thin layers of jam.

The rest of the day passed by in a magical Viennese swirl.

They walked the gardens of the Schönbrunn Palace, then returned to the hotel and luxuriated in the depths of the black marble bath, complete with Christmas bubbles scented with marzipan. Then their dinner was brought and served by a butler so stately that Gabe blinked.

'He looks more dukelike than *me*,' he said as the man made his dignified exit, and Etta gurgled with laughter.

Conversation flowed—easy talk, with both of them skirting any conversation that would remind them this was the end. Course followed course. Pheasant, goose ravioli, boiled beef and then gingerbread mousse. Each and every dish complemented the one before, and when it was over they stood by the window and gazed out over the still busy streets, illuminated in gold and white.

'Happy Christmas, Etta.'

'Happy Christmas, Gabe.'

As he took her hand to lead her to the bedroom it occurred to him that it *had* been. It had been the interlude he'd needed before harsh reality set in.

But now he needed to face his parents and set about carving out a new life.

Etta shifted on the bed, fought the idea of waking. She wanted to stay asleep, meshed in drowsiness, her mind and body still ensconced in the memories that fizzed and bubbled. The night had been magical—a magic wrought of Christmas and happiness, passion and sweetness and love.

Her eyes sprang wide in shock… *Love?*

Oh, no. No, no, no, *no*. Etta forced herself to remain still, to keep her breathing even as panic threatened to engulf her. This could *not* have happened.

It dawned on her that a noise had awoken her—it was still pitch-dark outside but a faint buzz provided a welcome distraction from the enormity of her stupidity. Until her brain and her ears connected. *Oh, God.* Was it her phone? Where *was* her phone? The phone she faithfully placed next to her bed every night. In case Cathy needed her.

Panic swarmed her brain cells as she scrabbled on top of a gold leaf cabinet. *Not there.* Scrambling out of bed, she tried to think… It must still be in her bag, probably nearly out of charge…

She ran into the enormous lounge, tried to recall where she'd dropped her bag, found it on the sofa and fumbled the phone to her ear.

'Cathy? Are you OK?'

'I'm fine, Mum. Actually I was worried about *you.* But I've just realised the time—did I wake you up? Sorry… I miscalculated the difference. We tried you twice yesterday. I wanted to tell you about…'

Etta sat perched on the chaise longue, listening to the babble of her daughter's conversation, and relief washed over her. Cathy was safe. But what if she hadn't been? What if she had been trying to get hold of her and it had been an emergency? What if the unthinkable had happened and Tommy had tracked her down? What if Cathy had needed her?

Guilt slammed into her, caught her breath.

'Mum? You sure you're OK? Your Christmas sounded pretty good… What's the plan now? Is the fake-girlfriend gig over?'

'Yes.' Etta forced brightness into her voice. 'It's over. I'll be flying out of Vienna today. I'll be in England when you get back, and we'll work out where to meet.'

She couldn't risk going home yet—there had been no sign of Tommy in Vienna, but there had been enough publicity that he would know exactly where she was.

Cathy's sigh carried down the phone and across the miles with gale force. 'Mum. *Please.* Let's drop the cloak-and-dagger stuff. We've already missed Christmas together. Let me meet Dad, let him into my life, and it will all be fine.'

The words sounded so reasonable but Etta knew she was wrong. 'I can't do that, Cathy. Your dad is dangerous and abusive.'

There came the memory of pain, physical and mental, of the sensation of worthlessness, the belief that she deserved to be hurt, the twisted certainty that Tommy loved her—*would* love her if she could only be less useless. She could not let Cathy be sucked into that vortex in her need for a father. A need *she* understood all too well.

'So the "cloak-and-dagger stuff" continues. In the meantime enjoy the rest of the cruise and I'll call you later.'

'Fine.' Cathy gusted out another tornadic sigh.

'I *do* get how you feel, Cathy, and I love you lots.'

'Love you too, Mum.'

Etta disconnected and tried to think—she was an idiot, a fool, a disaster zone. Once again she'd allowed herself to get sucked in. Gabe might not be Tommy, but that wasn't the point. The problem here was Etta—*she* couldn't handle relationships of any sort—not even a fling. Instead she flew out of control, lost perspective. Last time the cost had been her self-respect and her family. This time she might have lost her daughter.

'Stupid, stupid, *stupid.*'

'Who's stupid?'

Etta started and looked up to see Gabe standing between the open mirrored doors that separated the living room and the bedroom. Instant reaction shook her.

Get it together.

No matter what happened, Gabe must not suspect she'd fallen for him—*stupid* didn't even touch the sides of her folly.

Say something. Anything.

'Cathy. That was Cathy. She still wants to see Tommy.

Which is pretty stupid. But really I meant myself. I haven't exactly come up with a plan.'

Slow down, Etta.

She sounded deranged—like Daffy Duck on helium.

'Let her see him. Once.'

'We've been through this. I will *not* take that risk.'

'She loves you, Etta. Her loyalty is with *you*. Give her a chance to prove that. She'll see through Tommy.'

'You don't know what it's like to want a dad—to fantasise about the perfect man who will turn up and look after you. I *do* know.'

Somehow it seemed important that before she left, Gabe should know everything. She wanted him to understand, not to judge her and find her wanting. It shouldn't matter to her, but it did.

'I was a doorstep baby. My birth parents left me on the doorstep of a church in Henrietta Street. That's where my name came from. The authorities tried to trace my parents but they never came forward. I've tried to trace them too, but I haven't managed it. I have fantasised about their identity for years, and if someone turned up claiming to be my dad I'd believe whatever he said, whoever he was. Cathy will be the same.'

There was silence as he absorbed her words. Then he stepped forward and tugged her into a hug, and for a treacherous second she rested her head on the breadth of his chest and drew solace from his strength.

'That's tough. You must have so many questions.'

Stepping back, she knew with crystal-clear certainty that it was the last time he would hold her, and she could feel the crack appear in her heart. The pain made her catch her breath.

'I do. But I accept now that they won't ever be answered. My parents—my adoptive ones, I mean—assumed the worst. That my birth parents were drug addicts who simply didn't care about me. I think that's why they had trouble bonding with me. They were desperate for a child, and they convinced themselves and the social workers that it would all work out, but it didn't. They tried to *pretend* I was their child, but the whole time they were watching me, waiting for my blood to out itself. They tried to love me, but when Rosa came along they had an instant bond—they loved her without effort. I guess that didn't happen with my birth parents and me.'

Sadness touched her—what had been so wrong with her that they hadn't left her any clue as to her identity?

'You don't know that. They may have left you because there was no alternative.'

'Maybe. The point is, whether that's true or not, if they had turned up when I was a teenager and claimed to be saints I would have believed them—no questions asked. Cathy will be the same about Tommy.'

'No. Because Cathy has *you*. You had no one—you have always had to face things alone. Your adoptive parents weren't there for you when you needed them most. *Hell*. They weren't there for you at all. Little wonder you dreamt about your birth parents being perfect. Cathy won't do that. Trust yourself, Etta.'

His voice was deep with sincerity, but how could she trust herself when she'd blithely fallen in love with Gabe? A man who wanted a suitable aristocratic wife or a playboy lifestyle...a man who eschewed love and closeness.

She got *why*—Gabe had been packed off to boarding school, abandoned to the bullies, and expected to work it out for himself. He'd been brought up without love and believed that to show love was to show weakness. And Gabe wasn't a weak man. He was a man bound by duty and choice to follow a certain path in life. A path he couldn't share with Etta even if she wanted that. And she didn't—wouldn't risk what love did to her. How it messed with her head. She was safer, happier alone.

Yet misery weighted her very soul at the idea that she

would never see him again. Never touch him, laugh with him, or wake up cocooned in his arms. If she didn't leave now she'd cave, throw herself at him, and in the process lose all self-respect.

What was *wrong* with her? Her relationship with Cathy was forged in bonds of steel and love—how could she have let herself be distracted from that? For a man who didn't want her? Her lungs constricted and a band of grief tightened her chest. She *had* to get out of here.

'I need to go. Thank you for everything.'

Gabe's forehead was etched with a deep frown. 'Whoa. Not so fast.'

Gabe tried to force misplaced panic down. 'What's going on, Etta? I thought your plan was to leave tomorrow.'

Think, Gabe.

But for once his brain refused to cooperate. Strands of thought whirled and swirled and he couldn't correlate them, couldn't formulate a strategy.

Part of his mind was still trying to assimilate the extent of what Etta had faced in her life. To learn that she had been abandoned by her birth parents at the same time as learning she was adopted and then being rejected by her adopted parents... Little wonder she'd rebelled in a bid to win her parents' attention. But the consequence had been a plunge into an abusive relationship and a teen pregnancy.

Admiration seethed inside him as he looked at her, standing amidst the imperial grandeur. Yet for once he couldn't read her emotion—her expressive face was in shutdown, though she still rubbed her hands up and down her arms.

'It was, but I've changed the plan. I need to get to Cathy. Christmas is over and I need to be with my daughter. I need to talk to Steph and work out our next step. I need to get back to my real life. This week has been magical, and I'll never forget it, but it wasn't real. It was a fling—an interlude.'

Her lips turned up in a smile that didn't get anywhere near her eyes.

'Fun, with no strings attached, and now I need to move on.'

Strange how his own words seemed so hollow now. Panic rocked him back on his heels as he realised that he didn't want her to leave. *Insane.* What did he want? Another day? Another week? What difference would that make? He didn't know, but he knew he couldn't let her leave yet, had to make sure she was safe.

'We both need to move on,' he managed, the words redolent with strain. He forced his vocal cords into submission. 'But we need to make sure we do this right. We'll fly back to London together and go to a hotel. Then we can smuggle you out.'

'I may go and stay in Cornwall at the Cavershams' Castle Hotel. I can hole up there and—'

'Ethan could collect Cathy from the cruise ship and bring her to you.'

Ethan would protect Etta and Cathy, and that was the most important issue at stake.

'I can work out our next move from there. I'll start packing.'

There it was again—that near desperate urge to stop her, to take her into his arms and tell her he would keep her safe from Tommy, hold her close. But along with that came the surge of panic, the memory that closeness led to weakness, made you vulnerable to pain and loss and fear. If you let people close, you opened the door to pain. He'd nearly slipped up with Etta. Somehow she'd slipped under his guard and under his skin and he needed to get her out.

The best way to do that was to shut down all emotion.

This had to end now.

Yet he could sense the bleakness seeping in under his armour, trying to touch his soul.

CHAPTER SIXTEEN

Two weeks later

GABE LOOKED ROUND the lounge at Derwent Manor and wished he could shake the memories of Etta—it was absurd to wonder if he could smell a hint of vanilla in the air.

His parents glared at him across the room.

'What *is* going on, Gabriel?' His father's tone was testy, at best. 'You should be out there securing Lady Isobel Petersen.'

'Your father is right.' The Duchess's tone was glacial. 'Plus you shouldn't have asked Kaitlin to come. And, Kaitlin, you shouldn't have come—what will Prince Frederick think? It's his mother's birthday banquet and...'

For a moment Kaitlin looked as though she might respond with an unheard-of suggestion as to what Prince Frederick could do with the banquet, but instead she smiled her trademark smile.

'I'm sorry, Mother, but Frederick understands that my brother has to come first. I know Gabe wouldn't have asked us all here on a whim.'

Baulked, the Duchess turned to easier prey. 'As for summoning Cora...' Her green eyes stared down the table at the younger of her twins with disdain.

Cora grinned back cheerfully, clearly unfazed, and Gabe blinked. Marriage had morphed his diffident sister into a confident young woman, no longer cowed by her parents. *Marriage or love?* a small voice asked him as he recalled Etta's insistence that it was the latter.

'Don't worry, Mother. Rafael and I aren't staying here—we've booked into a hotel nearby so you won't need to see him.'

Gabe had little doubt that Rafael Martinez would rather eat dirt than stay with his in-laws, and he couldn't blame him.

'So, Gabe, why *have* you summoned us to this family conclave?'

His heart hammered in his ribcage. This was the moment of truth—the point in time when this nightmare would become completely real. Hope tugged at his heart as he looked at the aquiline features of his father and his mother's serene beauty. The same hope he'd felt all those years ago when he'd run away from school. That they would show empathy, understanding... Even then he'd known that love was too high an expectation.

Gabe closed his eyes briefly, braced himself, unclenched his jaw. 'I can't have children.'

The room rang, echoed with absolute silence. His parents' expressions morphed from disbelief to disdain and Gabe's heart plummeted in his chest. Disappointment and near revulsion twisted the Duchess's mouth into a grimace of distaste. As for his father—his blue-grey eyes were colder than the Arctic at its worst. He was looking at his son as if he could not believe that a Derwent could have let him down on so spectacular a scale.

Then Kaitlin spoke. 'Gabe, I am so sorry.'

As if her sister's voice had broken the spell Cora jumped up, moved around the table to his side, and pulled him into a hug. For a second he resisted, and then he hugged her back, before looking towards his parents.

'I know it's a shock—'

'A *shock*? It's a disgrace.' The Duke banged his stick on the floor. 'A let-down.'

'It's not Gabe's fault,' Cora said quietly.

'Fault is irrelevant,' the Duchess said. 'We need the next heir and now our son is unable to provide him.'

The look she gave Gabe was equivalent to one she might give to an experiment that hadn't worked to plan. Pain twisted his gut, but he refused to show it—after all, he had toughened up Derwent-style, and he would be damned if he'd let his parents see that their attitude hurt. He understood—always had understood—that the title, the land, the manor, and the Derwent name came first.

Yet in that instant his brain reeled as realisation socked him—that whole creed was *wrong*. Etta would *never* make Cathy feel like this—would be constitutionally incapable of it. He could almost hear her voice, knew exactly what she would say. *Nothing is worth more than your child's worth—their happiness and well-being is paramount.* Etta had lived her life by that principle and that made her truly wonderful. That was one of the reasons he loved her—she lived by her beliefs, had done so in the toughest conditions and won through.

What? Love?

That was preposterous. But true. The sheer incredibility of the knowledge, the strange joy that swirled inside him alongside panic threw his thoughts into turmoil.

Not now, Gabe.

'Actually, I have located the next heir. Matteas Coleridge. Late twenties, seems decent, lives abroad.'

'Never heard of him. Never heard the name.' The Duchess shook her head. 'How *can* you have let this happen?' For the first time there was a crack in her voice, as if the truth were sinking in. 'A line unbroken for centuries. And now, thanks to you…'

Cora spun round. 'How about thanks to Gabe for finding this other heir. I bet it wasn't straightforward. Plus, has it occurred to you how Gabe might be feeling? That he may be sad? Upset? Grieving? For himself? In his own right?'

'Cora. It's OK.' Gabe reached out and took his sister's hand. 'But thank you for the support. Truly, little sis.'

The Duchess turned a basilisk look on Cora. 'You always *were* vulgar, Cora. Marriage to a Martinez hasn't changed that.'

She rose to her feet and the Duke followed suit.

'We need to meet this Matteas Coleridge. Make it happen. If he is malleable and we deem it best you must step aside, Gabe.'

'*Excuse* me?' This time it was Kaitlin. 'You can't do that to Gabe. That's inhuman—and it's not your decision.'

'Enough.' Gabe kept his voice low but authoritative. 'This has been a shock. There is no need to make a decision yet. When it is the right time *I* will decide what I'll do.'

The Duke opened his mouth, but before he could speak Gabe rose to his feet.

'I think it's best if Dad gets some rest.'

The Duchess glanced at her husband's expression and gave a curt nod.

Once their parents had left the room Cora shook her head. 'They are *unbelievable*. But, Gabe, why didn't you tell us?'

'Because that's not what the Derwents do,' Kaitlin said as she leant forward in her chair, tucked a strand of red-gold hair behind her ear. 'But right now you need to tell us what we can do to help.'

'I don't think you can do anything, but I appreciate it that you want to.'

Kaitlin looked thoughtful. 'Was it Etta who found this Matteas Coleridge?'

'Yes.'

'Does she know the truth?'

'Yes.'

His sisters exchanged a glance.

'Do you love her?' Cora asked.

Yes, I do.

It explained so much. In the past two weeks there hadn't been a minute when Etta hadn't been in his thoughts. Everything brought back a memory of her—the smell of vanilla, the taste of venison, the sight of a woman with chestnut hair. Each thing made his heart ache because he missed her—missed her touch, the tilt of her chin, her smile, her chuckle, her courage. He missed Etta. Full-stop. Wanted her beside him, wanted to hold her, to protect her and…

And *enough*. How did this make sense?

Love made you vulnerable, opened up the route to pain and hurt.

But it also made you a better person.

Gabe knew he would do anything for Etta, and that if it cost him pain and hurt then that would be an acceptable price.

Only it didn't have to be like that. Being with Etta made him…*happy*. Her courage, her strength, her decision to take a leap of faith and have a fling with him, her vulnerability, her zest for life, her amazing ability to parent…

'Yes. I love her.'

Cora and Kaitlin looked at him.

'So what are you going to do about it?' Cora asked.

Two days later…

Gabe approached Etta's London address, crunched over the white layer of snow, smelt the tang of more snow in the imminent future. His nerves were stretched tauter than the proverbial tightrope as he mounted the stairs outside Etta's apartment block.

Easy does it.

Could be Etta wasn't even there. His conversation with Ruby Caversham had simply unearthed the fact that Etta was still in London.

He buzzed the intercom of her flat and waited.

'Hello?'

Relief at the sound of Etta's voice dropped his shoulders. 'Hi. It's me. Gabe. Derwent,' he added. 'Can I come in?'

There was a pause and he wondered if she would refuse. Then, 'Of course.'

The formality of her tone was not what he wanted to hear, but at least she was letting him in.

The intercom buzzed again and Gabe pushed the slightly dilapidated front door open and bounded up the stairs before Etta could change her mind.

Etta pulled the door open and led the way into a hallway separated from the rest of the flat by a closed door, painted a cheerful yellow. The hallway itself was an off-white colour that combined with the large mirror on one wall to give the tiny area an effect of space—a space well utilised with a coat and shoe rack.

She pushed the interconnecting door open to step into a small but welcoming lounge and headed to a spot behind a red sofa, her arms folded with more than a touch of wariness.

'Hey...' he said, his throat suddenly parched as he gazed at her.

Come on, Gabe.

He could do better than that. Only right now he couldn't—her beauty had caught his breath. Dressed in jeans and a dark red top, with her sleeves pushed up, chestnut hair pulled back with two clips he'd swear she must have borrowed from Cathy, she looked gorgeous.

'Why are you here, Gabe?' A small shake of her head. 'Sorry. That was rude. Would you like tea or coffee?'

He followed her gaze to the small kitchenette in the corner of the room, where again there was a feeling of cheer generated by the way Etta had combined clutter with clever use of space. Pots and pans hung from a handy contraption to the left of the sink. An array of fun mugs hung on hooks. A cork board was littered with notes and memos.

The sofa held a collection of cushions, presumably collected from various holidays, and stacked tables made the small area feel like home.

'I'm fine.'

'OK.'

Another silence and he realised he was procrastinating because of fear—pure and simple. Time to get on with it.

'How have you been?'

'Good. You?'

'Yup. Good. Where's Cathy?'

'Sleepover at Martha's.'

'So how come you're still in London?'

Etta took in an audible breath. 'I was going to get in touch with you. I was just waiting until…' Her voice trailed off. 'That doesn't matter. You're here now. I did what you suggested. I put my trust in my bond with Cathy and I let her meet her dad. She loathed him.'

There was a wonder in her voice, along with pride.

'Apparently he turned on the charm and at first it worked. Then he had a go at me and Cathy went nuts in my defence. He unravelled after that. Cathy says her curiosity is satisfied and she never wants to see him again. He was so angry he went out, got drunk, ended up assaulting someone, and is now back behind bars. I know he'll always be a danger, but both Cathy and I will keep seeing Max for martial arts training, and we've decided to live our lives. So thank you—you showed me that I could face up to Tommy and, most important, trust Cathy. That means the world to me.'

Pride and admiration filled him that Etta had been so brave, along with a feeling of satisfaction that she now knew and believed in her bond with Cathy and could lead her life untainted by fear.

'Don't thank me. *You* did it—you were the one brave enough to carry it through.'

'What about you? Your turn. Have you told your family about Matteas?' Her voice was brittle, her arms still folded.

'Yes. My parents do think I should consider standing aside if he comes up to scratch.'

'What do *you* think?'

'I'm not sure. That's why I'm here. I was hoping for your input.'

Etta's forehead creased in puzzlement.

'But I wondered if you'd mind coming back to Derwent Manor to discuss it.'

Gabe held his breath, the weight of hope that she would agree heavy in his chest.

'Now?'

'Yes. I'll drive you back later.'

Etta hesitated, and then nodded. 'Give me a minute to check in with Cathy.'

Ten minutes later Etta locked her apartment door, her mind whirring with an entire gamut of conflicting emotions, overridden by the megabuck question: what was Gabe doing here?

No big deal, Etta.

Gabe needed advice from one of the only people who knew the true facts. So she needed to focus on practicalities, not on the immense joy that wanted to surface at the sight of him. No way could she allow herself to reach out and touch him to check that he wasn't a hallucination from her dreams.

Yet she couldn't help but cast surreptitious glances across the car. Her body and mind absorbed his presence, stored the sight of his face, his blond hair, the depth of his blue-grey eyes, and the breadth of his shoulders into the Gabe Derwent treasure trove of her memories.

The drive to Derwent Manor was achieved in near silence as he concentrated on negotiating the roads through the snow that still cascaded down in lazy white flakes.

Once they arrived Gabe drove past the imposing walls of the manor and parked outside a dilapidated old building.

Gabe unclipped his seatbelt. 'What do you think?'

Etta studied the house—it was old, and in need of repair, but in her mind's eye she cleaned and plastered the walls, replaced the cracked panes of glass, resurrected the roof, and tended the neglected lawn.

'It has potential.'

'That's what I thought.'

He smiled at her then—a smile so full of warmth that her toes curled in her boots and the yearning to wrap her arms around the breadth of his chest had her scrambling to get out of the car.

'Could I have a closer look?'

'Sure, but first I want to show you something.'

Etta followed Gabe towards a small glade at the edge of the building and halted at the scene before her.

The spruce trees were alight with the twinkle of lights—a magical glitter that evoked memories of the first time she'd met Gabe at the Cavershams' Castle Hotel. In the middle of the wooded area a picnic table held a crystal vase overflowing with a burst of colourful flowers. The snow had slowed now, but still fluttered in lazy flakes to create a tableau that took her breath away.

Emotions jostled inside her: hope, perplexity, and wariness all attempted supremacy.

'Here.'

Gabe reached into the crook of the tree and produced a box, opened it and handed her a gold-wrapped package. Etta let out a soft sigh as his hand brushed hers and hurriedly attempted to disguise it with a cough.

'Open it.'

Etta complied, her fingers shaking as she gently tore off the embossed paper and opened the dark blue cardboard box inside. She lifted out an exquisite snow globe.

'Oh…'

Slowly she turned it in the dusky air and felt tears prickle her eyelids. Inside the globe were memories of Vienna—a miniature Ferris wheel, a Christmas tree, the palace, and a pair of ice-skaters. She shook it gently, watched the flakes swirl inside even as she tasted the cold tang of real snow on her tongue.

'It's beautiful. I'll treasure it and the memories always.'

'I wanted to say thank you.'

'For what?'

'For being you. And for showing me something precious.'

His voice was serious, yet with an overtone of warm chocolate that shivered over her skin. 'I don't understand.'

'You showed me the power of unconditional love. I thought everything in life was a barter, an agreement. You don't live *your* life like that. Your love for Cathy is and always has been without condition. From the minute she was conceived through to now. My parents don't work like that. We—Kaitlin, Cora, and me—we have always had to *earn* their approval. You are always there for Cathy, to help and support her regardless. You were there for *me* without any request for yourself. You went the extra mile at the fair—even bought champagne and cooked to celebrate its success. You gave up your own Christmas for Cathy's safety, but without martyrdom. Instead you made Christmas special for *me*, gave me a stocking.'

'You made Christmas special for me as well,' Etta pointed out.

Gabe shook his head. 'As part of a deal.'

'No.' Etta shook her head. 'There was no need to order pancakes, or set me up for a lifetime of self-defence. There was no reporter there to record *those* things. You didn't *have* to try and convince me to face up to Tommy, to trust Cathy. You're a good man, Gabe. I know that.'

'Thank you.' Gabe hauled in a breath and gestured to the

snow globe that she still held clasped in her hands. 'There's a compartment at the bottom. Open it.'

Etta did so and her mouth formed an O of disbelief as she saw the contents—an exquisitely delicate, multi-faceted diamond solitaire ring shone up at her. Her whole body stilled... her heart skipped a beat, somersaulted, and then pounded her ribcage as she tried to think.

Gabe stepped forward and picked up the ring. 'Etta. Will you marry me?'

'I...I...'

Yes, her brain screamed, *just say yes*. But she couldn't—not until she knew he was sure.

'But...I'm not suitable duchess material. I have nothing to offer on that score. And I don't want a marriage alliance based on what we bring to the table.'

Gabe visibly winced, then lifted one of her hands and held it against his chest. She felt the pounding of his heartbeat against her palm.

'I love you, Etta. With all my heart. That's what I am bringing to the table. All I have to offer is my love. All I want is the chance to try and win yours. I love everything about you. Your generosity, your loyalty and your beauty, your courage. I love it that you're funny and that you love traditions and spout facts and embrace routine. And, most important, when you're not with me I feel like there's a piece of me missing.'

Etta's head whirled at the sincerity on his face, at the genuine timbre of his deep voice, at the way his gaze held hers, blue-grey eyes alight with a flare she knew was the real McCoy.

'I love you and I want to spend the rest of my life with you. No one else. I know you need independence, but I can eat cereal in my PJs whenever you want. I also know that I need and I want to get to know Cathy better, and if you give me a smidgeon of hope I know I can make you love me.'

For heaven's sake, say something, Etta.

But emotions tied her tongue—sheer happiness jostled with a need to reassure him, to… 'Gabe, I love you more than I can possibly tell you.'

'You do?'

'I do.' She stepped forward, straight into his arms, and the feeling was so right her heart ached with happiness. 'I should have told you in Vienna but I panicked. I thought loving you would make me lose control and perspective, but it didn't. You helped me…showed me things about myself I didn't know. You made me believe in myself, trust in myself. You've shown me that love can be a wonderful thing, that we can be partners, make decisions together as a team. No one has to be in control.'

'So you'll marry me?'

'*Yes*. With all my heart.'

As he pulled her into his arms her head whirled with sheer joy.

'I love you, Etta, with my heart, body, mind, and soul.'

And as he slipped the ring onto her finger Etta knew that this was the best merger she could have ever made—an alliance based on love.

EPILOGUE

ETTA LOOKED AT her assortment of bridesmaids, all standing in the beautiful churchyard. The spring day was chilly but bright, and the sun glinted down from the cloudless sky.

'You all look stunning.'

The words were the absolute truth. Steph, Kaitlin, Cora, Cathy, and Martha all wore simple floaty chiffon dresses, short at the front and long at the back. Their outfits were fun yet elegant. Each was in a different shade—Cora in bold red, Kaitlin in teal-green, whilst Steph had opted for navy blue, and Cathy and Martha had decided on burnt orange and lemony yellow.

'Not as gorgeous as you, Mum,' Cathy said. 'But we *do* all look pretty fabulous. This wedding is going to rock.'

'Yes, it is,' Cora said. 'And, truly, you look beyond beautiful.'

For an instant nerves ricocheted through Etta even as she reminded herself of her joy in her dress—traditional ivory tulle with crystallised lace and gorgeous satin buttons and a chapel-length train. In a moment she would step forward into the historic church, which was bedecked with gloriosa and hyacinths and filled to the brim with aristocracy, celebrities, and royalty. All there to watch Etta Mason get married.

The realisation chased away her nerves. Because the press coverage, the many people she didn't know, the fact that she was on show, even the dress—none of it mattered. All that mattered was the fact that she would be walking down the aisle to Gabe, the man she loved with all her heart.

And there were some people who *did* matter in there. Such as her sister, Rosa, and her adoptive parents, to whom she had sent an invitation and who had agreed to attend. It was a first step, and Etta hoped it was a step towards reconciliation. Matteas Coleridge was also in attendance, in his new position as future heir. Because Gabe had decided *not* to step aside; he wanted to fulfil his role as Duke, not because of the kudos of dukedom but because he genuinely loved the manor and the Derwent lands.

Etta respected that, and she would stand by his side and support and help him as he would support and help her. As for children—that was something they would work out as they went along…the rights and wrongs of adoption…but Etta knew with bone-deep certainty that they would work it out together.

She took a deep breath and nodded at the women who surrounded her, and then she commenced her walk down the aisle. She had decided that she didn't want anyone to give her away. She was giving herself to Gabe, with a heart full of love and happiness. As she walked towards him and saw his awe-filled smile, his blue-grey eyes full of love, she looked forward to their future with joyful anticipation.

* * * * *

He knew exactly where to find her.

Watching the Trevi Fountain come to life, water spilling from it into the basin.

"Callie."

Her hips swiveled. Her head turned. Those soul-stripping eyes locked with his. "Hello, Joe. Tracking me down again?"

"We need to talk."

She gave a short laugh. "I thought that was my line."

He sat beside her on the edge of the fountain.

"Do you remember the last time we were here?" she asked after a moment, her gaze on the glistening water.

"I remember."

"I made a wish then. Should I tell you what it was?"

Joe wasn't sure he wanted to know. When he made a noncommittal sound, she angled her chin and pinned him with those incredible eyes.

"I wished for a dreamy romantic hero right out of the movies," she confessed.

"Sorry. Looks like you're zero for three." He didn't see himself as dreamy or romantic or heroic.

"Maybe I should make another wish." Eyes closed, she looked as though she was sorting through dozens of possibilities before settling on one. Then she sent the coin sailing toward the fountain.

"What did you wish for this time?"

She smiled. "You'll just have to wait and see."

* * *

Three Coins in the Fountain:
When you wish upon your heart…

CALLIE'S
CHRISTMAS WISH

BY
MERLINE LOVELACE

MILLS & BOON

First Published in Great Britain 2016
By Mills & Boon, an imprint of HarperCollins*Publishers*
1 London Bridge Street, London, SE1 9GF

© 2016 Merline Lovelace

ISBN: 978-0-263-92034-5

23-1116

Our policy is to use papers that are natural, renewable and recyclable products and made from wood grown in sustainable forests. The logging and manufacturing processes conform to the legal environmental regulations of the country of origin.

Printed and bound in Spain
by CPI, Barcelona

A career Air Force officer, **Merline Lovelace** served at bases all over the world. When she hung up her uniform for the last time, she decided to try her hand at storytelling. Since then, more than twelve million copies of her books have been published in over thirty countries. Check her website at www.merlinelovelace.com or friend Merline on Facebook for news and information about her latest releases.

Many, many thanks to Machaelie Halsey,
who let me pick her brain about counselling
techniques during lunch at Chili's, then read several
chapters while we were cooking Easter dinner.

Thanks, too, to Christy Gronlund,
who filled me in on the joys and stresses of
Children's Advocacy. You both made this book
so rich in detail and rewarding for me to write.

Chapter One

It started with the fountain.

That damned Trevi Fountain.

Callie and her two best friends *had* to take a long-dreamed-of trip to Italy this past September. Then she and Dawn and Kate *had* to defy the tradition that said just tossing a coin in the fountain would bring them back to Rome someday. Oh, no. The centuries-old tradition wasn't good enough. They *had* to make separate, secret wishes.

Kate's came true while the three friends were still in Italy, when she and her husband reconciled mere weeks away from a divorce. Dawn didn't realize her wish had been granted until she was back in the States and acting as surrogate nanny for a lively six-year-old. A few short weeks later, the laughing, flirtatious redhead had made the surprising and completely unexpected leap from carefree bachelorette to deliriously happy mother to Tommy and wife to hunky Brian Ellis.

Callie had made a wish in Rome, as well. One she hadn't shared with anyone. Not even her BFFs. It was too silly, too frivolous. And so not in keeping with her usual level-headed self.

That ridiculous wish was coming back to haunt her now. Every part of her thrummed with nervous anticipation as she helped Dawn and Tommy loop fresh pine boughs into Christmas wreaths for the doors of the Ellises' home. Luckily, the determined efforts of Tommy's three-month-old wheaten terrier pup to get into the action kept both the boy and Dawn so amused that neither noticed Callie jump when the doorbell rang.

The sound of the bell sent the pup into an immediate frenzy. His butt end whipped around. His claws skittered on the pine plank flooring. High-pitched yelps split the air as he careened out of the kitchen and down a hallway fragrant with the scent of the cloves and cinnamon and oranges in the Christmas potpourri.

"That'll be Joe."

Pushing to her feet, Dawn dusted the pine needles from the moss-colored turtleneck that clung to her generous curves and made her eyes appear an even deeper shade of emerald.

"His message said his plane would touch down at three and he'd be here by four." She slanted Callie a sly look. "Tall, dark, handsome *and* punctual. What more could a girl ask for?"

Nothing, Callie agreed, her stomach fluttering. Not a single, solitary thing.

Except…maybe…

There it was! That absurd coin toss again. How juvenile to wish Joe would let just a tiny smidgen of romance sneak through his solid, masculine, don't-mess-with-me-or-mine exterior. Hadn't he put his highly lucrative business interests on hold for her? Devoted considerable time and expense to tracking down the source of the ugly emails she'd begun receiving a few weeks before the trip to Italy? Shaking her head at her own foolishness, Callie followed Dawn, the wildly yipping terrier and Tommy down the hall.

"Joe promised he'd bring me a real, live boomerang from Australia," the boy reminded them as he charged for the door. "Hope he remembered it!"

He would. Callie didn't doubt it for a second. In the few short months she'd known Joe Russo, she'd come to realize that nothing ever escaped the steel trap of his mind.

They'd first met during a never-to-be-forgotten jaunt to Venice. At the time Joe headed a highly specialized personal security team guarding Carlo Luigi Francesco di Lorenzo, aka the Prince of Lombard and Marino, who also happened to be one of Italy's most decorated air force pilots. Carlo, Kate's husband, Travis, and Dawn's now-husband, Brian, had been involved in testing some hush-hush, super-secret modification to NATO special ops aircraft flying sorties from a base in northern Italy.

Callie and Joe had met again in Rome, when Travis surprised Kate with an elegant ceremony to renew their marriage vows. At that damned fountain! It must have been the stars in Kate's eyes as she reaffirmed her love. Or the mischievous sparkle in Dawn's when she announced she was flying home with the Ellises to assume duties as Tommy's stand-in nanny. Whatever the impetus, Callie gave in to her friends' urging that they all toss one last coin over their shoulders. Which was when she'd made that stupid, *stupid* wish.

Not ten minutes later, she'd found herself separated

from her friends and yielding to Joe Russo's quiet but relentless interrogation. As she'd soon discovered, the man hadn't transitioned from military cop to soldier of fortune to head of one of the world's most exclusive personal protection agencies without learning how to extract secrets from even the most reluctant interviewees.

He'd watched her, Joe had revealed. Saw how her shoulders braced every time she checked her email. Noted, too, how her eyes would flicker with distress before she withdrew even farther into her seemingly serene shell.

Callie tried to deny it. Tried to shrug aside his laser-sharp perceptions. She was too used to safeguarding the privacy of the children she'd represented as an ombudsman for the Massachusetts Office of the Child Advocate to spill their—or her—secrets. At that point Joe reminded her that she'd walked away from her job some weeks ago. He also pointed out that he could tap into any legal and/ or law enforcement agencies necessary to resolve whatever was scaring the crap out of her.

Callie still couldn't believe she'd broken down and told him about the threatening emails before she'd shown them to Kate and Dawn. Neither could her two best friends, for that matter. They'd let her know what they thought about that in some pretty forceful terms. But they got over their snit in short order and promptly threw a protective shield around her.

First, Kate insisted Callie stay with her in DC after their return from Italy. Then, when Dawn married and moved out of the elegant gatehouse designed for Tommy's live-in nanny, *she'd* insisted Callie take up residence there while Joe investigated the emails. And when the emails escalated from ugly to really scary, Joe tried to hustle her into protective custody.

Callie had drawn the line at that. She was staying in DC, hundreds of miles from her Boston home. She had four fierce watchdogs in the persons of Kate and Dawn and their spouses guarding her day and night. She'd turned over every threatening communication to the authorities, and Joe had exercised the legal system to gain access to the juvenile court cases she'd worked.

Enough was enough.

But her heart had still pounded each time she checked her emails. It pounded even harder every time Joe called or flew in to update her on his investigation. The kiss he'd laid on her last time he was in DC might also have something to do with the fact that she was holding her breath while Tommy yanked open the front door.

"Hi, Joe. Didja bring the boomerang? Didja?"

"You bet."

One of Joe's rare smiles flickered across his face. His cheeks creased, almost hiding the scar slashing down the left side. All Callie knew was that it was the legacy of a mission he wouldn't talk about to anyone, not even to Brian, Travis or Carlo. The angry red slash had faded in the past few months but still drew occasional startled glances.

Callie barely noticed it anymore. The rest of the package was too compelling. The broad shoulders now encased in a leather bomber jacket that had seen its share of wear, the square chin, the ice-gray eyes, the dark brown hair with its barest hint of a curl.

"Don't forget what I told you," Joe instructed as he stepped through the door and handed over a package wrapped in brown paper. "It's not a toy."

"I remember! Boomerangs are more than ten thousand years old. The aber...um...abra..."

"Aborigines."

"Yeah. The aborigines used to hunt with 'em."

While the boy tore at the brown paper, Joe nodded hello to Dawn before shifting his gaze to Callie. In their short time together, she'd discovered that his silvery eyes could turn as opaque and impenetrable as a Massachusetts coastal fog when he wanted, which was most of the time. But they glinted now with a triumph so clear and sharp that she knew instantly his sudden trip Down Under had yielded results.

"The emails!" she exclaimed. "You nailed the sender."

"To the wall," he replied with such savage satisfaction that Dawn whooped and flung up a palm for a joyous high five.

"All riiiight, Russo!"

The exuberant exclamation startled Tommy and the pup. Blue eyes wide, the boy clutched his boomerang to his chest and demanded to know what was going on while his pet made indiscriminate lunges at any and all adults.

"Down!"

Joe's low command caught the terrier in midlunge. It dropped instantly onto its haunches, looking as uncertain as a cuddly, curly-haired puppy could.

"Let me take your jacket," Dawn said in the sudden, blessed silence. "Then we'll go into the kitchen and you can tell us every detail."

"Mooooom."

Tommy stretched the single syllable into a mile-long protest that stopped Dawn in her tracks. Despite the butterflies in her stomach, Callie had to smile at her friend's goofy expression. The bubbly, irrepressible Dawn still wasn't used to being a mother to anyone, much less a blue-eyed imp with the face of an angel and enough energy to propel the Hubble Space Telescope into extended orbit.

"Joe's gotta show me how to make my boomerang come back," Tommy insisted. "Or..." He assumed an air of patently false innocence. "I guess I could take it outside and figure out how it works myself."

"Yeah," Dawn snorted. "Like I'm going to turn you loose with an ancient hunting weapon."

The Ellises' home was in an older part of Bethesda, just over the Maryland border from Washington, DC. The neighborhood consisted of gracious brick and stone houses set on large, tree-shaded lots. Their backyard was enclosed in mellow brick and graced by a fanciful gazebo now dusted with a light snow. It was also overlooked by a half dozen plate-glass windows, all of which were at risk despite Tommy's assurances that he would be *real* careful.

"We want to hear Joe's news," Dawn told the boy firmly. "Then we'll all put on our jackets and go out with you."

His lower lip jutted mutinously. "But..."

"Chill, dude."

Always a man of few words, Joe got his point across without raising his voice. Dawn flashed him a rueful smile as she created a diversion for boy and dog.

"Why don't you go into the den and get on the computer? You can pull up that website on the aerodynamics of boomerang flight your dad bookmarked for you. I bet Joe would like to see it after we talk."

Reluctant but outnumbered, Tommy caved. "'Kay. Just don't talk too long."

Still clutching his prize, he scampered off with the pup hard on his heels. Joe shrugged out of his jacket and raised a brow as Dawn hooked the well-worn leather on the hall coatrack.

"Aerodynamics of flight, huh?"

"What can I say? Brian and his first wife were both engineers. It's in Tommy's genes."

It was a measure of Dawn's basic warmth and security in her two-month-old marriage that she didn't want Tommy to forget his birth mother. Caroline Ellis had died of a brain tumor less than a year after her son's birth. Tommy had no real memories of her except those captured in the exquisite digital book Dawn had made for him using all her skills as a graphic designer.

"C'mon. I'll brew you some coffee while you tell us all."

Dawn turned to lead the way down the hall, so she missed the casual hand Joe laid at the small of her friend's back. Callie, on the other hand, felt the light touch right through her baggy purple sweater and cotton camisole.

When Joe called to say his plane had touched down, she'd almost dashed to the gatehouse to change, slap on some lip gloss and drag a brush through her mink-brown hair. She'd been thinking about taking Dawn's advice and getting the shoulder-length mass shaped at one of DC's elegant salons. With her life pretty much on hold these past weeks, though, she'd settled for just pulling it back in a ponytail or clipping it up.

She made a futile effort to tuck back some of the wayward strands as she and Joe settled in high-backed stools at the kitchen counter and Dawn plugged a fresh, single-cup, dark arabica blend container into the coffeemaker. As hot water steamed through the cup, the coffee's rich aroma competed with the sappy tang of the fresh-cut pine boughs on the kitchen table.

"Okay," Dawn demanded when the super-fast appliance delivered a steaming mug. "Talk! We've all been speculating like crazy since you took off so suddenly for Sydney. Tell us who the creep is who's been sending those emails and why."

Joe swiveled to face Callie. "Do you remember acting as ombudsman for a girl named Rose Graham?"

Frowning, she flipped through a mental filing cabinet of the cases she'd worked in her six years with the Massachusetts Office of the Child Advocate. Some files were slender; others were fat and crammed with tragic details. Still others were truly horrific. As best Callie could recall, though, Rose Graham's case file was one of the thinner ones.

"I remember the name."

"She was five when her parents duked it out in divorce court."

From the corner of her eye Callie saw an all-too-familiar mask slip over Dawn's normally expressive face. Her friend had been a young teen when her parents' increasingly bitter arguments led to an even more acrimonious divorce, with their only daughter caught smack in the middle. Kate and Callie had acted as buffers as much as possible, but sharing Dawn's heartache had been a significant factor in Callie's decision to pursue a master's degree in family psychology and accept an appointment as a children's advocate.

"The mother worked as a paralegal," Joe prompted. "The father was a software developer at one of Boston's ultra-high-tech medical research companies."

The details seeped back. Callie could visualize Rose Graham—fair-haired, small for her age and very bright.

"I remember the case now." Her forehead crinkled. "As best I recall, it was pretty open-and-shut. The child was well adjusted, doing fine in preschool and clearly adored by both parents. Judges are predisposed to leave a female child that young with the mother unless there's evidence of gross neglect or abuse. But..." Her frown deepened. "I'm pretty sure I recommended generous visitation rights for the father."

"You did, which was why we didn't give the Graham case as much scrutiny as some of the others. Only after I had my people go back and do a second scrub did we learn the father's company transferred him to their Australian office earlier this year."

"Uh-oh."

With a sinking sensation, Callie sensed what was coming. Otherwise amicable divorce and custody agreements could turn ugly when overseas travel was involved. The cost of the travel itself was often prohibitive, and the court couldn't discount the possibility a child taken outside its jurisdiction would not be returned. For that reason, Callie's report to the judge had contained the standard caveat requiring review if either of the parents should relocate outside the US.

"Rose's mother flat refused to let her daughter fly all the way to Australia," Joe confirmed.

"And the law firm she worked for tied her ex up in legal knots," Callie guessed. She'd seen that too many times, too.

"The father had to come back to the States so often for hearings and court appearances that he wiped out his savings and was forced to take out huge loans. As a result, he fell behind on child support."

Callie grimaced. "And that in turn led the state to institute proceedings to garnish his wages from his home company in Boston, only adding to his legal woes and burden of debt."

"He asked his company to transfer him back to Boston. He's been waiting for six months for a position to open up."

"In the meantime, his anger at the system festered."

"And then some." Joe shook his head in disgust. "I can't believe it took my people so long to break through the series of firewalls he erected. The man's damned good at what he does."

"But your people are better," Dawn commented.

"That's why I pay 'em the big bucks."

"So what happened when you confronted Graham?" she wanted to know.

"Pretty much what I'd expected. He acted astonished, then indignant. Then, when the Aussie cybercrimes detectives who accompanied me to his place of employment laid out the electronic evidence, he wouldn't say another word without an attorney present. After his lawyer showed up it still took some persuasion," Joe said with what both women suspected was considerable understatement, "but he finally admitted to fixating on the caveat in Callie's report as the root cause of his problems."

"Right," Dawn snorted. "Not the judge who signed the visitation order. Not his ex-wife or her team of lawyers. And of course not himself."

"Of course." Joe's silver-gray eyes frosted with icy satisfaction. "Bastard's in a world of hurt now. He'll be sitting in a cell for months while the US and Australia work out jurisdictional issues. Years, maybe, since the investigation and prosecution of terror-related cybercrimes takes far higher precedence in both countries than his threats."

Callie might have felt sorry for Rose's father if his vicious emails hadn't disrupted her life for the past three months. She'd have to pick up the pieces and get on with it, she realized. But first…

"Thank you." Reaching across the counter, she laid a hand over Joe's. "I appreciate all you've done for me. More than I can ever say. I hated involving you in the mess, but…"

"Hated me butting in, you mean."

"Well, yes. At first." She had to smile. "After all, we barely knew each other."

"A situation I've been trying to remedy."

He had. He most definitely had. Just remembering the hard press of his mouth on hers the evening before his sudden trip to Australia brought a wash of heat from the neck of her sweater. The heat surged even higher when Joe turned his hand, enfolded hers and brushed his thumb over her wrist in slow, easy strokes.

Callie didn't dare glance at her friend. Dawn wasn't the least bit hesitant to dish out advice or offer opinions. She and Kate had both already suggested—several times!—that strong, silent, super-macho Joe Russo had a serious case of the hots for the quiet, seemingly demure member of their trio.

Thankfully Dawn refrained from commenting on either Joe's thumb movements or the heat now spreading across Callie's cheeks. Instead she invented a quick excuse to depart the scene.

"I'd better go make sure Tommy isn't trying to test those aerodynamic principles in the den. Give a shout when you're ready to, uh, take the action outside."

The door to the den swished shut behind her, and a sudden silence descended. Callie was the first to break it. Her hand still in Joe's, she tried to ignore the skitter of nerves his stroke was generating and smiled up at him.

"I meant what I just said, Joe. I'm really, really grateful. And so relieved it's finally over."

"Me, too. It's been keeping me awake at night."

"I've lost sleep, too," she admitted. "I can't ever repay you for the man-hours you and your people put into the investigation."

"If it gets the shadows out of your eyes, I'll consider the debt paid."

His gaze locked on hers. "Your eyes are the damnedest color," he said after a small pause. "Not purple, not lavender. Sort of halfway between the two. First thing I noticed about you."

Well, Callie thought with an inner grimace, it wouldn't have been her ebullient personality or luscious curves. Dawn had the corner on those. And any stray male glances the flamboyant redhead didn't instantly capture, Kate's lustrous, sun-streaked blond hair and mile-long legs would.

"Thanks," she said for lack of a better response.

"I tried to find the right way to describe the color when I gave my folks your vitals," he said with a rueful grimace. "Couldn't bring myself to go with hyacinth or heliotrope. Their jaws would've smacked their chests."

Callie's own jaw almost took a trip south. These were the most words she'd heard Joe string together in one sitting. They were also the most surprising.

"So what *did* you go with?"

"Pansy."

Her nose wrinkled. "Lovely."

"Yeah, they are."

His hand tightened and tugged her closer. His other hand came up to slide under her hair. His palm felt warm on her nape, the skin hard and ridged in spots. She'd once read that expert marksmen fired thousands of rounds weekly to maintain their skills and developed shooter's calluses as a result.

Okay. She'd read that just a few weeks ago. When she was trying to weave a more complete picture of Joe Russo from the scant threads of his past that he'd shared with her. She was thinking of the still-gaping holes in that picture when he reclaimed her attention with a gruff admission.

"Those damned emails weren't the only thing keeping me awake."

He lowered his head but didn't swoop in and catch her by surprise, as he had the night before his abrupt departure for Australia. He gave her plenty of time to pull away, to ease out of his loose grip. So much time she was the one who leaned into the kiss.

That was all the encouragement he needed. With a low grunt, he pushed off his stool. She came off hers eagerly. The hand still wrapped around her nape moved up. He tipped her head back for a better angle and used his other arm to fit her against him. She strained even closer while his mouth worked hard, hungry magic on hers.

Within moments, Callie was aching for more. She wanted him out of his shirt. Out of his worsted-wool slacks and his Italian leather boots and...

"Caaal-lee."

She jerked her back and looked over her shoulder to find Tommy glaring at them with equal parts indignation and accusation. His pup wedged through the door with him and yipped, as if wanting to add his two cents to whatever was going on.

"Mom said you guys were still talking. But you're not. You're kissing 'n' stuff."

They hadn't actually gotten to the "stuff" part, but

Callie was thinking about it. Thinking hard. So was Joe, judging by the wicked tilt to his mouth.

"Yeah," he admitted, "we are."

Scowling, Tommy planted his fists on his hips. "When are you gonna be done?"

Joe slanted Callie a wry look. "How about we finish our…discussion…later? Somewhere private. Inaccessible to kids and dogs."

"Deal."

"All right, kid. Get your jacket and your boomerang and we'll go outside."

Chapter Two

When Joe stepped outside, he welcomed the clean, sharp bite of a DC winter. December was midsummer in Australia. During his flying visit, Sydney had been sweltering through usually high temperatures. As a result he enjoyed the brisk chill almost as much as he did Tommy the Terrible's determination to get his boomerang to fly.

Before making the first attempt, though, the boy fingered the fine-grained wood surface and gravely explained its aerodynamic principles to Joe. "See, this is a nonballistic missile."

"That so?"

"Uh-huh. It's different from ballistic missiles. They're, like, spears 'n' arrows 'n' bullets 'n' stuff. When you throw them or shoot them from a gun, they fly up in an arc till gravity pulls them down."

Which was about as cogent a distillation of ballistics as Joe had ever heard. He hid a grin as he thought of the hours he'd spent on the range as a raw recruit learning to calculate distance, velocity and trajectory.

"But a boomerang's different," Tommy continued, his face a study in fierce concentration as he fingered the intricate designs inlaid in the wood. "It's got this curved shape 'n' wide surface 'n' the top is conver… convey…"

"Convex?"

"Yeah, convex. Anyway, Dad says if you throw it right, it'll defy gravity as long as it has enough speed 'n' the rotation will bring it right back to you."

"Sounds like you've got the theory down. Want to put in practice?"

"Yes!"

Thankfully, Joe's Aussie contact had directed him to an indigenous arts and crafts store with a very accommodating owner. The man had hooked a Closed sign in his shop window and taken his customer to the soccer field just a half block from his store. It took patient coaching and several attempts before Joe eventually got the damned boomerang to return.

The Ellises' backyard wasn't anywhere near as large as a soccer field, but Joe figured it was adequate for Tommy's strength and throwing ability. Hunkering down on his heels, he shared his recently acquired knowledge.

"Okay, hold it in a two-fingered pistol grip."

"Huh?"

"Sorry. Hold it here with your thumb and two fingers. Tuck the other fingers into your fist. Good. Now lift the boomerang vertical to your shoulder. A little higher. Okay. It doesn't take a lot of effort to throw this. Just bring your arm back and hurl it forward."

Tommy's first attempt sent the boomerang plowing

straight down into the snow-dusted grass. The second whizzed past the pup's nose. The third actually flew off to the right, whirled and started to return before it ran out of speed.

"Joe! It was coming back!"

"I saw."

Thrilled with his throw, Tommy almost tripped over his pet in his eagerness to retrieve the boomerang. Joe figured he'd pretty well exhausted his expertise and leaned against the garden wall to let the boy enjoy himself.

He was a good kid. Make that a great kid.

Looking back, Joe could admit he'd harbored more than a few doubts when he'd heard Brian Ellis had brought his young son to Italy. At the time, Ellis, USAF Major Travis Westbrook and the playboy prince Joe and his team were providing special security for were in the final test phase of a highly classified NATO special ops aircraft modification. The mod had been designed by Ellis Aeronautical Systems, however, and the company's CEO was a widower who included his son and the boy's nanny on extended trips abroad whenever he could. Unfortunately, the nanny tripped and broke her ankle in the final and most critical phase of the test.

Joe didn't believe in luck. Not many men and women in his profession did. You considered every possible contingency, devised backup plans, worked out alternate escape routes and relied on training and instinct to get you out of tight situations. He was living proof that the formula worked...most of the time. When he looked in the mirror, however, he saw a graphic reminder of Curaçao and the one time his instincts were dead wrong.

Yet even he had to admit that chance or luck or whatever the hell you wanted to call it had played out in Italy. Kate and Travis Westbrook had hooked up again.

Fiery-haired Dawn McGill had stepped in as Tommy's temporary nanny. And Joe had met Callie Langston.

It hadn't been love at first sight. Not even, Joe recalled, instant lust. Callie would be the first to admit that most male glances slid right past her to snag on long-legged, tawny-haired Kate or laughing, flirtatious, extremely stacked Dawn.

Joe had experienced the same initial testosterone spike when introduced to the other two women. Right up until Callie had turned her head and nailed him with those purple eyes. But it wasn't until he saw her trying to disguise her reaction to those emails that she snagged more than a casual interest.

At first it was the cop in him. The military-trained investigator turned covert operator turned personal security expert. Then it was her insistence she could handle the problem herself. Then...

"Didja see that one, Joe? Didja?"

"I did. Good job, kid."

Then, Joe remembered, it was Brian and Dawn setting sparks off each other. And Kate and Travis getting back together. And the playboy prince putting the moves on Callie.

Carlo's heavy-handed seduction attempts had pissed Joe off more than they should have. They also got him thinking about things he hadn't allowed himself think about since Curaçao. Like someone to come home to. Hell, a *home* to come home to. And maybe, just maybe, a son like Tommy.

Suddenly impatient, Joe pushed away from the garden wall. "A couple more throws, kid."

"Not yet. I'm just gettin' good."

"Yes, yet. I want to finish talking to Callie. Besides," he added, taking a cue from Dawn's devious tactics, "your dad should be home soon. You don't want to wear out your arm before you show him your moves."

"'Kay. Four more."

"Two."

"Three."

"This one," Joe said in a tone that brooked no further argument, "and one more."

Inside the kitchen warmed by the dancing flames from a brick fireplace, Dawn and Callie cradled cups of steaming cappuccino and watched the action through frost-rimmed bay windows.

They'd just placed several calls. The first to Dawn's husband, Brian, to break the news that Joe had ID'd the originator of the emails. Another to the remaining member of their female triumvirate.

Kate had whooped with joy and relief and insisted they celebrate. Tonight. Before Joe disappeared again on one of his bodyguard gigs for some rock star or South American dictator. She and Travis would bring the champagne and sparkling cider. Dawn and Callie could take care of the eats.

They accomplished their assigned task by calling in a to-go order for tapas and paella at Paoli, a top-rated Mediterranean restaurant just a few blocks from the house. Which left them plenty of time to sip their cappuccinos and watch the outside activities.

"Joe's really good with Tommy," Dawn commented casually.

Too casually. Callie recognized that okay-whatever-I'm-just-saying tone. She buried her nose in the frothy brew and waited. Sure enough, Dawn plunked her own cup down and cut to the chase.

"C'mon, Cal. Give. To paraphrase my precocious little imp, what was with all that kissing 'n' stuff?"

Callie lowered her cup and met her friend's eager gaze. Her own, she knew, no doubt mirrored the welter of confusing emotions Joe Russo roused in her.

"I'm not sure. It's just… Well… Look, you've known Joe as long as I have."

"But not as well, obviously."

The drawled retort raised a smile, followed by a rueful grimace.

"The truth is, I don't know him as well as it might have appeared. Aside from the fact he can't—or won't—talk about his past, he's not exactly loquacious."

"No kidding. But back to that kiss. It wasn't the first, was it?"

"No."

"And?"

"And what?"

"Don't play innocent with me, sister. You might come across as all demure and innocent to outsiders, but Kate and I were peeking through the blinds when you sweet-talked Pimple Face Hendricks into dropping his drawers and showing off his prized possession."

"For pity's sake! We were, what? Eight or nine years old?"

"Old enough to know Pimple Face didn't have much to brag about. So spill it. Do you want Joe to deliver a repeat performance?"

There was only one answer to that. "Yes."

"Hallelujah! It's about time you took the plunge."

"Wait! I'm not exactly plunging into any—"

"The heck you're not. I can't count the number of studs Kate and I have fixed you up with in the past few years. After every date you've smiled your enigmatic

Mona Lisa smile and sent them on their way. Joe's the first male you've invited back for seconds."

"Dawn," Callie protested, half laughing and half embarrassed at how close that barb had hit to home. "It was only a kiss. Although…"

"Although what, Langston?"

She played with her half-empty cup. She couldn't understand her reluctance to share her silly wish with Dawn. God knows, they'd shared everything else in their lives. She hesitated another few seconds before yielding her secret.

"Okay, here's the deal. Remember when the three of us tossed coins in the Trevi Fountain that first time?"

"Of course I do. But you, Miss Priss and Boots, wouldn't make a wish. You insisted that just throwing in a coin satisfied tradition and we'd all return to Rome someday."

"Actually, I did make a wish."

"Which," Dawn guessed instantly, "involved Joe Russo."

"How could it? We didn't meet him until a week later, in Venice."

"Okay, okay. If you didn't wish for steamy, totally deviant sex with Mr. Macho out there, what was it? Please tell me it was something equally kinky."

"Since when are any of us into kink?"

When Dawn wagged her brows, Callie gave a rueful laugh. "All right. The wish was a little…fanciful."

"Are we talking satin sheets fanciful? Or whipped cream and melted chocolate? Or ice cubes and…"

"Dawn!"

"Ha! Do *not* go all prune-faced and prudish on me, missy. Just remember who advised Kate on the best brand of vibrator to buy when she and Travis separated."

"It was the same brand you recommend to me."

"Please stop annoying me with all these pesky details. Just tell me. What did you wish for?"

"Not what. Who. Louis Jourdan."

Dawn understood the reference instantly. She should, since she and Callie and Kate had drooled over the stunningly handsome '50s and '60s–era star during several all-night movie marathons as teens.

"God," Dawn breathed. "Do you remember him in *Gigi*? So suave and sophisticated and *hot*. The man made me want to jump straight from twelve to twenty."

"I think he was better in *Three Coins in the Fountain*," Callie mused.

She remembered the first time they'd watched the old classic. So many years ago. So many dreams ago.

"Did you ever notice how much Joe looks like him?"

That was met with a moment of startled silence.

"Now that you mention it," her friend said, recovering, "I can see the resemblance. Aside from that fact that Joe's eyes are gray, not brown, and he's probably four inches taller and considerably more muscled than our boy Louis, they're dead ringers."

"All right, I may be projecting a bit."

"Ya think? But, hey. Project away, girl. It's *so* romantic."

And *so* out of character. Despite the incident with Pimple Face Hendricks, Callie had always been the sensible, bookish one of the three. More into reading than boys in junior high. An honor student in high school. On scholarships all through college and her master's program.

Majoring in psychology had given her great insight into the vagaries of human behavior. Unfortunately, it had also reinforced her natural tendency to stand off to the side and observe. Six years at the child advocate's office, where she was sworn to protect her young clients' rights and privacy, had only added to her natural reticence. The often heartbreaking cases she'd worked had taught her to wall off her own emotions. Except, of course, from Kate and Dawn.

And now Joe.

He'd pierced her shell in Italy when he'd convinced her to tell him about the emails. He'd taken another whack at it with that kiss before he'd zipped down to Australia. The one he'd laid on her just a few moments ago had pretty well completed the conquest. Watching him now, coaching Tommy in the fine art of boomeranging, Callie could almost feel her outer barriers trembling like the fabled walls of Jericho.

"Well," Dawn commented in an obvious effort to validate Callie's wish at the fountain, "Joe certainly has what it takes to star in a few movies. They'd probably be more shoot-'em-up action flicks than romances, though." She hesitated a few moments. "It doesn't bother you, what he does?"

"It might, if I could pry more than the most superficial details about his clients out of him."

"Brian says Joe and his people were prepared to take a bullet for Carlo in Italy. Evidently the prince led a special ops raid that rescued some UN workers in Afghanistan. Or maybe it was Africa. Anyway, the group's leader put a bounty on Carlo's head. That's why he required beefed-up security when we first met him in Italy."

"Kate told me a little about that raid. Travis took part in it, too."

Dawn nodded. "I know I don't have to remind you that the constant fear and uncertainty, the never knowing where Travis was or how long he'd be gone or who was shooting at him, almost broke up Kate's marriage."

"No, you don't have to remind me."

Callie had been right there. She and Dawn both. Lending support and shoulders to cry on when Kate made the agonizing decision to end her marriage to the man she'd loved since high school. They'd been there, too, when Travis refused to let her go, insisting nothing else mattered if he didn't have her.

"Joe and I are nowhere near that stage," Callie said. "Or any stage, really."

"Tell that to your action hero." Dawn tilted her head in the direction of the window. "He looks like he has more than a kiss in mind."

Callie followed her nod and caught Joe's glance through the wide windows. He and Tommy and the pooch had finished and were heading in. When he jerked his chin in the direction of the gatehouse, she slid off the counter stool with more haste than grace.

"Kate said she'll leave work early," Callie reminded Dawn. "She and Travis should be here by six or six thirty."

"Brian's leaving early, too."

"Buzz me when they get here."

"You sure you want to be disturbed?"

Ignoring her friend's salacious grin, Callie met the three males at the back door. The pup danced around her while she dutifully praised Tommy's skills. Then Dawn lured her two boys into the main house with an offer of hot chocolate and whipped cream.

"Lots of whipped cream," she said with a wicked glance in Callie's direction.

Joe caught the less than subtle byplay. "Something going on I should know about?"

"Nothing important," she said as she led the way along the covered flagstone path to the gatehouse. Es-

caping the chill December air, she ushered him inside.
"Here, let me take your coat."

She hung it beside hers on an empty hook. The well-
worn bomber jacket carried his scent, she thought as
she took a discreet sniff. Sharp and clean and leathery.
It felt like him, too. Tough and resilient.

Oh, Lord! She had it worse than she thought if she
was standing here smelling his jacket. Hoping to heck
he hadn't witnessed the sniff test, she turned. Thankfully, he was looking around with interest.

"This is nice."

It was. Bright and cheerful, with floral chintzes and
bay windows that invited the outside in. The gatehouse
had provided Callie a cozy safe haven for almost two
months now. She hated the idea of leaving but knew she
had to pick up the threads of her life again.

The problem was, she had no desire to return to Boston or to her former career. Despite all the courses and
training and advice to the contrary, she'd let too much
of the heartache experienced by her young, helpless
and too often abused clients get to her. Even before the
emails, she'd decided to quit. Now all she had to do was
figure out what to do with the rest of her life.

She had no idea how much Joe might play in that. If
at all. The thought made her uncharacteristically nervous. To cover it, she responded to his comment with
a lively patter.

"The Ellises had the whole gatehouse gutted and re-
done for Tommy's former nanny, Mrs. Wells. The one
who broke her ankle in Venice. I don't think you met her."

"No, I didn't."

"Dawn's totally conflicted over that. She'd never
wish anyone harm, but she wouldn't have met Brian
and Tommy otherwise."

"And I wouldn't have met you."

Ohh-kay, Callie thought as he curled a knuckle under her chin. So much for small talk.

He tipped her face to his. "As I was saying before I got dragooned into boomerang duty, it wasn't just those damned emails keeping me awake these past weeks."

His voice got lower and huskier with each word. Combined with the brush of his thumb along her jaw, he managed to get every one of her nerves bucking.

"You're so beautiful."

The compliment touched a secret place deep inside her. She didn't lack confidence in herself or her abilities, but she'd spent a lifetime in Kate's and Dawn's more flamboyant shadows.

"When did you have your last eye exam?"

"I'm not talking the externals. I'm talking about what's inside. The quiet self-assurance. The serenity."

The happy glow faded a bit.

"I haven't felt all that self-assured or serene in the past few months."

"You hid it well, even from your best friends."

"There was so much happening in their lives. I didn't want to add to it."

"So you drew on your own inner strength, Callie. I admire that." His thumb made another pass. "You're the kind of woman I've been looking for. The kind I could come home to."

She didn't know why that doused the glow completely, but it did. She pulled back and searched his face. The scar didn't so much as enter into her thought process as she tried to interpret his expression.

It hit her a second later. Affection. That's what she was seeing. Admiration tinged with warm, genuine affection. Humiliatingly similar to what she saw on

Dawn's and Brian's faces when they played with their son's pup. The fact that Joe's was spiced with an unmistakable dollop of desire didn't soothe the swift, lancing hurt. Concealing her dismay, she eased out of his arms.

"Sorry, but I'm not sure I understand. What, exactly, do you mean by 'come home to'?"

"Well…" He paused, obviously searching for the right words and opted for a demonstration instead. "How about I just show you?"

He reached for her again and drew her closer. When his head lowered, Callie hesitated for just a moment before meeting him halfway. Her lips molded his. Her palms found his shoulders, circled his neck. It wasn't just affection, she told herself. She could taste his hunger, sense it in the arms that tightened around her waist.

When he widened his stance and positioned her between his thighs, she couldn't quite stifle a groan. She could feel him against her belly. A minor distraction at first. Then a hard, rampant bulge that shot heat from her midsection to every other part of her. She wanted this man. Ached for him. Would take him any way she could have him.

And when he scooped her into arms, she didn't hold back before responding to his gruff, "Which way to the bedroom?"

He undressed her with a skill that might have given Callie pause if she hadn't been so intent on matching him button for button, tug for tug. Her heart melted when he took time to sheathe himself. If she hadn't already been a little in love with him, his determination to protect her even in this most intimate act would've done the trick. That, and the fact that he drove her to sensual heights she'd never experienced before.

Every stroke, every kiss, every scrape of his late-afternoon bristles on her breasts and belly and thighs pushed her higher. She was panting when he parted her legs. Almost mindless with need when he entered her. Just enough sanity remained for her to take him along on the wild ride.

Her belly tight, she locked her calves around his. Her muscles contracted. *Every* muscle! She thrust her hips against his again, once more, and gave herself up to the roaring tide of sensation.

When they untangled, she came within a hair of succumbing to his offer of tomorrow and forever. Most likely would have, if he hadn't tucked her against him and stroked her hair. Slowly. Lazily. Again, with the same absent affection Dawn or Brian might stroke their son's puppy.

She didn't draw away. Didn't vocalize the return of her insidious doubts. Instead, she buried them deep as she and Joe took turns in the shower. He'd brought his carryall with him from the airport and changed into jeans and a misty-blue cashmere sweater that softened the steel gray of his eyes.

In deference to both the season and the occasion, Callie dressed up a bit in ballet flats, black tights with just a touch of silvery sparkle and a Christmassy green wool tunic. Twisting her hair up, she caught it with a jeweled butterfly clip she'd picked up on a foray to one of the DC area's many malls.

She was wearing her usual smile when she and Joe joined Dawn and Kate and their respective spouses to celebrate the end of her harassment.

Her calm smile stayed in place even when Kate and Dawn dragged her into the kitchen, using the excuse of making coffee for a tête-à-tête. Kate barely waited for the door to swish shut before she pounced.

"Details! The fat, pregnant sow wants details!"

Neither Dawn nor Callie bothered to point out that her tiny pooch barely even qualified as a baby bump.

"Rumor has it you and Joe got all close and cuddly this afternoon," Kate said. "Then you disappeared for several hours."

"Rumor being our gossipy friend here?"

"Hey!" Dawn protested. "Since when is any area of our lives off-limits? Seems like I can recall you two demanding every intimate detail when I got engaged the first time."

"And the second time," Kate admitted.

"And the third," Callie conceded.

"There! See? Turnabout's fair play. So how was it?"

"Pretty amazing, actually."

"You can do better than that, girl. On a scale of one to ten?"

"Twelve and a half."

"Way to go, Joe!"

Kate raised both palms and got slaps from the other women. Callie's was just a fraction slower than Dawn's, but the other two women picked up on that millisecond instantly.

"What?" Kate asked. "Twelve and a half didn't ring your bells?"

"They rang. Several times."

"But?"

She'd shared too many ups and downs with these women to hide her silly, niggling doubt from them. Still, she felt foolish even putting it into words.

"Turns out I want Louis Jourdan, and he wants Lassie."

Chapter Three

Dawn understood the reference to their earlier conversation, but Kate was totally confused. "Lassie? What's she got to…? Oh!" Her eyes popped. "Calissa Marie Langston, you sly thing! Just how kinky did you and Joe get this afternoon?"

"Kate! I was speaking metaphorically."

"Okay, now I'm really lost. How about translating for the verbally challenged? Where does Lassie come into this equation?"

Callie searched for the right words to frame her confused thoughts of a few hours ago. "Joe said I'm the kind of woman he could come home to. Not conquer worlds with. Not stand side by side with to battle the forces of evil."

"Okay," Kate said dubiously. "I guess that's a start."

"Some start," Dawn snorted. "I like Joe. What I know of him, anyway. And I love how good he is with Tommy. But he's not half as smart as I thought if he hasn't figured out Callie's the toughest one of the three of us."

"You and I know that," Kate agreed. "Travis, too. You gave him the most verbal abuse when he and I split, Dawn-O, but Callie sliced and diced him. The problem is, Joe hasn't seen that side of her."

"True." Dawn aimed a frown across the counter. "He stepped right into the role of big, strong hero to our help-less heroine. Okay, maybe not helpless," she amended when her friends opened their mouths on a simultane-ous protest, "but you have to admit you haven't been yourself, Cal. Not since you quit your job." She cocked her head. "It wasn't just stress or the emails, was it?"

"No. I was… I don't know." She rubbed absently at a spot on the marble counter with a fingertip. "I guess the best way to describe it is feeling restless. As though life was passing me by. I needed a change."

"You don't think getting involved with Joe would provide enough of a change?"

"Yes. Of course it would." With a determined shrug, she shook off her odd mood. "Assuming, that is, he wants to get involved."

"Yeah, right," Kate drawled. "As if you *can* get more involved than twelve and a half."

"Maybe not," Callie agreed, laughing. "We'll see. In the meantime, we'd better put that coffee on and get back to the guys."

As much as Callie hated to admit it, Kate and Dawn were right. She *had* played the helpless heroine. Worse, she'd been more than willing to let Joe step right into the role of the big, strong protector while she hid out here in DC. It was time to take charge of her life again.

But first, she decided as her gaze rested on the man

she'd opened her arms and the quiet corners of her heart to, she needed to find out just where Joe thought things between them might go. That could well color her decision on where to live and what new career paths to explore.

She approached the issue in her characteristically straightforward way. Serene and unruffled on the outside and nervous as all hell inside, she invited Joe to the gatehouse after they'd finished their coffee. The door barely closed before he had her backed against it.

"I like your friends," he muttered, nuzzling her hair. "But they talk too much."

"It's…uh…called conversation."

Oh, for pity's sake! All the man had to do was blow in her ear and she stumbled over her own tongue.

"Not where I hail from," he countered as his lips grazed her cheek.

The gruff reply reminded Callie of her objective. "We need to talk about that, Joe."

He raised his head. "Where I hail from?"

"Among other things. Your security team dissected my life during the investigation. They checked out my Facebook friends. Where I buy my bagels. I don't know anything about you."

The withdrawal was so subtle, so slight. His expression didn't change. He still pressed hard against her. Yet Callie sensed a few degrees of separation instantly.

"What do you want to know?"

"More than I can absorb with my back up against a door and your mouth three inches from mine." She edged sideways. "Should I make another pot of coffee? Or would you like a brandy? Dawn left the bar pretty well stocked."

"I'm good."

"Okay. Well…"

She led the way into the combination living room, den and study. Like the rest of the gatehouse, it had been furnished with an eye for comfort and color. Periwinkle-blue hydrangeas and lilacs in full flower patterned the overstuffed sofa and easy chair. The sixty-inch TV was mounted at easy viewing level, and a small niche housed a built-in desk with hookups for all the latest electronic gadgets. As a tribute to both the season and the temporary nature of her occupancy, Callie had put up only a three-foot tree decorated with ornaments she and Tommy had made the previous Saturday morning.

Kicking off her ballet flats, Callie sank into the plush sofa cushions and tucked one foot under her. Joe took the opposite corner. She did her best to ignore the hard thighs and broad shoulders showcased to perfection by his jeans and that cloudy blue cashmere.

Joe met her gaze with a steady one of his own. "I can't tell you much, Callie. Most of the ops I participated in while I was in the military are still classified, and those I work for my clients are confidential."

"I'm more interested in the basics. Where's home?"

"Originally? A little town in Texas you never heard of."

"Try me."

"Bitter Creek."

"You're right. I've never heard of it. Did you leave there to go into the marines like Brian? Or was it the air force, like Travis?"

Again, his expression didn't change. Neither did his inflection. Yet Callie could sense the gap widening.

"Army. Rangers. Then," he added slowly, reluctantly, "Delta Force."

She had no idea who or what constituted Delta Force but decided she didn't really need to know at this point.

"How long were you in uniform?"

"Nine years."

Longer than she'd spent at the Office of the Child Advocate. Like her, Joe had changed direction in mid-career. More curious than ever, she probed deeper.

"Why did you leave the military?"

"It was time," he bit out.

Okay. That was obviously not something he wanted to talk about. Well, there was one subject he couldn't avoid. Raising a hand, she feathered a finger over his still fading scar.

"And this? Where did you get this?"

He froze her out. That's the only way she could describe it. The icy mask dropped over his face so swiftly, so completely, that she blinked.

"That's not open to discussion."

Joe smothered a curse when she reared back looking as though he'd slapped her. Which he pretty much had.

No way he could tell her about Nattat, though, or his desperate, futile attempt to keep her safe. Exerting every ounce of will he possessed, he blanked out the all-too-vivid images of the mountaintop resort in the Caribbean and focused on the woman regarding him with such a bruised look.

"Sorry."

He scraped a hand over his jaw and forced Curaçao to the black pit where it belonged. The clean feel of his chin reminded him that he'd shaved after showering. He must have bristled like a hedgehog when he'd hustled Callie into bed earlier, though. Wincing inwardly, he could only imagine the whisker burns he must have left on her tender skin.

Hell! That was the wrong direction to let his thoughts take him. Exerting an iron will, Joe slammed the door on the image of this woman soft and hot and panting under him.

"Look, Callie, you'll just have to accept there's a big chunk of my past I can't talk about. All that matters is what's between us here and now."

"Funny you should say that. I was actually wondering about that, too." Those purple eyes skewered into him. "What *is* between us, Joe?"

Christ! Where were his alternate escape routes when he needed them? Sweating a little, he reached out. Cupped her chin. Felt a weird lurch under his ribs.

"I can only repeat what I told you earlier. You're a calm port. A safe harbor."

"Right."

She lowered her glance. Her lashes fanned against her cheek, as thick and dark as her shoulder-length hair. Joe had fantasized about that silky mass for the past few weeks. He didn't have to fantasize now. The sight of the dark locks spilling across the pillow had been even more erotic than he'd imagined. It was a sight he intended— hoped!—to enjoy on a regular and frequent basis.

So when she raised her eyes, her calm announcement came down on him like a collapsing brick wall.

"I'm going back to Rome."

"What?"

"Carlo texted me last week." She eased her chin from his hold. "He's offered me a job."

The quiet response triggered a welter of savage reactions. Before agreeing to provide Carlo Luigi Francesco di Lorenzo the high-level personal security his government had requested, Joe and his people had thoroughly researched the prince. The man might be short, balding and getting thick around the middle, but he'd descended from one of the oldest houses in Europe. He also commanded Italy's crack airborne special ops unit.

None of which mattered to Joe at the moment as much as the fact that di Lorenzo had racked up more hours in women's beds than he had hours in the cockpit of his C-130 Hercules.

"Did you know Carlo sits on the board of several charitable foundations?"

Her question brought a curt response.

"Yeah."

Grimacing, Joe raked a hand through his hair and fought to temper both his tone and his visceral reaction to the idea of Callie heading back to Italy on her own. Without Dawn or Kate. Or him.

"Di Lorenzo gave me a list of the organizations he's involved with when I agreed to provide enhanced security," he told her. "Most of his charitable activities are purely economic, but several…"

Joe caught himself. He'd built a reputation and a multimillion-dollar business based on absolute trust. He wouldn't breach a client's confidentiality any more than Callie would the privacy of the children she'd represented in court. Still, he couldn't hold back a terse warning.

"Several of the agencies he's involved with have ties to Africa and the Middle East."

"I know. The job he's offered is with one of those agencies. International Aid to Displaced Women."

Joe felt the tendons in his neck cord. Prince or not, if Carlo thought he could involve Callie in the type of activity he himself had needed protection from, the man had another think coming.

"IADW operates a sort of halfway house for female

refugees," she was explaining. "Women who've escaped or been driven out their own countries and have either lost their male protectors or been abandoned by them somewhere along the way."

"That right? And what does Carlo think you can do for them?"

The question carried more of a bite than he'd intended. So it was no surprise when Callie stiffened.

"Despite the impression I've obviously given you," she said coolly, "I'm neither helpless nor unskilled. At the least, I can help these women acquire a rudimentary English vocabulary, which many of them will need before being resettled in English-speaking countries. At best, perhaps I can ease some of the trauma they've gone through."

Cursing his lack of tact, Joe tried to recover. "Sorry. That came out wrong. What I meant was…"

What he meant was that he didn't like the idea of her working with or for Carlo di Lorenzo. Which was why he committed his second major blunder in as many minutes.

"Look, before you accept his offer, take some time to think about mine."

Her forehead puckered. "Did I miss something? What offer?"

"About coming home. To you."

Her jaw sagged. "Is this…is this a proposal?"

Her surprise knocked him back a step. Hell! He'd thought—been certain—she'd understood where this was going.

"Yes, it's a proposal," he said gruffly. "What'd you think it was?"

"I didn't… That is…" She gave her head a quick, disbelieving shake. "Joe, we barely know each other!"

"Not true."

She'd hit the mark when she'd reminded him that he'd had his people investigate every corner of her life. Joe suspected he'd uncovered a few things about her younger years she wouldn't want her parents to know. He chalked up those early escapades up to her more lively friends, though. Dawn, especially. The voluptuous redhead had started breaking male hearts while still a teenager. Luckily, she seemed to have met her match in Brian Ellis. As Joe had in this dark-haired, violet-eyed siren.

"I've seen your strength and grace under the pressure of threats, Callie. Plus," he added deliberately, "I'd say we got to know each other pretty well this afternoon."

"We certainly did," she agreed, recovering from her astonishment. "And it was wonderful. Off the charts, as Tommy's friend Addy would say."

He waited for the *but* he knew was coming.

"So I hope...I really hope...we can build on that mutual desire."

"With you taking off for Italy?"

"That's where we met," she reminded him, her gaze steady. "Where we can continue to meet. You may not be able to tell me much about your clients, but I gather Carlo's not the first European you've worked with. Nor, I suspect, will he be the last."

She had that right. Joe had put a number of potential clients on hold while he'd tracked the source of Callie's emails. He could pretty well choose the continent, the risk level and the degree of personal involvement in his next contract.

"We could see each other as often in Rome as we could in Boston," she said. "Maybe more often. If you want to make it happen."

Damned if Joe knew at this point.

He'd been so sure she would appreciate what he had to offer. Mutual respect. Sexual compatibility, which they'd more than proved earlier. Financial security. He knew she'd been living on her savings since she'd quit her job. Had thought she'd appreciate that while he wasn't the most expressive or demonstrative man in the world, he was rock solid. Unlike a certain Italian prince.

"I still don't understand. Why go all the way to Rome?"

She chewed on her lower lip. When she answered, Joe sensed she was revealing a part of herself she rarely shared with anyone other than her two friends.

"Your job takes you all over the world. But I grew up, went to school and have worked all my adult life within a ninety-mile radius of Boston. Aside from family vacations and a jaunt to Cancún with Kate and Dawn during one spring break, Italy was my first real adventure. I loved the color, the food, the people. And Rome…!"

A full-blown smile came out, so warm and radiant it slammed into his gut like a rifle butt.

"Oh, Joe! Dawn and Kate and I spent only a few days in Rome. I want more time to explore its rich history and culture. On my own…and with you whenever possible."

Okay. So maybe it wasn't such a bad idea after all. Wandering through the Forum with her. Sharing a bottle of chianti at the tiny trattoria he'd discovered a few blocks from the Spanish Steps. Making love in a hotel room with a view of the old city walls.

They could take the train up to the Lake District for a weekend at some opulent resort. Maybe zip over to Portofino, Italy's answer to the French Riviera. Now that the first shock had passed, Joe could see himself laying all Europe at her feet.

"I guess I can understand where you're coming from," he conceded. "I have one suggestion, though."

"What's that?"

"I think we should…"

He caught himself just in time. Dammit, he had to do this right. Had to appeal to this unexpectedly adventurous side of her personality. And that would necessitate a little more planning and execution on his part.

"I think we should sleep on it," he temporized. "See how we feel in the morning."

A gleam of laughter leaped into her eyes, but she answered with a solemn nod. "By all means, Mr. Russo, let's sleep on it. Your place or mine?"

His DC hotel room was modern and efficient but held none of the comforts of the gatehouse. Callie's smiling invitation to share it with him kicked his pulse into overdrive. It was hammering hard and fast when he tumbled her back onto the sofa cushions.

"Yours, Ms. Langston. Yours."

His internal alarm went off at its usual 5:00 a.m. He came instantly alert but had learned long ago to give no indication he was awake. That skill had saved his life several times, most recently in Curaçao.

Slamming the door on that memory, he kept his eyes closed and concentrated on recording sensory signals. He heard Callie beside him. Her breathy intake, her snuffling exhale. Not quite a snore but close enough to make him smile inwardly. He could feel her, too. Soft and pliant and warm against his side. Her scent filled his nostrils. The lemony tang of her shampoo. The faint, yeasty residue of their lovemaking. One whiff and he felt himself hardening. Only his self-discipline and

years of brutal training kept him from rolling her over
and burying himself in her hot, tight depths.

He lay quiet, mulling over everything they'd talked
about last night. Callie wanted to expand her world.
He could understand that. He'd explored damned near
every corner of it himself, both in the military and out.
Before she went traipsing off to Rome, though, he intended to make sure she wore his brand.

He disciplined himself to wait an hour. It was close to
six before he eased out of bed. No sign of the December
sun poked through the bedroom shutters as he dragged
on his clothes. He needed coffee in the worst way but
decided not to wake Callie. Instead, he jotted a quick
note and propped it on the kitchen counter.

He hit a Starbucks drive-through and infused the caffeine as he negotiated the still-light traffic in the south-
east corner of DC. As early as it was, he knew Frank
Harden would be at his desk.

He and Harden had served in Delta Force together
before going their separate ways—Joe as a merce-
nary for some years before starting his own protective services agency, Frank as a civilian analyst with
the Defense Intelligence Agency specializing in African affairs. Whip-smart and not shy about voicing his
opinion, Harden had progressed steadily up the ranks
at the DIA. His current senior executive service rank
equated to that of a major general, but neither he nor Joe
let that get in the way of the friendship they'd forged
all those years ago.

Joe called Harden's private extension when he was almost to the sprawling complex now known as Joint Base
Anacostia–Bolling. The base had been formed a few
years back by cobbling together the Anacostia Naval Sup-

port Facility and Bolling Air Force Base. Since the two installations sat side by side and ate up a big chunk of this corner of DC, Joe guessed the consolidation made sense.

As he'd anticipated, his workaholic pal picked up on the first ring.

"Russo, you mangy dog," Harden drawled in that laconic, down-home Mississippi twang that disguised his needle-sharp instincts and encyclopedic knowledge of all things African. "Where the hell are you, boy?"

"About two blocks away."

"Hot damn! I'll call down to gate B and clear you in."

As promised, Harden got him cleared through the main gate leading to the massive complex that housed DIA headquarters and a slew of other intel activities, like the headquarters of the National Intelligence University and the Joint Functional Component Command for Intelligence, Surveillance and Reconnaissance.

Harden had an underling waiting to escort his guest into the inner sanctum. Joe surrendered the lightweight Ruger LCR-357 that nested in his ankle holster, accepted a signed receipt for it, clipped on a visitors' badge and passed through the metal detector.

Harden's office reflected his exalted pay grade, but Joe had little time to enjoy the view. Rail-thin and every bit as gaunt as the day the two of them had tunneled their way out of a Sudanese prison, the bureaucrat delivered a bone-jarring thump to Joe's shoulder.

"Haven't heard from you since the cows came home. What've you been doin'?"

"Had a job in the Caribbean earlier this year." Joe could feel his insides curl but kept his tone casual. "Most recently at a NATO base north of Venice."

"Yeah, I heard something about that." Frank gestured to one of the armchairs facing his desk. "Rumor is your pal Ellis got a fat contract out of that gig. Some new avionics package for the entire NATO airlift fleet."

"Could be."

Joe knew damn well it was more than a rumor. He'd gotten to know Brian Ellis well during that NATO gig and at his request had recently completed a top-to-bottom scrub of his company's physical, industrial and cyber security. What had begun as a business association, however, had morphed into friendship.

"So what can I do you for?" Frank asked. "Or did you just come to gloat 'bout me being chained to a desk?"

"I need some info."

"Figured. Shoot."

"What can you tell me about a Rome-based charity called International Aid to Displaced Women?"

Joe left the Defense Intelligence Agency feeling marginally better about Callie's decision. Although Frank wasn't personally familiar with IADW, he had his people run a quick screen.

He also made a call to a contact at the State Department responsible for overseeing the US Refugee Admissions Program and the 6 billion dollars provided through the combined efforts of the Bureau of Population, Refugees and Migration and the US Agency for International Development. The contact's people in turn worked closely with a host of other agencies, including the Office of the UN High Commissioner for Refugees, the UN World Food Programme, the International Red Cross, the UN Children's Fund and the International Organization for Migration. Most of these organizations had special programs in place to protect the most vulnerable sectors of the population, including women and girls.

Harden's contact had verified that the Rome operation was legit. Equally important, there'd been no documented reports of terrorists or hard-core criminals infiltrating the population the agency cared for. That wasn't to say they couldn't. Given the growing number of women being recruited by groups like ISIS, the PLF and Sri Lanka's Tamil Tigers, programs that helped women enter or re-settle in other countries made tempting conduits.

Joe intended to go over the agency's refugee screening process with Carlo in some detail before Callie started work there. He made a quick call to his twenty-four-hour operations center and instructed the on-duty controller to check on an evening flight. The controller clicked a few keys and said there was a flight leaving Dulles at 5:40 p.m. Joe would have to hump to get everything done and be at the airport the required three hours early for international flights, but he figured he could make it.

"Okay, book it."

He then contacted the office of the director of the Na-ples film festival. Marcello Audi was worried that allow-ing a certain entry to be shown at this year's festival would put them on radical jihadists' hit list. He'd requested a thorough security assessment of all venues. Joe had planned to pass on the job, but Callie's little bombshell last night had triggered a swift reordering of his schedule. The Naples job would only take a few weeks, and it would put him less than an hour south of Rome. After that…

After that, he promised himself, he and Callie would settle on a permanent arrangement. One that gave them *both* a safe, comfortable haven. With that goal in mind, he steered his rental to the next stop on his hastily con-structed agenda.

Chapter Four

Callie sat curled up on the sitting room sofa, wearing loose, comfortable sweats and fuzzy slippers on her feet. She had fresh coffee in a Christmas mug and her iPhone within reach. She'd slept late—hardly a surprise given last night's strenuous exercise—and woken to find Joe gone. When she'd wandered into the kitchen, she found his note asking her to hold off calling Carlo until he got back.

She hoped he wasn't going to try to talk her out of Rome. He'd seemed to accept her decision last night, even admitted that he could see just as much of her in Italy as in Boston. She really wanted to contact Carlo and tell him she was accepting his job offer.

She itched to tell Kate and Dawn, too. And not just about Rome. There was this whole exciting, surprising, confusing matter of a proposal to share. They'd both already texted asking a) if she was awake b) if Joe was still there and c) whether she'd resolved the Lassie issue. She wanted to go over to the main house, huddle with Dawn so they could FaceTime Kate together. The three of them had shared so many secrets, so many of life's ups and downs. But Joe's note had asked her to wait, so she'd held off, prey to a slightly disconcerting tug of divided loyalties.

She was still feeling the tug when she heard a car pull into the drive. A quick glance through the front windows confirmed Joe's return. Uncurling, she was halfway down the hall before the bell rang. When she opened the door, he walked in looking every bit as tall and strong as he had when he arrived from Sydney yesterday, but *so* much sexier. Which, of course, might have something to do with the fact that she'd explored every flat plane and hard ridge of the body that went with his steel-gray eyes and square chin.

God! Was she totally insane? What woman in her right mind wouldn't jump at Joe's offer? Why *not* settle into a comfortable nest with him? Why *not* be there, waiting patiently, when he rolled in from one of his unspecified, no-questions-allowed assignments?

When he greeted her with a quick kiss and one of his rare smiles, her uncharacteristic self-doubt spiked again. But before she could give in to the sudden urge to tell him she was reconsidering her options, he preempted her with a brusque announcement.

"I talked to a buddy at the Defense Intelligence Agency. The International Aid to Displaced Women operation's legit."

"Good to know. Although…" She lifted a brow. "Did you think Carlo would invite me to work for an organization that wasn't?"

"Doesn't hurt to check."

"No, I guess not. Aren't you staying?" she asked when he made no move to shed his bomber jacket.

"Can't. Have some things to get done before I fly out this afternoon."

"Fly where?"

She'd blurted it out without thinking and half expected another rebuff. This time, however, Joe provided details.

"First to Rome. I told Carlo I want to review IADW's refugee screening process before you arrive. Then to Naples. I'll be doing some work—"

"Wait! Back up." She couldn't believe what she'd just heard. "You told Carlo that I was coming to Rome? To work at IADW?"

He blinked, as surprised by her sharp tone as she'd been by his abrupt announcement a few moments ago. "You said last night that's what you wanted. Did you change your mind?"

"No." A surge of irritation smothered her earlier doubts. "I would, however, have appreciated the opportunity to tell my prospective employer *personally* that I'd accepted his generous job offer."

"Oh. Yeah. Sorry." He scraped a palm across his chin. "It's just…"

"Yes?"

"You've seen the news coverage. The attacks in France and Belgium and other parts of the world. Some of those terrorists got into place by posing as refugees and entering through legitimate refugee resettlement conduits. I just want to make sure IADW isn't one of them."

Her irritation melted. A little. Even more when he brushed a knuckle down her cheek. His touch was warm. Soothing. Possessive.

"Keeping you safe's becoming my number-one priority, Pansy Eyes."

She had to smile at the endearment. And she could hardly argue with his desire to protect her. Not after she'd burrowed in this admittedly luxurious hole while he tracked down the creep who'd sent the emails. Yet the little corner of her mind that rejected the prospect of being wrapped in cotton wool for the rest of her life reared its nasty head again.

"Thank you, Joe."

She meant that. She really did. Still, she took a small, instinctive step back when he extracted a small jeweler's box out of his coat pocket.

"I know this is pushing things, Callie, but I saw this before I flew to Australia and asked them to hold it. I wanted you to check it out, see if you liked it. Now, with this Rome deal, I figured I'd take a chance."

"Joe…"

"It's not as flashy or sparkly as some I looked at," he said, flipping up the lid, "but it's almost the same color as your eyes. And the setting is kind of nice."

More than nice, Callie saw on a little intake of breath. It was exquisite. White gold, she guessed, spun into a filigree bouquet to showcase a gleaming oval amethyst. The end prongs were long-stemmed roses, the side prongs delicate leaves with a tiny dove nested between them.

"Joe, I…"

She floundered, tugged in a dozen different directions by the whirlwind of emotions this man roused in her. He noted her confusion with a small smile and pounced.

"It doesn't have to mean anything more than you want it to, Callie. Here, try it on for size." He slid it over her knuckle. "Good. It fits. I wanted you to have it before you took off for Rome."

She glanced up from the glowing amethyst and caught the glint of male satisfaction in his eyes.

"And," she guessed drily, "you wanted me to be wearing it when I meet with Carlo."

"Yeah, that, too."

The admission was totally unapologetic and so...so *Joe* that she had to smile.

"I like Carlo as a friend and now a prospective employer," she said. "That's all. Surely you know that."

"Of course I do. Doesn't hurt to reinforce the message, though." His gaze held hers, steady and unflinching. "You change your mind, or want to send a different signal after you get to Rome, just take it off. I'll understand."

Callie debated for some moments after Joe left. Her first instinct was to scurry next door, corner Dawn in her spacious home office and get Kate on FaceTime. A glance at the clock brought a swift revision to that plan. It was close to eleven o'clock, and her news was too momentous to share electronically. Two quick calls set up an emergency girls-only luncheon at an upscale eatery only a block from the thirteen-story high-rise on G Street where Kate worked.

Rushing into the bedroom, Callie exchanged her sweats and fuzzy slippers for boots, slacks and a roll-neck sweater. She angled a black angora beret sideways to keep her head warm and bundled up in a paisley scarf, gloves and the ankle-length khaki duster she'd snagged during a sale at Nordstrom.

She met a similarly muffled and extremely curious

Dawn on the flagstone walk connecting the main house to the guesthouse.

"What's the emergency?"

"I'll tell you and Kate together. You drive. You know your way around better than I do."

The light snow of the day before had pretty much turned to mush, but holiday decorations added bright touches of red, gold and green as Dawn negotiated DC's always busy streets. When she pulled up at the popular bistro and turned her Mustang over to the valet, the two women hurried inside.

It was still early, not yet eleven thirty, so Kate had been able to snag a booth by the round fireplace in the center of the restaurant. The noise level was still low enough for Nat King Cole's velvet-voiced rendition of "The Christmas Song" to provide the perfect complement to the crackle of flames.

Her tawny hair caught up in a smooth twist, Kate looked every inch the professional in a ruby blazer that hid her almost baby bump, white blouse and a flowing black skirt that draped over the top of her boots. She laid aside the menu she'd been examining and looked up expectantly as Callie and Dawn shed their outdoor gear before sliding into the booth.

"Okay, Miss Priss and Boots. What's so important that…oh, my God!" Jaw dropping, Kate grabbed the hand Callie was using to shake out her napkin. "This is *gorgeous*!"

Beside her Dawn gasped in surprise. "You stinker! Is that what I think it is?"

"Sort of."

"Sort of?" Kate angled Callie's hand from side to side. "What does that mean? Did you and Joe settle the Lassie question or not?"

"Not exactly. But we're working on it."

A server decked out in a sparkly red bow tie approached. Dawn waved him off with a quick smile.

"Give us a few minutes. We're talking some serious girl stuff here." She slewed around again. "Back to you and Joe and that hunk of quartz you're sporting. What's the bottom line?"

"The bottom line? Okay, brace yourself. I'm taking Carlo up on his offer of a job at International Aid to Displaced Women, and Joe wants me wearing his brand when I fly over to Rome on Thursday."

Her friends reacted with equal parts surprise and dismay.

"You're going to Rome?"

"This *Thursday*?" Dawn wailed. "You can't go this Thursday! Christmas is less than two weeks away. The three of us have gathered at one or the other's house every Christmas since, when? Fifth grade?"

"You've got Brian and Tommy to share it with now. And Kate and Travis. You'll have a house full."

"It won't be the same," she said stubbornly. "Wonderful, but not the same."

"The position I'll be filling has been vacant for several months," Callie explained. "The director—my new boss—is anxious to get someone in place."

"We're only talking another few weeks," Kate protested. "Surely your boss can wait until after the holidays."

"Evidently not." A small smile played at the corners of Callie's mouth. "From what I can gather based on my brief conversation with Carlo this morning, he's a bit intimidated by the woman."

Her friends shared another astonished look. Neither Kate nor Dawn could envision any mere female intimidating Carlo di Lorenzo. The cocky Italian Special Forces pilot with the string of royal titles after his name had racked up hundreds of combat hours. According to the paparazzi, he'd also charmed his way in and out of the same number of bedrooms.

"This director must be a real witch," Kate warned. "You sure you want to work for someone like that?"

"I'll be in Italy," Callie said softly. "Remember what happened to you there? And to you, Dawn?"

That silenced the other women for a few moments. Kate went all dewy eyed thinking of the surprise ceremony Travis had arranged at the Trevi Fountain to renew their wedding vows. Dawn could only grin at the memory of the sparks she and Brian had struck off each other when they'd met in Venice. She came out of her reverie in time to wave the waiter away again.

"What about Joe?" Kate asked. "He's content to let you zip off to Rome as long as you're wearing his ring?"

Callie gave a small huff. "Not hardly. By the time he got around to slipping it on my finger this morning, he'd already contacted a pal in the Defense Intelligence Agency and had them check out the organization I'll be working for. Then he told Carlo that he's flying in tonight to do a scrub of the center's screening procedures. And he set up a job for himself in Naples."

"Naples is only an hour south of Rome."

Kate should know. She'd researched train schedules and driving times and every possible tourist sight for their trip to Italy a few months back.

"So Joe informed me." Callie fingered the ring again. "He also informed me that all I have to do is take this off and he'll drop out of the picture, no harm, no foul."

"Oh, that's romantic," Dawn snorted. "Please tell me he didn't use those actual words."

"Pretty close."

"Well? Are you going to remove it?"

"No." Sighing, Callie shook her head. "Not now, anyway. I'm still trying to sort out how I feel about him."

"How *do* you feel? Right this exact second."

"Happy. Confused. Excited. And," she admitted with a reluctant laugh, "completely in lust."

Neither of her friends could argue with that. Or talk her out of relocating to Italy. Resigning themselves to the inevitable, they helped Callie tie up the loose ends she'd left dangling when she'd taken refuge in the Ellises' gatehouse.

"I'll zip up to Boston," Dawn volunteered. "I can sort through your closet and send you what you'll need in Rome. But what do you want me to do with rest of it? Your furniture, your houseplants, your ton and a half of books?"

"The books and furniture will have to go in storage. I'm pretty sure Mrs. Eckstein, my neighbor, will take the plants."

"How about your lease?" the fiscally minded Kate asked. "Does it allow you to sublet?"

"The lease is actually up for renewal at the end of next month. Since I'm not giving them the required sixty days' notice, I'll probably have to forfeit January's rent and my security deposit."

"Let me handle that. As for Rome, you shouldn't have any trouble using your credit card for purchases or withdrawing cash at an ATM. But you should open an account at a local branch and transfer some operating funds, just in case. I'll get the paperwork started, if you want."

"Thank you. Thank both of you!"

The gratitude came straight from Callie's heart. Yet

she had to suppress a stupid little twinge at how easy it was to cut all ties to the life she'd lived in Boston for six years.

Oh, for…! What was her problem? This was what she wanted. What she'd wished for at the Trevi Fountain! Adventure. Romance. A whole new chapter in her life.

"Won't you need a license to practice in Italy?" Dawn asked, still working the logistics in her mind.

"I would, if I was working in an Italian treatment facility or setting up my own practice. That's not the case here. The IADW center is physically located in Rome, but it's governed by an international body with different credentialing requirements. According to their standards, I'm actually *over*qualified for the work I'll be doing."

"And your parents?" Kate put in. "Have you told them you're zipping off to Europe?"

"Not yet. I wanted you guys to be the first to know. I'll call them after lunch."

They'd be surprised, Callie knew, but not particularly concerned. Since moving to a seniors-only retirement village in central Florida six years ago, her retired teacher mom and former postal worker dad had become totally immersed in new hobbies and activities. Including, she remembered with an inner smile, their latest passion for bird-watching. She hadn't told them about the vicious emails, and they'd voiced only mild curiosity about her extended stay in DC.

"So you're really going to do it," Dawn said, breaking into her thoughts.

"I am."

"In that case we need to celebrate with our favorite Italian drink." A smile and an uplifted finger brought the patient server to the table. "We want three Bellinis—two regular and one virgin for the pregnant lady."

The young server looked confused. "I don't know if there is such a thing as a virgin Bellini."

"Tell the barkeep to improvise," Dawn instructed airily.

Despite her friends' wish that she would wait until after the holidays, Callie stuck to her decision to report to her new job the following Monday. She flew out of Dulles late Thursday afternoon and thoroughly enjoyed the unexpected and unaccustomed luxury of an upgrade to business class compliments of Joe. When she landed at Rome's Leonardo da Vinci Airport early Friday morning, she zinged off a text to let Kate and Dawn know she'd arrived.

She cleared customs with the intention of spending the day setting up the small flat that came with her new job and the weekend exploring the neighborhood around it. She hadn't included Joe Russo in her plans, however. Looking like Italy's answer to Patrick Dempsey in snug jeans, a black turtleneck and his tan bomber jacket, he met her in the arrivals terminal and welcomed her with a hard, hot kiss. She was still recovering from that when his take-charge personality emerged.

"Are you totally wiped?" he asked as he steered her to the baggage claim area.

"Not wiped at all. I slept most of the flight in lie-flat leather luxury." She hesitated, but innate honesty made her ask. "I saw that the upgrade was charged to JLR Security. It won't be billed as a business expense, will it? If so, I'll reimburse you."

He glanced down at her, amusement flickering in those stone-gray eyes. "Not to worry. I use a top-fifty

accounting firm. They keep my personal and professional accounts straight."

"Good to know. Except I'm used to paying my own
way. I don't expect—or want—you to pick up the tab
every time we're together."

"Well, we shouldn't have many expenses in Naples
this weekend. I'm meeting with my prospective client,
so my time will be charged to him."

"Naples? I can't go to Naples this weekend! I've got
too much to do here in Rome."

"You might want to reconsider. Today's the feast of
Santa Lucia. I'm told her day sort of officially kicks off the
Christmas season. Marcello—my prospective client—has
invited us to join him and his family for their traditional
dinner tonight. It would give me a chance to get to know
him in an informal setting, assess what kind of man he is."

"But…"

The rumble of the baggage conveyor belt cut off her
protest. By the time Joe had snagged her two suitcases,
she'd reassessed her priorities. From the sound of it, this
meeting was important to Joe. Unpacking and settling
into the apartment could wait.

Or not. To her surprise, he'd planned for that, too.
After asking if she needed anything other than her roll-
on for the weekend trip, he turned her bags over to the
associate waiting beside a slick black SUV.

"This is Emilio Mancera, head of my operations here
in Italy."

"Ciao, Emilio."

"Ciao, signorina. *Benvenuto a Roma.*"

Dark eyed, curly haired and the possessor of a proud
Roman nose to go with the muscles that bulged under
his fleece pullover, the thirtysomething Italian loaded
the bags in the SUV.

"I will take these to your apartment, *sì*? And make sure the kitchen contains all you need."

"I, uh, *sì. Grazie.*"

He conducted a brief exchange with Joe in swift Italian before giving Callie another cheerful ciao and departing.

She glanced at Joe while he beeped the locks on a second SUV in the adjoining space. Why hadn't she picked up on the fact that he spoke the language when she'd first met him here in Italy? It was just one more gap in her knowledge about this man and his past. Gaps she intended to bridge. Starting now, she decided after they'd left the parking garage and hit the bright, brittle December sunlight.

"You sounded pretty fluent in that exchange with Emilio. Where did you learn Italian?"

"Here and there. My five-month gig with Carlo considerably expanded my vocabulary. Although," he added with a sardonic tilt to his head, "most of it can't be repeated in polite company."

"Do you speak any other languages?"

"Some Spanish. A little French. Enough Portuguese to ask directions to the closest bar."

"Portuguese? I'm impressed."

Shrugging, he aimed for the airport exit. "You take a job in Angola, it helps to be able to communicate with the local cops."

Callie tried to sketch a mental image of Africa. She knew Angola was near the continent's southern tip but couldn't place it on the east or west coast.

"What did you do there?"

He shot her a quick glance. Callie kicked herself, thinking she'd crossed the line again. She was suppressing a twinge of resentment at being shut out of his past when he decided to let her in a bare inch or two.

"How much do you know about Angola?"

"Nothing, I'm embarrassed to admit."

"It sits on huge mineral and petroleum reserves, and its economy is among the fastest growing in the world. Problem is, a handful of wealthy elites control the economy."

"Which makes them prime targets," Callie guessed.

"Exactly."

Okay, he'd cracked the door. She pushed it just a little harder.

"Your client was one of these incredibly wealthy elites?"

His expression didn't change but Callie could sense him drawing into himself. Again.

"Dammit, Joe. You brought up the job in Angola. You can't just leave me hanging. Yes or no? Was your client one of these wealthy elites?"

"No."

Well, she'd set herself up for that one. She was about to let the grudging remark go when he surprised her with a terse follow-up.

"She was at the other end of the spectrum," he said, his jaw tight. "A young, passionate member of parliament who wanted to curb the elites' power. My team and I smuggled her out of the country the day before her appointment with a firing squad."

"Good grief! Where is she now?"

"Dead."

The single syllable hit like a glass of ice water to the face. When Callie recoiled against her seat back, Joe wrenched his gaze from the road.

"An assassin got to her in Curaçao." His tone was as cold as his eyes. "And I got to him."

Her breath stuck in her throat. She had to swallow twice before she got out a quavering, "Good."

As shaky as it was, her endorsement seemed to pull Joe from the dark cave of his memories. The taut angle of his jaw eased. So did the tension cording his neck above his jacket collar.

"Helluva a way to kick off what I'd planned as a fun weekend," he growled.

Still startled by the piece of his past she'd pried loose, Callie forced a smile. "I'm sure it'll be fun. How could a traditional Italian family dinner be anything but?"

Blessedly ignorant of the noisy, exuberant, exhausting evening ahead, she relaxed in her seat and vowed to keep the conversation away from dark subjects as they hit the autostrada and rolled south.

Chapter Five

Since Joe's client didn't expect them until late afternoon, they made the drive down from Rome in leisurely stages.

They stopped first at the Abbey of Monte Cassino. Perched atop a steep precipice overlooking the main road to Rome, the abbey had become a key objective in the Allies' push north during WWII. Their efforts to dislodge the Germans resulted in a murderous battle than caused more than 190,000 casualties and left the abbey and town at its base in smoking ruins. Rebuilt after the war, Monte Cassino now offered visitors a glimpse of its original medieval glory. The grim history of the battle and accompanying artifacts interested Joe, of course, but Callie delighted in the priceless manuscripts and religious treasures that had been taken to Rome for safekeeping and returned to the abbey after the war.

Closer to Naples, the warm Mediterranean currents

chased the chill from the air, and the temperature rose. Callie wiggled out of her wool duster and tossed it in the backseat. Joe did the same with his leather jacket. When they left the autostrada for lunch at a trattoria recommended by Joe's prospective client, they opted to sit outside on a vine-draped patio. The setting was idyllic but it was the cloud-wrapped mountain in the distance that held Callie's fascinated gaze.

"Is that Vesuvius?"

"Looks like it."

"Do we have time to visit the ruins of Pompeii?"

"Not if you want to do them justice. Maybe tomorrow. Or Sunday, before we head back to Rome."

Not quite believing that she was actually here, in the shadow of Mount Vesuvius, she took the friendly server's recommendation and ordered a local specialty of sausage served with broccoli rabe. Joe went the more traditional route of pasta in a red sauce, with meatballs served separately as the second course.

Feeling deliciously lazy afterward, she expected them to head into Naples. Instead Joe skirted the city's sprawling outskirts.

"Signor Audi lives in the city," he explained, "but his family's ancestral farm is another forty-five minutes south. Or more correctly, their ancestral ranch."

"They raise cattle?"

"Water buffalo. They've got about three hundred head on their ranch."

"What in the world do they do with... Oh! They make mozzarella?"

"The best in Italy, according to Signor Audi."

Despite her extensive reading, Callie couldn't imagine how the big, plodding, wide-horned water buffalo had migrated to Italy. From Asia, probably, herded across the Mongolian steppes by nomadic tribes. Or maybe imported by the Arabs who'd invaded Sicily. But there was no denying mozzarella had pretty much become associated with all things Italian.

Still, she wasn't prepared for Campania's rich grass-lands. Wide, rolling pastures bordered the road and stretched all the way to the sea that could be glimpsed through tall, thin cypresses and silver-barked eucalyptus trees. Dotting these pastures were herds of black buffalo grazing placidly or wallowing contentedly in man-made ponds with sloping ramps. The air wafting through the SUV's vents carried a mix of grass and salt sea air, along with an earthy hint of dung.

When the navigational system pinged a few minutes later, Joe turned left and drove through a pair of stone pillars. A cypress-lined road led them past more fenced pastures and ended in a broad yard bordered on one side by a long, narrow building with huge roller brushes at its entrance.

"Is that a car wash?" Callie asked in surprise.

Joe's glance flicked from the brushes to the gleaming stainless steel tank truck parked at the building's far end. "I'm guessing that's the barn where they milk the buffalo. They probably have to scrub 'em down first to make sure the milk stays clean."

Her mind boggled at the thought of one of those huge buffalo going through a series of washes and waxes like the family car. Trying to visualize the process, she looked around the rest of the yard with some interest. Older buildings and sheds constructed of local stone housed tractors and various other pieces of farm equipment.

A rambling, two-story residence sat a little farther down the road. Surrounded by ancient cypresses that stood tall and spear straight, its varying levels suggested it had been added to numerous times over the years. Like the other buildings, it, too, was constructed of stone covered almost entirely with a pale yellow plaster. U-shaped terra cotta tiles delineated the varying roof lines, and bright green shutters framed its many windows. Flowers spilled from window boxes, stone urns, even the wooden bucket dangling over what must have once been a working well.

Adding to the color were the scattered children's toys…a red-and-blue plastic Big Wheel, a hot pink bike with training wheels and sparkly handlebar streamers, a forgotten doll with the pale hair and blue gown of Princess Elsa from *Frozen*.

Callie was thinking of all the times she'd watched that particular video with Tommy when two dogs raced from behind the house and offered a raucous greeting. One was a mottled gray and black of an indeterminate breed, the other a small collie. They were noisy but not vicious, as evidenced by the greeting they gave Joe after he exited the SUV and squatted to let them sniff his hand.

Callie climbed out as well and breathed in the pungent tang of a working farm overlaid with the perfume of so many flowers. She was letting the dogs scope her out when a woman strode out of the house. In boots, tight jeans and a loose-knit sweater, she moved with the careless, casual grace that seemed as natural as breathing to so many Italian women.

"Signor Russo, Signorina Langston, welcome. I am Arianna Audi de Luca." Her dark eyes were friendly, her handshake firm. "My father apologizes that he is not here to greet you. He and my husband are at the barn. One of our buffalo has gone into the milking chamber and does not wish to come out. She can be very stubborn, that Domenica, but she'll usually come to Papà when he whistles to her."

"Domenica? Is that her breed?"

"No, no, it is her name."

Callie's glance swept past her to the hulking black animals in the pasture. "You name them all?"

"Not all. But this one is like a pet, yes? When she was but a tiny calf, she followed my brother and me everywhere." Head cocked, Arianna issued a smiling invitation. "If you're not too tired from your journey, perhaps you would like to meet her? And see something of the milking process?"

Callie wasn't about to pass up the chance to see the cow wash in operation. "I'd like that."

Joe seconded the idea, and their hostess gave them a quick history as she led them back toward the barn. With each step the scents of fresh-cut grass and dung edged out the flowers a little more.

"With Papà and my brother so busy in Naples, my husband and I manage the farm. It's been in our family since the sixteenth century. We have a framed copy of the original deed in the office."

Her expression turned serious.

"There are many cruelties in this business, but my family has spent much time and money over the years to make ours humane. As you'll see, we use the voluntary milking method. We also hold to the strict sanitary standards required for DOP certification. *Scusi.* DOP stands for *denominazione di origine protetta.* It means our mozzarella meets the highest government standards for quality and excellence."

Angling to the left, she pointed out a wide metal chute that led from the pasture to the giant roller brushes. Several large bovines waited patiently in the chute while others milled near its mouth.

"The females come when they wish to be milked. Since it is all done by machine, they do not have to follow a set schedule. They enter here and…"

The sudden rumble of an engine starting and gears engaging interrupted her.

"Ah! Papà has convinced Domenica to leave the milking chamber. Now the others may enter. But first they take a little bath, yes?"

Streams of water arced across the barn entrance, the giant rollers whirred into action and the lead buffalo in the chute ambled up the low ramp. Tail swishing, it disappeared into the mist.

"Amazing," Callie murmured. "They're not afraid of it at all."

"I think they consider it a spa treatment," Arianna replied, laughing. "We give them jets of cool water in the heat of summer, warm water in winter."

Dodging the spray, she ushered them through a side door and into a spacious work area. "This is the office, where my husband takes care of all the necessary forms and endless paperwork. And here…"

She opened another door to show a small room with stainless steel counters and an impressive array of laboratory equipment.

"Here is where I spend much of my time."

Callie could see why. A quick glance at the framed degrees on the wall beside the door indicted Arianna Maria Patrizia Audi had earned a bachelor of science in organic chemistry from Stanford and a *laurea magistrale* in *biotecnologia agricola* from the University of Pisa.

"I'm working to increase the conjugated linoleic acid

content in our herd's milk," she informed them. "There's some evidence it possesses anticancer properties. It may also affect insulin response. Sadly, the science is not there yet. One can only keep researching."

After the high-powered cow wash and pristine lab, Callie wasn't surprised to see the single worker in the milking area wearing immaculate white coveralls, a hairnet and plastic booties over his shoes. He didn't appear to have much of a job, however. Just stood by as the newly scrubbed buffalo meandered into a narrow chamber. A second later, a robotic arm slid under her. The animal got another wash, this one from a gentle up-spray, then six flexible tubes snaked upward. Like cobras, they curled and wove and latched onto their prey.

"Good grief!" Astonished, Callie watched for some reaction from the buffalo, but she didn't so much as blink her long, curling lashes. "How did those cups magically attach to her udder?"

"They're equipped with optical cameras and lasers that detect the exact position of each teat. Once attached, the cup will rinse the teat again with warm water and gently massage it to stimulate the premilk. That gets flushed into a side line, then the rest will flow through the main milking line and empty directly into the truck you see outside for transport to our plant in town."

"No wonder Domenica didn't want to leave the chamber," Callie couldn't help commenting. "She must really enjoy all that flushing and massaging."

"She does," Arianna confirmed with a laugh. "What female would not?"

Both women glanced at Joe. He merely lifted his brows, but to Callie's surprise and secret amusement a faint tinge of red crept into his cheeks.

Would she ever understand this man? Only this morning he'd admitted taking out an assassin, and now here he was, embarrassed to hear two women discussing udders and teats. Smothering a grin, she listened as their guide continued.

"Once the milk stops flowing, the cups disengage and the udders are washed again, then sprayed with disinfectant."

They followed the chamber's current occupant toward the exit. The buffalo entered another chute that led to the pasture, and Arianna and her guests emerged into the yard.

"That was *so* interesting," Callie said. "I had no idea cattle milking had become so mechanized."

"Not all farms are as progressive as ours. And there... Ah! Here is Papà."

Callie's first, startled thought was that the gentleman who hurried toward them looked just like Rossano Brazzi, the hunky Italian actor who'd starred alongside Louis Jourdan in *Three Coins in the Fountain*. Tall, tanned, wavy haired and full lipped, he greeted Joe with a hearty handshake and Callie with a traditional kiss to both cheeks.

"I'm so pleased you could join us, Signorina Langston. I see Arianna has been showing you a little of what makes our mozzarella the best in Campania."

"She has, and I must say I'm very impressed."

"You will be even more so once you taste it. Please, let us escort you to the house and introduce you to the rest of the family."

Four hours, two dozen or so relatives, several glasses of wine, a ginormous platter of pasta and six different flavors of mozzarella later, Signor Audi asked his daughter to entertain Callie while he took Joe into his study for a private discussion. Not that she needed entertaining. She was so stuffed she could barely move. She was also beginning to feel jet lag creeping up on her. Comfortably ensconced on the sofa, she was more than content to listen with half an ear to the buzz of conversation conducted mostly in Italian and watch Arianna's two young children setting candles into ornate ceramic holders to be lit in honor of Saint Lucia.

"It's a tradition for us," their mother explained, her feet up and her ankles crossed on a hassock. "One that dates back almost a thousand years. Lucia means light, yes? She was martyred on this day in December, which under the Julian calendar was then the winter solstice."

"The shortest day of the year," Callie commented.

"Exactly! So for us the lighting of candles signals the end of the dark winter as well as the beginning of the twelve days of Christmas. When we light the candles, we sing her song and give the children sweets and small gifts."

"'Santa Lucia.' I know that song."

She should. The famous Neapolitan hymn had been recorded by everyone from opera greats like Enrico Caruso and Luciano Pavarotti to modern-day classical crossover star Hayley Westenra. Even Elvis Presley had sung it in one of his most popular movies, *Viva Las Vegas*. Movie buffs that they were, Callie, Kate and Dawn had watched the classic starring Elvis and Ann-Margret a half dozen times.

"You have another interesting Christmas tradition."

Callie nodded to the A-frame crèche that occupied an entire corner of the room. It was the largest and most elaborate she'd ever seen. Five, maybe six feet tall, it contained several tiers of shelves filled with wrapped gifts, fragrant pine boughs, small candles and far more figures than she was used to seeing in a Christmas nativity scene. Some of the exquisitely detailed and gorgeously painted figurines wore the simple robes of shepherds and goat herders. Others were garbed in what looked like costumes from a dozen different historical eras, including modern-day soccer garb.

"I've never seen soccer players in a manger scene before."

"That, too, is very Neapolitan," Arianna told her. "We add new figures to our crèche every year, and the new addition doesn't always have biblical significance. It could be a famous person from the past, a great opera star, even a president or politician." Grinning, she pointed to a figure in modern clothing. "Do you see that grim gentleman there, on the far right? That's our current prime minister. Papà added him this year. He feels the poor, misguided soul needs as much heavenly exposure as he can get."

"We have a few politicians in the States who could use more, too."

"You would probably see many familiar figures for sale on Via San Gregorio Armeno. That's where the artisans who make the cribs display their wares. You *must* stroll down that street while you're in Naples. You'll see nothing else like it in the world."

"I'll certainly check it out if I have time before we head back to Rome."

"Ah, yes. Papà tells me you are to work with Carlo di Lorenzo." Her voice took on a cautious note. "You've met him before?"

"Several times."

"*Bene.* Then you know to expect the most extravagant offers to jet away with him to Casablanca or Hong Kong."

"His last offer was Dubai," Callie confirmed.

"And Joe?" Arianna asked curiously. "He knows this about Carlo?"

"He does."

Callie didn't realize she was fingering her ring until it drew the other woman's gaze.

"That amethyst is gorgeous, and the setting so unusual."

"Thank you. I'm still not quite used to it."

"I begin to understand." Arianna's dark eyes danced. "If Joe Russo gave you that beautiful ring, not even Carlo di Lorenzo can mistake its message. Whether he will choose to heed it, however, is another matter altogether."

"Sounds like you know the prince pretty well."

"I, too, have been invited to fly away with him. But," she added on a merry laugh, "that was before I settled down with a husband, two bambini and three hundred water buffalo."

When Joe and Signor Audi returned, Callie confessed she was starting to feel the combined effects of her long flight, the delicious dinner and several glasses of wine. They made their farewells a few moments later and left with invitations to visit again, an exchange of phone numbers and a promise from Arianna to call Callie the next time she was in Rome. They must do lunch, the buffalo rancher declared, and shop at some of the city's elegant little boutiques.

"I hope she does call," Callie said as she settled in the soft leather seat. "It would be nice to hit the shops with a friend."

She wanted to stay awake for the short drive into Naples. She would really like to experience the city for the first time bathed in moonlight. She was also eager to see the colorful Christmas lights Arianna said were strung from building to building in alleys so narrow that second- and third-story residents could almost shake hands with neighbors living across the street.

She remembered clicking her seat belt. Remembered her head lolling against the back rest. The next thing she knew Joe had opened the passenger side door and was unclicking her belt.

"Whrarwe?"

"At the hotel. C'mon, sweetheart, let's get you to bed."

The parking valet took the SUV, and Joe took her arm. While he checked them in, Callie registered sleepy impressions of a lobby with more marble than the pyramids of Giza, a wide circular staircase draped with exquisitely decorated garlands and a Christmas tree that soared three or four stories.

Once in their suite, her jet lag hit with a vengeance. Close to comatose, she left a trail of clothes from a sitting room graced by a massive sofa to a bedroom dominated by a four-poster bed draped with shimmering, champagne-colored silk. In bra and panties, she crawled under the covers. A sleep-starved corner of her mind registered the small thud of Joe placing their carryalls on the bench at the foot of the bed. The faint whisper as he undressed. The dip of the mattress when he slid in and pulled her against him. His chest was warm against her back, his thighs hard under her butt. With a sound halfway between a sigh and a whimper, she snuggled closer and sank into oblivion.

She woke to thin shafts of sunlight sneaking through the drapes and hazy realization she was still spooned against Joe. She smiled in perfect contentment and went back to sleep.

It could have been moments or hours before she blinked awake again. Pushing up on one elbow, she discovered the other half of the bed was empty and the covers neatly smoothed. The only sound disturbing the stillness was the faint honk of a car horn outside the draped windows.

"Joe?"

No answer from either the bathroom or the spacious sitting room visible through open double doors. Tossing back the covers, Callie padded to the bath. Each step brought the delicious sensation of her feet sinking into inch-thick silk carpet. The room itself stopped her in her tracks.

The decadent bath was a symphony in marble— gleaming black-and-white squares on the floors, dove-gray patterned with what looked like real gold swirls on the walls, a matching slab of gold-toned stone on the countertops. The walk-in shower was as large as the kitchen in her Boston apartment, and the claw-foot tub sat in regal splendor on a raised dais.

Good grief! This hotel suite must cost a fortune. She felt an uneasy twinge thinking back to yesterday, when she'd insisted on paying her share of expenses. Then she remembered Joe saying his prospective client would pick up the tab. The mozzarella business must be booming.

Joe's business, too, if he catered to such super-wealthy clients. He and Callie had never discussed either the size or the financial base of his company. They'd had no reason to. Just one more aspect of the Joe Russo enigma she knew nothing about.

Thinking of the gaps in their knowledge of each

other, she padded to the shell-shaped sink with its gold faucets and arching swan's neck spigots. None of the fixtures showed a single water spot despite the obvious signs Joe had used them earlier—his razor, shaving cream and aftershave were lined up in precise order beside a leather shaving kit. He'd even folded back the top sheet of toilet paper, she noted with some amusement.

Her immediate needs attended to, she snuggled into one the hotel's plush robes and headed back into the bedroom to discover that Joe had picked up the clothes she'd discarded the night before. He'd also unpacked the rest of her things. They hung beside his at evenly spaced intervals in a wardrobe of ornately carved burled walnut.

"Well," she murmured to her reflection in the wardrobe's mirrored doors, "whatever else the man's done in his checkered past, he learned to pick up after himself."

Evidently you could take the man out of the military. Much harder to take the military out of the man, she mused as she surveyed the sitting room that he'd left in the same neat order. Newspaper folded. Glossy magazines aligned on the monster coffee table. Room service tray with its contents stacked, placed on a hall table near the door. Note folded and propped against the vase centered on a round table inlaid with a dozen different kinds of wood.

The message in the note, like the man himself, was short and succinct.

Checking out film festival venues with Sig. Audi.
Back by 3:00 p.m.

A glance at the mantel clock above a fireplace faced with green marble indicated it was almost 10:00 a.m.

She'd been out cold for thirteen hours. The basic need for sleep taken care of, she now had to deal with another. She'd left Audi Farms last night convinced she'd never eat again. Her stomach was now singing an entirely different tune.

She'd call room service, she decided, and grab a quick shower while waiting for breakfast to be delivered. After that she'd go explore. But first...

She searched the brocade curtains covering the entire wall, hunting for their pull cord then realized they operated electrically. She hit one switch, and the heavy brocade whirred back. A second switch opened the blackout curtain underneath. As soon as it parted, brilliant sunlight flooded in. Momentarily blinded, Callie took a step back and squinted through the glare.

"Oh. My. Lord!"

Stunned, she fumbled for the latch of the double doors that opened onto a wide balcony. A brisk breeze tugged at her hair. The balcony's marble tiles were cold against her bare feet. On the street below, traffic honked and diesel fumes tainted the air. What sounded like a jackhammer was going at it somewhere not too far away. Callie didn't see or hear or feel any of it. The view from the balcony utterly and completely enthralled her.

Naples in all its chaotic glory spilled down the hill below and spread its wide, sprawling arms to embrace the impossibly, incredibly blue Bay of Naples. Vesuvius towered above the far side of the bay. The clouds that had shrouded its peak yesterday had dissipated. Today the cone wore a wreath of glistening white snow.

Enchanted, Callie leaned her elbows on the stone baluster and reveled in her bird's-eye view of jumbled streets and narrow alleys strung with washing and ropes of colored Christmas paper. Far below was what she guessed was the main piazza. A majestic cathedral dominated one side of the square. To its left was a 1890s-looking building with a fanciful glass dome. And facing the cathedral was a mile-long structure with a facade interspersed with dozens of statue-filled niches.

Whirling, Callie rushed back inside. The heck with breakfast. She'd grab a croissant or a roll and some coffee on the go. She had to get out and explore.

She scrambled into slacks and a lightweight sweater, bunched her hair into a scrunchie, slapped on some lip gloss and added a quick postscript to Joe's note. Then she was out the door.

Chapter Six

Callic was almost through the lobby before she remembered Arianna mentioning a street she shouldn't miss. A quick detour took her to the concierge's desk.

"But yes, madam," he said when she asked about a street where they sold crèches. "It is the Via San Gregorio Armeno. Let me show you where it is."

He pulled out a tourist map and circled what looked like a short alleyway but warned her it was difficult to find.

"It's best to take a taxi, madam. And may I suggest other sites nearby worthy of a visit?"

"Yes, please."

"Here, just a few blocks away, is the Museo Cappella Sansevero, with its magnificent statue of the Veiled Christ. And here is the Basilica of San Lorenzo Maggiore. It's located at the exact center of the ancient city of Neapolis. There is a new museum here that gives the history of this area, from the Greeks to the Angevins and down to the present day. You can also visit the excavation of the Roman market once located on this spot."

"Thank you, I will."

"But be careful, madam. These spots are very popular with tourists, and thus with pickpockets. I suggest you drape the strap of your purse across your chest and keep it in front of you, yes?"

Callie thanked him again and studied the map while the bellman summoned a cab. Not that her studying did much good. She gave up even trying to read street signs as the cab rocked through a series of hairpin turns and zoomed down the hill. With each turn the streets got narrower, while the buildings got older, darker and a little grimier.

The taxi driver let her off at the head of the street of the crèche makers. As the concierge had warned, the narrow lane was jammed with tourists. Callie kept a careful hand on the purse she'd looped across her chest and plunged into the throng.

Via San Gregorio Armeno was everything Arianna had said it would be! In shop after shop, brightly lit windows displayed crèches made of wood or cork or gorgeously decoupaged cardboard. Some were small, some huge and multitiered. A number of them featured mechanical windmills or waterfalls or baaing sheep. Artisans were hard at work in many of the shops, hand-painting terra cotta shepherds and oxen and angels.

Other artisans crafted the figures from different eras that fascinated Callie as much as they did the other tourists. Arianna hadn't exaggerated. Statuettes of famous political figures, rock stars and athletes crowded next to the holy family, the magi and the shepherds. Callie recognized a good number. William and Kate with their own little angels. The US president. The Irish musician and world-renowned philanthropist Bono.

As one shopkeeper explained in excellent English, it was the ultimate goal of all Italian entertainers to find themselves on the Via San Gregorio Armeno.

"As soon as they become famous, they want the statue. Here is the great Pavarotti. And the young Anna Tatangelo, who sings like an angel. And this is Giuseppe Fabiano, the footballer who goes to jail for not paying taxes."

Callie dutifully admired the array of modern figures but decided to go traditional on a gift for Joe. The beautifully crafted four-inch statue of Joseph, Mary's husband and protector, depicted both strength and nobility of character. A fitting start to the crèche—and family—she and her very own Joseph might build together.

In another shop she found a Kristoff, the iceman from Disney's *Frozen*, for Tommy, and a flame-haired angel for Dawn. For Kate she chose a wicked caricature of a former US presidential candidate her friend had heartily despised. She left the street pleased with her purchases but not quite sure she fully appreciated the irreverent sense of humor that would juxtapose the sacred and profane so exuberantly.

The tantalizing scent of something hot and yeasty lured her to a bakery halfway down the next block. Since it was already past noon, the cases displayed both pastries and open-faced sandwiches. A slab of pizza bread tempted her, but she decided she'd rather share a real Neapolitan pizza with Joe and settled instead for coffee and a ricotta-filled pastry. Flaky and topped with powdered sugar, the roll melted in her mouth. She lingered over the coffee, people watching and enjoying the hustle of the busy street. She would've stayed longer if not for the desire to be back at the hotel when Joe returned.

Once out on the street, she headed for her next stop. After several wrong turns and an appeal to a passerby for assistance, she found the entrance to Cappella Sansevero tucked off a side street. The printed brochure that came with the entrance fee explained that it had once been the private burial chapel of the prince of Sansevero, who'd hired some of Italy's most famous artists and sculptors to embellish his family tomb. The statues and frescoes and painted ceiling were magnificent, but the life-size statue of Christ draped in a thin shroud transfixed Callie. The veil was carved from the same marble block as the statue and was so seemingly transparent that the wounds on Christ's hands, feet and side showed plainly.

She stood by the velvet cord roping off the statue for long moments, only half hearing the Gregorian chant piped into the chapel through hidden speakers. When she finally turned to leave, she was sorry Joe hadn't been there to share the experience with her. So she was both surprised and delighted when a cab pulled up less than a half block later and a tall, broad-shouldered figure emerged.

"Joe! How did you find me?"

"The concierge said…"

The rumble of a truck drowned him out. He waited for it to pass before crossing the narrow street. He was in a suit today. Probably because he'd been meeting with the directors of the Naples film festival and touring the various venues. But he'd tugged off his tie, popped the top buttons on his dress shirt and hooked on a pair of mirrored sunglasses. Callie had to admit he looked as hot in his big-important-executive uniform as he did in his jeans and bomber jacket.

When he'd crossed the narrow street, she greeted him with an eager question. "Have you seen the Sansevero Chapel? It's just down the block."

He hadn't, so Callie made a return visit. The Veiled Christ struck an even deeper chord on second viewing. Its vivid portrayal of Christ's suffering was deeply embedded in her memory when they reemerged into the sunlight filtering through the narrow alley.

"Did you have lunch?" Joe asked.

"Coffee and a roll about an hour ago. I was hoping we could share one of Naples's famous pizzas."

"So was I. Matter of fact, I asked Marcello Audi for the address of his favorite pizza joint. Let's grab a taxi."

His earsplitting whistle brought a cab whipping over to the curb. When he checked an electronic note on his phone and rattled off the address, Callie marveled again at his fluent Italian. She passed the short ride telling him about the mob on the street of the crèche makers and the incredible diversity of nativity figures offered for sale. Only after they'd been shown to a table on the second floor of a tiny restaurant overlooking the bay and placed their order did Callie remark again on the concierge's efficiency in putting Joe on her trail.

"He just told me where you were headed," he said with a shrug. "I tracked you via your phone."

"How?"

"It has a GPS chip."

"Yes, but I thought…"

Confused, she sat back as their aproned waiter delivered their caprese salads and a carafe of chianti. She poked at the thick wedge of mozzarella in the salad, wondering if it came from the Audi farm, while the server poured the ruby-red vino into thick water glasses.

"You thought what?" Joe prompted when the waiter departed.

"I've used the Find My Phone app before to pinpoint its location when I thought I'd lost it. But I thought...no, I'm sure I had to enter my password to access the app."

"You do. I don't."

"Why not?"

"My tech folks developed a program that unscrambles the password."

He said it so calmly, so casually. As if hacking into someone's cell phone was just a routine part of his everyday routine.

"Doesn't the phone have to be turned on to be unscrambled?"

"No."

"So you can track anyone, just by the number?"

"Pretty much." A brief smile flitted across his face. "We offered the program to Homeland Security some weeks back. They want it but are still wrestling with the legalities."

Frowning, Callie poked at her salad again. Although she considered herself a liberal in most respects, the Boston Marathon bombing had tilted her to the right when it came to curtailing the civil liberties of suspected terrorists. She hardly fell into that category, however.

Still frowning, she met Joe's bland gaze. "I'm not sure I like the idea of being on an electronic leash."

"Comes with the ring, sweetheart."

The blunt, masculine possessiveness behind that statement left her sputtering indignantly.

"Dammit, Joe. The fact that I'm wearing your ring doesn't mean I want you to take control of my life."

A shuttered look dropped over his face, spurring her irritation.

"I appreciate your wanting to look out for me," she said firmly. "I do *not*, however, appreciate you preempting my decisions. Like letting Carlo know I'd decided to accept his offer before I had a chance to tell him myself. Or arranging this weekend in Naples, as delightful as it is, when I have so much to do in Rome. Or…"

"I protect what's mine." His eyes had gone cold. "Any way I have to."

A hot retort rose to Callie's lips. She bit it back as she remembered the little bit of his past that he'd shared with her on the drive down from Rome.

"The woman you smuggled out of Angola. The one killed by an assassin in Curaçao. Were you…were you in love with her?"

A muscle ticked in one side of his jaw. He sat unmoving, his expression so closed she thought he wouldn't answer. When he did, she had to strain to hear him.

"I'm not sure you'd call it love. Nattat was fiery and outspoken. And so damned uncompromising. We argued as often as we…"

He broke off, leaving Callie to fill in the blanks. Right. They'd argued as often as they'd indulged in wild, animal sex.

She dropped suddenly clenched fists to her lap. She'd never for one moment imagined she could be jealous of a dead woman.

"She wore her tribal headdress like a badge of honor," Joe continued after a moment. "She hated the Portuguese who'd plundered her country. Hated the native-born Angolans doing the same. As the youngest member ever elected to parliament, she was an unrelenting thorn in their sides." His jaw worked. "It was only a matter of time until the bastards got to her."

The jealousy bit harder, sharper. Callie couldn't imagine a greater contrast between herself and a young, passionate Angolan member of parliament. She suspected Joe had never categorized this crusader for human rights as a calm port to come home to.

Ashamed of the thought and green-eyed monster nipping at her, Callie said quietly, "She sounds like an amazing woman, Joe."

"Yeah. Amazing. Also stubborn as hell and too prone to take risks."

"Which I'm not."

He hiked a brow.

"Okay, I may be a little stubborn at times," she conceded, "but I'm not inclined to take risks. So I don't need to be wrapped in cotton wool. Or kept on an electronic leash."

He didn't like it. She could tell by his closed expression.

"I mean it, Joe. We have to respect each other's boundaries."

He gave that a polite few moments' consideration before shaking his head. "I'm not made that way, Callie. I can't turn it on and off."

She stared across the table with a confusing sense of having reached an impasse. Intellectually, she flatly rejected the idea of being considered any man's possession. Training and experience, however, had taught her some primitive instincts were so deeply imprinted on homo sapiens' DNA that society's civilizing influences could never eradicated. The instinct to protect one's mate was certainly one of those instincts.

Unfortunately, she'd worked too many cases where that protective, possessive instinct spilled into jealousy and domestic violence. Could that happen with Joe? Given his admittedly violent past and dangerous present occupation, Callie couldn't deny the possibility. Yet every primitive instinct *she* possessed said she had nothing to fear from him.

Still, they needed to establish some of those boundaries she'd mentioned now, before they went too far down the path to misunderstanding or distrust. Their pizza arrived before she could marshal her arguments, however. Just as well, she decided. Better to finish this discussion back at the hotel, in the privacy of their opulent suite.

"Ecco! Pizza margherita."

The waiter positioned the pie on the stand in the center of the table with a dramatic flourish and proceeded to serve them a piece. The single slice slopped over the edge of Callie's plate and smelled of crusty dough, sweet tomatoes, mozzarella and fresh basil. Her first bite confirmed it tasted even better than it looked.

"Oh, God! This is unreal." She took another bite, swiping at strings of cheese and savoring the explosion of spices and sauce. "Do you know why they call it *pizza margherita*?" she asked Joe. "I read somewhere it's named after a queen."

"Right. The wife of King Umberto the first or second. Maybe third." He caught a wayward mozzarella strand, tucked it back on his half-devoured slice. "When Umberto and his wife visited Naples and tried pizza for the first time, she said the colors reminded her of the Italian flag."

Callie could see why. The bright red tomatoes. The white mozzarella. The green of the basil leaves.

"So they named it after her," she commented. "Would

those be the same royals who built that humongous palace in the main piazza?"

"Their descendants, I'd guess, a couple centuries removed." He downed another man-sized bite. "The palace is on the way back to the hotel. It's pretty impressive. We could tour it, if you'd like."

"I would. And tomorrow, we *have* to visit Pompeii before we head up to Rome."

"Deal."

They opted for a self-guided tour of the grand palace, aided by a free app they downloaded to their cell phones. The wide marble staircase was impressive enough. The opulence of the salons above boggled Callie's mind. The salons ran into each other, one after another. The blue room. The red. The gold. Each containing priceless works of art, lavishly decorated baroque furniture and some really strange objects brought from the four corners of the world as gifts for the Bourbon kings. Joe held the sack with her purchases while Callie spun in slow circles, her phone to her ear, trying to take in the magnificence.

Pleasantly tired after her day of exploring, she relaxed against Joe's side during the taxi ride back to the hotel. She'd enjoyed the afternoon so much that she toyed with the idea of just taking things with Joe as they came, one speed bump at a time. Especially since those little bumps occurred between stretches of such thrilling and intense pleasure.

Like the stretch that began after they crossed the lobby and the elevator doors pinged shut. In a swift move, Joe backed her against the paneled wall. His mouth came down on hers, hard and hungry and demanding the response that flared instantly in her belly.

She didn't even try to temper it. Didn't hold back. *Couldn't* hold back. There was nothing gentle in the kiss. Nothing tame or affectionate. The heat in it ignited an answering flame that she knew burned hot in her face when he raised his head.

"Been waiting to do this since I picked you up at the airport yesterday morning. Damned near killed me when jet lag got to you last night." He dipped his head, took another taste, muttered against her lips, "Tell me the palace didn't wipe you out."

Since his hands were as busy as his mouth, Callie could only gasp an urgent negative. "The palace… didn't…wipe me…out."

The hum that rose from his throat conveyed equal parts relief, satisfaction and a hunger so fierce that every nerve in her body leaped with anticipation. She had time for only a fleeting prayer that the elevator wouldn't stop to let anyone else on before it hit their floor. Then Joe raked both hands into her hair, dislodging the scrunchie, and wedged a knee between hers. His mouth devouring hers once more, he rocked her with a pleasure so intense she almost lost it right there.

The elevator made it to their floor without any stops, thank God, and their suite was only a few doors down the hall. Callie spent those few yards raking a hand through the hair now tumbling around her face and tugging at the hem of her sweater. A useless exercise, since Joe swept her into his arms as soon as he'd keyed the door. Her sweater rucked up again and her hair got caught against his shoulder, but she didn't even wince when the kick he aimed at the door sent it banging into the jamb.

He had to dip to set the security lock and flip on the electronic Do Not Disturb sign. Callie grabbed his shoulders to keep from being upended and held on as he cut through the sitting room. She was still clinging like a monkey when they hit the bedroom.

Housekeeping had been in, she saw as Joe made straight for the four-poster draped in champagne-colored silk. The gold tassels decorating the bed's richly embroidered comforter marched in a straight line along its hem. A half dozen or more similarly tasseled pillows in varying shapes and sizes sat banked against the carved headboard.

They promptly shot all that neat precision to hell. Joe didn't take time to yank down the spread. Didn't bother shoving the pillows out of the way. He dropped to the bed with Callie still locked against him.

She wasn't sure who attacked whose clothes first. They probably went at it simultaneously. She got his dress shirt off without too much trouble, but Joe was quieter and much quicker. He was feasting on her bare breast while she was still trying to shove his slacks down his lean, muscular flanks. Frustrated, she nipped him on the shoulder. Then nipped again, harder.

That got his attention. His head shot up. Surprise glinted in his eyes.

"You trying to tell me something, tiger?"

"Yes," she panted.

The surprise deepened. "Interesting. Didn't think you were into rough stuff."

"I'm not!" She wiggled under him, fighting the slacks again. "But I could use a little help here."

When he rolled to one side and shucked the rest of his clothes, Callie didn't hesitate. Taking full advantage of having him on his back, she swung a leg over his hip even before his shoes and pants hit the floor. A quick push brought her upright. Another wiggle scooted her back a few inches. Straddling his thighs, she had full access to his rampant sex.

He was rock hard and slick to her touch. And salty when she scooted back a few more inches and contorted enough to take him in her mouth. She couldn't remember ever doing this before. Couldn't remember wanting to. Yet having Joe at the mercy of *her* hands and thighs and busy, busy lips shot her into a new sexual stratosphere. She'd gone beyond registering anything other than his taste and his scent and his feel when he gave a hoarse grunt that could have signaled pleasure or protest.

"Callie. Sweetheart." He nudged her shoulders. "Let me... Crap!"

Joe being Joe, he insisted on giving her the same pleasure she'd given him. Much to Callie's secret delight, however, it took him a few moments to recoup his strength. Hiding a grin, she wallowed in a trough of feminine superiority right up until the moment he had her digging her nails into the spread and moaning in a long, shuddering, shattering release.

It was a while before they recovered enough to sluice off in the mammoth shower and wrap up from neck to knees in the hotel's plush terry-cloth robes. As Callie walked back into the bedroom busily towel drying her hair, Joe winced at the red scrape on her neck.

"Sorry 'bout that whisker burn."

She looked up from under the towel and smiled. "No complaints on this side. It was worth... Oh!"

She stopped dead. Eyes round, jaw slack, she gaped at the scene outside their floor-to-ceiling windows. Dusk had begun to darken the sky, and a fat, full moon hung just above the stone balustrade of their balcony.

"It's just like in that song," she breathed in delight. "The one about the moon hitting your eye like a big pizza pie."

Whipping back her hair, she wrapped the towel turban-style around the still-damp mass and shoved her feet into the hotel-provided slippers.

"Let's go out on the veranda."

"Go ahead. I'll get some Pellegrino and join you."

While she arrowed straight for the veranda, Joe detoured to the minibar to retrieve two dew-streaked bottles. The chilled water in hand, he took a moment to study the robed and turbaned figure transfixed by her view of the moon-washed bay. She'd turned up the collar on the robe and belted it tighter around her waist against the cooling evening air. Elbows propped on the railing, she leaned forward just far enough to showcase her nice, trim butt.

God, she was gorgeous. She didn't think so. No surprise there. She'd grown up in the shadow of her two friends and tended to retreat into the background whenever Kate or Dawn took center stage. Not because they were smarter or prettier or more accomplished. Because she was so comfortable in her own skin that she felt no need to compete for attention. Which was one of the reasons Joe had known almost immediately Callie Langston was right for him. He admired her quiet presence. Envied her serenity.

He didn't have much of either in his own life. Not that he lived on a razor's edge 24/7. Sometimes he went months between a high-profile client like Carlo di Lorenzo or a seriously vulnerable target like the Naples film festival. Even on the job, Joe had learned to make stress work for him. It kept him and his team alert. Kept them alive. It was those few hours when the adrenaline rocketed through the roof, those days and nights when sleep wasn't an option, that left him craving a quiet sanctuary to return to after a particularly hairy gig.

He did have a sanctuary or two already. He maintained a house close to his operations base in Houston. Kept a private retreat in the Colorado Rockies. Paid a month-to-month lease on apartment in LA used for strictly business purposes. The places were comfortable. Some might say luxurious. But sterile. Empty. He wanted someone like Callie to fill that emptiness.

Joe's fists tightened on the bottles. No, dammit! He didn't want someone *like* Callie. He wanted *her*.

Looking back, he knew now that he hadn't wanted Nattat this badly. Yeah, he'd lusted for her. Broken every rule in the book for her. Even killed for her. But she'd never stirred this gut-deep need to cherish and protect and…and…

Hell! No point trying to analyze whatever it was Callie stirred in him. Enough to just roll with it. Which he did, at least until she straightened and came inside.

"It's colder than it looks out there," she announced with a little shiver.

He hefted the Pellegrino. "Want something that'll raise more heat than water?"

"No, that's good. Besides, after all that wine we had with our pizza, I need to have a clear head."

"For?"

She gave the ends of the robe's belt a little tug. "I enjoyed today, Joe. This whole weekend. But we need to talk."

Chapter Seven

We need to talk.

Exactly what every man wanted to hear from his woman. Hiding a grimace, Joe arched a brow. "Long talk or short?"

"That depends on you."

His euphoric mood of just a few seconds ago went down in flames. Just your basic crash and burn, he thought sardonically as he gestured to the sitting room.

"Might as well get comfortable."

She curled into one end of the curved-back sofa and tucked her feet under her. Joe took the middle cushion. Not close enough to crowd her, but within reaching distance. Just in case he had to resort to emergency measures. Passing her one of the bottles, he braced for the worst while she unscrewed the cap and took a long swallow.

"I debated whether to have this discussion, Joe. I enjoyed this afternoon so much. This whole weekend. Especially the past few hours," she added with smile.

The smile didn't hack it. "Cut to the chase, Callie. What's this about?"

Unperturbed by the gruff demand, she nodded. "All right. You told me you're not into flowery phrases or stringing together lots of adjectives, so let's keep it simple. If you had to describe what you feel for me in just two or three words, what would they be? And *please* don't say 'a calm port in a storm.'"

Christ! Where'd that come from? He'd thought... been sure...she'd understood it was a compliment. Digging deep, he settled on some lines of Scripture his gran had drilled into him as a kid, accompanied more often than not by the smack of her palm alongside his head.

"Three words? How about 'faith, hope and love. But,'" he added gruffly, "'the greatest of these is love.'"

Her eyes widened in surprise. *Payback,* he thought with a stab of fierce satisfaction, *for the crash and burn.*

"Isn't that from the Bible?"

"First Corinthians, chapter thirteen."

"I didn't know... That is..." She floundered for another moment. "Are you a regular churchgoer?"

"Not according to my grandmother."

"You have a grandmother?" she echoed faintly.

"Most people do," he drawled.

"You've never mentioned her. Or your parents. Are they still alive?"

"Never knew my father. Mom died when I was six. Gran took over then."

"Is she still alive?"

"Alive and kicking. She lives only a few blocks from me in Houston."

It'd taken some persuasion to get the feisty octogenarian to leave the home she'd raised him in. Joe had made sure she was comfortable there, that house had every modern convenience known to man. But three years ago arthritis all but crippled her and Joe finally convinced her to move to Houston. She was in a wheelchair now and quoting Bible scriptures to the attendants at a luxurious assisted-living center.

"How often do you…?" She stopped, drew a breath. "Never mind. We'll get to that later."

He waited, letting her circle back to whatever had spurred this need for this little talk.

"Why 'faith, hope and love'?" she finally questioned.

Resigned, Joe dug a little deeper. "Faith, because once you give your loyalty, it stays given. Dawn and Kate are living proof of that."

"I guess," she murmured, not quite convinced.

"Hope, because…" He held that deep purple gaze. "For the first time in longer than I can remember, the future holds promise."

Her doubt melted, her voice softened. "And love? Are you in love with me, Joe?"

What the hell? Did she think he went around proposing to every female who looked at him sideways?

"You're the first…the only…woman I've asked to marry me."

"So that's a yes?"

"Didn't I just say that?"

"Not exactly. Say the words. I'd like to hear them."

He opened his mouth, but her too-innocent expression knocked the simple phrase back down his throat. The little witch! She was jacking him. Playing him like a trout on the end of a six-pound line.

"I love you. And now…" Thunking his Pellegrino down on the coffee table, he plucked hers out of her hand and leaned in. "Your turn. What do you feel for me? Three words. Spit 'em out."

She didn't blink, didn't hesitate. "I love you. I didn't realize how much until this moment."

"Right. Okay. Good."

Callie knew better than to smile, but it took some doing. He sounded every bit as flustered as she had a few moments ago. Taking pity on his obvious confusion, she laid a hand on his forearm.

"Will it help if I tell you that you're the first man… the *only* man…whose ring I've worn?"

"It helps," he said, recovering. "It also makes me wonder where this 'we need to talk' sh…stuff came from."

She acknowledged the barb with a nod and took a moment to gather her thoughts. Her religious education had been sporadic at best. One parent was a lapsed Catholic, the other agnostic. They'd both pretty much left her to find her own way. But she'd attended enough weddings to have more than a passing familiarity with the love verse Joe had just quoted.

"Isn't there something in that First Corinthians chapter about love not insisting on having its own way?"

"Verse five. Why? What's your point?"

"Remember what you said this afternoon? When I told you I don't like being on an electronic leash?"

"Hell, Callie. Is that what this is all about? The phone-tracking app?"

"The app's part of it. Mostly it's about establishing and respecting the boundaries I mentioned."

She chewed on the inside of her cheek, needing to get this right. Whatever future they might build together depended on the next few moments.

"You told me you couldn't turn your instincts off and on, Joe. I don't want you to turn them off. Not com-

pletely. Some primitive corner of my psyche thrills to
the idea of a strong, protective mate."

He managed to look both vindicated and baffled. "I
repeat, what's your point?"

"The point," she said patiently, "is that I want to be
a full partner in this relationship, not some pampered
pet. I want you to explain up front about any security
issues or actions that involve me. Or us. Or you, for
that matter."

"The process isn't always that deliberate. There are
times…too many times…when I have to go with my
gut."

"I get that. I do. And I'd be a fool to tell you to ignore those gut instincts. It's the other times. The ordi-
nary you-and-me times. I need to know you won't just
assume you know best for me."

She reached for his hand. Hers was still damp and
chilled from the Pellegrino bottle, his warm and sin-
ewy. The contrast wasn't lost on her.

They were so different, she and Joe. They came from
disparate backgrounds, apparently. Had followed widely
divergent career paths. And they were certainly at the
opposite ends of the spectrum when it came to bruis-
ing, bare-knuckle experiences.

And yet in many ways they were very much alike.
Both self-contained. Both confident of their own abilities. Both, she thought with a warm halo around her
heart, seemingly in this for the long haul.

"Promise you won't make unilateral decisions, except in extraordinary circumstances."

He grabbed at the out. "Extraordinary circumstances.
Okay, I can live with that."

"I mean it, Joe. Starting here, starting now, we're
equal partners in this adventure. Deal?"

He thought about it for a second or two, then raised her hand and dropped a kiss on the back of it. The gesture was so courtly and un-Joe-like that she almost melted into a puddle right there on the hotel's thousand-dollar-plus sofa.

"Deal."

He released her fingers and reached for the belt of her robe instead. It loosened with a single tug. With a satisfied grunt, he curved his palm over her thigh.

"As your full and equal partner, I vote we adjourn to the bed."

"The bed we just left a few moments ago?"

"Yeah." He slid his hand higher. "That one."

A cold, gray drizzle obscured the bay the next morning, but Callie held Joe to his promise to take her to Pompeii before they drove up to Rome. Fortified by the hotel's sumptuous Sunday brunch, they checked out and hit the road.

The nasty weather actually did them a favor by whittling the hordes of tourists down to the hardiest few. Bundled against the chill in her long duster and the paisley scarf looped twice around her neck, European-style, Callie shoved her left hand in her pocket. Joe held onto her right and kept it tucked in the pocket of his leather jacket.

She appreciated his steadying grip as they navigated the cobbled streets. Drifting fingers of fog made the time-worn stones slick and treacherous. They also blanketed the ancient ruin in eerie silence, almost as if the terror of that day in 79 AD had never happened. Yet every excavated dwelling, every scrap of tiled floor or line of decapitated marble columns rising out of the mist gave grim evidence of Vesuvius's destructive power.

"Hard to believe all this lay buried for more than a thousand years," she murmured.

Even harder to believe the hot ash and molten lava had spewed out of the volcano with such speed that Pompeii's citizens had no time or place to run. They had died where they cowered. Or in the case of a noticeably pregnant woman, where she lay. Callie bit her lip as she studied the plaster cast made from the hardened hollow where the woman's body had once been entombed in layers of ash. She'd tried to shield her head with one arm. The other cradled her stomach and unborn babe.

The tragic figure had Callie blinking back tears. She couldn't help thinking of Kate and her emerging baby bump. She hated to miss her friend's exciting time of discovery and impending birth. Hated missing Christmas with Dawn and her new family, too. Her choice, she reminded herself. Her choice. But she made a silent promise to call her friends as soon as she got settled in her new apartment.

That led to a reminder of the job waiting in Rome and the center sheltering desperate female refugees. She stared at the cast of the long-dead woman, thinking that all these years later, death and destruction still rained down from the skies. Man-made now, more often than not, and every bit as devastating. So many tried to escape it. So many needed help.

"I've seen enough," she told Joe. "Let's go."

The dank, heavy mist continued to roll in from the coast as they drove north. Traffic moved at a slow crawl for most of the way. When they finally crested one of Rome's seven fabled hills, angry black clouds had piled up over the city and added to the fast-descending darkness.

The deluge hit moments later. As if navigating the capital's labyrinthine center wasn't enough of a challenge, the torrential downpour turned to slush, then fat, wet snowflakes that gave the SUV's oversize wipers a run for their money. With grim thanks for GPS, Joe followed the system's precise directions to the flat he'd checked out before picking Callie up at the airport three days ago. The parking gods must have been smiling. He squeezed into a space just a few yards from the entrance, unloaded their carryalls and caught Callie's arm for a quick dash through the snow.

The flat wasn't much. One bedroom, one combination kitchen, eating area and living room, with a tiny bath tucked in a corner. But it was on the third floor of a recently renovated building with solid security and located only a few blocks from the women's center where she'd be working. Still, he'd had Emilio, his contact here in Rome, install a fingerprint-activated electronic keypad on her door and new bolts on the windows...which, under the terms of their recently negotiated agreement, he felt obligated to tell her about.

"Was that really necessary?" she asked, eyeing the polished brass hardware that gleamed bright and new against an old but very solid door.

"Probably not. Here, press your palm against the scanner. Fingers flat. Now roll them a little. Right to left. Good."

Feeling a little like a felon being fingerprinted by Rome's *polizia*, she submitted to what she hoped was the last of Joe's electronic gadgets.

"The super has an override code," he said as the door clicked open. "Just in case."

Callie didn't move. "Do you have the code, too?"

"Yeah, I do." He turned and gave her a cool look. "You have a problem with that?"

"Not if you call or text me before you use it."

"Damn." His mouth twisted. "There goes my plan to surprise you when you come home and find me wearing nothing but a smile and big red bow."

It was so deadpan—and so unexpected—that Callie blinked before choking out a laugh. "Trust me. If I walk in and find you in a big red bow, I'll be *extremely* surprised."

"Too late. You ruined it. I'll think up something else." He nudged the door with his carryall. "You want in or not?"

Once inside, Joe flicked on the lights and waited while Callie explored her new home.

It was perfect, she thought in delight. Absolutely perfect. The warm yellow walls dispelled the winter gloom, and the furnishings were an eclectic mix of modern and shabby chic. The kitchen consisted of a two-burner stove with a single-rack oven, a small fridge and cloth-covered cupboards. The eating area held only a narrow drop-leaf table and two chairs that could be turned around to augment seating in the living area. That room's solitary window faced the street and the buildings directly opposite. Roll-down shutters would block the streetlights and traffic noise.

Entranced, she opened a door to the bathroom. A stool, a sink and a shower surrounded by a circular curtain suspended from the ceiling, all squeezed into what she guessed might once have been a closet.

The bedroom just beyond contained only a double bed, a nightstand and a hand-painted wardrobe. But to Callie's great joy, it also boasted a glass-paned door that opened onto a minuscule balcony that seemed to hang suspended in midair. Snow-dusted buildings stair-stepped down the steep hill below. And in the distance a floodlit dome was just visible through the curtain of snow.

"Is that St. Peter's?" she gasped.

"Looks like."

Thrilled, she twisted the knob and stepped outside for a better look. Skirting a dime-size café table with a single chair, she gripped the wrought-iron railing with gloved hands. Rome had enchanted her during her brief visit with Dawn and Kate a few months ago. Awestruck by the snowy scene spread out before her, she fell completely, irrevocably in love.

More in love, she amended as Joe edged past the rickety little table to join her. Overwhelmed, she turned and framed his face with her gloved hands. The light spilling through the glass-paned door illuminated one side of his face. The scar was lost in shadow. Where it belonged, she thought fiercely. His past had made him the man he was now, but the future belonged to her. To both of them.

"Thank you," she breathed. "For Naples. For Pompeii. For being here with me. This whole day's been perfect."

"You're welcome. It'll be even more perfect," he added with a hopeful waggle of his brows, "if Emilio stocked your kitchen with something quick and easy to fix."

From the sublime to the practical. Laughing, Callie came back to earth.

And now that he'd mentioned it, she was ravenous, too. After that ginormous brunch at the hotel in Naples, she'd vowed to cut out all carbs for the next week. Touring Pompeii and the long, slow drive back to Rome sent that vow down the tubes.

"Let's take a look."

They shed their coats and crowded into the tiny kitchen. Emilio had indeed stocked the fridge and tiny pantry. Callie inventoried paper-wrapped Parma ham, a thick wedge of Asiago cheese, garlic cloves, onions, Roma tomatoes, potatoes, eggs, coffee, creamer, some canned soup, a bottle of Tuscan red and, of course, several variations of pasta.

"How about an omelet?" she suggested. "That's quick and easy."

"I hit the omelet bar at breakfast."

"Soup?"

"Tell you what. I spotted a trattoria on the corner. Why don't I just go down and get two takeout orders of veal scaloppine?"

"Oh, God, that sounds wonderful. But I hate for you to go back out in the snow."

"Not a problem." He snagged his jacket off the chair where he'd draped it. "I'll be right back. You open the wine and get settled."

Before she accomplished either of those tasks, Callie had a far more important one to attend to. It was just past six Rome time. A little after noon in DC. Digging her phone out of her purse, she dropped onto the edge of the bed and hit Kate's speed-dial number.

"Callie! Travis and I were just talking about you. How's Rome?"

"Absolutely incredible." Her gaze locked on the window. "At this precise moment I'm sitting on the side of the bed in my apartment, looking through the balcony door, watching snow blanket the dome of St. Peter's."

"Get. Out."

"I kid you not! Hold on while I get Dawn on the line."

Their friend answered on the second ring and shouted over the din in the background. "About time you called."

"What?"

"I said, it's about time you called."

"I can barely hear you. Where are you?"

"Sunday brunch at Paoli's. Where are *you*, and more important, what the heck took you so long to contact your best friends?"

"I've been a little busy."

"That's what I tried to tell her," Kate put in. "She wanted to call you, but I twisted her arm and made her wait until you got your feet on the ground."

"I waited," Dawn groused, "but I didn't like it. So spill it, girl. No! Hold on, I need to go someplace without all these decibels."

Callie heard a thump, a muffled voice, the clash of pots and pans. Then blessed silence.

"Okay," Dawn announced breathlessly. "I'm in the ladies' room. Wait a sec while I put the seat down. There. I'm good. Now talk. How's Rome? What's happening with you and Joe?"

"Rome is clean and bright and dusted with snow from top to bottom. And Joe…"

Callie didn't spin out the pause deliberately. She just needed a couple seconds to sort through everything that had happened in the three tumultuous days since she'd landed in Italy.

"We've been together this whole time. After he picked me up at the airport Friday morning, we drove down to Naples to meet with his prospective client. Then…"

"Wait. Back up. You crawl off a plane after a nine-hour flight and he takes you to Naples for a business meeting?"

"Actually, we went for a sort of pre-Christmas feast with Signor Audi and his family. At their water buffalo ranch."

Dawn made a "huh" noise but Kate caught the connection immediately.

"Buffalo, as in mozzarella cheese?"

"As in a dozen different varieties of mozzarella, all of them scrumptious."

"And you went to the source of these dozen different varieties?"

"We did! Honestly, it was so interesting. The buffalo get scrubbed, massaged, milked and scrubbed again. All done robotically."

"Sounds fascinating," Dawn commented in a voice that clearly indicated otherwise. "Back to Joe. Three whole days with Mr. If I Tell You I'll Have to Kill You, and you haven't changed your mind?"

"No," Callie said at the same moment the sound of a loud flush came through the phone. "Just the opposite."

"What? I can't hear you."

"I said Joe and I are great. Fantastic. Wonderful."

"Wow," Dawn murmured after a short silence. "Those must have been some three days."

"They were. I'll zip off an email tomorrow with all the juicy details."

"And pictures," Kate insisted. "We want pictures of your apartment and where you work."

"Will do. Say hi to Travis and Brian and Tommy. I love you all and miss you already."

"Give Joe our best. And Carlo, when you see him."

"Will do," Callie promised again. "Ciao for now."

She clicked off and pushed off the bed. Her first

order of business was to uncork the wine and let it breathe. She wasted a few moments hunting for a corkscrew until she realized the cap was a twist-off. Interesting. One of her coworkers back in Boston had been a self-professed and completely unapologetic wine snob. Devin would no doubt have heart palpitations if he had to twist rather than uncork and meticulously decant.

Smiling at the thought, she went ahead and set the table with the silverware and pretty red-and-yellow napkins she'd found in her hunt for a corkscrew. No wine goblets, but the wavy green water glasses would do nicely.

That homey task done, she transferred the carryalls to the bedroom. She left Joe's on the bed but unpacked her toiletries and stuffed the clothes she'd worn over the weekend in the laundry bag she found hanging in the hand-painted wardrobe. Her two suitcases were in the wardrobe, too, left there by the so-efficient Emilio. She pulled one out, but before she could lug it to the bed to unpack, her phone chirped. The succinct text message made her grin.

Coming up. Using the override.

Ha! Who said you couldn't teach an old dog new tricks? Still grinning, Callie went to join Joe for her first meal in her new home.

Chapter Eight

Joe stayed the night, taking up more than his fair share of the double bed, and had to leave early Monday morning.

"I'll be in Zurich until Wednesday," he told Callie as he tucked his shaving kit into his carryall. "Then I have to fly back to the States. You've got Emilio's number. Call him if you need anything before I get back."

"Any idea when that might be?"

"Not sure. I'll try to make it before Christmas, but I have to put together the team I promised Marcello Audi I'd bring in the first week in January. Some top people to beef up electronic surveillance at his venue sites. More to conduct hands-on training for his security staff."

She nodded but suffered another silent qualm about the prospect of spending Christmas on her own in Italy. Her decision, she reminded herself fiercely as Joe zipped his carryall. Her decision.

Besides, if the center was as short-staffed as Carlo had indicated, she wouldn't have time to feel lonely. Or so she thought, right up until she walked Joe to the door of her tiny apartment.

"Have a safe trip home."

"Plan to." He curled a knuckle under her chin and tipped her face to his. "Good luck at the center. You sure you can find it?"

"Two blocks to the north and one to the east? I think so. But if I have any trouble," she promised solemnly, "I'll use the directional finder on my phone."

"Whatever works." He took the hit with a philosophical shrug and made a slow pass over her lower lip with his thumb. "Don't let the heartache you find there get you too down."

Easier said than done, she knew. She still carried painful memories of some of the children's cases she'd worked in her heart.

"I plan to stay too busy to get down."

"After meeting *il Drago*, I can pretty much guarantee you will."

"*Il Drago*? The dragon? I hope that doesn't refer to my new boss."

"Carlo's tag for her, not mine. It fits, though. The woman put us both through the wringer when he told her I wanted to review the center's refugee screening process."

"Wonderful. You pissed off my new boss. Exactly what I needed to hear before my first day on the job."

His mouth curved in one of his rare grins. "My money's on you, Pansy Eyes. Just aim one of your cool, we-need-to-talk looks at her and she'll fold like *washi*. Thin Japanese paper," he said in answer to her blank look. "They use it make origami and wrap gifts to burn in honor of their ancestors."

This man amazed her. He really did. Bible verses. Japanese origami. Fiery tribal beauties. Hired assassins. She was still trying to fit all these facets of his personality into their respective niches when he dropped a quick kiss on her lips.

"Call me," he ordered as he headed down the narrow S-shaped stairs. "Let me know how today goes."

"I will."

He'd hit the first floor landing before she remembered the Christmas gifts she'd purchased in Naples. She leaned over the railing to call him back, but he was already out the door.

Damn! He could've taken Dawn's and Kate's and Tommy's back to the States with him. Opened his, too, while he was here. She'd have to FedEx the others and keep his until his return to Rome. Hopefully in time for Christmas.

She gave the high-tech palm pad a sideways glance as she wandered back into her new home. Joe's presence had made the two rooms seem cozy. Okay, crowded. Now they felt empty, sucked of their vitality.

All right. Enough of that. She had things to do, places to go, people to see. With a determined roll of her shoulders, Callie shook off her deflated feeling and set to work unpacking the suitcases Emilio had delivered.

Not that she had all that much to unpack. She'd based her wardrobe choices on a study of Rome's average winter temperatures and her preliminary research into the shelter run by International Aid to Displaced Women. The center's residents were older than the children she'd worked with for the past six years. They'd lost their husbands, their families, all ties to their native lands.

Some had survived unimaginable horrors. Callie knew they'd relate more to jeans and a sweater than a tailored black pantsuit.

An hour later she emerged into a city that had come alive after its snowy night. The sun was a bright sphere, the air frosty. Tucking her chin in her scarf and her hands deep in the pockets of her duster, Callie set off for the center.

The Monday morning traffic had churned the streets to slush, but the wrought-iron balconies and green-painted shutters adorning the buildings on both sides of the street still sported downy white eyebrows. School kids with monster book bags clumped by in oversize boots. Housewives bundled up against the cold clutched fishnet shopping bags as they headed to the local butchers and greengrocers. Office workers stood elbow to elbow at espresso bars, munching pastries, scanning folded newspapers and getting the necessary caffeine jolt to jump-start their day.

When a patron exited one of those tiny cafés, the scent of fresh-ground coffee and hot croissants lured Callie inside. She studied the chalkboard menu while waiting in line and managed to order in her few phrases of broken Italian. The white chocolate cream concoction came in a glass with a silver handle and was topped with a frothy heart almost too pretty to slurp. She carried it and a still-warm croissant to a stand-up counter and consumed both while studying the framed black-and-white photos filling every square inch of wall space.

Many were from WWII and depicted US soldiers who must have chosen this little café as a favorite gathering spot. Others looked like they were from the late '40s and early '50s. Callie spotted an extremely well-endowed Sophia Loren in one, a Jack Kennedy look-alike in another.

Intrigued, she edged closer to examine the scrawled signature. It *was* Kennedy. Young, impossibly handsome, flashing that famous grin, with his arm hooked over the back of a chair occupied by a pouty blonde Callie didn't recognize. She would've liked to take a closer look at some of the other celebrities, but a quick glance at the clock above the bar sent her back out into the bright, cold morning.

A quick turn brought her to her new place of employment. Identified only by the street number above its door, the three-story building that housed the IADW center blended in with its neighbors. Like them, it was stuccoed, only this was a deeper terra-cotta red than either of its neighbors. Marble pediments decorated the first-floor windows; green shutters framed the others. Callie noted the absence of any security cameras and felt a tingle at the back of her neck as she remembered Joe's comment about terrorists using refugee centers as conduits to the West.

Although he hadn't mentioned it—probably because he hadn't wanted to scare her—she suspected these centers could become targets, too, for extremists at both ends of the spectrum. Ultra-right neo-Nazi types stirred to fury over the influx of "foreigners" might present as much of a threat as leftist revolutionaries seeking to exploit the residents' hopes and fears.

With these—hopefully remote!—possibilities in mind, she pressed the bell centered in a dented and slightly rusted speaker box.

"Sì?"

The single syllable came across as clipped and distinctly impatient.

"My name is Callie Langston. I'm…"

"Finally! Come in. I'm in the storeroom. Down the hall, last door on the right."

The locked clicked, and Callie stepped into a foyer tiled in gray marble. A graceful arch led from the foyer to a long hallway. Doors opened off either side of the hall, and at the far end a graceful marble staircase spiraled upward.

She made her way to the last door on the right as instructed while admiring the Murano glass sconces and elaborate ceiling medallions that suggested the center had once been home to a fairly well-to-do family. She was only a few feet from her destination when a thump and a curse sounded from its open door. A quick glance inside showed a cluttered office and a rail-thin woman with short, flyaway white hair. While Callie watched, the woman shoved aside a carton with a logo that depicted what looked like a giant green hand cupping a dark-eyed baby in its palm.

The hearty shove sent the box careening into a stack of similarly marked cartons. They wobbled wildly, precipitating another muttered curse and a quick jump forward from Callie. Between them, the two women managed to keep the tower more or less upright.

The save didn't appear to afford the older woman much satisfaction. Hands on hips, she scowled at the stack, as if daring it to take another wobble. Only after she'd stared it down did she turn a look of unalloyed disgust on Callie.

"I've told this group again and again we need supplies for women and adolescent girls."

Her English was thick and heavily accented.

"Do they listen? No! Do they keep sending diapers and teething rings? Yes! Does my *idiota* intern accept their shipments? Every time!"

Despite her skeletal thinness and dandelion-fine white hair, she looked so fierce Callie half expected her to aim another kick at the precariously stacked boxes. Instead, she drilled the newcomer with a pair of startlingly blue eyes.

"The prince insisted I take you on as my deputy. Your credentials are impressive, I'll give you that. Far better than the one you're replacing. But if you think working with us at the center will convince the prince to offer more than weekends in Monte Carlo or Antibes, you should think again."

"*Excuse* me?"

"Ah! So he didn't tell you? No, of course he would not. He will wait for the right moment."

"Look, Signora Alberti… You are Signora Alberti, aren't you?"

"*Sì.*"

"Look, Signora Alberti. The prince is a friend. A good friend. But if you don't wish to accept me based on my credentials, that's your prerogative."

"*Magari.*"

"I'm sorry," Callie said stiffly. "I don't know that word."

"It means… How do you say in America? *I wish.*"

Callie opened her mouth, but before she could tell the Wicked Witch of the East to take her job and stuff it, the director flapped an impatient hand.

"*Non importa.* I will know soon enough if you're as hopeless as the others. Come along. I'll introduce you to the staff who aren't in session. You'll meet the rest at lunch. The residents, too."

During the next hour, Callie's initial impression of an irate, dandelion-haired virago who waged war with innocent boxes underwent a swift reevaluation.

Despite her abrupt manner, Signora Alberti's staff appeared to adore her. The two mental-health techs, one Italian and one French. The nurse-practitioner from Corinth, Greece. The three translators who between them spoke eleven different languages. The multinational kitchen crew busy cleaning up after breakfast. Even Signora Alberti's *idiota* assistant, who turned out to be an Italian grad student working at the center as part of his hands-on training for a master's in cognitive therapy from La Sapienza, one of the oldest and most prestigious universities in Europe.

Unfortunately, the intern's English was as limited as Callie's Italian. After struggling to communicate using the impatient director as an intermediary, they agreed to compare notes at a later date. Hopefully, when they'd each gained a little more facility with the other's language.

Staff intros over, Alberti gave Callie a tour of the upper stories. The second floor contained an arts and crafts area, a library, a TV room and a series of dormitory-like bedrooms, each two bedrooms linked by a shared bath. The third floor was entirely bedrooms. All but one were occupied.

"We try to match roommates who speak the same language or at least practice the same religion," the director said. "It's not always possible, of course, but we try."

"How long do the residents stay here?"

"We've placed some in jobs and homes within a few weeks. Others..." Her shoulders lifted. "Others stay much longer."

"Can they go out? Get their nails done or go to..."

"Of course they can," Alberti snapped. "This is a shelter, yes? Not a prison."

Properly chastised, Callie was given a tour of the first-floor meeting and counseling rooms, then shown her office. It was directly across from the director's and sparsely appointed. A desk, two chairs, a metal file cabinet. Delicate sconces hinted at the house's former glory, and pale squares marked the walls where pictures or portraits must have once hung.

The director jabbed a finger at the flat-screen computer monitor sitting dead center on the desk. "We update our case files daily. All counseling sessions you have with residents, either one-on-one or in group. No excuses. No delays. Operating procedures require that we change the password once a week. When we remember," she admitted grudgingly. "This week it's Aleppo221."

"Got it."

The director tipped her chin toward a row of black binders perched atop the metal file cabinet. "Those notebooks contain our operating procedures. They're in Italian, but have been translated in English and Arabic. You need to review them along with the case files, also in Italian and English. You've got some time now. We have lunch at noon, yes? There's a group session you should sit in on at two this afternoon. And I've scheduled you to teach the beginning English class at four. It's been on hold waiting for your arrival. Can you handle that?"

"Yes, ma'am."

"Simona," she said with an irritated chop of her hand. "Call me Simona."

With so many new experiences bombarding her, Callie took the precaution of jotting down the password before she forgot it. Years of inbred caution had her reversing the digits, however. That done, she logged on and opened the oldest file.

She thought she'd seen the full spectrum of family tragedy. As she worked her way through the computerized case files, she realized she'd barely scratched the surface. Her throat got tighter as she read family histories that included everything from mass murder to honor killings to kidnapping and rape.

A number of the seventy-three women currently residing at the center had lost every living relative to war. Others had suffered pain and humiliation at the hands of vengeful husbands or fathers or brothers. Two girls barely into their teens had been sold into sexual slavery and experienced appalling degradation before escaping their captors by hiding in a dung cart.

Yet when Callie accompanied her boss to lunch, they entered a room filled with lively chatter. The meal was served buffet-style in what must have been the original owners' grand salon. The fare was hearty lamb stew fortified with green peas and couscous, the preferred drink a fragrant apple tea. The women present appeared to be primarily Middle Eastern and African, with a sprinkling of Europeans. They sat at tables of four or eight. The clusters appeared cultural for the most part, with the Muslims in modest robes and hair covered by veils or scarves, the others in more flamboyant dress.

One sat alone. Head down. Shoulders hunched. Head scarf covering her hair, her very pregnant belly evident even under her loose robe. She refused to look up even when Simona stood and called for attention. Pausing at intervals to allow the translators to keep up, the director introduced the newest member of the staff. After a flurry of smiles and welcomes in several different languages, the women got on with their lunch.

Callie waited for a lull in the director's conversation with the woman on her other side to nod discreetly at the solitary diner.

"Who's that?"

Simona followed her glance. "We call her Amal, but we don't know her real name. She washed ashore in Greece a month ago, we think from a boatload of Syrian refugees that sank off the coast. If so, she was the only survivor. She won't…or can't…tell us anything about herself or her life before she arrived here."

"Is she due soon?"

"Nikki Dukakis, our nurse-practitioner, thinks it could be within the next few weeks. We don't have facilities here for a nursery, so she'll move to another center when she leaves the hospital."

How sad, Callie thought, and how frightening it must be to give birth in a strange land surrounded by people you don't know and can't communicate with, only to be shuffled from one facility to another. She couldn't help remembering the plaster cast of the pregnant woman in Pompeii and felt a wrenching hope this mother-to-be would find a safe harbor for herself and her child.

A number of the residents came up after lunch to welcome her, some shyly, some with warm smiles. Callie then sat in on the two o'clock group session conducted by one of the mental-health techs. Despite having to work through an interpreter, the tech did a very credible job getting the women to participate.

At four o'clock Callie walked into the beginning English class feeling nervously inadequate. She soon found she didn't have to worry. The seven women and one teen in the class were eager to learn, and the teaching aids included very basic flash cards, picture books and whiteboards. The youngest class member, named

Sabeen, had a wide gap between her front teeth and seemed to take special delight in repeating sibilants like "sleep" and "snake." With each whistle, she'd giggle, slap her palm over her mouth and set the colored beads at the ends of her hundreds of tiny braids to dancing a merry tune. Having read her case file only a few hours ago, Callie could only marvel at the kidnapping victim's resilience.

Simona had indicated the staff were welcome to eat dinner with the residents, although most preferred a little separation after their long days. Night duty rotated among the paid staff and involved either sleeping at the center or remaining at home, close to a phone.

Since it was Callie's first day on the job, she opted to have dinner at the center. She shared a table with a woman from northern Iraq whose husband and three sons had been beheaded by ISIS last month. A former university professor, she spoke English and kept the conversation focused deliberately and exclusively on Callie. Where she was from. Where she'd gone to school. Why she'd come to Rome. Why the United States had invaded her country, then plunged it into chaos. Well aware she had to earn these women's trust, Callie answered as honestly as she could.

The night air was cold and brisk when she walked back to her apartment, accompanied by dark-haired, dark-eyed Nikki Dukakis. The nurse-practitioner lived only two streets over and invited Callie to have dinner the following evening with her and her husband.

"Simona is coming, too," she said. "And Carlo, if he has returned to Rome. My Dominic is with the Greek Trade Commission. He does business with Carlo, which is how I came to work at the center. But I'll do my best to keep them from talking trade embargoes all night."

She waved a cheerful goodbye at the corner, and Callie climbed the stairs to the third floor. Fumbling off her glove, she activated the scanner and let herself into the two rooms that were already beginning to feel like home. Her first order of business was a hot, steamy shower. Her second, snuggling into warm pj's. Her third and most important, calling Joe.

"Hey," she said when he picked up. "How's Zurich?"

"Cold. Snowing. Traffic pretty much at a standstill. But I got done what I needed to."

"So you're going to fly back to the States tomorrow?"

"If the airport stays open. Your turn. How was your first day?"

"Exhilarating. Exhausting. And really, really humbling. These women have been through so much, Joe. I spent most of the day waffling between a burning desire to help and questioning whether my puny skills are up to the task."

"They are. How'd you get along with *il Drago*?"

"I'm on probation until I prove I'm not just another do-gooder Carlo foisted on her. Which might be kind of tough, since I hope to do good and Carlo *did* foist me on her."

"Like I said this morning, my money's on you. Hang on, I've got another call." He returned a few seconds later. "Sorry, I need to take this. I'll call you back."

"That's okay. I'm pooped. I'll talk to you tomorrow. Good night, Joe."

"Night, Pansy Eyes."

Her voice lingered in Joe's mind as he reconnected with the caller he'd put on hold. "Yo, Frank. What's up?"

His Defense Intelligence Agency buddy didn't waste

time on chitchat. "A report just crossed my desk I think you should know about."

"I'm listening."

"Someone's been making inquiries about the place you had me check out a few days back. Very casual, very innocuous inquiries. They were buried deep in a flurry of other chatter."

"And?"

"And up until these queries surfaced, we were pretty sure we'd taken this particular someone down."

Joe's stomach went tight. "Can you give me details?"

"Not over an open line."

Joe vowed instantly to depart Zurich within the next hour, snow or no snow. If he couldn't fly out, he'd either drive or jump a high-speed train to whatever airport was still open. Once there, he'd charter an executive jet if necessary.

"I'll see you tomorrow."

He cut the connection and stood for a moment, hefting the phone in his palm. The ink had barely dried on the deal he'd cut with Callie. No wrapping her up in cotton wool. No ignoring mutually agreed-to boundaries. No unilateral decisions…except in extraordinary circumstances.

The problem was, he didn't know how extraordinary these circumstances might be. Serious enough for Frank Harden to contact him, certainly. And troubling enough for Joe to pull out all the stops to get back across the pond. Until he was in possession of some cold, hard facts, though, he couldn't see worrying Callie. Besides, this was obviously not something that could or should be discussed over the phone.

Refusing to admit he was rationalizing, he stabbed a speed-dial number and connected with the on-duty controller at his twenty-four-hour operations center. "I need out of Zurich tonight and into DC tomorrow. Any way you can work it."

"I'm on it, boss."

By the time he'd thrown his toiletries in his shaving kit and stuffed his spare clothes in his carryall, the controller called back to confirm the Zurich airport was still open.

"You're in luck. Flights look iffy for later tonight, but right now they're keeping the runway plowed and the planes deiced. I got you on Lufthansa leaving for New York in two hours and the shuttle from there to DC. You'll have to hustle to make it."

"I'll make it."

Chapter Nine

Callie got up early enough the next morning to make a quick cup of coffee. Just one, though. What she really wanted was one of those sinfully rich white-chocolate espressos at the little café she'd discovered yesterday.

The air was still crisp and cold. Bundled against the chill, she wove through the backpacking school kids and early shoppers. The scent of hot, strong coffee and fresh-baked pastries welcomed her when she ducked inside the café. While she waited for her croissant and espresso in its elegant, silver-handled glass, her gaze roamed the framed black-and-white photos. There was Sophia Loren again, and Jack Kennedy. And a helmeted general in jodhpurs and a low-slung holster.

Patton? Could that really be Patton?

Her glass in one hand and the croissant in the other, she tried to edge past the stand-up counter crowd for a closer look. She was almost there when one of the patrons closed the lid of his computer and turned to leave. She jumped back to avoid a collision but sloshed some foamy white chocolate on his sleeve.

"Oh! *Scusi!*"

The man muttered something that didn't sound too complimentary under his breath and grabbed a napkin to dab at his jacket sleeve.

"I'm sorry," Callie said in English. "I hope it didn't get in your laptop."

He jerked his head up and stared at her with unfriendly eyes. Then he turned on one heel and shouldered his way unceremoniously through the crowd.

"Ohhh…kay," she said to his back, "And no, I didn't splash hot coffee on my hand and burn myself, but thanks for asking."

Shrugging off the incident, she enjoyed the croissant and what was left of her espresso, then headed for the center.

Her second day on the job turned out to be even busier than the first. She sat in on another group therapy session at nine and attended an occupational assessment workshop at eleven. With the aid of a translator, a job placement specialist gently probed a sad-eyed, stoop-shouldered young widow for possible employment choices.

Callie joined a table of three women at lunch. Although English wasn't their native language, all three spoke it with varying degrees of proficiency. One, the victim of a vicious disfigurement by a jealous husband, hid the gaping hole where the tip of her nose had been cut off behind a veil. A native of Bangladesh, Leela had contacted an IADW outreach worker after that same loving husband had driven her out of their home with a whip.

"Simona says the doctors can fix my face," she murmured in soft, very British English. "She says she will tell Prince di Lorenzo to arrange it."

"Which he will do," one of the other women said with a smile. "He lives in fear of Simona, although he is twice her weight and so much older."

Weight, Callie agreed with. But older? Although she didn't know his for sure, she would guess the prince was somewhere in his mid-to-late thirties.

Her glance shot to the center's director seated at a table across the room. With her snowy hair and lined face, Simona certainly looked to have some years on him.

Leela followed her glance and said quietly, "She has suffered greatly, our Simona. Although she does not speak of it, it's said her hair turned white overnight."

Callie was still digesting that startling revelation when the subject of their discussion pushed away from her table and gestured for the newest member of her staff to join her. Once in the hall, the director posed a curt question.

"Are you qualified to conduct trauma therapy?"

Callie had used a trauma-focused approach with some of the children she'd worked with. Getting them to expose their memories and fears resulting from abuse or other trauma required a delicate touch, however.

"It's been a while…"

The tentative response sent an impatient flicker across the director's face. A younger face, Callie could see now, than her white hair and the deep grooves creasing her cheeks would indicate.

"Is that a yes or no?" she asked curtly.

"Yes."

"*Bene!* I want you to work with Amal. Maybe you can connect with her. God knows none of the rest of us can."

"I'll try my best."

"You do that. You do that."

Callie had to conduct an extensive search for the pregnant woman. She finally found her tucked in a corner of the second-floor arts and crafts room. She was almost completely hidden behind an artificial palm that the center's Christian residents had draped with handmade stars and silver tinsel. The small crèche under the palm reminded Callie of the purchases she'd made in Naples. She would take them out of their wrapping when she got home, she decided, and set up a little bit of Christmas in her apartment. Kate and Dawn and Tommy would just have to wait for their gifts. But first...

"Hello, Amal."

The quiet greeting startled the other woman. She whipped her head around, her dark eyes frightened, and made an instinctive move to shield the clipboard in her lap. Callie caught just a glimpse of a pencil drawing on the top sheet of the paper before the loose sleeve of Amal's robe covered it.

One glimpse was enough. With hardly more than a dozen bold strokes, the woman had masterfully interpreted the clean, fluid lines of Michelangelo's *David*.

"Oh," Callie breathed. "That's beautiful." She gestured in an attempt to overcome their language barrier. "Please, may I see it?"

Amal's arm remained firmly positioned over the sketch. The fear had left her eyes, but there was no mistaking the message they now conveyed. Ignoring the back-off signal, Callie did a quick scan of the room. The game table held a pencil and small pad for score-keeping. She grabbed both.

"I took a few art classes in school," she confessed as she dragged a chair over and positioned it next to the stone-faced woman. "Mostly art history, although I do like to draw. Unfortunately I'm not very good."

According to Simona, their best guess was that Amal had survived the tragic sinking of a refugee boat from Syria. Callie didn't know a word of Arabic. But she'd used art therapy with children many times in her previous job and knew it could cross generational barriers. She hoped it would cross language barriers, as well.

"This is me." She sketched a fairly decent female figure with longish hair. "This is where I'm from."

She added a quick backdrop of Boston's skyscrapers, although she knew each stroke was a calculated risk. The US and its allies were waging an air war in Syria. Amal's father or brothers or husband might have fought—might *still* be fighting—either with or against rebel forces. Yet everything Callie had been taught, every nugget of experience she'd gained over her years as a counselor, dictated that she lay a foundation of honesty.

"And this is you."

Flipping to a clean page, she stretched the limits of her artistic skills with a quick portrait of a figure wearing a head scarf. Then she held the sketch out to the silent woman at her side.

"Where are you from?"

Callie knew she risked alienation by pushing too hard. Possibly total and irrevocable shutdown. Yet the longer Amal hesitated, the harder Callie's heart hammered. Finally the other woman reached for the pad, but her hand trembled so violently that she snatched it back.

"It's okay," Callie said quietly. "You're safe here."

She knew Amal couldn't understand her. Knew, too, that platitudes meant little to a woman who'd lost everything. She held her breath as Amal retrieved the pad. Then slowly, so slowly, the other woman sketched a backdrop to the solitary figure.

Despite the small size of the canvas she had to work with, the layers came together in stark, minimalistic detail. Bombed buildings. Piles of rubble. Children with eyes too large for their skeletal faces. Just as slowly, she added another rendering of Michelangelo's *David*. Curly haired. Square jawed. With fierce eyes and a lethal-looking semiautomatic held waist high.

"Is this…" Callie had to stop, pull in a breath. "Is this your husband?"

Her question drew no response. The other woman stared down at the sketch for long moments. Then her pencil lashed out. Suddenly. Violently. Slashing from right to left so viciously that the paper shredded and Callie had to grab her wrist to stop the desecration.

"Amal! It's okay! You're safe here. You and your baby. You're both safe."

With a guttural sound, the other woman jerked free and thrust out of her chair. Her own sketch jammed tight against her chest, she whirled and ran out of the room.

Callie didn't go after her. She wanted to. Ached to. But training and experience kept her riveted in place. The next move—if there was one!—had to come from Amal.

Still, doubts stung like an angry swarm of wasps as she went downstairs to her office and powered up her computer. Simona's instructions had been specific. Case files were to be updated daily. No excuses, no delays. Any counseling sessions with residents, either one-on-one or in group, went in their file.

Callie curved her fingers over the keyboard while she organized her thoughts. Then entered the password, pulled up Amal's case file and battled the excruciatingly slow system to detail her failed attempt to bridge the communication gap. The entry complete, she grimaced at the flickering screen. So much for proving to Simona Alberti that she wasn't just another of Carlo's do-gooders. She logged out, wondering how long it would take before the director jumped down her throat.

Simona pigeonholed her that same evening, not long after Callie arrived at Nikki Dukakis's spacious flat.

Nikki's husband answered the door. The Greek was seriously gorgeous and wreathed in the same hot, spicy aroma that wafted from the rear of the apartment.

"I'm Dominic Dukakis," he said as he took her coat, hanging both it and her shoulder bag on an antique clothes tree in the hall. "And you must be Carlo's American."

Not quite sure how to respond to that one, she merely smiled and held out her hand. "Callie Langston."

"Come in, come in. Nicola's in the kitchen. I'll tell her you're here and fetch you a glass of wine. Or would you prefer ouzo?"

"Wine, please. Red, if you have it."

"Of course."

"Simona's here, too," he said as he gestured to a wide archway that opened onto a high-ceilinged room. "If you care to join her, I'll bring your wine."

"'Carlo's American,'" Simona echoed sardonically

when Callie joined her. "I've no doubt you'll wear that label until his next 'friend' takes your place."

"I've worn worse."

The calm reply earned a sharp look from the director, followed by a reluctant nod. "I don't doubt you have. I read your update in Amal's file," she added in a quick change of direction.

Callie braced herself, but to her surprise, the snowy-haired Simona gave her an unexpected stroke.

"You accomplished what none of us have been able to do. You connected with her."

"Only for a few moments."

"You connected," Simona repeated.

Encouraged by the unexpected praise, Callie shared her thoughts. "Amal whipped a detailed background sketch out so quickly, with such bold, sure strokes. I'm sure she's had formal training. She's that good."

"What are you thinking? That she might be an established artist?"

"Very possibly. I'm going to surf the net and see what I turn up. In the meantime, I'll try to connect with her via art again. Perhaps use it as a springboard for trauma therapy, as you recommended, or adult cognitive behavioral therapy."

Simona cocked her head, her blue eyes piercing. "You're trained in adult CBT?"

"I worked primarily with children in my last job, but I volunteered one weekend a month at the Boston VA hospital. We found CBT to be a very useful tool when working with patients suffering from post-traumatic stress."

The director glanced away. "*Sì,*" she murmured. "It can be."

Whatever she was seeing, it wasn't the impression-istic rendition of Mykonos's famous windmills that occupied a good portion of the far wall. Callie knew better than to probe. Not that she would anyway in a social setting. Instead she stood quietly until the Italian shook off her memories and deliberately changed the subject.

"We don't make Christmas a big celebration at the center, you understand."

"I would guess not, since so many of the residents are of different faiths."

"We try to accommodate those who are Christians, however. So if you have no plans for…"

"Here you are." The interruption came from Dominic, who returned with a bowl-shaped glass. "This is from the vineyard of Katogi and Strofilia, in northern Greece. Although Carlo would never agree, I think you'll find it as good—or better!—than any Italian red. And speaking of our xenophobic prince," he said as the doorbell jangled, "that will be him."

Callie could never quite pin down what it was about Carlo di Lorenzo that seemed to expand whatever room he entered. It certainly wasn't his appearance. The man was a fireplug, as wide at the middle as he was through the shoulders. What's more, his shiny bald spot had crept forward another inch or two since Callie had last seen him at Dawn and Brian's wedding. But his dark eyes danced above his luxuriant handlebar mustache, and no woman alive could remain immune to his obvious delight as he crossed the room, his hands outstretched.

"Calissa, *cara mia!*"

"Ciao, Carlo."

He took her hands in both of his and raised them to his lips with a dramatic flourish that had her smiling, Dominic grinning and Simona rolling her eyes.

"You grow more beautiful every day, Calissa. But

this…" He dropped his gaze to her ring and twisted his lips in exaggerated sorrow. "I couldn't believe it when Joe told me that you were engaged. Surely you cannot mean to marry that block of wood. Not when I have offered to show you the delights of Marrakech and Bali."

"Her," Simona said with a small snort, "and a hundred other women."

"Ah, yes." With a spectacularly unsuccessful attempt to hide a grimace, the prince released Callie's hands and turned to face his nemesis. "Dominic told me you would be here, *il Drago*."

Callie stiffened, expecting fireworks, but Simona Alberti seemed to take the label as a tribute.

"And you still came. How very brave of you," she drawled, the sarcasm as sharp as dagger points.

He drew himself up to his full height, which put him almost at eye level with the director. He looked, Callie thought, like a mastiff going nose to nose with a whip-thin greyhound. Simona didn't appear the least intimidated, but before either of them went for the throat, Nikki strolled in from the kitchen.

"Sorry, everyone. I must confess I'm a better nurse than cook. Dominic, my darling, get Carlo a drink. And check the dolmades."

Sending her husband on his way with an airy wave, Nikki kissed Callie on both cheeks and received one of Carlo's flamboyant greetings.

"Ciao, Nicola. You're far too beautiful for that lump of Greek clay you're married to. Since I can't convince Callie to run away with me, perhaps I can talk you into abandoning Dominic and allowing me to show you the wonders of—"

"Yes, yes, we know," Simona interrupted with unconcealed irritation. "Marrakech or Bali or the South

Pole. Now, for pity's sake, may we stop this nonsense and discuss something actually important?"

"By all means," Carlo returned with soft, silky menace. "Please tell me, Madam Director, what's so important that we must dispense with civility?"

Whoa! Callie had only ever seen the prince at his most charming. This combination of haughty aristocrat and ice-edged commander made her blink and Nikki step in hastily to defuse the situation.

"It's the computers, Carlo. Simona and I were talking about them before you arrived. They're old and slow."

Callie couldn't help recalling her frustrating session just a few hours ago. "Not just the computers. The wireless router, too. The signal's so weak it takes forever to get online."

"When we can get on at all," Nikki put in.

"If I'm to submit the ridiculously detailed reports you and the board require," Simona said tartly, "I must have the tools to do it."

"*Madre di Dio!*" Palms up, Carlo surrendered with a return of his urbane smile. "How can I withstand the onslaught of three such determined women? I'll get you what you need."

The promise won delighted thank-yous from Callie and Nicola and a curt nod from Simona.

"See that you do." The brusque order wiped the smile off Carlo's face. If the director noticed his sudden scowl, however, she ignored it. "Nikki, I think I smell something burning. Shall we go help Dominic in the kitchen?"

"*Ochi!*"

Their hurried departure left Callie standing beside an obviously irate Carlo. A growl rolled up from deep

in his chest as he shot narrow-eyed darts at their re-
treating backs.

"She never allows me the last word, that one. Never!"

Callie had no trouble guessing which she he referred to.

"If she were one of my troops, I would have her up on
charges of insubordination," he steamed. "But does she
care that she shows me little respect? Does she worry
that the entire board quakes every time she comes before them? No, damn her, no. Instead, she makes me
burn to kiss that condescending smirk off her face every
time I'm with her!"

Callie jaw went slack. Mouth open, she gaped at the
furious prince and fumbled for a response. *Any* kind
of a response. Thankfully, she was saved by the bell.

The loud jangle brought Dominic's head popping out
of the kitchen door. With it came a cloud of gray smoke.

"Carlo, *aprire la porta, per favore.*"

The prince balked, obviously torn between answering
"*la porta*" and making a quick call to the fire department. He threw out a spate of urgent Italian and Dominic
returned what Callie sincerely hoped were hearty reas-
surances. Still, she decided to retrieve her phone from
the purse she'd left hanging in the hall and keep it close
at hand. Just in case. She'd taken only a few steps, however, when she got her second shock in as many minutes.

"Ciao, Giuseppe."

With a mix of surprise, confusion and pure joy, she
watched the prince greet the former chief of his special
security detail with a hearty thump on the shoulder.

"I thought you'd left Rome," di Lorenzo commented.

"I flew home last night and did a quick turnaround."

"That was indeed quick. But why would you…"

He broke off as Joe's glance shot past him and fixed
on Callie.

"Of course." The prince's mustache lifted in a wicked grin. "I would not leave her alone too long, either, were I you."

"Yeah," Joe drawled. "That was pretty much my thinking."

Callie had recovered enough to take exception to that bit of blatant chauvinism. Which she would certainly have done, if Joe hadn't sniffed the air and suddenly stiffened.

"Jesus! Is this place on fire?"

"I'm not sure," Carlo admitted. "I'll go see."

Joe took advantage of his departure to cross to where Callie stood and brush his mouth over hers. As light as the kiss was, she felt the scrape of the bristles darkening his cheeks and chin. She also took note of the red rimming his eyelids and the deep creases bracketing his mouth.

"What's happened, Joe? Why did you turn right around and fly back in Rome?"

"Not here," he said with a small shake of his head.

She didn't bother to ask how he'd known where to find her. She did, however, want to know why he hadn't held to his end of the bargain they'd negotiated a few days ago.

"How come you didn't let me know you were coming right back?"

"Check your phone."

Frowning, she dug it out of her shoulder bag and discovered it was in silent mode. She'd set it on vibrate before the therapy session she'd sat in on this morning, she now remembered, and had forgotten to take it off. She also discovered two voice mails, both from Joe, and four texts, two from him and one each from Kate and Dawn.

"You need to leave the ringer on, Callie."

"I don't want it going off during therapy sessions."

"Then keep it in your pocket, not your purse. So you'll feel it vibrate."

"Why?" she asked again. "What's going on?"

"We'll talk about it at your place. Right now we'd better…"

A wild clanging shrieked through the air. Callie winced and clapped her hands over her ears, thunking herself with the phone in the process.

"Smoke detector," Joe shouted over the din. "Open the door and some windows. I'll see what the hell's happening in the kitchen."

Stuffed grape leaves. That's what was happening. Tight little rolls filled with ground lamb, rice, chopped onion, minced garlic and fragrant spices.

Once they extinguished the fire, Nikki and Dominic and their guests discovered that one of the dolmades had somehow tipped out of the baking pan and fallen unnoticed to the back of the oven. It toasted to a blackened crisp before igniting and setting the remaining appetizers and a pan of souvlaki ablaze.

The cleanup didn't actually take all that long. Dominic drenched the charred remains in the sink, then carried both pans out to the balcony while Nikki assured anxious neighbors their homes weren't about to go up in flames. In the meantime Carlo, Joe, Simona and Callie waved dish towels to dispel the acrid smoke.

Dominic joined their effort after his trip to the balcony. Flapping a towel vigorously, he threw Joe a curious look. "Have we met?"

"Name's Russo. Joe Russo. I came to find Callie."

"Oh. Well, thanks for helping out here, Joe."

"No problem."

* * *

Fifteen minutes later their collective efforts had replaced most of the smoke with cold night air, and Nikki had been introduced to her uninvited guest. Like Dominic, she thanked Joe for coming to the rescue, then suggested they all repair to a nearby restaurant.

"We promised you dinner," she insisted. "It'll take a while yet for the apartment to totally air out, and I don't intend to turn the stove on again tonight. Maybe ever. I did mention, didn't I, that I'm a much better nurse than cook?"

"You are," Simona confirmed before adding a tart, "thank goodness."

Laughing, her husband retrieved their guests' coats and shepherded them out into the night. Still puzzled by Joe's unexpected return, Callie tucked her arm in his and asked quietly whether they should beg off dinner.

"No, this'll work. I need to talk to Carlo. I'll get him aside for a few minutes at the restaurant."

His discussion with the prince took place in a quiet corner of the bar. Callie watched them from the table in the noisier eating area, Joe's head bent close to Carlo's, the prince listening with a frown.

Both men wore neutral expressions when they rejoined the group, and Callie was forced to bridle her unease until she and Joe returned to her apartment some two hours later. She waited until they'd shed their coats and gloves and scarves, dumped some grounds in the coffeemaker and pointed to the kitchen chairs.

"Now," she demanded when they faced each other across the tiny table. "Why are you here? What's going on?"

"Someone's been making inquires about the center. Someone my contact at the Defense Intelligence Agency thought had been taken out."

"Taken out? As in…?"

"Made dead," Joe said flatly. "Bastard was driving a vehicle that took a direct hit from a drone five months ago. My contact thinks now the driver might've been someone who looked so much like the target that whoever called in the strike got it wrong."

"And this…this target is interested in the center? Why?"

"We're not sure. Best guess is because he knows one of the current residents."

That might be their best guess, but there were others. Callie knew Joe well enough now to sense he was holding back. Shielding her. Trying to protect her from the big, bad, ugly world.

"What are the other possibilities?"

"They're a stretch, Callie. Not credible threats."

"Tell me."

He didn't want to frighten her. She could see it in his eyes.

"Tell me."

He answered reluctantly. "One scenario says the women at the center have forsaken their honor by fleeing their homelands and adopting the decadent ways of the West."

"So they should be punished. As if they haven't already been punished enough," she added savagely. "What else?"

"It's the other side of the same coin. You people at the center are working a hidden agenda. In the guise of helping refugees, you're forcing them to deny their heritage, their religion."

"So *we* should be punished."

"Like I said, these scenarios are out there. Not credible."

"Credible enough for you to jump on a plane and come straight back to Rome," she pointed out.

He couldn't argue with that, and Callie couldn't believe they were actually sitting here talking about drone strikes and retaliating against helpless women who'd already suffered so much.

This was Joe's world, she thought with a fist-size knot in her throat. And now hers.

"How much did you tell Carlo?" she asked after a futile attempt to swallow the lump.

"Enough. He's going to advise the other members of the board."

"What about Simona? You have to tell her, too."

"Carlo and I plan to brief her tomorrow."

"She's not going to like this."

"Got that impression." Joe's gray eyes flickered with something she might have mistaken for amusement under other circumstances. "Funny, I've never known di Lorenzo to go six shades of pale at the mere mention of a woman's name. Your boss must put him and the rest of the board through the wringer."

Callie didn't comment. She still hadn't quite processed the prince's earlier outburst, wasn't even sure now that she'd heard him correctly.

"I thought I'd camp out here for a few days," Joe said casually. Too casually. "Or we could move to a hotel. It would give us a little more space."

She glanced around the tiny apartment with its bright yellow walls and incredible view. She hadn't put much of a personal stamp on it yet. Just angled the kitchen table so she could drink in the sight of St. Peter's dome with her morning coffee and set out the nativity figures she'd bought in Naples. They rubbed shoulders on her postage stamp of an end table. Dawn's flame-haired angel, Tommy's Disney figure, Kate's despised political candidate and the traditionally robed Joseph.

Her gaze shifted from the Virgin Mary's protector to her own. With a sense of inevitability, Callie accepted that her Joe wasn't going anywhere any time soon.

"Let's stay here."

Chapter Ten

Joe had agreed to meet Carlo at the center at eight thirty. Their plan was to beard the director in her den before the problems and events of the day distracted her or fired her temper.

He woke at his usual five o'clock and lay in the shuttered stillness, trying to shift his focus from the warm butt nested against his groin to the sparse data Frank Harden had shared.

The known aliases of the terrorist supposedly taken out by the drone strike. A list of atrocities attributed to the man as verified through human, signal, geopolitical and open-source intelligence. A blurred photo taken from a half mile away. The date, time and coordinates of the airstrike that had—supposedly—taken him out. There was nothing to suggest the bastard had survived the hit. Nothing, that was, except the recent queries about the center operated by IADW.

The probes themselves were innocuous enough.

None would've triggered an alert if not for the fact they'd been made on the same laptop previously owned by the target of the strike. A laptop that went off-line at the precise instant the drone hit. A laptop that had come back online only two days ago.

US cyberspooks had pinpointed the source of the transmissions. By triangulating cell towers and satellite systems, they'd zoomed in on a squalid, teeming tenement in Palermo, on the island of Sicily. A door-to-door search by Italian security forces hadn't yielded the laptop, however, or any indication of who might have powered it up.

Joe had his own people working the problem—his cybersecurity folks at home, Emilio Mancera here in Italy. The affable Roman had met him at the airport last night, gotten a quick briefing and put one of his own men on a flight to Palermo an hour later.

If the residents of that squalid tenement had withheld any information from the police, Emilio's man would squeeze it out of them. He knew the island, knew the inner workings of the criminal element that still flourished there. Knew, too, that the Mafia had shed its skin several times over the decades. They were still heavily into narcotics and protection rackets, of course, but now funneled their profits into legitimate businesses like shopping malls and hotels and apartment complexes...all built by a construction industry that operated on bribes, kickbacks and corruption. Without a single twinge of conscience, Joe had given the green light to apply all three if necessary.

In the meantime, he and Carlo would work the problem from this end. Starting with a thorough scrub of the backgrounds of each and every resident at the center and...

"Nmmg."

The indistinct mumble was accompanied by a twitch that sent Joe's thoughts sliding sideways. He held himself still, his breath stuck in his throat, as Callie wiggled again.

She couldn't seem to find a satisfactory position. With another mumble, she straightened one knee. Bent it again. Canted her hips. Thrust her bottom, and put Joe in an instant sweat.

"Callie. Sweetheart."

He tried to ease back a few inches. She wiggled again and locked onto him with the precision of a laser-guided heat-seeking missile. Smothering a curse, Joe shifted his head on the pillow and threw a glance at the window. His internal clock said it was still predawn. The blackened shutters confirmed that.

Hell! No way he could hold out until six or seven. Not hard and hurting like there was no tomorrow. If he and Callie hadn't ended last night with an extended tussle between the sheets, he might've rolled her over and initiated a repeat performance. But she'd collapsed on his chest, and Joe had barely found enough strength to drag up the covers before they were both out.

He'd let her sleep, he decided, and use this quiet time to contact his cybergeeks. He'd check in with Emilio, too. But not here. Somewhere that served thick, black, vein-opening coffee.

Callie was still dead to the world when he returned with two espressos and a paper sack of fresh-baked pastries. It didn't take long for the seductive aromas to penetrate her consciousness. Especially after Joe held a still-warm *cornetto* mere inches from her nose. She blinked awake, stared owlishly at the marmalade-filled bun and slicked her tongue over sleep-dry lips.

"Does that taste as good as it smells?"

"Only one way to find out."

An arm snaked out from under the blankets. Fingers latched onto the sticky sweet. Three bites later, a tousled head of mink-brown hair popped up.

"Any more where that came from?"

"On the kitchen table. Espresso, too."

He smiled as she lit up like the gaudy Christmas decorations strung across the streets outside. Rolling out of bed, she dragged a blanket around her like a tent and made for the kitchen.

"I waited for you to wake up to take a shower," he commented. "I'll make it quick."

She was too busy exploring the contents of the bag to do more than flap a distracted hand.

Joe emerged fifteen minutes later showered and shaved. Callie took considerably longer, but the results were definitely worth the wait. The steamy shower had left a delicate blush on her cheeks, and her hair fell in glossy, raisin-dark waves above a sky blue turtleneck sweater. The worry was back, though, shadowing her eyes to a purple so deep they looked almost black.

"What time did you say Carlo is going to meet us at the center?"

"Eight thirty. But it might be better if you stay out of this one."

"Why?"

"Your boss is already torqued at me for asking to review the center's screening process. Even more at Carlo for insisting it happen. No need to get her pissed at you, too."

Callie didn't comment but had to admit she was secretly happy to stay out of the line of fire.

Unfortunately, she didn't stay out of it long.

Bundled in boots, jeans, a warm sweater and her wool duster, she huddled close to Joe's side for the short walk to the center. Carlo was already there and looking none too thrilled with the task ahead.

Callie peeled off with a murmured "good luck" and headed for her office to prepare for the nine o'clock group session. When she came out twenty minutes later, notebook in hand, Simona's door was closed. The thick panel didn't quite block the sound of raised voices, though, or the thump of something banging down on the desk. Simona's palm? Carlo's fist?

She didn't stick around to find out. But when she got to the session room, the news that the mental-health tech who normally conducted this group therapy had called in sick added another wrinkle to the day. Luckily, the group was a small one. Only one translator and four participants: the two teens who'd escaped brutal sexual slavery, the disfigured wife from Bangladesh and the sad-eyed, stoop-shouldered young widow. Hiding her nervousness at being thrust into the role of facilitator as opposed to observer, Callie picked up where they'd left off yesterday.

"We were talking about how we see ourselves, and how what we've experienced colors our self-image."

She waited for the translator, then picked her way carefully over sensitive ground.

"Too often when something bad happens to us, something we can't control, we think it's our own fault. We feel guilty, anxious. Unable to make decisions or relate to others."

The woman from Bangladesh drew her veil tighter across her mutilated face and murmured something Callie couldn't quite catch.

"I'm sorry. What did you say?"

"A leper," Leela said in her soft, British-accented English. "I feel like a leper. I show myself to no one."

The thinner of the two teens spoke next. A single word, muted, reluctant.

"Unclean," the interpreter translated. "After what was done to her, she feels unclean."

Callie nodded and looked to the other two participants. The young widow shrank back against her chair and shook her head, but the second teen, the one named Sabeen, chose to speak out. Usually so happy and giggly, she launched into an angry spate that set the beads at the ends of her braids dancing and the words whistling through the gap in her front teeth.

"She, too, feels dirty," the interpreter related, hurrying to keep. "She bathes two or three times a day but cannot wash the smell of those pigs off her skin, out of her hair."

As if to emphasize her feelings, the girl grabbed a fistful of the braids and shook them angrily.

"Sabeen says she would cut them off. All of them. As she would cut off the thing between the legs of every man who took her."

"Well..."

Callie was treading delicate ground here. For all she knew, those colorful beads denoted rank or marital status in the tribe these girls had been abducted from. They'd chosen not to return to their tribe, however, deciding instead to make a tortuous journey to another country, another way of life.

"Why *not* cut them off?" she asked gently. "The

braids, I mean. Although I think castrating the pigs who hurt her is a pretty good idea, too."

The question was obviously one the girl had debated before. A host of emotions flickered across her face, not least of which was fear of losing the last vestige of her identity in this foreign world.

Callie waged a similar internal debate. She was here to facilitate, not direct. Enable, not lead. Yet she couldn't force herself to remain detached and neutral and merely nurturing. Something drove her to bridge the seeming impossible gulf between these women's world and her own.

"Hang tight," she instructed through the interpreter. "I'll be right back."

She hurried down the hall to her office, throwing a quick glance at Simona's closed door as she went. She didn't hear any raised voices or loud thumps and couldn't decide whether that was a good or bad omen. Joe could be pretty intimidating when he wanted to, she knew. Carlo, too, as she'd discovered last night. Simona would have to be made of kryptonite to stand up to both of them. And after having known the director for all of two days and a few hours, her money was on the director.

Once in her office, Callie riffled through her desk drawer for a pair of scissors. She found them in a bottom drawer, then rooted around in her purse for her handy-dandy little travel mirror. Clutching both objects, she hurried back to the session room.

"I haven't suffered as you have," she told the other women through the translator. "I haven't experienced anything that could even remotely compare to what you've suffered. But, like you, I'm beginning a new life in a new place. So I think... No, I *know*. I'm ready for a new me."

Brandishing the scissors, she held the mirror at arm's length and tried unsuccessfully to wield the scissors with the other.

"I could use some help here. Will someone please hold the mirror for me?"

The interpreter looked as hesitant as the four residents. When none of them replied, Callie dropped the mirror, grabbed a hank of her hair, and hacked off a good eight inches.

Leela sprang to her feet, half laughing, half scandalized. "Buddha preserve us!"

Her veil slipped, revealing a glimpse of her horrific disfigurement, before she threw the ends over her shoulder again and grabbed the scissors.

"I will do it. But only if you really wish me to."

"Whack away," Callie instructed cheerfully.

Within a remarkable short period of time, hair lay in heaps on the floor. Callie's dark brown. Sabeen's black braids. Leela's hennaed tresses.

Sabeen kept slapping her hand over her mouth to contain her giggles, but her infectious laughter soon drew a half dozen curious residents. Then Nikki. Then an obviously irritated Simona.

"What goes on here?"

"Hair therapy."

Grinning, Callie shook her short, surprisingly curly locks. She felt pounds lighter and thought she looked like a completely different person. Unfortunately, her boss wasn't impressed.

"*Hair* therapy? Is that some new American fad?"

The scorn behind the question cut as sharp and as

deep as the words themselves. Smiles slipped. Expressions turned worried. Sabeen passed a nervous palm over her new buzz cut.

"It's hardly a fad." Callie's response was cool and level. "You might want to read Dr. Elaine Boyer Barrington's *Adaptive Therapies for Female Adolescents.* Her work merely reinforces the basic fact that a teenager's hairstyle is one of the most obvious indicators of her feeling of self-worth. So obvious, in fact, that therapists too often fail to ascribe it the significance they should."

Simona's brows snapped together, but she didn't challenge Callie in front of the others. Instead, she merely glowered and issued a terse command.

"I want to speak with you. In my office."

"Of course. I'll just sweep up the hair and…"

"We'll take care of it," the translator said quickly.

"Thanks."

With a smile and another toss of her short, who-would've-guessed-it curls, Callie followed her boss. Simona marched down the hall, her back stiff and her chin held at a combative angle.

"Adaptive therapies?" she huffed. "Dr. Elaine whoever Barrington? If I go online and do a search, will I find either?"

"I'd be very surprised."

"So you invented all that nonsense?"

"No, I didn't. I knew Elaine in grad school. She was a very innovative thinker but switched careers after earning her PhD. Last I heard, she and her husband were operating a treetop guest lodge in Tanzania."

Simona stopped with one hand on the doorknob of her office. Blue fire shot from her eyes. "Are you playing with me? If you are, I'll tell you now I'm not in the mood for it."

No kidding. Didn't take a genius to see her meeting with Carlo and Joe hadn't gone well and Callie was about to take the heat for it.

"Well," she said with a calm smile, "the treetop lodge might be in Zimbabwe."

Those blue lasers narrowed dangerously. Callie kept her smile in place but felt the narrowness of her escape when the director whirled and thrust open the door. She stomped in, waited for Callie to follow, then slammed it shut and wasted no time on preliminaries.

"The prince and your fiancé shared some disturbing news."

"Joe told me about it last night."

Simona resorted to the classic Italian gesture. Bringing the fingertips of one hand together, she waved it up and down. Despite her short time in Rome, Callie had seen the gesture often enough to know the most polite interpretation was *What the hell?*

"I cannot not believe this. My center, the target of inquiries by a dead terrorist! It is not to be believed."

Her accent thickened with each word, along with her indignation.

"I think," Callie replied carefully, "that we should trust Joe's instincts."

"The prince most certainly does," her boss huffed. "He informs me—*informs* me, you understand—that your Joe considers our security totally inadequate."

Callie couldn't help thinking of the rusted panel beside the front door. "Well..."

"The prince also informs me," Simona fumed, "that your fiancé sends one of his subordinates to install additional equipment."

Emilio Mancera, Callie guessed, Joe's very efficient head of operations here in Rome.

"I don't see why you would object to a little additional security," she said cautiously.

"Ha! You see no problem?" Bristling from the ends of her superfine white hair to the tip of her indignantly quivering nose, Simona folded her arms across her chest. "Then perhaps you agree that Carlo and your fiancé should have access to our case files."

"What?"

"Ah. So you didn't know?" The director assumed an expression of fake surprise. "Your fiancé didn't tell you that he wants to sit down with us? To go through every case file?"

"No, he did not."

Callie was more indignant than she'd been in longer than she could remember. At Joe, for not discussing this with her before springing it on her boss. At Simona, for thinking she would condone such a breach of ethics.

"And if he *had* discussed it with me," she added icily, "I would've given him the same answer I suspect you did."

Her obvious ire defused some of the director's. Simona's chin lost its pugnacious thrust and a satisfied smirk replaced her fake surprise.

"But, yes! I told him, '*Non lasciatevi la porta si colpisce nel culo sulla via d'uscita.*'"

Callie had picked up enough Italian to string "*porta*" and "*uscita*" together. "I got it. You told him not to let the door hit him in the ass on his way out."

"*Sì!*"

She bit her lip. She wasn't ready to let go of her indignation just yet, but the thought of this tiny sprite of a woman unceremoniously booting Joe out of her office shaved off some of its sharp edge.

"Well," she admitted after a moment, "I probably wouldn't have given him that exact answer. But close enough."

"Are you sure, Calissa? You really feel this way?"

"For pity's sake, Simona…"

"Do not fire up at me! Carlo and your bedmate have given me enough grief."

"Our intake interviews and case files are privileged information. Carlo must know that. Joe, too."

He had to. He couldn't have been in the security business without smacking up against privacy laws. Although… With an inner grimace, Callie shoved the suspicion that he might've found a way around, over or under a few of those rules and regulations to the back of her mind.

"Carlo does indeed know it," Simona confirmed, "but he says he will take the matter to the board. We will soon be caught in the middle of a fight."

"It won't be my first time."

"Yes?" The director cocked her head. "You've battled with this fiancé of yours before?"

"We've had a few differences," Callie conceded, "but we sat down and discussed them like rational adults. We'll do the same in this instance, too."

"Ha!"

"We will! But…" she said, coming off her haughty stand, "perhaps I'd better take another look at our operating procedures. I read through them my first morning, but I want to be sure I didn't lose anything in translation."

She was thoroughly acquainted with the standards of patient confidentiality as detailed in the American

Psychological Association's code of ethics, of course. She could also quote title and chapter of Massachusetts law that codified those standards. Her initial review of the center's operating procedures had indicated that IADW's policies mirrored APA's. Basically, client information and records of therapy sessions were confidential, with several internationally recognized exceptions.

One of those exceptions involved any reasonable suspicion of child abuse. Callie was intimately familiar with that provision. She'd had to exercise it far too often while acting as an ombudsman for children caught between warring parents or kids seemingly lost in the foster care system.

Belief that a client will harm himself or someone else was another exception to confidentiality laws. Callie had been forced to exercise that option on several occasions, as well.

She hadn't worked as much with the criteria involving lawsuits and court-mandated therapy sessions, however, and would have to dig deeper to make sure she fully understood IADW's position on each of them.

Crossing the hall to her own office, she retrieved one of the dusty black binders from atop the metal file cabinet. She still had her nose buried in the notebook some thirty minutes later when the sound of footsteps outside her door brought her head up. Expecting Simona, she blinked in surprise.

"Joe! I didn't hear the bell. How'd you get in?"

"Please." He gave her a pained look. "Tommy Ellis could pick the lock on the front door blindfolded. The one on the back door's even worse."

"Simona told me you'd decided to beef up our security."

"Just met with Emilio. He'll purchase the equipment and install it himself. What'd you do to your hair?"

She'd forgotten all about her new do. Lifting a hand, she combed her fingers through the curls. "I call it adaptive therapy. Like it?"

"Yeah, I do. Makes your eyes look even bigger. And speaking of therapy…" He wedged into the narrow space in front of her desk and claimed one of the two chairs. "I expect Simona also told you that she stonewalled Carlo and me a while ago."

"She told me you wanted access to our case files. She also said she, quite correctly, refused."

"Correctly?"

"Those files contain privileged information, Joe. You know that."

"They also contain intake interviews that document your residents' nationality and where they entered the refugee aid system. One of those interviews might reveal a link to the drone strike."

"Not every resident's home of origin is documented," Callie countered, thinking of Amal's shrouded past. "And even if that information *is* in the record, it's protected. We couldn't disclose it without the written consent of the individuals involved."

"So get their consent."

He said it so coolly. So matter-of-factly. As though extracting information was a matter of time, patience and technique, not ethics. A little shocked, Callie pressed him to understand.

"Joe, please. Listen to me. Most of these women have been severely traumatized. Simona, Nikki, the professionals here at the center…they've worked with them for weeks and in some cases months. I'm just beginning to make a few tentative connections. Yesterday, with a sketch pad. Today with this."

Her hand went to her hair again. Raking the shaggy curls. Standing them on end.

"I have to earn their trust, Joe. That won't happen if I ask them to sign a document they may not understand. One that strips them of the little privacy and dignity they have left."

He studied her through eyes that had gone as opaque and as impenetrable as the fog that rolled in across Boston Bay.

"What about our connection?" he asked after a long moment. "Our trust? You don't believe I could protect their privacy and dignity?"

She flinched and searched for a possible compromise, however shaky.

"Let me talk to Simona."

He nodded. Once. A brief dip of his chin. Then he pushed out of the chair. "You do that. And tell her Emilio should be here before noon."

"Wait! Where are you going?"

"I've got some business to take care of. I'll see you later."

Chapter Eleven

Joe labeled it a strategy session. Carlo, still smarting from the wounds he'd received during the morning's firefight with Simona, declared it a war council. Dominic Dukakis thought he'd been invited to the prince's palatial apartment on Via Zanardelli to discuss yet another proposed amendment to the hotly debated Greece-Italy pipeline.

He learned otherwise shortly after the three men gathered around a burled walnut table in the library. Leather-bound first editions lined the shelves that ran the length of two walls. Gilt-framed portraits of Carlo's ancestors covered every square inch of a third. The fourth boasted velvet-draped windows that give an unobstructed view of the Pantheon's colonnaded portico. None of the three men were interested in Emperor Hadrian's architectural gem, however.

When Joe explained the reason for the meeting to

Dominic, the Greek diplomat didn't bother debating the nebulous nature of the threat. Desperate refugees were wading ashore in his county by the thousands. Most carried with them hope for a better life. No small few, Dominic knew, carried a buried—sometimes burning— resentment toward the Western nations that had bombed or strafed in the ceaseless battle against terrorists. That one of those terrorists might have survived a direct strike and was now making inquiries about the center where Nicola Dukakis worked was all her husband needed to know.

He also didn't waste time sympathizing when Carlo related Simona's flat refusal to grant access to the center's computerized case files. His wife was a highly skilled nurse-practitioner, licensed to diagnose and treat in Greece, Macedonia and Italy. Dominic was well aware of the laws governing patient privacy and the confidentiality of medical records. Instead of railing at the system, he wanted to know what had to be done to protect the women who lived and worked at the center, his wife included.

"Emilio's there now," Joe reported. "He's installing new electronic locks with touch pads and putting motion detectors on the ground-floor windows."

Shuffling through a stack of papers, he extracted a schematic detailing all three floors of the center's interior and exterior.

"We're also installing surveillance cameras that feed to our twenty-four-hour monitoring service. Here, here, here and here."

Dominic's brows winged up. "Simona's fiercely protective of the residents' privacy. I'm surprised she consented to cameras, much less to twenty-four-hour monitoring."

"She agreed to exterior surveillance only." Joe shot Carlo a quick look. "But we're adding unobtrusive interior cameras that can be activated with the flick of a remote switch."

"By unobtrusive I assume you mean hidden."

"Correct."

"And you haven't told Simona about them?"

"Not yet."

The Greek blew a soundless whistle. "I sincerely hope I'm not in the line of fire when she discovers what you've done."

"She won't. Not with Emilio doing the installing."

"You live dangerously, my friend."

"Comes with the territory."

"Speaking of your man Emilio," Carlo put in. "Did he hear from *his* man in Palermo?"

"He did," Joe reported grimly. "His guy squeezed every contact, legitimate or otherwise, but got nothing. Whoever powered up that laptop knows how to cover his tracks."

Carlo muttered a curse while Joe shuffled the papers again and slid one across the table.

"This is a copy of the center's daily schedule. Also a list of outings planned for the next two weeks. I'll have someone shadowing each outing."

The list ran the gamut from shopping excursions to a walking tour of streets lit with holiday lights to attendance by three of the center's Christian residents at the pope's traditional Christmas Eve Mass.

"*Christós*," Dominic muttered when his gaze snagged on the last item. "Fifty or sixty thousand people jam into St. Peter's Basilica for that Mass. Another four hundred thousand fill the square outside to watch it on huge screens. Your men will have a time keeping watch on these three."

"They'll manage."

Carlo picked up from there. "I spoke to a contact at *Questura Centrale*. He agreed to step up patrols by uniformed police in the area around the center. I've also briefed the commander of the ROS."

The *Raggruppamento Operativo Speciale*, or Special Operations Group, was an elite arm of Italy's national military police, specifically established to combat terrorism and organized crime.

Dominic nodded his approval of these measures and voiced a key question. "What can I do?"

"The same thing Joe and I intend to do. Become more involved in center activities. For the next few weeks, at least."

"That may not be easy to pull off," Dominic said slowly. "Some of those women have been severely traumatized by the very men who should have protected them. Nikki understands this. Simona even more so. She allows only three men to work at the center, two cooks and one mental health tech, and Nikki says she personally vetted each of them."

"Which is why it must be the three of us," Carlo responded. "*Il Drago* can hardly object to a casual visit by Nikki's husband or Callie's fiancé. Or," he added with a twist of his lips, "the chairman of the board she supposedly reports to."

Dominic looked skeptical but withheld comment as a phone pinged. All three men instinctively checked their devices, but the text message was for Joe.

"Emilio's almost done," he reported, pushing back his chair. "I'll use checking his work as an excuse for another foray into the dragon's den."

* * *

He activate the override code on the shiny new touch pad Emilio had installed beside the front door but took care to announce his arrival by texting Callie. Her answering text was short and succinct.

I'm in session. Wait in my office.

Another text pinpointed Emilio's location. Joe found his subordinate crouched beside a low sill in a small storage room at the end of the first-floor hall. Its single window was almost obscured by stacked boxes and metal shelves jammed with an assortment of office supplies. Muttering to himself, Emilio scraped at what was probably three or four centuries of paint with a sharp-edged knife.

"These windows," he snarled to Joe in idiomatic Italian, "they're a bitch."

"Need help?"

"No, this is the last. But I could use some mineral water. Or better yet, a stiff shot of grappa."

Joe was more than happy to comply with the first request. It gave him an excuse to conduct a visual surveillance of the kitchen. He'd already studied its floor plan and assessed every possible ingress and egress point. Still, nothing compared to direct eyeballing.

The unmistakable aromas of Italy hit him the moment he pushed through the swinging door. Garlic, olive oil and the sweet, heavy cream of fettuccine Alfredo. Both of the regular cooks on the center's list of employees were present. One was busy grating fresh Romano while his associate stirred several steaming pots. When Joe asked for mineral water, the stirrer merely stabbed the tip of his spoon in the direction of a stainless steel refrigerator.

Once every nook and cranny was imprinted in his mind, Joe made his way back down the hall. A quick glance in Callie's empty office confirmed she hadn't finished her therapy session. Simona's office across the hall also stood vacant. But when Joe approached the storage room at the end of the hall, Emilio's tense voice stopped him in his tracks.

The Roman tried Italian first. Then French. Then English. Each iteration was more pleading than the last.

"It's okay. It's okay. Please! Don't do anything rash."

Every instinct on red alert, Joe dropped into a crouch. He shifted the water bottle to his left hand and dropped his right to the lightweight Ruger nested in its ankle holster.

"I see what you want," Emilio said. "No! It's okay! It's okay! You do it. Take my knife. Go ahead, take it."

Joe was still in a crouch, still strung wire tight, when he caught the soft thud of footsteps on the stairs at the far end of the hall. He spun around and spotted Callie frozen halfway down the spiral staircase, her eyes wide and questioning.

He put a finger to his lips. She got the message, but only to the extent of creeping down the remaining stairs on tiptoe. Cursing under his breath, Joe signaled for her to stay the hell back.

She froze in place again, her entire body rigid as she, too, caught the faint whisper of what Joe guessed was a naked blade slashing through cardboard. Emilio's voice followed a few second later.

"There. Take as much as you want." A pause, a gentler tone. "When's your baby due?"

Oh, God, Callie thought. That was Amal in there

with Emilio. Amal, who never spoke a word but could sketch like this century's answer to Michelangelo. Amal, who might give birth any day, surrounded by strangers. Callie knew she should intervene. Should let the other woman know she wasn't…

"My name's Emilio."

She held her breath as Joe's associate waited a beat. Two. Three.

"And you?" he said softly. "What's your name?"

The tableau played out in vivid high definition inside Callie's head. The dusty storage room. The impossibly handsome Roman with his buffed-up biceps and bedroom eyes. The pregnant refugee who'd lost everything. She'd just decided to terminate the agonizing inquisition when she caught a whisper so faint she almost missed it.

"They…they call me Amal."

Callie couldn't move, couldn't breathe. Astounded, unbelieving, thrilled, she locked on Joe. He transmitted an unmistakable signal to keep silent as Emilio spun out the tenuous thread.

"Amal? That's a pretty name."

Painful seconds ticked by. Callie had almost given up hope when Amal answered in tortured whisper.

"The name is a mockery."

"Why?"

The reply was low, tortured. "In Arabic it means 'hope.' But I have none."

"Why?" Emilio asked again.

So calm. So unthreatening. Yet the single word provoked a fierce response.

"You could not understand!"

"Then tell me. Explain why you're so frightened."

Callie inched closer to Joe. She felt like a world-class voyeur but wasn't about to interrupt this fragile conversation. To her intense disappointment, it was terminated a moment later.

Amal burst out of the storage room. Her robe flattening against her distended belly, she flew past Callie and Joe. Emilio emerged almost on her heels. His handsome face contorted into a scowl as he watched her rush up the spiral staircase.

"She shouldn't run like that. She could trip," he worried. "Hurt herself or the baby."

"What was that about?" Joe demanded. "What was she doing in the storage room?"

"I'll show you." Emilio went back into the dusty storage room and returned a moment later with a still-wrapped ream of copy paper.

"Here. This is what she was after." His glance cut to Callie. "She seemed desperate for it. Why don't you take it to her?"

She knew where to look this time. As she'd anticipated, Amal had taken refuge in the corner half-hidden by the potted palm with its mantle of tinsel and silver balls.

Once again Callie signaled her presence with a soft hello. And once again the mother-to-be looked up with wide eyes and refused to return her greeting.

"Emilio…the man downstairs…he said this is what you wanted."

Callie placed the ream on the table beside Amal. Despite the other woman's blank-eyed stare, a dull red crept into her cheeks.

"You know you can have as much paper to draw with as you wish. You've only to ask."

The red deepened.

"I heard you downstairs," Callie continued gently.

"You and Emilio. I'm so glad you speak English. I've been wanting to tell you something."

That produced not much as a flicker of response but she refused to give up.

"I'm completely in awe of your artistic ability," she told the other woman. "Perhaps…perhaps we could visit some of Rome's museums together. The Borghese and the Sistine Chapel top my list."

Amal's lashes swept down, but not before Callie caught the spark that leaped in her dark eyes. Hiding her own excitement, she took that for a yes.

"The Sistine Chapel might be tough to get into this close to Christmas," she said in a deliberately conversational tone. "So many tourists here for the holidays. Why don't I go online and see if I can get us tickets for the Borghese?"

She did a quick mental shuffle of her schedule. "How about tomorrow? I'll talk to Simona and see if I can move the English class to one o'clock instead of four."

She waited a few beats. "Amal? I won't push if you don't want to go. Just tell me yes or no."

The nod was short and excruciatingly slow in coming.

"Great!" Excitement shooting through her, Callie wasn't about to give the other woman time to change her mind. "I'll go downstairs right now and check on tickets."

Joe and Emilio were still in the hall. They were deep in conversation but broke off as she approached.

"Is Amal all right?" the Roman asked with concern stamped across his face.

"She's fine. I can't believe you got her to speak to you. That's the first time she's verbally communicated with anyone."

Callie wanted to kiss him. Almost did.

"You cracked the door, Emilio, and I squeezed through after you. Amal agreed to go to the Borghese with me tomorrow afternoon. I'm going online now to see if I can reserve two tickets."

"Make it three," Joe said. "I'll go with you."

"Four," Emilio put in.

Callie hesitated. "I'm not sure that's a good idea. I barely got her to agree to go with me."

"Reserve four," Joe instructed. "If she balks at an escort, Emilio and I will keep our distance. Neither of you will see us in the crowd."

"And if there is a problem with tickets," his associate added, "my cousin's wife's brother works at the museum. He'll get us in."

Callie didn't have to resort to Emilio's relatives. She reserved four tickets for a 2:30 p.m. entrance time. She also printed out the brochure containing a map and description of the exhibit rooms and took it upstairs.

"We're all set," she told Amal. "I hope you're as excited as I am."

The gleam in the other woman's eyes was answer enough. Callie prayed that including an escort wouldn't kill it.

"Is it okay if my fiancé comes with us?" she asked. "And Emilio, the man you met downstairs. When I told them what we were planning, they both said they'd like to go."

She felt a little guilty withholding the fact that neither man was driven by a burning desire to view the Borghese's art treasures. Not guilty enough to explain the reasons for their presence, however. Primarily because Joe stressed that the precise details of the drone strike were still classified. Secondarily because Simona had yet to advise Callie on how much or how little to tell the residents.

She saw the reluctance in Amal's face and moved quickly to counter it. "That's okay. They don't have to come with us."

They'd trail along behind instead.

Callie's guilt kicked up another notch. Her professional conscience pinging, she realized she couldn't keep shading the truth like this. She'd destroy her tentative connection with this woman before it even took root.

She'd just decided to cancel the outing, or at least delay it until the security scare was over, when Amal finally communicated verbally.

"The one downstairs," she whispered in a low voice.

"Emilio?"

"He has a kind face."

That wasn't how most women would see it, Callie thought in surprise. With his melting brown eyes, noble nose and sensual mouth, Emilio Mancera was a Roman god come to life. But the fact that Amal had at last deigned to speak with her thrilled Callie so much that she instantly agreed.

"Very kind. So it's all right if he joins us? He and my fiancé?"

Amal nodded.

"Okay!" Feeling as though she'd just scaled a ten-thousand-foot mountain, she shoved the brochure she'd printed at Amal. "Here's a brochure of the museum. You can study the layout before we go tomorrow. And I checked. They have wheelchairs available if you get too tired or the baby starts to weigh you down."

The other woman's hand dropped to her swollen belly. She hesitated for long moments before revealing the first hint of her past. "We walked for many days, my babe and I. Many nights. We do not need a wheelchair."

Callie couldn't help thinking of Joe's thwarted request to review the residents' intake interviews and case files. She came close, so close, to asking Amal where she'd walked *from*. And who she'd left behind.

She resisted the urge. First, because anything Amal shared with her would still be considered privileged information. Second, because Callie's instincts warned her not to push too hard, too fast.

"Okay," she said instead, "no wheelchair. We'd better take a taxi to the museum, though. You and the baby may be able to walk that far. I can't."

Once back downstairs she confirmed arrangements with Joe and Emilio and left them to finish whatever security improvements they had left while she updated Amal's case file. That done, she braced herself to brief Simona on the breakthrough, as tentative as it was.

As she suspected, the director had yet to fully recover from her contentious meeting with Carlo and Joe. When Callie tapped on her door, she snapped out a "Come in," and looked up to give her deputy a decidedly unfriendly glare.

"Have you seen these locks your fiancé's installed?" she fumed. "They read palm prints."

"I know," Callie responded. "He had one installed at my apartment, too."

The pencil Simona was balancing between two fingers seesawed back and forth, hitting the desk repeatedly. Tap. Tap. Tap. Each tap louder and angrier than the last.

"So tell me," she demanded. "What's to stop this 'security expert' you're engaged to from running these prints through various international databases?"

"I asked him about that."

The pencil hit the desk again. Faster. Harder.

"Did you? And what did he say?"

"The same thing he and Carlo told you this morning. Any prints provided voluntarily outside a therapy session aren't protected by client-counselor confidentiality."

"Perhaps not," Simona fired back. "But running these voluntarily provided prints without their owners' consent violates their privacy."

"You'll have to argue that with Carlo. Joe said the prince got a legal opinion on the matter."

"Oh, yes," Simona huffed. "He did. From one of the half dozen judges he has tucked in his back pocket. One who apparently thinks the safety and security of the masses override our residents' rights to privacy."

After almost witnessing the Boston Marathon bombing firsthand, Callie's own feelings were too contradictory to argue the point.

"Actually," she said instead, "I came in to tell you about Amal."

"What about her?"

As she described the incident with the ream of paper and the subsequent proposal to visit the Borghese, the director's angry pencil stilled.

"And she agreed to go with you?" Simona asked incredulously.

"She did." Callie couldn't help grinning. "I booked tickets for two thirty tomorrow afternoon. Assuming you don't mind me moving the English class up to one p.m., that is."

"Of course not."

To her relief, her boss relaxed into a smile. The result was a Simona Alberti that looked years younger.

Young enough, Callie thought with an inner grin, to have snared the reluctant interest of Italy's playboy prince.

"You've gotten more from Amal in a few days than the rest of us have in a month," Simona said.

"I can't claim all the credit. Emilio coaxed her into talking to him. That broke the ice."

"This fellow, Emilio. What do you know about him?"

"Nothing other than the fact that he works for Joe."

"Are you sure it's wise to include both men in this trip to the Borghese?"

"Amal seemed okay with it."

"Don't forget that drawing you told me about. The one she destroyed. The male figure in that sketch may well represent someone she fears."

"Or hates," Callie agreed, remembering how viciously she'd slashed the drawing.

"Whatever the emotion is, it's obviously very close to the surface. Be careful you don't unintentionally trigger it."

Callie took the warning to heart but could only hope an excursion to one of Rome's most famous museums would trigger joy, not hate or fear.

Joe spent the afternoon helping scan the staff and residents' palm prints into the electronic keypads Emilio had installed at the front and back entrances. Per Simona's strict orders, they made sure everyone understood they could use the palm pad or punch in an override code. Since the code consisted of sixteen alpha and numeric digits, neither Joe nor Emilio was surprised every resident went with option A.

Joe disappeared for a while after the key pads were up and running but was waiting in the little café across

the street when Callie left work that evening. He noted
with approval that she'd dressed for the December night
in her long duster, a warm scarf and gloves After a
quick exchange with the man sharing his table, he
dodged the traffic and joined her.

"Who's that?" she asked with a glance at his companion.

"One of Emilio's crew. Are you up for a walk?"

"Sure. Where to?"

"Via Condotti. We've both been cooped up all day. I
thought you might like to stretch your legs and see the
shops all decked out in lights."

And Joe needed to buy her a Christmas present. With
everything else going on the past few days, it had almost slipped his mind.

"Ooh!" She breathed a delighted puff into the frosty
air. "I've been dying to see Via Condotti. When Kate
researched our trip this fall, she told us it's *the* street
for high-end shopping. We couldn't afford to buy anything in those absurdly expensive boutiques, but we'd
planned to cruise them anyway."

That sealed it. Her present would most definitely
come from Via Condotti.

"And at Christmastime," she related in delight, "the
window decorations are supposed to be spectacular."

Not just the window decorations, they soon discovered. The entire street was festooned for the holidays.
Monster chandeliers of twinkling white lights illuminated the thoroughfare from the foot of the Spanish
Steps to its intersection with Via del Corso. Shops tout-
ing names like Prada and Gucci and Valentino all tried
to outdo each other with spectacular displays. But Joe
and Callie both agreed Fendi took the prize.

A wide band of blue lights belted the Italian designer's four-story building. As if that wasn't eye-catching enough, the Fendi's signature logo sparkled in the white lights that comprised the belt's massive buckle. Like icing on an extravagant cake, the largest tree Joe had ever seen dominated the traffic circle in front of the store.

"Wait!" Callie dragged him to a halt and yanked her cell phone out of her purse, then stretched out her arm. "I have to send a selfie of us to Kate and Dawn."

Joe flinched. Years as a Delta Force operative had conditioned him to shy away from having his picture taken. His instinctive aversion had ramped up since Curaçao. He didn't need a visual reminder of that failed mission. Not when he could see one every time he looked in the mirror.

"I'll take the picture," he told Callie. "You don't need me in it."

"Yes, I do! Dawn and Kate were so bummed we wouldn't be together at Christmas. It's the first time since we were kids." She waved an arm at the glittering display. "I want them to see you and me together, enjoying all this."

"You've shared *every* Christmas since you were kids?"

"It's not all that hard to pull off when you grow up in the same small town," she retorted. "Hold still."

Okay. He could pose for one shot. For Callie. Still, he angled his head to hide the scar as she stiff-armed the phone. Her reach wasn't long enough. She barely caught the two of them in the frame, much less the lights.

"Let me do it."

He cradled her against his chest and framed them against both the tree and the belted building.

"Oh," she enthused. "That's better."

It was. Much better, Joe agreed. He had Callie in his arms and Rome lit like a Christmas tree behind him. Any thought of Curaçao faded. So did the worry that had goaded him like a vicious spur since Frank Harden's call. For the first time, Joe felt the joy of the season seep into his bones.

He took the shot, then Callie twisted in his arms.

"Take another."

She pushed up on her toes. Her arms hooked around his neck. Her mouth went from cool to hot as it molded his. With his arm still extended, Joe could only hope he would hit the right button on the camera app as he hooked his other arm around her waist and tugged her against him.

The applause pulled them apart. That, and a laughing suggestion from some men who'd stopped to watch the show. Luckily, the suggestion was in Italian. When Joe responded with a grin and lowered his arm, Callie grabbed the phone and switched immediately from camera to photo mode.

"Oh, my God! These are great. Look at that tree. And the Fendi belt! Hold on, I have to send the pics to Dawn and Kate."

Her thumbs flew. When she'd finished, he took her elbow and steered her toward the store entrance. Once again she dragged him to a halt.

"Joe! I can't afford anything in there."

"I can."

"We talked about this. Remember? I want to pay my own way."

"Christmas presents aren't part of that agreement."

"Maybe not. But I'm not into designer bags or belts or boots. Tell you what," she said when he started to protest. "You can buy me a print at the Borghese tomorrow. Something pretty I can frame and hang on my bright yellow walls."

He gave in, but only because he was already considering another gift…which turned out to be a smart move, because they never made it to the Borghese.

Chapter Twelve

The other half of her bed was empty when Callie
blinked awake the next morning. She groped for her
phone and peered owlishly at the digital display. Ugh!
Six fifteen. Her alarm wouldn't go off for another forty-
five minutes. She snuggled under the duvet again but
couldn't go back to sleep. The stillness in her tiny apartment was too loud.

"Joe?"

No answer. Not that she'd expected one. She stretched
lazily and wondered how in the world the man could
slide out of bed, shower and/or shave, dress and depart
without making normal human sounds.

Giving up the battle after a few more minutes of
snooze time, she stuffed her feet into slippers and
wrapped the duvet around her like a tent. When she
padded into the kitchen area, she found a note propped
against a large takeout coffee and a paper sack containing fresh ricotta-filled pastries.

"Bless you," she muttered as she pried the lid off the coffee and scanned the note. Surprise, surprise. Joe had some business to take care of.

She hitched up the duvet and carried the coffee back to the bedroom with her. In what was sure to become a daily habit, she ducked out on the tiny balcony to get her daily fix of the view. Night still shrouded the city, but the sky to the east showed streaks of purple and red. She still couldn't quite believe she was standing here, suspended above the rooftops of Rome and gawking at St. Peter's softly illuminated dome in the distance.

The frosty air drove her back inside. That, and the urge to take another look at last night's selfie. Plunking down on the side of the bed, she traded the coffee for her phone and scrolled through the photos she'd taken in the past week. As much as she missed Kate and Dawn, her Christmas season was turning out to be truly magical. Sharing Saint Lucia's day with the Audis. Mingling with the throng in Naples's street of the crèches. Last night's stroll through Via Condotti with its amazing display of lights.

She lingered over the selfie and had to smile at how Joe had positioned her in the shelter of his arms. Always the protector. Always the guardian.

Good thing they'd established boundaries this early in their relationship. Without those boundaries Callie knew it would be all too easy to succumb to the seductive promise of being petted and pampered. Now if only...

The phone vibrated in her palm. Joe, she thought. Calling to give her whatever details he could about the task that had gotten him up so early. Instead her boss's name came up on the caller ID. Surprised and just a little alarmed by the early call, Callie switched instantly from silent to speaker mode.

"Hi, Simona. Is everything okay?"

"No! Everything is *not* okay." Anger, hot and scorching, jumped through the speaker. "I want you at the center in fifteen minutes."

"Why? What's…?"

"Fifteen minutes! Not one minute later. *Capisce?*"

Agitation had stirred the director's accent. It was so thick and heavy Callie struggled to separate the furious words.

"If you take longer," her boss fumed. "If you are not here then, do not bother to come in. Just pack your bags. Go home!"

"Simona! Wait! Tell me—"

Too late. She was talking to dead air. Callie wasted several precious seconds debating whether to call her boss back. It wouldn't do any good, she realized. She needed a face-to-face to sort out whatever had Simona in such a fury. Tossing her phone aside, Callie raced for the bathroom.

She was out the door nine minutes later. Her duster flapped around her ankles as she hurried through streets just coming alive with morning traffic. With each step, she tried to figure out what she'd done to infuriate her boss.

Maybe it was her unconventional hair therapy. Had that backfired? Had one of the teens suffered a traumatic loss of identity after hacking off their long, beaded braids? Or Leela? Was the mutilated wife now mourning the loss of her hair? Could she feel it added to her disfigurement? Think that not even surgery would help her now?

Or was it Amal? Dear God, had she pushed Amal

too hard? Dragged the agreement to visit the Borghese out of her? Precipitated a panic attack? Her stomach clenching, Callie could visualize the pregnant woman springing out of bed, grabbing her pencil and viciously slashing another drawing.

With her thoughts roiling, she rounded the corner and blew out a relieved breath. Whatever had precipitated the director's summons apparently hadn't included a call to outside authorities. No police cars, no fire trucks, no ambulances or flashing strobes of any kind were parked in front of the center. The terra cotta building sat dark and silent, showing only the dim outline of a single lighted window on the ground floor.

Her office. That was her office.

More confused now than apprehensive, Callie slapped her palm against the keypad and yanked the door open. She started down the dimly lit hallway but had taken only a few steps when she caught the back-and-forth of angry voices coming from her office.

Simona. And Carlo. Trading such fast and furious Italian that Callie couldn't catch even a gist of their heated conversation. She was about to call out when something banged against the metal file cabinet and Simona issued what sounded like a sneering taunt. Then, suddenly, the taunt ended on a squawk.

Uh-oh. This was not good. Not good at all.

Like a bright red warning light, the prince's startling revelation that he itched to kiss the condescending smirk off the director's face flashed in Callie's head. She almost turned tail and ran. A sharp crack and a growled curse held her in place. Her imagination running riot, she decided she'd better make her presence known. Like now.

"Simona? Carlo?"

She heard a rattle. A thump that sounded like the legs of her office chair hitting the floor. Her boss's angry acknowledgment.

"In your office!"

The tableau that greeted her confirmed her worst fears. Simona bristled with fury and Carlo's cheek sported a fat red blotch.

"You, uh, wanted to see me?"

"No." Simona's arm whipped out. A rigid index finger stabbed at the flickering screen of Callie's desktop. "I wanted you to see this."

"Why did you boot up my computer?" Callie asked in confusion. "Did yours crash?"

"*I* didn't boot it up. It was on when I got here."

Thoroughly confused, Callie looked from her to Carlo and back again. "Who turned it on, then? Nikki? One of the mental-health techs?"

The prince rubbed his cheek and took it from there. Shooting an angry glance at his nemesis, he answered stiffly.

"None of the other staff members have come in yet. *Il Drago* found the computer on when she arrived. At which point she called me and started ranting about my having another judge on my payroll. One who would authorize access to your case files."

A chill slithered down Callie's spine. "Someone… someone got into my case files?"

"So it appears," Simona threw at her. "Unless you forgot to log out and shut your computer down last night."

"Of course I logged out!"

Carlo aimed another glance at the director and tried to soften what was feeling more and more like an inquisition. "Are you certain, Callie?"

"Yes!"

Or...

Frantically, she searched her memory. Images flashed by like a slide show. She'd talked to Amal. Confirmed the tickets for the Borghese. Gone down to her office. Logged on and updated the case file. Logged out and hurried to brief Simona on the breakthrough.

Another series of images popped into her head. Of Joe helping Emilio scan the staff and residents' palm prints into the new electronic key pads. One after another. With plenty of time in between to take a break. Amble down the hall. Scope out Callie's office.

No! She wouldn't go there! She couldn't!

Despite the fierce self-denial, a sick feeling curled in the pit of her stomach. She'd jotted down the password, she now remembered. Aleppo221. She'd reversed the digits but acknowledged now that wasn't much of a challenge for a determined hacker.

Her office was too small and crowded to get to her desk. The sick feeling spread from her stomach to her lungs as she uttered a bleak request. "Simona, look under the blotter."

"Why?"

"Just do it."

The director took two steps and jerked up the blotter. The violent movement dislodged the sticky. It floated free and drifted down to lie on the desktop like an accusing yellow eye.

"You wrote down the pass code?" Simona breathed fire. "And left it where any *idiota* might find it?"

Callie couldn't answer. Couldn't breathe. But she could visualize the yesterday's scene as if it replayed in high definition.

Joe and her. Standing toe to toe in this same office.

Not every resident's home of origin was documented, she'd informed him. And even if was, the case file containing that information was protected. She couldn't disclose it without the written consent of the individuals involved. And she could hear his answer. As terse and sharp as a hammer striking iron.

So get their consent.

She staggered back a step as another scene spun through in her mind, too vivid to block. Joe and Emilio. So clever. So skilled. Circumventing legal requirements by plugging an absurdly long override code into the keypads at the center's front and back entrances. Then waiting in the hall when Callie dashed upstairs to tell Amal she'd booked museum tickets.

No! Joe wouldn't search her desk. He wouldn't hack into her files.

Would he?

Stabbed through the heart by sudden, crippling uncertainty, Callie spun on her heel. She ignored the director's sharp command to come back. Ignored Carlo's urgent plea to talk this through. She wanted no part of either of them. No part of the pain that clawed at her heart.

Joe was bent over a map of Rome when his phone buzzed. A quick glance at caller ID showed Carlo's photo and phone number. He hit Connect, knowing his friend's face would flash up on the other end.

"Yeah?"

"We need you at the center," the prince barked. "Now!"

His pulse kicked. "Why?"

"Simona. She called me. Callie, too."

"Callie's there?"

"She was. She just stormed out."

"On my way."

* * *

Callie wandered aimlessly. She didn't notice the city springing to life around her, had no idea where she was. She couldn't focus enough to identify any landmarks.

Her thoughts centered on Joe. Only Joe.

He'd promised, she thought, her heart twisting. That morning in Naples. Before they'd explored Pompeii. He hadn't liked being pinned to the mat. Still, he'd agreed that theirs had to be a marriage of equals. Reluctantly, she remembered, and only after grabbing the out she'd offered him with both hands.

Extraordinary circumstances. That was the out. Had he used it? Made a unilateral decision to access the files?

Blind to the traffic beginning to churn the streets, Callie turned a corner. Two seconds later she stopped dead. Oh, sweet Jesus! Not the fountain! Not now, with the silly, *stupid* wish she'd made three months ago rising up to mock her.

She turned away. Made it several yards down one of the three streets leading away from the fountain before she surrendered to its inexorable pull. Her feet dragging, she turned and retraced her steps.

Thankfully, it was too early for the usual horde of tourists. Only a hardy few had braved the cold to add their contribution to the more than three thousand euros tossed in the fountain's basin every year. The offerings of these early risers hit with dull thunks. Callie saw why when she threaded through the sparse crowd.

How appropriate! How ironically appropriate! Rome's iconic fountain was bone dry.

With a hiccuping laugh, she sank onto the steps leading down to the basin. Last night she'd wandered Rome's beautifully illuminated streets and marveled at how magical the city was at Christmas. Now it felt as cold and empty as the fountain and too dreary for words.

Yet… Dammit! She hated to tuck tail and scurry home like a scolded child. Yes, she'd screwed up. Yes, she'd left a barely disguised version of her computer's password where person or persons unknown might find it. But every time she tried to pin Joe's face on that nebulous someone, her heart stuttered.

Shoulders hunched, nose sniffling in the cold, Callie burrowed her chin in her coat collar and stared unseeing at Oceanus and his pawing steeds. Joe hadn't violated her trust. He wouldn't. The certainty seeped into her heart slowly. Steadily. Replacing the doubt with a soul-deep relief.

She had no idea how long she'd been sitting there, lost in thought, when an excited exclamation pierced the cold morning air.

"Oh! Look!"

Callie's glance cut from the wide-eyed coed just a few feet away to the fountain. It came alive right before her eyes. Water trickled into the top basin. The sun had arced high enough now to add a frosty sparkle as the stream filled that marble bowl.

"They've turned on the fountain." The young coed a few feet away threw Callie an excited grin. "Isn't that awesome?"

"Totally."

The trickle gained volume. The top basin spilled into the second. Its overflow emptied into the third. That overflow fanned sideways. Soon the splash into a half dozen marble shells filled the air. Breathlessly, Callie watched as the giant circular basin at the fountain's base began to fill.

* * *

Joe didn't need a GPS lock to know exactly where to look for her. Sure enough, he spotted her huddled against the cold and sitting shoulder to shoulder with a young woman sporting a Stanford University backpack. The two of them were completely absorbed in the spectacle of the Trevi Fountain coming to life.

He hung back, remembering the last time they'd gathered at this same fountain. Him, Carlo, Travis and Kate, Dawn and Brian and Tommy. And Callie, of the pansy eyes and serene smile. He still found it incredible that none of her friends had seen the worry she'd hidden behind that Mona Lisa facade. Even more incredible that he'd pierced her stubborn defense and gotten her to trust him.

That trust now hung by a thread. After Carlo's terse account of the confrontation at the center, Joe knew she had to think he'd betrayed her. Rehearsing and discarding a dozen different approaches, he settled for simply saying her name.

Her hips swiveled. Her head turned. Those soul-stripping eyes locked with his. "Hello, Joe. Tugging on my electronic leash?"

"We need to talk."

She gave a short laugh. "I thought that was my line."

The coed flashed an uncertain look from her to Joe and back again. "Do you want me to hang with you awhile?" she asked Callie.

"No. But thanks for the offer."

"You sure?"

"I'm sure. Go ahead, make a wish."

The twentysomething pushed to her feet, all long-legged grace and unfettered energy. She tipped her backpack off one shoulder and rooted around in its cavernous depth for several moments.

Joe preempted her and produced a coin. "Here."

She hesitated and threw another glance at Callie. At her nod, the college student accepted the euro with a mumbled, "Thanks."

Joe sank down in the spot she'd just vacated. Hip to hip, he and Callie watched the young woman face away from the fountain. The euro sailed in a clean arc over her shoulder and splashed into the half-full basin. She turned, spotted the ripples, and gave a jaunty thumbs-up before joining several others her own age for a flurry of group shots and selfies.

"I hope she gets her wish," Callie murmured.

Joe didn't answer for the simple reason that he didn't think a reply was required. Beside him, Callie drew up her knees and rested her chin on the flap of her coat.

"Do you remember the last time we were here?" she asked after a moment, her gaze on the glistening water.

"I remember."

"We made a wish then, Dawn and Kate and I. Should I tell you what my wish was?"

Joe wasn't sure he wanted to know. When he made a noncommittal sound, she angled her chin and pinned him with those incredible eyes.

"I wished for a dreamy romantic hero, *à la* Louis Jourdan," she confessed.

"Who?"

"He was one of the stars in the original movie version *Three Coins in the Fountain*."

Right. Nothing like losing out to some '50s-era matinee idol he'd never heard of.

"A dreamy romantic hero, huh? Sorry, sweetheart. Looks like you scored zero for three."

"Actually," she countered, "I think I scored three for three."

He was still digesting that when she scooted around on the step so they were knee to knee. Pulling off her glove, she feathered her fingertips across his cheek.

"I don't want movie star flash and dash, Joe. I want a real hero. One who's earned his stripes the hard way. One who would never lie to me or betray my trust."

He captured her hand and held it against his cheek. "I didn't hack into those files, Callie."

"I know."

"Nor did any of my crew."

"I know." Her mouth twisted in a grimace. "I admit I freaked when Simona confronted me this morning. It was such a shock, coming out of the blue like that. But once I got here, once I took time to think things through, I knew you wouldn't renege on our agreement."

Joe wanted to let this moment spin out. Given a choice, he would've kept the ugliness at bay until their butts froze to the cold marble step. Unfortunately, he didn't have that option. He needed to bring Callie up to speed and get them both back to the center.

"We've verified the breach didn't originate in-house," he told her. "The hacker overrode the password and powered up your computer from a remote device."

"Device?" She glanced quickly from side to side and lowered her voice. "Like a laptop?"

"Yeah."

She took a moment to process that. "You said he overrode the password. So he didn't use the one I scribbled on a note and stuck to the underside of my blotter?"

"No, but remind me to teach you some of the finer points of computer security."

"Oh, Joe! I'm so glad. Well, not *glad*. But I thought…

Simona and I both thought…" She blew out a frosty breath. "Well, let's just say I was getting ready to pack my bags."

Joe could have relieved everyone's mind about that a lot sooner if he'd instructed Emilio to activate the interior cameras he'd installed yesterday. The hidden eyes would've picked up anyone entering or exiting Callie's office.

Well, that hurdle was now cleared. According to Carlo's terse account, he'd informed an outraged Simona that the cameras were in place and were going active until further notice. Di Lorenzo hadn't related her response.

"Have you determined the location of this remote device?" Callie wanted to know.

"Not yet. But we're close."

They damned well should be, with cybergeeks on two continents pulling out all the stops. Joe's people, DIA, NSA, their Italian counterparts, even Brian Ellis, whose skunkworks cadre sat elbow to elbow with the members of the Military Satellite Communications Systems division at Los Angeles Air Force Station.

"We're also close to tagging which files he went into, if any," Joe told her. "Once we have that information, we can talk to the subjects. And hopefully nail down who's so interested in them, and why."

"That's skirting pretty close to the line," Callie worried. "Simona might object."

"Carlo can take that one on. From what he's told me, he and Simona have been duking it out all morning."

"Um. Not quite *all* morning."

Joe cocked his head. "You know something I don't?"

"Maybe. When we get back to the center, you might want to ask Carlo if his cheek still stings."

"Huh?"

"Just ask him. In the meantime…" She got up and brushed off the seat of her coat. "I guess we should head back. I'd like to find out if I still have a job."

"Hold on." Joe unfolded his tall frame. "You say you got your wish. I sure don't see myself as dreamy or romantic or much of a hero, but what the hell. As long as it works for you."

"It works. Believe me, Joe, it works."

"Maybe. But this is what works for me."

Her nose was cold, her lips almost as chilled. They warmed under his, though, and sent a welcome heat rolling through his veins. When he raised his head, the smile in her eyes confirmed that all was right between them.

"Since that seems to have worked out so well," she said, "maybe I should make another wish."

"Sure you want to tempt fate twice?"

"Pretty sure. Do you have another euro?"

He watched as she took the coin and assumed the proper position with her back to the fountain. Eyes closed, she looked as though she was sorting through dozens of possibilities before settling on one. Then she sent the coin sailing to join the others in the basin.

"You going to tell me what you wished for this time, too?"

"Only after it comes true," she laughed.

Joe still had the specter of a supposedly dead terrorist hanging over him. Still had a hinky feeling in his gut that things were about to break. Yet that laugh made him feel a thousand pounds lighter.

The feeling lasted for all of five minutes. Just until he and Callie were weaving through the jumble of tourist stalls beginning to open for business on the Via Delle

Mutate. They were still several blocks from the center when Joe's phone buzzed. One glance at caller ID had him whipping up the phone.

"Russo."

"He's there." Frank Harden's voice stabbed through the instrument. "In Rome."

Chapter Thirteen

With Harden's warning ringing in his head, Joe hit speed dial and called for another war council at the center ASAP. By the time he and Callie got there, Emilio and Dominic were on their way. Carlo hadn't left the center yet. They found him pacing the hall, nursing a cup of coffee and a fierce scowl.

"Where's Simona?" Callie asked. "I need to know if I still have a job."

"Upstairs. One of the residents is ill."

"Oh, no! Is Nikki with her?"

"Not yet. Dominic just texted. She's coming in with him."

"I'd better go up and see if I can help."

She shed her coat and scarf, tossed them in her office, and hurried up the stairs.

That left Joe to relay Harden's terse message. When he had, Carlo cursed and tossed his half-empty cup in a trash can.

"It's not yet eight o'clock and the morning has already become a nightmare. First *il Drago* wakes me from a very pleasant and most interesting dream. Then she drags me down here, only to fling accusations at me about bribing half the judges in Rome. And then, when I try to deny the absurd charge, she snorts and says I probably wouldn't remember who I've bribed, anyway."

Having worked the prince's security for several months, Joe would bet his last dollar that Carlo was more riled over the forgetfulness charge than the bribery. Sure enough, the prince tugged at one end of his mustache and sputtered indignantly.

"She all but called me senile. Me!"

Callie's earlier remark teased at Joe's brain. He wanted to ignore it. And he didn't want to hear any further details in what could turn out to be a very awkward situation. But Carlo's outrage demanded a response.

"So you, uh, offered to prove that you're still young and virile?"

"What? But no! I merely kissed her."

Joe tried, he really tried, to block the image of Carlo laying one on Simona Alberti.

"So," he said when the image wouldn't go away, "she whacked you a good one."

"A *very* good one." His outrage subsiding, Carlo slipped into a rueful grin and rubbed his cheek. "I should recruit her for the Stormo Incursori, no? My commandos could use someone who packs as much firepower in one arm as that one does."

"Better we brief her on Frank Harden's call," Joe suggested, pulling the prince back to the present. "She needs to know whoever hacked into the case files is here, in Rome."

Carlo nodded, but any plans to make the director

aware of the threat took a sharp U-turn when Callie
flew halfway down the stairs. Her eyes wide under her
cap of curls, she leaned so far over the wrought-iron
rail that Joe almost shouted a warning.

"Amal's in labor," she announced excitedly, "and
Simona says the baby's crowning! I've already called
nine-one-one. We need scissors or a sharp knife and
some string."

She whirled and flew back up the stairs, leaving the
two men to exchange looks of sheer male panic.

"Do you know anything about delivering a baby?"
Carlo asked with a touch of desperation.

"Only what's in the special ops medical handbook.
You?"

"The same."

Swallowing a groan, Joe took off at a lope. "I'll hit
the kitchen. They'll have a knife. Maybe some string.
You check the offices."

Like Carlo, Joe had spent years in clandestine ops.
More years prior to that as a military cop. During those
years, he'd put his emergency medical training to the
test more times than he wanted to count. Most recently,
he remembered like a bayonet to the heart, in Curaçao.
Cursing, he shoved that bloody scene out of his head.
This was here. This was now.

As he raced for the kitchen, he dredged up a mental
image of the special ops medical handbook. There was
a chapter on obstetrics, he remembered. Not anywhere
as detailed as the chapters dealing with treating battle-
field injuries, of course. But pretty damned thorough.
The subheadings faded in, faded out, jumped into focus.

*Stage One: Onset of cervical changes and uterine
contractions.*

Stage Two: Full dilation and birth.

Stage Three: Delivery of the placenta.

Okay. Okay. Callie said the baby was crowing. That meant Amal had already progressed to stage two.

Images from the memorized manual flashed into Joe's head. Diagrams of the female reproductive organs. Other diagrams showing a fully formed baby in the birth canal. Instructions on assisting a breech birth. How to do a…

What the hell was that incision? Damned if he could remember the medical term for a cut might be necessary to keep the baby from tearing the vaginal wall and ripping into the rectum, causing a bacterial infection that could kill both mother and child.

Christ Almighty!

He slammed into the kitchen and scared the crap out of the two cooks preparing what smelled like spicy breakfast frittatas. Good thing they recognized Joe from his survey of ingress and egress routes or he might have been smacked in the face with a giant frying pan. Still, they tensed and looked ready to let fly when he grabbed a long knife from the preparation counter.

"The director… Signora Alberti…she needs this." Whirling, he plunged the blade into a pot of boiling water. "And string. *Corda.* Do you have *corda*?"

One of the cooks pointed his spatula at a drawer in the counter. Joe pawed through the jumble and found a roll of plastic twine. He was out of the kitchen and halfway to the stairs when he remembered Emilio. Juggling the knife and twine, he got his phone out of his pocket and stabbed a speed-dial number.

"Where the hell are you?"

"I'm just parking."

"You have your med kit with you?"

"In the dash. Why?"

"It's got sterile gloves, right? Gauze? And scissors. We need scissors."

"*Mio Dio!* What's happened?"

"A baby. That's what's happening."

"Amal? Is it Amal?"

"Yeah! Now get your ass in here!"

Callie's only experience with live birth had occurred when she was nine or ten years old. One otherwise uneventful Thursday evening, the gray-and-white cat who'd adopted her some years previously had mewled and pawed a nest in Callie's fluffy pink bedspread. With no further ado, Boots proceeded to deliver seven adorable kittens.

This birth looked to be considerably more nerve-racking for everyone involved. A panting, white-faced Amal half sat, half reclined in her favorite chair in the arts and crafts room. Hidden behind the artificial palm draped with handmade stars and silver tinsel, she'd obviously been sketching when her pains first stabbed into her. Her pencil and a head and shoulders crafted with her signature bold strokes lay at the side of the chair, kicked out of the way by Simona and Leela.

The director now knelt between Amal's knees. The center's emergency medical kit and a stack of folded white towels were close at hand. Leela crouched beside the straining woman, gripping her hand and murmuring encouragement in her precise English. Another woman, one whose name Callie couldn't remember, stood on Amal's other side and dabbed her sweat-streaked face with a cool cloth.

Other residents crowded the hall and corners of the large room. As Callie hurried past them, she thought for a heart-wrenching moment that she could tell those who'd had—and lost—children by the mix of hope and desolation on their faces. Aching for them, she issued a breathless report.

"Scissors and some string are on the way, Simona."

"Good, because this little one's about to make his or her debut." The director was calm, cool, rock steady. "Push now, Amal. Push. Once more. Ah, there he is. I'm holding his head. One more… Wait. Wait!"

She flashed a look over her shoulder and caught Callie in a relentless stare. "Grab one of those towels. Now kneel beside me and support the baby's head. No, don't elevate it. Just hold it steady."

Still calm, still steady, the director explained what she was doing to the panting mother. "The umbilical cord is wrapped around your baby's neck. That's not uncommon. My second baby came the same way."

Callie barely registered the words. Her entire being was concentrated on the folded towel that cradled the tiny head crowned with wet, matted black hair.

"There," Simona said. "I'm loosening the cord, making the loop bigger. Now the shoulders can slip through. All right. Push."

When the baby slid into Simona's hands, none of the women in the room uttered a single sound. The incredible drama gripped Callie, too. She could hardly breathe as Simona gently turned the baby over and cleared its mouth with a gloved finger. Then the baby's lusty wail broke the spell. Relief and excitement pulsed through the room in palpable waves.

"It's a girl." The director's voice wavered for the briefest instant as she wrapped the baby in a clean towel and placed the bundle in Amal's outstretched arms. "A beautiful little girl."

Joe heard the pronouncement as he angled his way

through the crowd at the door. Carlo was right behind him, and he could hear Emilio thundering up the stairs. He wanted to believe their services weren't needed but knew they weren't in the clear yet. Someone still had to cut the cord…and take care of the afterbirth. He was hoping to hell he could pass the knife and twine to someone more qualified to perform those tasks when he caught the wail of a siren. It was followed almost instantly by Carlo's fervent prayer of thanks.

"Grazie a Dio!"

Nikki arrived on the scene the same time as the EMTs. Only too happy to yield her place to professionals, Callie pushed to her feet. As she edged around the potted palm, she spotted Amal's discarded sketch. She swooped it up to keep it from being trampled by the medical team but was too absorbed in the continuing drama to give the portrait more than a passing glance.

She was still holding it when the EMTs transferred Amal and her baby to a gurney and wheeled them out. Nikki went with them, leaving Simona to share warm hugs with Leela and the woman who'd mopped Amal's sweaty face. She hugged Callie, too, in a rare moment of pure sentiment.

As the crowd of residents slowly dispersed, Simona went into a bathroom to wash off the blood and fluids. When she came downstairs some time later, she was wearing a borrowed skirt so long it dragged the floor and a T-shirt obviously donated by the younger of the two teens. A female rock star Callie didn't recognize flashed a dazzlingly white smile across Simona's breasts.

"Good, you're still here."

She crossed to Callie, standing in the hall with Joe, Carlo, Emilio and Nikki's husband, Dominic.

"I'm sorry I railed at you earlier about the password. After you ran out, Joe told us someone hacked the case files via a remote device."

"No," Callie protested. "You were right to be angry. It was stupid of me to write the password down."

"Well, that's water under the bridge."

"It is?" Carlo asked, feigning amazement. "Am I hearing right? Is *il Drago* tempering her fire?"

"Not when it matters," Simona warned.

"Ah. Then I must assume you won't apologize to me."

"You assume right," Simona huffed. "You deserved to have your face slapped."

"I was not speaking of that." The mocking gleam in his eyes softened. "But since you mention it, *cara*, I must tell you it was worth the pain."

To the surprise and acute discomfort of their audience, a tide of red crawled up Simona's creased cheeks. She countered it with a reply that dripped unadulterated acid.

"Then what *were* you speaking of?"

"Hmm. Let me think." Carlo pretended confusion this time. "I'm trying to remember."

He glanced from Joe to Emilio to Dominic, his expression comical.

"*Santa Maria!* I must be growing senile." He turned a helpless look on Simona. "Did you…? Did you…? Help me, *cara*! Did you accuse me of having judges in my pocket?"

Her reply was a glacial stare.

Callie caught her breath as the light of battle leaped

into the prince's face. Thank God Joe intervened before blood was spilled.

"Why don't we take this to your office, Simona? I need to tell you about the call I got earlier this morning while Callie and I were on our way back to the center. I briefed her and Carlo, but you and Emilio and Dominic need to know the latest."

The director glared at him, obviously reluctant to surrender the field. But concern for her charges won out over her private war with the prince. Hitching up her ridiculously long skirt, she headed for her office.

Carlo didn't try to disguise his disappointment at her capitulation. Joe, Dominic and Emilio, however, shared a glance of profound relief. Callie ignored all four as the director's calm, steady assurances to Amal echoed in her mind.

That's not uncommon.

My second baby came the same way.

She let the others go on ahead. Simona's words kept ringing in her head.

Callie was a trained psychologist. She'd studied at two of the most reputable universities in the United States. If her ego had needed stroking, she could've hung her framed diplomas in her office. Yet every day, every client reinforced how rarely life conformed to textbook case studies.

Simona's past was obviously as complex and tortured as Joe's, yet they'd both defied the odds. Somehow, some way, they'd drawn on inner reserves to emerge stronger and more resilient than anyone would've predicted.

And Amal, or whatever her real name was. She'd given birth surrounded by strangers. No screams. No tears. Only muffled grunts as she delivered the child she must pray would grow up in a safe, stable world.

Humbled again by Amal's courage, Callie glanced at the portrait she'd scooped off the floor. She'd almost forgotten she held it and swore softly when she saw her nervous fist had crunched the paper. Carefully, she smoothed the folds.

As before, Amal's talent astounded her. The bold, confident strokes. The clean lines. The pride and…

Wait! She knew that face! But how? Where?

She made the connection just seconds later. Amal had sketched the same face a few days ago. So arrogant. So beautiful. Then she'd slashed the sketch, over and over and over, until she'd obliterated it.

Callie had thought then—she *still* thought—the drawing represented some unidentified, unspecified male figure from Amal's past. A masculine amalgam that summarized her deep-seated hate and fear.

Yet the longer Callie stared at this portrait, the more convinced she became it wasn't an abstract rendering. This man had lived and breathed. His face was so real and alive and…

Oh, God! She'd seen him! Just the other morning! She'd spilled white chocolate espresso on his sleeve, then earned a fierce glare when she'd asked if the foam had seeped into his computer. His *laptop* computer.

Barely able to breathe, Callie gripped the sketch in suddenly icy hands. Could this man be the target? The one who'd escaped the drone strike? Had he made those online queries about the center? And hacked into the case files? The possibilities were too real and too frightening to ignore.

Her heart thumping, she hurried down the hall. A few yards from the director's office, she abruptly stopped.

She could hear the conversation inside. Joe. Simona. Joe again. Their low voices competed with the warnings now firing through her mind.

Amal had sketched this portrait here, at the center. A place that promised her sanctuary and every expectation of privacy. Was this drawing covered by client-counselor privilege? Would Callie violate that privilege if she showed it to outsiders?

As soon as the thought occurred, she killed it. If the man in this sketch was who Joe thought he might be, he represented a potential danger to Amal. Possibly everyone at the center. Callie would take full responsibility for showing the portrait to appropriate authorities.

She pushed through the door and thrust the crumpled sketch at Joe. "Amal drew this. I don't know who the man is, but I've seen him. Just a few days ago. At the café around the corner. He was having espresso... and he had a laptop with him."

The others crowded around to study the portrait.

"Anyone recognize him?" Joe asked.

When no one did, he whipped out his phone and snapped several quick shots.

"I'm forwarding these to Harden and my own people," he said, his thumbs working. "To you, too, Carlo, so you can send them to your contacts in the *polizia*. Emilio, I want you to zap a copy to every man on your crew. Have them canvass the neighborhood. Start with the café where Callie spotted this guy. And get someone to the hospital. I want a watch on Amal's room 24/7."

"Do you think she's in danger?" Simona asked sharply. "Her and the baby?"

"I don't know. Let's hope to hell she can answer that. You'd better come with me. You and Callie."

"It might be better if Emilio talks to her," Callie suggested.

Joe's glance sawed into her. "You think I might frighten her?"

The scar. He thought she was worried about the scar. Her chin lifting, she met that absurdity head-on.

"You have to admit you can be pretty intimidating when you want to," she replied calmly. "But I was thinking of yesterday morning. Emilio actually got Amal to talk to him. And she told me that she thought he had a kind face."

Joe snorted, and the others all turned to study the face under discussion. It immediately turned brick red. Thoroughly embarrassed, Emilio said gruffly that he'd be happy to accompany them to the hospital.

The Ospedale San Giovanni Addolorata was a massive complex in the heart of Rome, located right behind the Egyptian obelisk and within sight of the Colosseum. Interactive displays in the hospital's main entrance depicted its long history, while plexiglass cutouts in the tiled floor gave glimpses the long-buried ruins of the home of Emperor Marcus Aurelius's mother.

A call to Nikki confirmed that Amal and the baby had already been transferred from the ER to the maternity ward. Getting to the ward proved quite a challenge. Signs directed Callie and the others to another building, then to two different banks of elevators and, finally, to the wing containing the obstetrical delivery suites, nursery and neonatal intensive care unit. Their small group drew several glances along the way. Particularly Simona in her gaudy borrowed T-shirt, dragging skirt and flyaway dandelion hair. Blithely ignoring the stares, she marched up to the nurses' station where Nikki was filling out forms.

"How are they?"

"Fine. The doctor has examined them both. The baby's in the nursery, and Amal's getting cleaned up a bit. I'll need some help with this paperwork." Nikki made a helpless gesture at the forms. "She still won't give us her name or any other identifying information."

"I'll talk to her. What room is she in?"

"Three twelve. Second door on the left."

When the director headed for the room, Nikki gave Callie a quick smile. "You did well this morning."

"I didn't do anything. Amal and Simona did all the work."

"Well, the result was worth their effort. The baby's beautiful."

"You said she's in the nursery?"

"She is. There's a viewing window just there, down the hall."

Nikki went back to her paperwork, Emilio went in search of coffee and Callie waited for Joe to finish checking his text messages.

"I wanted to make sure my contacts received the sketch," he told her when he finished. "They have, and they're running facial recognition programs. If he's in the system, we'll ID him."

"I'm going to see the baby. Want to come with me?"

"Sure."

The shades were up, giving an unimpeded view of the plastic bassinets in their stainless steel stands. Most were empty. The babies were probably with their moms, Callie guessed, being nursed or bathed or cuddled. Only three bassinets were occupied.

In one, the baby wore a blue stocking cap. The other

two wore pink. Both still had the scrunched-up red faces of newborns, but the baby on the left had to be Amal's. The silky black hair peeking below her stocking cap was a dead giveaway. That, and the name on the bassinet. Callie had to squint to make out the hand lettering. When she did, she caught her breath.

Simona. Amal had named her baby Simona.

The rightness of it put a smile around Callie's heart. She hoped it would put one around the director's, too.

"Which one is Amal's?" Joe asked.

"The one on the left."

"How can you tell?"

"Look at the name on the bassinet."

Like Callie, he had to squint. Unlike her, though, he wasn't as confident about the rightness of it.

"I don't know much about your boss's past," he said quietly. "Carlo doesn't, either. Only that she was married once and lost her family in some kind of natural disaster. Hard to imagine how someone who's lost so much will feel about having a namesake."

"I think she'll love it," Callie murmured. Her gaze lingered on the pink stocking cap and tufts of black hair. "Cradling that little head in my hands this morning at the moment of her birth was the most amazing thing I've ever experienced."

With a last glance at the baby, she angled away from the window.

"We haven't talked about having kids, Joe. How do you feel about having a namesake?"

"Just say the word." One of his rare smiles tipped his mouth. "Kate and Dawn would probably advise you to take a trip down the aisle first, but I'm ready any time you are."

"I'm ready, too. For both."

It took a moment for that to register. When it did, his smile became a full-fledged grin. "How does a Christmas wedding sound?"

"Oh, I would love that! But I can't fly home, even for a few days, and leave Simona in the lurch."

"So we have the wedding here."

"But…"

"Kate and Dawn. Yeah, I know. Reminds me of that old saying."

Callie arched a brow.

"If a frog had wheels, it wouldn't bump its butt."

Her other brow rose. "What does that mean?"

"Damned if I know. Gran says it all the time, though." Curling a knuckle under her chin, he tipped her face to his. "Let me work the details, Pansy Eyes. All you'll have to do is—"

"Joe! Callie!" Nikki waved to them. "Simona wants us to join her in Amal's room."

Chapter Fourteen

"He is my husband's brother."

Amal didn't look at them. Gripping the hospital blanket with white-knuckled fists, she stared at wall above their heads.

"He was to drive the car. The one that was hit. But he suspected someone had betrayed him. Coward that he is, he sent his brother to die in his place."

She dropped her gaze, glaring at them as her words gained heat and fury.

"My husband was not like him! He was gentle and kind and would have nothing to do with his brother's hate-filled friends! That's why they tricked him into driving the car. Why he followed at a safe distance, sending messages on his computer to others in their cadre, waiting to see if my husband sprang the trap they'd suspected."

Her fists convulsed on the blanket. Her face, her eyes, her body language all conveyed rage.

"He would kill me, too. I knew what he had done. He could not let me live to tell of his shameful cowardice. So I fled. And when the boat sank and I swam ashore, I told no one my name. Told no one where I'd come from."

She stopped, breathing hard and fast as the memories tore at her. Then her fire shaded to fear.

"I thought we were safe, my baby and I. Now Simona says… She says he may be here. In Rome. Is that true?"

Joe didn't pad the truth. "We think so."

"You must find him! Please! Before he finds me and my baby."

"We plan to. Until we do, Emilio will stand guard. He and the *polizia*. They'll protect you and the baby."

"I'm staying, too," Simona announced. "Callie, you'll go with Joe back to the center, won't you?"

"Of course."

"Explain what's happened to the staff and other residents. Show them the sketch and tell them to be especially aware when they go out."

They were in the SUV, just pulling up at the center, when Joe got a call from Carlo. He screeched the vehicle to a halt with a terse explanation.

"One of Emilio's crew spotted him. He's having espresso at the same little café where you bumped into him. The *polizia* are on their way. Wait here at the center."

She knew better than to suggest she should go with him. Joe didn't need to be worrying about keeping her safe. She wanted him to focus on keeping himself safe! Her heart banged against her ribs as he shouldered the door open.

"Be careful!"

"I will."

He tore off the moment she hit the keypad and was safely inside. The café was just around the corner. She would hear the sirens when the police arrived. Only if they hit the sirens, she amended. They might not want to alert him.

She had no idea how long she stayed rooted just inside the door. Her hands shoved in her pockets, she repeated again and again the wish she'd made just a few hours ago at the Trevi Fountain.

And then it was over.

No flash, no bang, no police sirens.

Just Joe pulling up in the black SUV to deliver another quick report. Callie spotted the monster vehicle through a front window and ran outside almost before he'd braked to a halt. The driver's side window whirred down, and Callie hung on the door while he shared the news.

"We got him. Bastard was too busy banging away on his laptop to realize we had him in our sights. He tried to run when the *polizia* arrived." His mouth tipped in a wolfish grin. "Didn't get far."

"Are you sure it's him? Amal's brother-in-law?"

"Almost one hundred percent. Carlo's going to the hospital with one of the police officers. They'll nail down the last one percent."

"Thank God!"

"I'm heading downtown to share what I know with the anti-terror unit." He put the SUV in gear but kept his foot on the brake. "When I get back, we need to finish the discussion we were having at the hospital. The one about namesakes and Christmas weddings."

Callie was so overjoyed that the worry and fear might

finally be over that she would have married him right there, in the street. She settled for leaning through the window and hooking an arm around him to drag him down for a kiss.

"You take care of the bad guy. I'll take care of the wedding."

Naturally, her first call was to Kate and Dawn. She couldn't wait. Still standing in the street, she woke first one, then the other and had to assure both that she hadn't yanked them from sleep because she was hurt or had been in an accident or had dumped Joe.

"Just the opposite. We're getting married."

"When?" Dawn shrieked.

"Where?" Kate yelped.

"That depends on whether Brian's corporate jet's available in the next few days."

"To fly you home?"

"To fly you guys here. I know it's short notice and you've probably got family coming for Christmas. Brian's folks, or yours and Travis's, Kate. But if you can make it, I would—"

"Don't be stupid. Of course we'll make it. Just tell us where you want us when."

"Christmas Eve. Here in Rome. I haven't worked all the details yet. I'll get back to you as soon as I do."

"What about your folks?" Dawn asked. "The jet has plenty of room if they want to come."

"Thanks for the offer. I doubt they'll want to fly over, but I'll call and check."

She gripped the phone, suddenly teary eyed with emotion and drippy nosed from the cold.

"This has been the most amazing morning," she sniffed. "I almost got fired and I helped deliver a baby.

Then Joe and Carlo took down a really, really nasty bad guy. Oh, and I tossed a coin in the Trevi Fountain. The wish is already coming true."

"All that in one morning?"

Kate sounded amazed, but Dawn zeroed in instantly on the most significant of those events.

"Hot damn! The fountain scores again."

Callie gave a watery laugh. "Okay, I'm standing on the sidewalk freezing my ass off. I've got to go inside and make a bunch more calls. I'll get back to you as soon as I firm up the arrangements. Ciao. And thank you!"

Before she could start working her growing mental list of to-dos, she had to brief Leela and Sabeen and the other residents on the visit to the hospital. They greeted the news that both mother and baby were doing fine with happy smiles.

"We will visit her," Leela declared. "And take gifts for the baby."

Callie left them making arrangements and hurried to her office to make her own. It was still too early to contact her folks, so she called Carlo, intending to just leave a voice mail asking him to call her when he could. He picked up halfway through her message.

"Oh, I'm sorry. Are you at the hospital?"

"We're still on the way. I just spoke with Joe. He tells me you're to be married. Congratulations, *mia bella*, although I can't understand why you would wish to tie yourself to such a lout when you could fly with me to—"

"Yes, yes, I know. Casablanca or Antibes or wherever. Why don't you take Simona? You know you want to."

"Ha! She would not consider it for a moment." He hesitated a beat, two. "Would she?"

"You won't know until you ask. In the meantime, I might need a favor."

"You have only to name it."

"I haven't checked yet what kind of license or permit we'll need to get married in Italy on Christmas Eve. If it turns out there's a bureaucratic tangle, do you think you could you get one of your judges to slice through it?"

"Certainly. And may I make a suggestion? My home here in the city boasts a very large salon. It would give me great pleasure if you and Joe would have the ceremony there. With a supper to follow, perhaps?"

Callie's initial thought had been to hold the ceremony here at the center. Having it at the prince's palazzo would make it a treat for the residents and so very, very special for both Joe and her.

"Oh, Carlo, thank you! That would be wonderful!"

"*Bene*! I'll take care of getting the judge to conduct the ceremony, too, if you wish. One of those many in my pay," he added drily.

"Yes, and thank you again!"

She disconnected feeling slightly dazed. In the space of ten short minutes, she'd nailed down the time, the place, the matrons of honor, the judge, the wedding supper. That left a dress…and a ring for Joe.

She knew exactly how to nail those down, too. Yanking open her desk drawer, she searched for the business card she'd brought back from Naples with her. Luckily, she got through to the buffalo ranch and reached the person she wanted on the first try.

"Ciao, Arianna. It's Callie."

"How good to hear from you. How are you enjoying Rome and your new job?"

"I love both."

"We must have lunch when I come up to Rome. Perhaps next week, yes? I still have a few presents to buy and haven't seen the lights of the Fendi building yet."

"That's why I'm calling. Joe and I strolled down Via Condotti the other night, but those boutiques are way out of my price range. I thought maybe you could recommend a shop where I could get a wedding ring for him and a dress for me."

"But yes! I frequent many excellent shops. When is the wedding?"

"Christmas Eve. I know it's short notice, and I'm sure you have plans to spend that evening with your family, but we would love if any or all of the Audi family could attend."

"But yes!" she exclaimed again. "And I will drive up tomorrow. It's Saturday and all the Christmas shoppers will be out, so we must start early. Can you meet me at Caffè Domiziano, in the Piazza Navona? Shall we say nine o'clock?"

"I'll be there!"

Unbelievably, every hastily contrived plan came off without a hitch.

With Arianna's enthusiastic assistance, Callie found the perfect dress and a simple gold band for Joe. Carlo sent his head chef to consult with her on the menu for the wedding supper and lined up a judge to perform the ceremony. After filling out reams of paper, she and Joe obtained a special license and arranged for a representative from the US consulate to act as a witness.

When Amal and the baby returned from the hospital, the refugee broke down in tears and shared her real identity. As Callie had suspected, Rasha Hadid was a highly regarded artist whose work was on exhibit in museums in Damascus and Cairo and Athens. And now that she no longer had to fear her brother-in-law, she could accept the position she'd been offered as an adjunct professor at the University of Thessaloniki. But first, she and the baby must attend the wedding of two to whom they owed so much.

As joyous as Rasha's return was, Callie's happiness brimmed over even more on Christmas Eve morning. She and Joe drove separate cars out to Ciampino Airport to pick up Kate and Dawn and their husbands. Joe wheeled the monster SUV. Callie drove a smaller and more manageable Fiat from Emilio's fleet. They parked at the terminal that handled executive jets and were waiting when the sleek Gulfstream with the Ellis Aeronautical Systems logo on its tail swooped in for a landing. To their delight, the first person to exit when the stairs were let down was Tommy. He raced over to them with his usual energy and promptly announced he wasn't worried about Santa finding him in Rome.

"Dad says his radar is better than the one on the Gulfstream even, 'n' he'll leave presents for Buster back at home. Doggy treats 'n' stuff. Grandma and Granddad are taking care of him. They're gonna make sure he doesn't eat poop. Dogs do that sometimes."

"Good to know," Joe said solemnly, then shook hands with Travis and Brian. "Thanks for making the trip on such short notice."

"No way we could miss seeing the last of the Inseparables bite the dust," Travis assured him. He nodded to the three women wrapped in a fierce group hug punctuated by sniffles and tears of joy. "How long has it been since they've seen each other? Three weeks?"

"Closer to two," Brian drawled.

When they finally untangled, Callie gave all four males a quick kiss before sweeping Dawn and Kate toward the Fiat. "Six o'clock. Carlo's palazzo. See you there."

"Yeah," Joe confirmed, "you will."

Callie steered through Rome's center with maximum concentration and minimal wrong turns. Kate and Dawn twisted to see the Fendi building as they zipped past. The decorations weren't as awesome in daylight as in the photo Callie had texted, but they both vowed to hit the high-end shopping street before they flew back to the States. Fifteen minutes later Callie squeezed into a parking spot and took them up to her apartment.

They oohed over the warm yellow walls and ahhed over the view of St. Peter's from the tiny balcony. Then they shed their coats and got down to the serious business of checking out the contents of the boxes sitting on the bed and the dress bag hanging on the closet door.

Chapter Fifteen

Callie couldn't have imagined a more stunning setting for a wedding than Carlo's palazzo. When she and Kate and Dawn emerged from the limo Joe had sent to pick them up, they had to fight to keep from gawking at the elegant facade and butler who'd been waiting for them. As tall and aristocratic as his employer was short and muscular, the tuxedoed majordomo bowed and ushered them inside.

He must have sent some silent signal to the prince. As Callie and Kate and Dawn were shedding their coats, Carlo descended a flight of marble stairs wide enough to drive a tractor up. Looking astonishingly royal in a dress uniform crossed by a red sash studded with glittering medals and decorations, he greeted Kate and Dawn with kisses to both hands and cheeks.

His greeting to the bride was no less extravagant. "Ah, Clarissa. You look so beautiful. Are you sure you—"

"Yes," she interrupted hastily, cutting him off before he could make yet another offer to whisk her off to parts unknown. "I'm sure."

But she had to repeat her suggestion of a few days ago. "Why don't you take Simona? You know you want to."

"I did ask her," he answered with a scowl. "Her reply still burns my ears."

Laughing, Callie stooped to drop a kiss on his cheek. "I know you. You're too much like Joe to take no for an answer."

"Perhaps. Perhaps not. But now…" He crooked his arm. "You break my heart, Clarissa, but do me such great honor by asking me to give you away. Shall we go upstairs?"

Her friends led the way. Dawn had brought a gown in her favorite green. Kate wore one of deep crimson. The rich hues formed a glowing complement to the garlands draping the stone balustrade. Callie's heart tripped as she mounted the marble stairs under the watchful eyes of what looked like ten or twelve generations of Carlo's ancestors.

Banks of poinsettias ringed the second-floor landing. As Carlo led her past the glorious color, Callie could hear an unseen baritone singing "Santa Lucia." She'd now adopted the hymn as her own personal anthem. The baritone was good, she acknowledged, but she intended to download Elvis's version the next time she logged into iTunes.

Then the same majordomo who'd met them downstairs opened a set of double doors. Beyond was a salon as long as the nave of a cathedral and almost as high ceilinged. Rows of gilt-edged chairs lined the salon's parquet floor. Callie blinked in surprise when she saw every seat was filled.

As though perfectly timed, the hymn finished and a string quartet launched into Mendelssohn's wedding march. Carlo squeezed Callie's arm and they followed Kate and Dawn down the aisle between the chairs. She smiled as she recognized the guests. Emilio and his crew. Marcello Audi, his daughter, Arianna, with her husband and kids. Sabeen and Leela and the other residents of the center. Amal and her baby in the second row with Simona.

Callie had to suppress a gasp at the director's altered appearance. Simona had tamed her flyaway hair and actually applied some lip gloss and blush. Even more astonishing, her floor-length skirt and fitted jacket of wine-colored velvet looked as though they might come from one of the boutiques on Via Condotti. Callie felt Carlo's start of surprise and had to hide a grin.

Travis and Brian and Tommy were in the front row. The men smiled and the boy beamed as Callie floated past. They were her family now, as much as Kate and Dawn. Integral threads in the fabric of her life.

But it was the man waiting for her at the end of the aisle who filled her heart. So tall, so awesome in his hand-tailored tux. Her very own Louis Jourdan, Callie thought with a lump in her throat.

"I must ask," the prince murmured, pressing her arm to his side. "Are you *sure* you're sure?"

She gave a helpless laugh. "Oh, Carlo. I've never been surer of anything in my life."

Then she put her hand in Joe's, and her Christmas wish came true.

* * * * *

Don't miss Dawn's and Kate's stories, part of the
THREE COINS IN THE FOUNTAIN *series:*

THIRD TIME'S THE BRIDE
"I DO"... TAKE TWO!

*Available now wherever Mills & Boon books
and ebooks are sold!*

MILLS & BOON®

Cherish™

EXPERIENCE THE ULTIMATE RUSH OF FALLING IN LOVE

A sneak peek at next month's titles...

In stores from 17th November 2016:

- **Winter Wedding for the Prince** – Barbara Wallace *and*
  The More Mavericks, the Merrier! – Brenda Harlen
- **Christmas in the Boss's Castle** – Scarlet Wilson *and*
  A Bravo for Christmas – Christine Rimmer

In stores from 1st December 2016:

- **Her Festive Doorstep Baby** – Kate Hardy *and*
  The Holiday Gift – RaeAnne Thayne
- **Holiday with the Mystery Italian** – Ellie Darkins *and*
  A Cowboy's Wish Upon a Star – Caro Carson

Just can't wait?
Buy our books online a month before they hit the shops!
www.millsandboon.co.uk

Also available as eBooks.

MILLS & BOON®

EXCLUSIVE EXTRACT

Crown Prince Armando enlists Rosa Lamberti to find
him a suitable wife—but could a stolen kiss under the
mistletoe lead to an unexpected Christmas wedding?

Read on for a sneak preview of
WINTER WEDDING FOR THE PRINCE
by Barbara Wallace

"Have you ever looked at an unfocused telescope only
to turn the knob and make everything sharp and clear?"
Armando asked.

Rosa nodded.

"That is what it was like for me, a few minutes ago.
One moment I had all these sensations I couldn't
explain swirling inside me, then the next everything
made sense. They were my soul coming back to life."

"I don't know what to think," she said.

"Then don't think," he replied. "Just go with your
heart."

He made it sound easy. Just go with your heart. But
what if your heart was frightened and confused? For
all his talk of coming to life, he was essentially in the
same place as before, unable or unwilling to give her
a true emotional commitment.

On the other hand, her feelings wanted to override
her common sense, so maybe they were even. As she
watched him close the gap between them, she felt her
heartbeat quicken to match her breath.

"You do know that we're under the mistletoe yet again, don't you?"

The sprig of berries had quite a knack for timing, didn't it? Anticipation ran down her spine ceasing what little hold common sense still had. Armando was going kiss her and she was going to let him. She wanted to lose herself in his arms. Believe for a moment that his heart felt more than simple desire.

This time, when he wrapped his arm around her waist, she slid against him willingly, aligning her hips against his with a smile.

"Appears to be our fate," she whispered. "Mistletoe, that is."

"You'll get no complaints from me." She could hear her heart beating in her ears as his head dipped toward hers. "Merry Christmas, Rosa."

"Mer…" His kiss swallowed the rest of her wish. Rosa didn't care if she spoke another word again. She'd waited her whole life to be kissed like this. Fully and deeply, with a need she felt all the way down to her toes.

They were both breathless when the moment ended. With their foreheads resting against each other, she felt Armando smile against her lips. "Merry Christmas," he whispered again.

Don't miss
WINTER WEDDING FOR THE PRINCE
by Barbara Wallace

Available December 2016

www.millsandboon.co.uk

MILLS & BOON®

Why shop at millsandboon.co.uk?

Each year, thousands of romance readers find their perfect read at millsandboon.co.uk. That's because we're passionate about bringing you the very best romantic fiction. Here are some of the advantages of shopping at www.millsandboon.co.uk:

* **Get new books first**—you'll be able to buy your favourite books one month before they hit the shops

* **Get exclusive discounts**—you'll also be able to buy our specially created monthly collections, with up to 50% off the RRP

* **Find your favourite authors**—latest news, interviews and new releases for all your favourite authors and series on our website, plus ideas for what to try next

* **Join in**—once you've bought your favourite books, don't forget to register with us to rate, review and join in the discussions

Visit **www.millsandboon.co.uk**
for all this and more today!

MILLS_WEB